# HOUSE OF GLASS

## Merryn Allingham

# HOUSE OF GLASS

First published in Great Britain 2018 by The Verrall Press

Cover art: Berni Stevens Book Cover Design

Copyright © Merryn Allingham

ISBN 978-1-9997824-4-3

Merryn Allingham asserts the moral right to be identified as the author of this work.

# Chapter One

'Grace Latimer?' The voice was a little too energetic for this early in the morning. I held the receiver at a distance and took a gulp of strong coffee. 'Speaking.'

'Hi! This is Nick Heysham. You probably don't remember me.' There was a pause while I struggled to recall the name. 'We met last month at the Papillon — at the Gorski retrospective.'

Another pause, and then he added, 'I gate-crashed.'

A vision of a startlingly yellow shirt and suede trousers swam to mind. The trousers had clearly seen better days. He had come alone, I remembered, and was evidently not part of any of the noisy groups sipping their champagne. I'd suspected then that he hadn't been invited — for one thing, he'd been far more interested in the paintings than the people.

'Yes, I remember you.' I was cautious. 'How did you get my number?'

'A little amateur sleuthing.'

It wouldn't be that difficult; the staff at the gallery would be unsuspicious. Most of them existed in worlds of their own. They would have given my number to the Yorkshire Ripper if he'd called.

'How can I help?' I tried to keep my voice polite while hoping he'd called me in error. I had a mountain of work and this was a conversation I didn't need.

There was a deep intake of breath at the other end of the line. 'It's like this…I've been asked to do a project, a research job, and I've run into problems. I think you'd be able to sort it for me.'

'And why would that be?'

I could hear frost feathering my voice. A man, who gate-crashed Oliver's party and spoke to me for all of ten seconds, seemed now to be expecting I'd ride to his rescue.

'You're a pretty impressive woman, Grace, amazing qualifications and so on. In historical research — and that's what I need.' He sounded pleased he'd explained everything to my satisfaction.

'So can I be clear, Mr Heysham? You want me to do the research that you will then get paid for?'

'Nick. And it's not exactly like that.' He sounded sheepish. 'The job is paying very little as it is — but I can buy you a drink.'

'I believe I can do that for myself, but thank you for the kind thought.'

'I thought you might be interested. It's the Great Exhibition.'

'What about the Great Exhibition?' I knew I should put the phone down, but I couldn't prevent a small surge of interest. More than a small surge since I had written extensively on the subject. Before, that is, I settled for an easier life.

'Missing plans,' he said hopefully. 'Lucas Royde?'

Royde, I knew, had been the darling of Victorian architecture, but I'd never before heard of his connection to the

Great Exhibition.

'Can you be more precise?'

'Royde is supposed to have designed some kind of pavilion for the Exhibition, his very first commission, but I haven't been able to track the plans down. I was hoping you might know something.'

I didn't, but his words had got me thinking. Was there really anything in this, or was I just willing there to be? I was debating with myself whether or not I should simply bid Nick Heysham farewell when he seized on my silence.

'Can we meet? There's a wine bar just around from the Papillon.'

'I'm in Hampstead, not Hoxton.' That was something I shouldn't have divulged. I could have him knocking on my door in the time it took to hop on a Northern line train.

'Not today then. But tomorrow perhaps?'

My sigh was audible. 'I'm at the gallery tomorrow. I can give you a few minutes after work.' The faintest hint of a mystery was sufficient, it seemed, to ensure my surrender. My life must be more of a wasteland than I'd realised.

'Early evening?'

'Six o'clock at the wine bar.' I was unusually brusque, but I doubted it would have any effect, and it didn't.

'Great. Thanks, Grace. See you there.'

'Dr Latimer —' I began, but the phone went dead.

I sat holding the receiver for some time. Nick Heysham might be perfectly harmless, a little eccentric perhaps and overly enthusiastic. On the other hand, he might be a clever manipulator and turn out to be the stalker from hell. I shouldn't have agreed to meet him. Perhaps I should run it by Oliver first. No, I wouldn't do that. Too much of my life was already run by Oliver.

The sudden thought had me feeling guilty. I was grateful to Oliver. He had been immensely generous, kind, too, but over time I'd discovered he was a man who liked to control — events, people — and it had begun to grate. The phone call had come out of nowhere, and that was probably its appeal. That and the smallest possibility of uncovering something new. The researcher in me had risen to the bait and a small voice had whispered that, even at this late stage, I might take the art world by storm. If nothing else, finding a missing piece of Victorian art might help to bolster my spirits. They were worryingly dismal these days, and they shouldn't be. For the first time in my life I had security and the love of a good man. That should be enough, and yet somehow it wasn't.

I turned back to the papers on my desk and the letter from Marigold Carmichael surfaced from the pile where I'd hidden it two days ago. There was no escape from the latest in a long line of complaints from this most demanding of clients. It seemed Mrs Carmichael had become newly enraged by my suggestion that the 'original features' of White Heather Cottage had been added some time in the 1950s. Naturally she was gathering expert opinion to disprove my theory.

No wonder I felt low. It wasn't just Marigold Carmichael and her ilk, it was the work itself. What kind of a job was it researching the history of other people's houses, most of them vastly uninteresting except to their owners? No kind of job was the answer. Not, at least, for a woman facing the watershed of thirty. A stop-gap, a dead end, until the next foreign buying trip, the next gallery event, when for a short time I would blossom at the head of Professor Oliver Brooke's entourage. I wasn't sure how I had walked into this life. I used to have plans, ambitious plans, but then Oliver had come along and somehow they had been put on hold. I hadn't struggled. After years of turmoil, I had settled for an easier life, a simple life. But simple had gradually metamorphosed into dreary, and I had only myself to blame.

# Chapter Two

By ten minutes past six the following evening, Nick Heysham had not made an appearance. The wine bar was humming, excited chatter almost drowning the wail from the stereo system. I was hoping that none of the Papillon staff would decide they needed a drink before they left for home, but just in case I'd found a seat in one of the bar's darker enclaves. I'd spent a frustrating afternoon at the gallery and had no wish to encounter any of Oliver's colleagues again. I'm sure they saw me as an interloper whose visits interrupted their pleasant routines. I was still trying to tidy up paperwork from the Gorski show, but getting their co-operation was painful and I'd managed to do almost nothing.

I craned my neck around a gargantuan palm that obscured my view of the door, but there was still no sign of Nick. Five more minutes, I thought, then time is up and I can leave with a clear conscience. I should never have agreed to meet him, but when he phoned I'd been working against a deadline and wanted to lose him as quickly as possible. If I were honest, though, I'd only said yes because for an instant an implausible search had sent a ripple of colour through my life. And it was implausible: what possible excitement could the Great Exhibition provide? It was a terrain that had been so thoroughly sifted by generations of researchers that it was now barren. I gathered up my bag and took my coat from the nearby rack.

'Sorry I'm late.' Nick Heysham emerged from behind the palm, breathing heavily. 'I lost a wheel on the corner of Gosset Street.'

'Lost a wheel! Your car lost its wheel?'

'Bike. Remember I work for a pittance.'

'What's happened to the bike?'

'I abandoned it. It has no one to blame but itself. The brakes have been faulty for weeks, but losing the wheel was the last straw.'

His nonchalance in the face of potential death made me blink, but he appeared wholly unperturbed. He was dressed in frayed jeans and a tee shirt that proclaimed Same Shirt, Different Day. At least it looked clean. He glanced briefly at my empty glass and ordered two large glasses of white wine. I was about to quarrel with this high-handed behaviour when I took a sip. It was surprisingly mellow. He might be short of money, very short by the look of him, but somewhere in the past he had acquired a knowledge of good wine.

'Thanks for coming.' He smiled engagingly and I found myself drawn into studying his face.

He was eminently paintable. A strong jawline, dark hair and very blue eyes. He could have sat for a study of any Romantic poet, except for the expression. That was as far from soulful as you could get.

'Thanks for coming,' he repeated, and I realised just how hard I'd been staring. I flushed with annoyance.

'I've only got half an hour — you better fill me in on

details.' It wasn't like me to sound so ungracious.

He grinned, rightly gauging my embarrassment. 'I take it you've heard of Lucas Royde?'

'Of course I've heard of him. He was probably the most influential of all Victorian architects.'

'Right, well this is the thing. The Royde Society is putting on a celebration to mark the centenary of his death. They want to do a life-size mock-up of one of his designs and use that as the venue.'

'So where's the problem?'

'They've decided to focus on Royde's beginning rather than his final years. So the design has to be his earliest project — that's the problem.'

'I can't see why. It must be well documented. You said something about a pavilion for the Great Exhibition, but I think you'll find it was a chapel — 1852?'

'Hey, you're pretty good.' He smiled his approval. 'Royde designed an Italianate chapel for the Earl of Carlyon.'

'A very individual take on an Italianate chapel,' I corrected him, recalling shreds of my past studies. 'His design got rave reviews and was copied any number of times over the next few years.'

'Really?'

'Forgive me, Mr Heysham.'

'Nick.'

'Forgive me, Nick,' I steepled my fingertips together in deliberation, 'but you seem to have only the haziest idea about Royde. Why would the Royde Society ask you to research his plans?'

He looked a little self-conscious. 'My sister works in events management. They asked her to come up with the goods. And she asked me.'

'Your sister? So this job…'

'Pure nepotism, I'm afraid. But I need the money. And I *am* a freelance writer with plenty of research under my belt. Lucy thought I could manage it. I thought so, too, but it turns out I can't. And that's a shame — I've just about got through the nice, fat cheque from *Art Matters* and I'm almost penniless.'

'What were you doing for *Art Matters*?' I found it difficult to imagine the man, who sat opposite me, writing with any sensitivity on art.

'I did a series of profiles on significant Eastern European artists. Gorski was the last.'

'Hence the gate-crashing.'

'Sorry about that.' He didn't sound too sorry. 'I needed to see his paintings before they went on general display. It worked, too. The magazine paid me well, but now their bounty is gone.' His tone was mournful, but almost immediately he recovered his bounce. 'That's where you come in.'

'Me?'

'Yes, I need to find those plans for the pavilion — if they exist.'

'The Victoria and Albert has the archive for the 1851 Exhibition and probably the Royde papers, too.'

'So I gathered from the net, but not all of them, it seems. That's the difficulty. They have the stuff on the Carlyon chapel, but nothing earlier.'

'Are you certain there was anything earlier?'

'The Society is convinced there was. They reckon Royde spent a couple of years in Italy, Lombardy I think it was then, came back to England around 1850 and then got involved in some way with the Great Exhibition. They imagine he was engaged to design one of the hundreds of display spaces.

But I can't find a trace.'

'So what do you want from me?'

'Could you discover whether there's anything earlier than 1852? You've probably got a lot more sources available than I can tap into.'

He exuded a confidence I didn't feel. I sipped my wine slowly while I thought it over. Did I really want to get involved? All I could do was conduct the same search in which Nick had already failed. It was unlikely to yield a different result, although it was possible a specialist's eye might alight on something he'd missed. I knew I was probably fooling myself, but even so I couldn't prevent a slight frisson of anticipation.

'I don't have other sources, as you call them, but I'm willing to look through the papers at the V and A. There may be something you've overlooked, although it's doubtful.'

His face smiled pure pleasure. 'You're a pal,' he said breezily. 'And if you do come up with anything, I'll stand you another drink.'

'That goes without saying.'

And for the first time I allowed myself to smile back at him. I could see he was momentarily stunned by the difference. I've been told I look ten years younger when I smile and a great deal more fun. And my eyes, which often seem misty and indeterminate, become an electrifying green. I watched his stupefaction with some amusement.

'How long have you been a freelance writer?' I asked. It was time to lighten the atmosphere.

'Too long!'

My eyebrows must have risen and his voice became defensive. 'Four years, maybe a bit more. I've never had what you'd call a 'proper' job.'

'Nor me,' I confessed.

'How come? You look pretty well set up.'

'Looks can be deceptive. I spent years as a student and now I fritter my time away investigating the history, if there is any, behind people's houses. It's mostly a vanity project for them — and for me, I guess.'

'But what about the gallery? Don't you work there?'

'Odds and ends when I'm needed. My main role is hostess at events like the Gorski. Oliver Brooke owns and runs the gallery. Actually he runs three galleries, the one here in London, one in Bristol and one he's just opened in Newcastle.'

'Busy man.'

'Successful man.'

'So why, if it's not an indelicate question, aren't you involved in running any of these galleries multiplying across the face of England?'

I took my time to answer. 'Oliver prefers me to take a background role. I manage my own small business, but I need to be on hand to accompany him on buying trips or trade fairs, new exhibitions, that kind of thing.'

Nick finished his wine before he said flatly, 'He's your partner.'

'Yes, he's my partner.' My response didn't sound hugely enthusiastic even to my ears, and he was encouraged to probe.

'How did you meet?'

'Oliver visited my uni when I was an undergraduate. He gave a lecture on gallery management. I got talking to him afterwards and the upshot was that he took me on for work experience at the Papillon during the summer. He even paid me.'

'Generous!'

'He is very generous.' I was suddenly serious. 'He funded me through my postgraduate studies. I couldn't have made it without him.'

I wished I hadn't told him that. He was a stranger, and here I was spilling personal information all over the place. I tried to change the subject.

'Have you had much published, apart from the series you mentioned?'

'Bits and pieces. It doesn't amount to much.'

I must have frowned because his protest was instant. 'You don't know how difficult it is to get published.'

'That's where you're wrong. I know very well. You must have to take on other jobs— unless you have a wealthy family supporting you.'

'Wealthy family, yes. Supporting me, no. My father washed his hands of me when I refused to follow him into the law.'

'And your sister? She hasn't followed in his footsteps either, it seems.'

'Lucy? No. But that's okay with Dad because she's a girl, would you believe? He set her up in business — events management. Did I mention that?'

I nodded.

'I don't think he ever expected to see a penny of his money back, but amazingly she's turned out to be businesswoman of the decade. My brother is the most successful barrister in his chambers, which leaves me as the family failure.'

'Hardly. *Art Matters* is a prestigious journal. If they thought you were good enough to publish, you should get other offers.'

'That's what I thought, but it hasn't happened. I've been

hanging around on the off chance that some eager editor will get in touch — I've written a corker on art fraud in Romania — but no one's interested. So it will soon be back to waiting tables.'

'And that's presumably why you contacted me?'

'I've worked really hard on the papers from the Exhibition,' he assured me. 'It's not that I want you to do my work for me.'

I allowed myself a slight smile since that was precisely what I did think. In response, he leaned across the table, his body tense. 'I figured that if you looked through the stuff at the V and A and came to the same conclusion, then I'd be justified in telling the Royde Society that earlier plans simply don't exist.'

'And you can happily advise them to use the Carlyon chapel for their nostalgia fest, meanwhile collecting your fee en route?' I finished for him.

'If they do pay out when they get the news — I'm not convinced, these cultural societies are often tightwads. Anyway, if they do pay, I'll stand you dinner.'

'My reward is rising all the time. How can I refuse?' It was a very slight mystery, but any mystery was an event in my present limbo, and there was always a chance I might strike gold. 'I'll have a look through the V and A archive once I've settled Mrs Carmichael,' I found myself saying.

'Who's she?'

'She is my current burden — sorry, client. I'll give you a ring when I know more.'

He got up to go, pulling down the tee shirt that had ridden up to reveal a neatly compact body. 'Thanks, Grace, you're about to save a dying man,' he said, and started off at a sprint.

'Hadn't you better leave me your number? Do you have a card?'

'*Please.* Do I have a card?!'

He grabbed the menu and looked hopefully around for a pen, as if one might materialise out of the air.

'Here.' I handed him my silver ballpoint and he scribbled on the menu. 'And I'll have it back.' He was half way to the door again.

'Sorry, but there's a pawnbroker around the corner,' he joked, and handed me back the pen.

\* \* \*

Perhaps not such a joke. Nick Heysham appeared to live on the edge of respectability. Oliver would not approve. He would see him as a liability and wonder why I'd taken it into my head to befriend him. But when I broached the subject over dinner that evening, he seemed relaxed about the idea of my undertaking research for someone I hardly knew and without any likely recompense. His mind was on other things.

'I've an idea to move the Gorski up to Newcastle next month.' He absently stroked the small, spiky beard he'd managed to grow in recent weeks. 'The exhibition worked brilliantly at the Papillon, and we did a good deal of extra business from it.'

'Do you think Gorski is well-known enough in Newcastle?'

It was a foolish thing to say. Oliver was very strong on the notion of 'art for the people.' But at the same time he was good at spotting the next big thing, which is why he lived in a large house in Hampstead and drove a top-of-the-range Mercedes.

'Don't be snobbish, darling. The art world there is buzzing. Think of the Baltic, the Laing, the Shipley.'

I thought about them while he began to clear the table.

'We might take a trip together.'

'To Newcastle?'

'Yes, of course to Newcastle.' He sounded a trifle impatient at my obtuseness. 'If the exhibition is as successful as I expect, we must celebrate.'

He was loading the dishwasher in a distracted fashion, imperilling some very expensive china. He always performed household chores in a kind of disassociated way, as if they were being done by someone else. He straightened up with the last rattle of cutlery and allowed a smile to lighten his customarily austere expression.

'We could travel on from Newcastle. We haven't had a real holiday for a long time and we'd enjoy a few days in the Highlands.'

I tried to smile back convincingly, but wondered why Oliver always talked about 'we.' He made the decisions and I went along with them. It was feeble and a small part of me felt ashamed at taking this road, but the past was still writ large in my mind, and that was my excuse.

As it seemed I would shortly be hoisted northwards, I decided I should make a start on Nick's research as soon as possible. I knew for a fact there were volumes of papers involved in the Great Exhibition, and they would all need to be checked. Once Mrs Carmichael was placated. And she would be. Tomorrow.

# Chapter Three

In the event it was nearly a week before I tripped up the sweeping grey arc of steps to the front entrance of the Victoria and Albert museum. Mrs Carmichael had been speedily dismissed, but a new client, Leo Merrick, had been phoning me constantly and growing more agitated with each call. He had begun to renovate a partly derelict building in Silver Street in the East End — he thought it had once been a school — and had hit problems. Not the everyday problems of a dodgy roof or an inefficient drainage system. No, this problem was a ghost.

His wife, who was refusing to visit the site again, let alone live there, swore she had felt, heard, even seen, a deeply unhappy spirit. Since exorcism didn't feature prominently in my list of skills, I couldn't see how I could help. But he was adamant that if I could discover more of the history of the building, it would in some miraculous fashion show him the way forward. I wasted a lot of time trying to persuade him otherwise, but in the end I agreed to find out what I could.

The statue of Prince Albert looked benignly down as I passed through the revolving glass doors, exchanging the noise of Cromwell Road for the hushed echo of footsteps.

Even on a busy weekend, the bustle of bodies and the swell of chatter were muffled by the sheer scale of the place. Today, with few visitors, the building seemed more than ever cathedral-like. Immense arches stretched into the distance, long vistas of ornamented stonework, this morning lit by a pale sun.

The National Art Library was where I was headed and once through its double doors, I took a numbered disc from the board and signed myself in. The smell of old leather, a soft light trickling through the arched windows, were comfortably familiar, yet I was still surprised to be here. A eureka moment was highly unlikely, and it was a measure of my restlessness that I'd started on a path that was almost bound to lead nowhere. Even so, a few hours in the hallowed quiet of the Reading Room was something to enjoy.

I changed my mind the minute a young librarian pushed a loaded trolley towards me. I had always known the store of papers would be large, but never appreciated quite how large.

'I've chosen the papers I think will be most useful for you,' he said cheerfully. It must have taken him most of yesterday to put together the huge cache, and I wished I could feel grateful.

'There's more?'

His dark brown eyes lit with amusement. 'Certainly there is. But if you get through these, you can ask for me at the desk and I will bring them. Paolo Tarelli.

'I'm Grace Latimer. You're from Italy?'

He nodded. 'Here for a year as an intern — and I am learning all the time. The Great Exhibition — phew! Who would have known there was so much?'

'Not me for one.' I would be here all day and more if I had

to stagger my way through the pile of boxes he'd parked beside my reading desk. It was a far larger collection than I had ever tackled, but I'd agreed to do the research and a woman's word is her bond.

'Thank you for your help, Paolo.'

'Buona fortuna!' He gave me a wry grin, and left me to it.

I took a deep breath and considered where best to start. The obvious was usually a good place. The original proposal for the Great Exhibition of the Works of Industry of all Nations, 1851, contained illustrations, plans, elevations and sections from the working drawings of the building contractors, but though the overall structure of the Exhibition Hall was clear, there were no mentions of individual display spaces or their architects and sponsors.

The official Catalogue issued by the Royal Commission was more forthcoming, with detailed accounts of the exhibits and at the very back, a list of the architects employed on the grand project. This was just what I needed, and it looked as though I'd be able to return my trolley largely untouched. But I searched the Catalogue in vain for the name of Lucas Royde. The list was of practices rather than individual architects, and I'd no idea whether Royde had worked as an employee when he returned from Lombardy or set up his own business immediately. Trying to discover which practice he might have worked for, if any, meant researching every partnership on the list. And even if I managed it — a monumental task — their records were almost certain to be incomplete.

Deflated, I turned to the trolley again and pulled out a box that contained prospectuses from every exhibitor. I had no idea who might have sponsored Royde's display space, if it ever existed, and that meant I would have to trudge through every single book, from raw materials to machinery to manufactures. And there were sixteen whole volumes.

I broke for lunch around book number nine, and by then my eyes were raw. A deep longing to be elsewhere took hold of me, but I hate to be beaten and a cheese and tomato sandwich later, I abandoned the idea of an early escape and drove myself back to the Reading Room. In my absence the surrounding desks had acquired a clutter of students and bags.

'Looks as though you've got your hands full,' the girl two seats away whispered loudly.

'More than my hands,' I muttered.

I was beginning to dislike Nick Heysham with a passion. After hours of reading and several moments when I thought I might just be on to something, not a single solid clue had emerged to bring me closer to my goal, and I still had seven more boxes of prospectuses to trawl. My eyes wandered upwards to the ironwork balustrade which encircled the room and I began idly to calculate the number of books it held, losing count somewhere around the second wall. It was time to return to volume ten.

\* \* \*

By five o'clock I'd discovered nothing, and I'd had enough. Any thought of professional glory had fled and I was ready to ring Nick and tell him he was free to say whatever he wanted to the Royde Society. His concerns were no longer mine. A hot bath and a glass of wine were. I started to repack the papers on the trolley and dislodged the final box, which was labelled trade advertisements and trade cards. Sheer curiosity pushed me to open the box and flick through the various publicity sheets. There were dozens of them, advertising the most diverse assortment of goods: Henry Edwards' highly esteemed custard powder (with directions) to make custards without eggs, Dewar's brown Durham mustard, Appold's centrifugal pump for draining marshes. Beneath the pile of advertisements lay price lists that told me how much J. S. Fry's chocolate and cocoa cost in 1851, or how much money I would need to afford Anderson's Exhibition patent Victoria car. Fascinating stuff but useless for my purpose.

I felt foolish in having invested my hopes in so little. Irritably, I bundled price lists, trade cards and advertisements back into the box. There was one I hadn't seen before that now caught my eye, a beautiful picture. In fact, a beautiful painting of a scarlet-and-black wall hanging. Its vibrant colours and intricate patterns were exquisite. According to the motto beneath, the hanging was made of silk from the Veneto.

'Ah, Italian silk.' Paolo had emerged from whatever inner sanctum the librarians inhabited, and was looking admiringly at the poster I'd held up to the light. 'My grandmother had a bedcover very like this. But does it help your search?'

'I'm afraid not. There's no obvious connection. The name of the company selling the silk has been largely obliterated. See here.'

'And there is nothing else?' He gave a sad shake of the head.

'Well, if I'd been around in 1851 I could have seen this work of beauty — what does it say? — the writing is so faded.'

'You could have seen it in a pavilion constructed in association with Daniel de Vere and Partners, Great Russell Street,' he read out.

'I wonder what 'in association' means? De Vere's could have been middlemen who imported the silk perhaps, or maybe they were the company charged with marketing the goods — maybe even producing this advert?'

'Could they be the architects you're looking for?'

'If only that were true. But I suppose de Vere *is* a notable name.'

So notable, in fact, it hadn't registered with me on my original trawl through the list of architectural practices. I felt my heart beat a little too loudly.

'I need to check something,' I said hastily.

I scrabbled my way back through the discarded mounds of paperwork and pulled out the official Catalogue. Once again, I skimmed the list of practices, but there was no trace of de Vere and Partners. Then I read the column backwards, from bottom to top. I don't know what I expected to find that would be different. But still no de Vere. I began to feel a tingling at the base of my neck.

'You have found something?' Paolo asked hopefully.

'I'm sorry, I'm keeping you.' I sounded distracted. 'You must be wanting to close the doors.'

'No, please, Grace. This is exciting. You think this poster is important after all?'

'I could be on a wild goose chase.'

He looked startled. 'A goose chase?'

I relaxed into a laugh. 'Sorry — what I mean is the advertisement might not be significant. Even if de Vere's were the original architects for this wretched pavilion, they could have been replaced by another practice, one that *was* listed in the Catalogue.'

'And if they weren't?'

'In that case, we have a firm of architects who designed

an Exhibition space for a company selling Italian silk — and the Italian connection might be important — a firm who doesn't feature on the Exhibition's official list. It's possible that Lucas Royde, the man I'm chasing, worked for them - a firm that isn't listed but does have an address. This one,' and I pointed to the poster.

A clue at last!' Paolo said delightedly and, to my surprise, gave me a warm hug.

# Chapter Four

**H**is pleasure was premature. I'd still no idea of the precise nature of de Vere's business and I'd have to find that out; or rather, Nick Heysham would. I strolled towards South Kensington station thinking over what I should say to him. Away from the thunder of the Cromwell Road traffic, it was a pleasant enough walk in the late afternoon sun through tree-lined side streets, and I took my time. I should have been as delighted as Paolo that I'd found any kind of clue, but during the slow walk any euphoria I'd felt evaporated. In retrospect, it seemed such a tenuous link that I couldn't in all faith imagine it would stand up to scrutiny. But since I wouldn't be the one scrutinising it, I was happy to pass on the information. I reached for my phone and called the number Nick had given me.

'Grace, hi! Great to hear from you.'

I wondered if his enthusiasm was a permanent state. It could prove wearing if I saw too much of him. But that was unlikely. There was no longer a reason for me to be involved since I'd gone as far as I could in satisfying my researcher's curiosity. If he wanted to take it further, he could.

I thought I'd get straight to the point. 'I haven't very exciting news for you. I've spent all day reading, but without a single mention of Lucas Royde coming to light.'

There was quiet at the other end of the line.

'That *could* be exciting,' he said eventually. 'I can report to the Society I've had an expert confirm my initial findings that the Carlyon chapel was the first of Royde's designs.'

'I'd rather you didn't bring me into the conversation.'

'It surely can't hurt to mention you.' He sounded almost indignant. 'Come on, help a guy out!'

Annoyance at being coerced must have communicated itself in my silence, because his tone changed abruptly. 'Listen, Grace, it would help me sound convincing if I could say I'd consulted an expert, and I won't name you.'

'You're not being realistic. They'll want to know the person you've talked to.'

'I guess so, but I can skirt round that. No worries.'

I was sure he could since he seemed fluent in not quite telling the truth, but I didn't fancy being dragged into his scheming. I decided it was time to plant a question in his mind.

'There was *something* you might want to follow up.'

'What's that?' He sounded taken aback. Good.

'Among the stacks of paper I waded through today, I found an advertisement for a company selling fine Italian silks. I couldn't read the company's name, but the advert mentioned an associated firm who might just be architects.'

'So?'

'If they *were* architects, they're not listed officially in the Exhibition Catalogue, and that's odd.'

I could hear I'd lost him, but he was trying to keep up. 'Why wouldn't they be listed?'

'Any number of reasons — maybe a printer's error, maybe the silk merchant changed his architects and it's the later practice that appears in the Catalogue.'

'I'm sure this is fascinating stuff to you, but I'm grappling with why it's important.' His enthusiasm had deserted him at last and I decided to be kind.

'If Royde worked on a pavilion for the Exhibition, it may not have been under his own name. He may have worked for one of the architects listed in the back of the Catalogue, or he may have worked for a firm that *doesn't* appear there.'

'I don't see how that gets me any further.'

'It probably doesn't, but it may be worth a try. He doesn't appear in the Catalogue under his own name, and if you can't trace him working for another architect, then you can be pretty sure there's no connection between him and the Great Exhibition.'

He was uncharacteristically quiet, and it was clear I was going to have to spell out his options.

'As I see it, you have the choice of going through the official Catalogue and checking every architectural practice on the list in the hope of discovering from their records who they employed in 1851. Or you could take a chance and just research this one firm, who seem mysteriously to have been omitted from the record — that is, of course, if they *are* architects.'

He caught on fast. 'I'll take a chance.'

'I thought you might. The name is de Vere and Partners, and they operated from Great Russell Street. It's possible that if they were architects, their offices are still used for the same purpose. The buildings are very old there and sometimes stuff doesn't get jettisoned from one generation of workers to another. They might have something hiding in the attic!'

'I'll get on to it, although it sounds like a dead end.'

'More than likely, but this is the only clue you have and once you've investigated, you can claim your prize from the Royde Society with a clear conscience.'

'Whatever would that be?' His voice bubbled with laughter. Nick Heysham was bouncing back and it was probably time to go.

'Let me know if you turn anything up.' I was quite certain I wouldn't hear another word from him.

'Sure thing. And thanks. I won't forget that drink.'

'Dinner, wasn't it?' I teased. 'I've just spent a day immured in the V and A's Reading Room for you.'

'I'm glad you enjoyed it,' he said, and I didn't think he was joking. I went to put the phone down and then, 'Hey, Grace, are you still there? Where do you think I should start with de Vere's?'

I took a deep breath. 'Kelly's first, to confirm they *were* architects.'

The unvoiced question hung in the air. 'Kelly's Post Office London Directory of 1851,' I said crisply and rang off.

* * *

I left Hampstead underground station and turned into Heath Street. Sometime during my journey, the weather had undergone a transformation — from warm sunlight to cold splinters of rain that sliced their way determinedly through an inadequate jacket and short skirt. The walk home seemed interminable, and I arrived at Lyndhurst Villas cascading water. Oliver darted out into the hall as soon as he heard the key, but my drowned state seemed to pass him by.

'Where on earth have you been?' was his greeting. He didn't wait for a reply. 'I've been trying to get you all day.'

I felt myself bristling, but said as reasonably as any sodden person could, 'I mentioned last night that I was working at the V and A today.'

'You had your phone switched off.' His tone continued accusatory.

'The museum has a strict policy, you know that.' I was trying to stay patient, but my pressing need for a hot shower was beginning to triumph.

'What I do know was that I wanted you and you weren't available.'

His neck was mottling to a dusky red, which was always a sign he was seriously upset. He liked me to be on call and felt entitled to my attention, and I had one more attempt at placating him.

'Oliver, I'm sorry, but I had no idea you were in desperate need of my services.' It came out rather more sarcastically than I intended.

'Your services, as you call them, are exactly what I needed. And I've had to wait for hours to get them.' He pursed his lips. Very early in our relationship, his ex-wife had been anxious to tell me that Oliver was a 'petulant' man and on a very few occasions I've had to agree. This was one of them.

'So, what is it?'

'What?'

'Why have you been trying to contact me?'

'I'm moving the Gorski earlier than expected. The present show at Newcastle is closing — it was never a good choice and done against my advice. The upshot is that we need something else to fill the Papillon and pretty damn quickly.'

'And?'

'And I was depending on you to make the necessary

arrangements. Except you weren't around to make them.'

His harping was getting hard to take, as though I were an employee who'd fallen down on her duties, but I managed to keep a tight rein on my temper.

'I'm sorry you were inconvenienced,' I said as mildly as I could, 'but I'm not your PA. I do have a job of my own.'

He actually sniffed. 'If you can call it a job.'

'What exactly do you mean by that?'

'I mean it's not serious, darling.' He saw me looking shocked and tried to bluster his way out, while managing to dig an even deeper hole.

'It's a casual thing, temporary.' He waved his hand around as though dismissing the very notion that a job existed.

'In other words, it's nothing work,' I finished for him. 'Why don't you say it? But then you were opposed to my taking the job I really wanted, even though you paid my student fees for years.'

His face was annoyingly calm. 'I saw you had great promise and I was happy to help you fulfil it, but we agreed when you were offered the post at Sussex that you wouldn't have been happy there. Universities stifle creativity.'

'You agreed,' I corrected him angrily. 'And what's so creative in researching mundane houses for people with too much money? Or, for that matter, in project managing exhibition schedules?'

I caught sight of myself in the rococo mirror, precisely placed to reflect two milk-white cherubs sitting face-to-face on the shelf opposite. Right now the glass was reflecting something a little different: flushed cheeks and glittering eyes. My unruly curls had started to dry in the warm air and were now corkscrewing in every direction, a visual metaphor for the snakes of spleen rampaging through me.

Oliver must have taken a good look at the virago in front of him and decided on compromise. 'You know I consider your house research business has real potential,' he coaxed. 'I wouldn't have sponsored it otherwise. Right now, though, it's surely not the most important thing in our world, is it?'

'Not when it interferes with your plans apparently.'

'The whole point of setting you up in your own business was that you'd be free to help me when I needed it.' His tone now was resigned, patient. 'Without you, I've had to cobble together some very ad hoc arrangements.'

'That's good.'

'It isn't. It will probably be a complete shambles.'

'I'm sure not,' I said briskly, and went upstairs.

I stripped off each item of wet clothing and threw it as far away from me as I could, as though I were stripping off every unwanted layer of my life. I was deeply, deeply angry. I despised the work I did and now it appeared Oliver had joined me. His pretence that it was important was sickening. The house research had been his idea and his money that had set up the business. It was a way of keeping me occupied until he needed my help. I'd always known the deal, but this evening the disdain in his voice had shredded me. He had barely disguised his contempt.

I ran a hot shower and spent a long time staring at the bathroom tiles. Even these were Oliver's choice and not mine. I had always hated their black and white geometric precision. Oliver's mix of antique and minimalism could make me nostalgic for my sister's chintz, though goodness knows I'd shown enough distaste for that before I had left for good.

When I came back into the bedroom, he was sitting on the huge bed that dominated the room and looking drearily down at the polished wood floor. He seemed to have shrunk into himself, or else one of the denim shirts he affected had mysteriously grown. He looked up as I closed the bathroom door and his expression was pleading. We had never quarrelled quite so starkly before.

'Grace, I'm sorry.'

I didn't reply. I still found it difficult to speak to him.

'I shouldn't have dismissed your work in that unpleasant way.' He sounded ashamed, which I suppose was a start.

'No, you shouldn't have.'

'It was a wholly unacceptable thing to say.'

That was a favourite word of Oliver's, 'unacceptable.' It didn't really describe what I thought of his remarks.

'Grace, darling, look at me.'

I looked at him, but it didn't appear to be the right look.

'I was very wrong,' he began again, and I wondered how long the recital was going to take. I started to ruffle through my bedroom chest to find some clean pyjamas. I was tired out and needed to go to bed.

'I was very wrong,' he repeated, 'I lost my temper. That was unacceptable.'

There it was again. I pulled on pyjama bottoms and searched for a tee shirt. He shifted his position on the bed so that his gaze could follow me as I moved around the room. He seemed to gain confidence from my silence because he abandoned his penitent's speech and went for vindication.

'I've had a most trying day, although I'm sure you don't want to hear. But some very difficult clients and then this Newcastle business on top of it and Sue is an experienced gallery worker but completely hopeless at organising. I was left to do it all on my own.'

Did he expect me to sympathise? I wondered.

'You're a wonderful companion in all kinds of ways.' His voice was suddenly much softer. 'Don't let's continue this fight. I'm sincerely sorry.'

He looked and sounded contrite. 'I couldn't do without you, you know. I depend on you in so many ways. I know you still hanker after the university job, but it really wouldn't have been a good idea.'

I was tempted to ask why not exactly, but my antagonism had begun to melt. Who doesn't want to be needed? The appeal had hit me where it was supposed to. In any case, I hated conflict. I knew from bitter history that nothing positive ever came from it, only damage. And after all, it was Oliver who had helped set up my business, Oliver who kept it going in the lean times. For years I'd been happy enough to accept his bounty, along with his whims, because at heart he was a good man, a kind man, and I wasn't being strictly fair. I went over and kissed him on the cheek, and he pulled me down towards him, stroking my face and hair in just the right way.

The ringing of a phone shattered the moment. I was happy to leave it to ring, but Oliver got to his feet, grumbling. I followed him downstairs to the sitting room.

'Yes. Who? Just a minute.' He'd plucked my phone from my handbag.

'It's a Nick Heysham. Something about the V and A.' Oliver's mouth was pursed again and I damned Nick for calling me.

'It's a dry cleaners.' His voice sounded tinny.

'What?' I hadn't a clue what he was talking about.

'Great Russell Street, number twenty-two. It's a dry cleaners.'

'You went to Great Russell Street?'

'I'm there right now. De Vere and Partners were architects, like you said, and these were their offices. But there's no trace of them — no trace of any architects, for that matter.'

'It was always a long shot,' I soothed. 'At least now you can say you've explored every avenue.'

'I'm not sure.'

Oliver was banging dishes rather too loudly in the kitchen, and I was anxious to finish the call, but this was tantalising. Had Nick discovered something after all?

'Why aren't you sure?'

'There's nothing to be gleaned from Royde's workplace, but what about where he lived?'

'It's possible, I suppose, but that seems an even longer shot.'

'Worth pursuing?'

The noise from the kitchen had escalated. 'You'd have to consult the census to find his address,' I said quickly. 'You're lucky — there was one taken in 1851.'

'I figured the date, but I don't know the borough he lived in. Theoretically I could be searching to doomsday.'

'Don't exaggerate. If he worked in Great Russell Street, he must have lived reasonably close.'

'Are you sure about that?'

'Almost sure. Horse-drawn buses travelled across London, but I'm imagining Royde was a junior employee and wouldn't have afforded the daily fares. Most likely he walked, as most people did. So his lodgings aren't going to be that far from his office.'

Oliver's voice cut brusquely across the conversation. 'I've cooked pasta, Grace. Don't be long.'

The last thing I wanted to eat was pasta. I didn't want to eat at all. But it was Oliver's way of expressing remorse and here was Nick Heysham spoiling it for him. Nick wasn't giving up on the call either.

'It might be sensible then to draw a three-mile radius from Great Russell Street,' he was saying. 'But there'll be more than one census district involved, won't there?'

'Three at least, maybe four: Holborn, Bloomsbury, St Pancras and possibly Westminster. Look, Nick, I have to go. I'm sure the search won't take as long as you fear.'

'Would you —'

'No, I wouldn't.'

'Just two districts.'

'What do you mean, just two? I've been staring at print all day, and I'm very tired.'

'You can leave it until tomorrow,' he conceded generously. 'And if both of us look, we'll be speedy. Promise. Lucas Royde isn't exactly a common name.'

Oliver was in front of me now, the bowl of pasta balanced precariously on a tray and threatening to tip into my lap. 'Would it be too much to expect you to respond when I call?' All self-reproach had disappeared, and his voice was hectoring. 'Or are you intent on ignoring me today?'

I looked at him and felt sudden dislike.

'I'll take Bloomsbury and Westminster,' I said into the phone, and rang off.

Oliver remained where he was standing, looking thunderous. 'Nick Heysham?'

'You remember,' I said lightly, 'he wanted some help with a query on the Great Exhibition.'

'And that's what you were doing at the V and A?' His neck was again mottling alarmingly.

'Yes.'

'All day?'

'Pretty much.'

'So while I was battling to stay upright, you were engaged on this footling quest, researching things that don't matter for someone that doesn't matter.'

'If you put it like that, yes.'

I wasn't going to apologise. Oliver was probably right and I'd wasted my time. But there had been several moments in the day when I'd been quickened into life, moments when I thought I might be on the verge of discovery. And for once, I hadn't suffered a single headache.

His thunderous expression had been replaced by one of incomprehension. With elaborate care, he put the tray down on the Pembroke side table. Then, muttering irritably, he retreated to the sofa and disappeared behind the daily broadsheet. I judged it wise to abandon the pasta and go to bed. I didn't have to feign tiredness.

# Chapter Five

Tired I may have been but I slept badly, and was still tossing from one side of the bed to the other when the doorbell rang out its full Victorian chime. It was enough to rouse a whole village, let alone a body hovering in and out of sleep. I crawled to the front door expecting to find our doleful postman, complaining as always of the climb up to Lyndhurst Villas, but it was Nick Heysham's patched jeans and Young, Gifted and Slack tee shirt that greeted me.

'Quite a walk,' he said cheerfully, his breath coming short, 'but worth it. What a view — like sitting on top of the entire city.'

I was taken aback at finding this newly-minted lover of nature on my front steps and stood motionless in the open doorway. He took the opportunity to invite himself in.

'Nice pad,' he said, looking around approvingly. 'Where's Bluebeard?'

I ignored him and slunk into the kitchen in search of coffee. I needed sustaining. He followed me and looked around admiringly.

'What a kitchen! High-tech heaven. Not what I expected after those very expensive antiques in the hall. I like the mix.'

'Are you by any chance thinking of setting up as an estate agent?'

'Didn't sleep too well?' he queried sympathetically.

'No, I didn't, and you coming here uninvited at —' I had to push back a tumble of curls from my eyes '— ten in the morning...' I stopped, not quite believing the clock.

'Yeah, ten o'clock, Sleeping Beauty.'

'Have you eaten a book of fairy tales for breakfast?' I felt waspish.

'If I had, I wouldn't be so hungry. Any chance of some toast?'

I ignored him again and smacked down one of the coffees I'd made. With a resigned sigh, he settled himself at the kitchen table.

'Sorry about last night.'

'Sorry?' I played dumb.

'You know, Oliver. I could hear his fury in Great Russell Street. I didn't mean to cause havoc.'

'Then perhaps you'd better stop intruding into my life,' I said tartly. 'I was havoc free until you got involved.' Not strictly true, but I wanted him to feel at least a little guilt. I needn't have bothered.

'Red Lion Square — that should cheer you up.'

'What? Where?' I wasn't in any state to play guessing games, but luckily neither was he.

'Red Lion Square. I found him. Royde.' He couldn't keep the excitement from his voice.

I opened my eyes a fraction more and squinted at him. 'For someone who not so long ago wanted to grab the money and run, you've become very keen on this mystery.'

'Strange, isn't it? I'm sort of hooked now on finding him.'

'So what did the census tell you?'

'Quite a bit. In 1851 he was twenty-six years old and listed as an architect. He was sharing the house with the landlady and three other men, all in their twenties, another professional guy but also two working men — a baker and a saddler.'

'They were both skilled crafts.'

'Is that important?'

'It means they could afford to pay a reasonable rent. Their lodgings wouldn't have been luxurious, but quite acceptable.'

The word made me think of Oliver. He must have left for the gallery hours ago. I didn't know what more needed to be done for the move, but he had obviously thought better of waking me to tell me. I finished my coffee and decided to put my companion straight.

'If you're expecting me to go with you, I'm afraid you've had a wasted journey. I have to visit the Papillon this morning. But I'll walk to the underground with you if you can wait for me to dress.'

He seemed startled at the idea I wasn't about to fall in with his plans.

'But you've got to come. This is a joint quest now and —'

'No, it isn't.'

'You haven't heard me out yet.'

'I don't need to.'

He reached across the table and grasped my fingers. 'Come with me this morning, Grace. Just this once and then I'll *never* bother you again.'

I hastily retrieved my hands. 'I'm sorry, but if you want to carry on with the search, it's your business, not mine.'

'At least come to Red Lion Square. It's in Holborn, on your way to the gallery.'

His geography seemed slightly awry, but it would only mean a short stop-off, and it seemed oddly important to him that I went along.

'Okay, but then that's it,' I said with what I hoped was finality.

'Agreed. Mind if I take a look around while you're getting ready?'

'You will in any case.' I left him making for the conservatory.

I pulled on the nearest thing to hand, which happened to be skinny jeans, pumps, and a Day-Glo tunic. Nick Heysham was someone for whom you dressed down. It hadn't been my aim, but he appeared to like what he saw. Noticing his appreciative smile, I told myself I'd need to be cautious. He wasn't an unattractive man. In fact, he was very attractive, just not my kind of man: I've never been a fan of Tigger-type enthusiasm. Still, I must be on my guard, careful to keep this trip strictly business. I didn't want my relationship with Oliver to get any more complicated than it already was.

* * *

Less than an hour later, we turned into Red Lion Square. It was one of those civilised London spaces that occasionally you come upon when you least expect it, an oasis surrounded by noisy, traffic-filled roads. A small, neat garden was at its centre, guarded by black-painted iron railings. I'm sure it must have looked very much the same in 1851.

Number eight was no different from its neighbours, except for the bright yellow door. In Royde's day the Georgian terrace would have been relatively modern but originally built for a large family, with its three main floors plus basement and attic. By 1851 it must have ceased to be a family residence and been let out to respectable tenants. I wondered which room or set of rooms Royde had inhabited. There was nothing to tell us.

'Well,' Nick let out a sigh of disappointment. 'Nothing.'

'What were you expecting?'

'I don't know, some indication the guy had lived here, I guess.'

I thought about that. 'It is strange there's no blue plaque. He was a celebrated man in his time, hugely influential on the future of architecture. They put up plaques for far less important people.'

Nick leaned against the house railings and peered down into the uncovered basement window. I hoped the local Neighbourhood Watch wasn't too active. 'Perhaps nobody knows he ever lived here if there are no records to say so, except a page from an old census.'

'Perhaps not.' I turned to face him. 'But it's still odd. The whole thing is beginning to feel odd. We have an Exhibition space he's supposed to have designed, but it's missing from the records. Now we have a house where we know he lived, but that hasn't received official recognition either. It's as though an entire swathe of his early life has been erased.'

Nick shrugged his shoulders. 'Blue plaques are pretty arbitrary — there's not a lot of sense to where they pop up — and it could be what you thought, that Royde didn't design anything before 1852. He might never have worked for de Vere's and it's a coincidence he lived close to their offices.'

I didn't think so, but I couldn't fathom it out. I wondered whether Lucas Royde had prospered in Red Lion Square, whether it was in this house he'd gained notice for his work on the Great Exhibition and started his long climb to fame and wealth. Or had his life been very different here? Had this been an unhappy lodging, a transient resting place from which those early plans had mysteriously disappeared? For long minutes I stood gazing silently at the house, as though by simply looking I could draw out its secrets.

# Chapter Six

*London, late January 1851*

Lucas Royde banged the door of number eight Red Lion Square behind him and almost jumped down the flight of steps. He was late, and it would not look good. This was only his first month working for what many considered the best architects' practice in London. As he ran, he straightened his necktie and began hastily to button up a newly acquired frock coat. The rawness of an English winter demanded every particle of warmth.

He had risen at dawn and draped himself in as many blankets as he could find. Then, hunched over the small worktable he'd purchased for his room, he had become so engrossed in his design that time had vanished from sight. He was working on decorative tiles, new and exciting shapes, new and exciting colours. Curve by intricate curve, angle by angle, he'd been creating another image to add to his portfolio. The tiles were to shine with the most brilliant of tints — ultramarine and cadmium, he thought. Massed in their glory, they would look sublime. It was a relief to immerse himself in this precise world of colour and shape, for it helped to blunt the disappointment he was beginning to feel with the new life he'd embraced.

He hurried along Proctor Street then swerved left into Bloomsbury Way. Though it was still early, a few threadbare pedlars were plying their wares and the beggar who squatted at the entrance to the Bull and Mouth was already alert to any likely dispenser of largesse. The hard flagstones bit into his thin shoes and puddles left by the overnight rain began to soak upward into the soft leather. His footwear was made for Italian streets, he reflected, not the dirt and grime of a London January. He thought nostalgically of Verona and the long summer days spent in its piazzas.

He could have stayed, braved the rumours, since Marguerite was to return to France and he would see her no more. She would be married in Paris, as she'd always planned, and the idle talk that swirled around the small Italian town would have died stillborn. But Marguerite was not the only reason he had left a place and a people he loved. He was destined for great things. It sounded ridiculous when he said it aloud, but he knew its truth as he knew the very limbs of his body. He would do great things, push the skill, the artistry, that resided within him to its limits, make his audience sit up and take notice. It was the opportunity to light a grander stage that had impelled him towards this new life in the capital of the world.

Bury Place, as he rounded the corner, looked even shabbier in the dingy light of early morning. The detritus from the Saturday market had not yet been cleared, and there were rotting vegetables in the gutter and clouds of paper scraps whirling in a wind that every minute was growing more vigorous. He bent his head against its ice. He had come to this forbidding city for opportunity, but what in fact did that amount to? At the moment, it seemed little. A small, dark desk wedged between the walls of a small, dark cubicle and a succession of journeyman tasks. Adjusting a moulding, filling in a background, labelling forgotten plans: work fitting only for an apprentice.

Surely once his creativity and skill were recognised, he would be entrusted with more ambitious assignments. He would fulfil his mother's dreams for him and justify the harsh scrimping that had bought his architect's training. Except... future projects were likely to be no more to his taste than present trifles, for they would have at their centre a style that repelled him — Gothic, the dream child of the north. De Vere's were ardent in pursuing the current craze and too many of their projects involved the wilful destruction of beauty, the mellow loveliness of ancient English churches refashioned into mediaeval pastiche.

Enmeshed in these bleak thoughts, he narrowly averted an accident with a horse and carriage travelling at speed along Great Russell Street. He had reached his destination. Once through the double doors that guarded an imposing entrance, he saw immediately he was the last to arrive. One or two morose assistants looked up from their desks and even the draughtsmen in the connecting office bobbed their heads in surprise at his late arrival. And it *was* late, he noticed, the massive oak clock that hung on the far wall showing well past eight. He inched his way past the long trestle that housed the plans for de Vere's current commissions and slid into the cubicle opposite. Then made a show of shuffling papers, as though the latest paltry chore was a matter of great import.

Fontenoy, whose desk faced his, gave a broad wink and whispered rather too loudly, 'It must have been quite an evening, Royde!'

His fellow workers smirked in the background. A handsome face and a protracted sojourn in the Italian states had been sufficient for them to decide that Lucas was a ladies' man. Such a reputation was wholly undeserved, he thought. His affair with Marguerite was over, and there were to be no more delicate entanglements. From now on his work would be his life, his every sinew focussed on gaining recognition for his talent.

At ten o'clock, Fontenoy pushed his papers aside and prepared to leave for the coffee house in Grays Inn Road. He would fetch two pints of hot tea and serve them to his fellows on the dot of ten thirty. The ceremonial walk to Holborn was a source of great pleasure among the assistant architects and they eagerly looked forward to days when the duty fell to them. It signified half an hour of freedom, a time to breathe fresh air and if they were clever, to run small errands for themselves. It was petty, Lucas thought, but then office life *was* petty. Its regimentation was as killing in its way as the work itself.

He was doodling idly when the door to the inner sanctum opened abruptly and Mr Daniel de Vere strode out among his underlings. As always, de Vere was dressed with meticulous propriety. A multi-coloured paisley vest sandwiched between dark tailcoat and narrow dark trousers was the only suggestion of an artistic disposition. The assistants wielded their pencils ever more energetically, hoping their employer's presence would be brief and they would be left in peace to drink their tea when Fontenoy returned.

'Royde?' De Vere's voice was soft but assured.

He was being singled out for his tardiness, Lucas thought, and seemingly about to receive a public reprimand.

46

'Royde,' de Vere repeated, and then, 'Come through, I wish to speak to you.'

Lucas looked up, his blue eyes wary, but de Vere was smiling graciously. He got to his feet and followed the man back into the proprietor's walnut-panelled room. The hiss of whispers in the outer office was evident even before he had closed the door behind him.

Once through the door, he became aware of another presence. A man was standing with his back to the wall of deep windows that gave on to Great Russell Street. The visitor must have entered through the back entrance of the building. He was a bulky man of average height, dressed in the pinstripe uniform of business, his moustache short and spiky and his expression chilly.

De Vere turned to his guest. 'Mr Renville, may I introduce our newest recruit, Mr Lucas Royde. Mr Royde is recently arrived from Lombardy — I am sure that will prove most helpful — and comes to us with the most excellent references.'

De Vere gave a melancholy smile at Lucas. 'Royde, this is Mr Edward Renville, a new client.'

Both men took stock of each other, and neither felt any liking. There was an uncomfortable silence following the polite handshakes until de Vere gestured to them both to take a seat, while he barricaded himself behind the fastness of a large mahogany desk. Despite the precision of his dress, his desk was amazingly cluttered: sheaves of plans fought for space with drawing implements and open books were piled one upon another. Tiers of shelving above the desk overflowed with files so battered they leaked paper at every corner.

De Vere struck at the silence. 'You are only lately arrived

in England, Royde, and may not know that Mr Renville is a most important dealer of Italian goods.'

'The most delicate silks in the world and the very finest of Venetian yarns,' Edward Renville interjected, his thin voice at odds with his appearance.

Daniel de Vere coughed delicately. 'Mr Renville has come to us with a most interesting proposal.'

His tone suggested that such interest was muted. 'Mr Renville intends to display his wares at the Great Exhibition, which is now only four months away, and is desirous of having an Exhibition space designed and built to show his goods to their best possible advantage.'

Then to underline the importance of his words, he added for Lucas's benefit, 'The Exhibition is likely to be one of the greatest events of the century.'

Renville nodded solemnly. This time he spoke at length and his voice was as clipped as it was thin, as though he were unwilling to give more time to each syllable than absolutely necessary.

'My business is thriving, Mr Royde. Turnover continues to increase and I have little need to seek further business.' He almost swelled physically as he made this claim. 'However, as Mr de Vere has said, the Exhibition is likely to be one of the greatest moments of a great century. Such an important enterprise as Renville's should not be absent. We need no introduction to the *cognoscenti*, but it is only right and proper that the rest of the world has an opportunity to know and appreciate our matchless quality.'

The man is a pompous ass, Lucas thought. And why choose me for the dubious honour of working for him? His employer answered his question almost immediately.

'Mr Royde is newly qualified but is an architect with

immense potential. At the moment, he is not engaged on a major project for us and can give immediate attention to your requirements.'

Lucas silently translated. This is a job that de Vere considers trifling and hardly worth the effort. But Renville is a new client who may offer more substantial work in the future and he is reluctant to turn him away. I am available and I come cheaply.

Renville was now looking even chillier, his silver-grey eyes veiled in frost. He began flicking imaginary dust from his lapels in a gesture redolent with disdain, signalling clearly that he considered he was being fobbed off with an inexperienced assistant. That was not what he was used to; he looked likely to walk away.

Eager to placate his awkward client, Daniel de Vere hurried on. 'I think you will find that Mr Royde's knowledge of the Italian states will add enormously to the project. He will be the right man to design you a fitting backdrop for your exquisite silks.'

The visitor looked unconvinced, but then a calculating expression flitted across his face. 'I had expected to employ someone a little more experienced, de Vere,' he said, chopping at the words in his thin voice. 'We will need to talk cost.'

'Naturally,' de Vere responded smoothly.

Lucas felt vastly irritated. He might as well not be in the room. It was a bargaining process between two powerful men, and he was a mere pawn. Whether or not he wished to design for Renville was immaterial. He would have to. But despite its disagreeable source, the commission was sounding interesting. A display space created especially for the sensuous silks of Italy; he might even infiltrate his beautiful tiles into the design, and then the rest of the world, as Renville had put it, would see them at last. It might just be his breakthrough — a goodbye to the Gothic pillaging, the cramped cubicle, tea at ten thirty.

'Mrs Renville will be in charge of the project.'

They had risen from their seats, readying themselves for the obligatory farewell, but at this statement both de Vere and Lucas blinked.

'Mrs Renville?' de Vere queried.

'My wife,' Renville said curtly, as though it explained everything.

Then, seeing their blank faces, he said in a tone verging on the acerbic, 'You cannot think that *I* would have time to supervise something so…' and he struggled to find a properly dismissive word, '…frivolous. I have a business to run.'

Daniel de Vere swallowed hard and when he spoke, a newly abrupt manner signalled that he knew himself to have judged rightly in delegating this small undertaking to the most junior of his staff.

'The project will be carried out in whatever way you think fit.'

'Good.' Edward Renville drew himself up to his full height and looked through them. 'Our dear Queen opens the Exhibition on May the first and Renville's must be ready. As it happens my wife is Italian and an artist herself. She will oversee the design and make sure it is right for our merchandise. She has a sharp eye, not as sharp as mine, but sharp enough. Most importantly, she will ensure the business does not incur unnecessary expenditure. In that she will have my full support, do not doubt.'

The slightest of smiles creased the corners of his mouth. He seemed delighted he had trampled any likely opposition. With this final admonition, he lodged his top hat firmly on his head and turned to shake hands with Daniel de Vere. Lucas was accorded a brief nod.

'I will bring her here,' he announced. 'This afternoon. You will need to get started.'

Both men looked taken aback. 'No time like the present.' Renville gave a satisfied grimace. 'But before I sign anything, I will need to see the small print, de Vere.'

He wrenched open the door to the outer office and stalked a pathway through the interested minions.

'Well, Royde,' de Vere said in a judiciously controlled voice once their visitor was out of earshot, 'You should hold yourself ready this afternoon for a visit from Mrs Renville.'

Then as he made to return to his room, he added quietly, 'Remember, they are the clients. They decide. But do try to steer the lady away from anything too elaborate. Something quite simple, I think, something quite modest. Yes, modest, that's the word.'

And his office door closed with what seemed a sigh of relief.

# Chapter Seven

Lucas wandered back to his desk, unsure of what to think. He had disliked Renville on sight, but if an architect only worked for those he took in immediate liking, he would starve. Had he not this very morning bemoaned the lack of satisfying work, and daydreamed of a chance to show his skill? And here was a commission that might open up any number of possibilities. He had been in England for only a few weeks and knew little of the Exhibition, but from a brief scan of the newspapers he had a measure of its likely importance. Discussion in the press was frequent and wide-ranging, from arguments over admission prices, to warnings against opening the Exhibition to 'foreigners', to the moral panic whipped up by some that Hyde Park would be overrun by socialist demonstrations. The mere fact of so much discussion suggested there would be a very large audience, an audience for his work as much as for Renville's goods. Realising this, he had begun to feel a thrum of enthusiasm, his tiles a kaleidoscope of colour and shape, dancing through his mind.

But then the blow had fallen. He was not to be free to plan as he wished, free to win over this admittedly difficult client to a striking and innovative design. He would have someone looking over his shoulder the entire time, and the end result would not be his. It would be a mishmash of ill-fitting tastes. Not only that, but it was a woman with whom he had to contend. He was to be supervised by a wife who was 'artistic.' It couldn't get much worse. She would be one of those wispy, middle-aged females who had taken up watercolour painting as an antidote to the crushing boredom of domestic life, and would be replete with unsuitable suggestions he would have to pretend to take seriously. One by one, he would have the fight of his life to dismiss them from consideration. And with Renville huffing in the background, he was unlikely to win. At this moment, even the Gothic seemed preferable.

'Working for a woman, eh?'

Unheard, Fontenoy had come up behind him. Lucas was still astounded at the way news found its way around the office almost instantaneously. He didn't reply, and Fontenoy went on with his teasing.

'Now I wonder why DV chose *you*?' De Vere was always known by his initials in the office. 'Could it be those blue eyes and that charming smile are likely to loosen the Renville purse strings?'

'Don't you get tired of singing the same song?' Lucas returned in some exasperation. 'Having a female supervising the project will not make the slightest difference.'

He lied, he knew. It would make it twice as hard. If she wasn't fey, she would be a dragon desperate to exercise some influence in the world. Married to an autocrat stuffed full of his own importance, why wouldn't she?

Fontenoy raised sceptical eyebrows, and Lucas was goaded into defending himself. 'Mr de Vere chose me to lead the project before ever he became aware that Mrs Renville was to be involved.'

Fontenoy's eyebrows stayed where they were.

'It's simple. I'm the logical choice. Renville sells Italian silks and I've spent the last two years in Lombardy.' He might as well make it sound important, even though his role had already been downgraded.

'Ah, that would explain it, then.'

His colleague gave a smirk and went back to his work, leaving Lucas feeling depressed. His earlier small enthusiasm had vanished and the Renville design no longer carried any possibility of advancement. Instead, it was a dead end towards which he must trudge. He had no choice, he told himself; he was an employee and did what his employer requested. But the opening of the Great Exhibition on the first day of May was beginning to sound like a date that could not arrive quickly enough.

*  *  *

The summons came halfway through the afternoon when Lucas was indifferently leafing through the firm's scrapbook of Gothic mouldings, searching for new options to present to a dissatisfied client. His colleagues again looked up from their desks when his name was called and again were disappointed to discover they were not to be party to the introductions. Like her husband before her, Mrs Renville had slipped in through the rear of the building.

'*Buona fortuna!*' whispered Fontenoy wickedly, as Lucas made his way towards the office door.

The blinds had been drawn against a low afternoon sun, and it took some while for Lucas to focus in the darkened room. The burly outline of Edward Renville was the first shape to emerge. He was standing by de Vere's massive desk, tapping the wood with impatient fingers. He looked towards the door as Lucas entered and made only the barest of acknowledgments before embarking on introductions.

'I have brought Mrs Renville to meet you, Royde. As I intimated, the Exhibition space will be largely my wife's concern. But that should not worry you — she will do a good job of overseeing the work. She has flair and will be happy to advise, will you not, Mrs Renville?'

Lucas looked at the woman addressed and felt his heart sing. She was at least twenty years younger than her uncompromising spouse, and a thousand times more attractive. She was bareheaded, and her long, dark hair was drawn back smoothly from an oval face and fastened into a knot from which one or two curls escaped with joyous abandon. Her heritage was betrayed in the smooth olive complexion and the soft brown eyes that even now were smiling out at him. Women's fashions were often unflattering, he thought, even downright ugly, but the light blue silk dress Alessia Renville wore did nothing to conceal her beautiful form. In the warmth of the office she had unbuttoned her woollen cape and Lucas caught a glimpse of full but shapely breasts and a neatly nipped waist.

When she spoke, the accent was hardly detectable. 'I am pleased to meet you, Mr Royde. I am most interested in design, though I cannot pretend any expertise. But it will be a great pleasure to work alongside you.' Her gentle voice seemed to reach into him and give a little tug at his soul.

He stood as though rooted to a few square inches of floor, unable to think at all sensibly. He knew he had to pull himself together. This was a business meeting, and she was his client's wife.

He moved towards her and took her proffered hand. 'It

is a great pleasure to meet you, Mrs Renville,' he said in as neutral a voice as he could manage. 'Our shared acquaintance with Italy is sure to result in a most successful collaboration.'

Seeing a deep frown appear on Renville's face, Daniel de Vere interposed. 'Mutual experience will make for an excellent beginning, but naturally the collaboration will be an entirely English one.'

'Entirely,' Alessia Renville added unexpectedly. To Lucas's ear her tone held a note of gentle mockery, but when he shot her a swift glance, her face was without guile.

Her husband gave a loud harrumph and once more collected his hat from the desk.

'We must be leaving,' he announced abruptly. 'I still have many hours of work before me.' His contemptuous glance dismissed the notion that this could ever apply to an architect. 'And I must first escort my wife home.'

'Of course,' de Vere said smoothly. 'Will Mrs Renville be coming to our offices for consultations? If so, I would be happy to make my room available to her whenever she wishes.'

'Royde will come to our house,' his uncomfortable guest stated baldly. 'Next week, Thursday at two in the afternoon. Bring some ideas for my wife to see. Once she has agreed them, we will make a start since time is of the essence. The Exhibition site has been under construction since last September, I believe, and is already well developed.'

Lucas was confounded. Surely even this philistine must realise he would need time to create a design that matched the perfection of Renville silks. But there was little point in arguing. Edward Renville was a rich man, who expected his demands to be met.

'If development of the site is already at an advanced stage,' he said in a voice tight with annoyance, 'it would help to know the location of the space you have been awarded.'

'You will need to discover that for yourself. What I want to see are plans — and quickly. Space at the Exhibition is heavily oversubscribed and only my considerable influence has obtained one.'

Lucas gave up. The man was an ogre and a stupid ogre at that. He could not keep the contempt from his face, but before Renville had noticed the affront, his wife had collected her bonnet from a nearby chair and was holding out a gloved hand.

'Till next Thursday then, Mr Royde.' She gave him a gentle smile.

'*A giovedì,*' Lucas repeated quietly, holding her hand for just a shade too long.

The unexpected music of Italian provoked a glowering expression in Edward Renville and without further pause, he ushered his wife through the side door and out into Great Russell Street.

# Chapter Eight

Red Lion Square had proved a disappointment to us both. 'We're not doing any good here.' Nick's feet shuffled impatiently. 'We should go. That coffee seems a distant memory and I'm hungry as well.'

The nearest coffee shop wasn't the smartest of places, but I could see why Nick had been attracted when we'd passed it earlier. Its display window was crammed with carbohydrates, and he reached the counter in double-quick time and was already shuffling through his pockets for change. If this was his usual diet, I couldn't imagine how he managed to keep a neat, muscular figure. If life was at all fair he should be consigned to the muesli and pasta regime Oliver maintained was excellent for fuel and form, not confections of sugar and pink icing.

Between mouthfuls of doughnut, he attempted to sum up what so far we'd managed to discover, and that was very little. He sounded despondent and I felt the same. Something about this search had got under both our skins, but what it was I couldn't put my finger on. It was as though there were something hidden beneath the surface, not just the missing pavilion and missing plaque, but something else we didn't know or understand that was leading us onwards. Except at the moment we weren't going anywhere.

'I say we go to Norfolk,' he said unexpectedly. He wiped the last sugar particles from his mouth.

'Norfolk?'

'There are different stories, but the Royde Society thought he came from Norfolk. We could go there, try and find where he lived, discover any clues to his early life. We might even be able to speak to some of his descendants, get to know any family gossip that's been handed down.'

The goose chase had just got wilder, and I thought it time to bring him down to earth. '*We* aren't going anywhere. And if you decide to make the trip yourself, you'll find it very difficult to discover where Royde lived and almost impossible to trace a family who knew him.'

But Nick refused to be put off. 'I think it's a great idea. It's not as if there's anything to find here. And Lucy told me the secretary of the Society was convinced Royde was brought up in Norfolk. She said he travelled to Italy from there.'

'But where's the hard evidence of a Norfolk connection?'

'She mentioned something, though I don't remember it exactly. At the time all I could hear was my sister saying there was work for me… it might have been something to do with the kind of house Royde built for himself when he retired.'

'The house was near Taunton, I think. I saw a picture of it once — brick, flint and coursed cobbles — unusual for Somerset, although it was a traditional Norfolk mix in the nineteenth century.'

'There you are, then.' He sounded smug.

'It's nowhere near enough. You'll need to ask your sister to find out more from the Society. Are you seeing her soon?'

'Unlikely. We don't socialise — she prefers to keep me in

the background. I don't quite fit the canapés and cocktail circuit.'

He was smiling, but something about the tone of his voice made me think he wasn't as happy with the situation as he made out. I was curious.

'What about the rest of your family? Do you see them?'

'Christmas, but I guess that's it. They're in Gloucester-shire.'

'That's not exactly the end of the world.'

'No, it just feels like it. Not Gloucestershire, but the whole family set up. And since I declined my father's kind offer of a career in law, I haven't been the most welcome visitor.'

'You're not counting on acting the prodigal son, then?'

'Why would I? Do you fancy the role of prodigal daughter?'

His casual comment knocked me off balance. 'I don't have parents.'

For the first time since I'd met him, he looked concerned. 'I didn't realise. Sorry. I have a big mouth.'

'There I'd have to agree, but it wasn't your fault.'

'So, no family?'

'A sister,' I said, and my voice was strained. 'An older sister, much older.'

His face invited confession and I blurted out, 'She brought me up, but we don't speak.'

'Too bad.'

There was an awkward silence, and he quickly reverted back to Norfolk. 'I really think we should go. It might do you good.'

I didn't know what he meant by that, but going to East Anglia was the last thing I intended. 'You've only the very flimsiest proof that Royde had connections with Norfolk.

You can't go haring off there on a whim. I certainly can't. I've an exhibition to move.'

Those very blue eyes gazed at me steadily. 'You're still working for Oliver Brooke, then?'

'Why wouldn't I be?'

'I heard the way he spoke to you last night. I didn't think you'd take that kind of shit.'

'Oliver was stressed.' I felt the need to defend him.

'Still…' He looked at me thoughtfully as if weighing up how much to say. 'When I first saw you across the Papillon's white space, I thought you a bit dizzy, a bit frivolous. Blame the blonde curls or maybe that you only came up to my shoulder! But you have claws, Grace, and I'm wondering why you don't use them.'

I wanted to tell him to mind his own business, but his expression was warm and friendly and I couldn't. 'Oliver has been good to me.' The only person who ever has, I thought, but that went unsaid. 'I owe him a great deal.'

He must have heard the edge in my voice and decided against pursuing the subject. Instead, he relaxed back into his chair. 'So there's nothing more we can do?'

'Nothing — and I must get going.' My phone rang as I bent to retrieve my handbag. I was tempted to ignore the call since I was already running late.

'Must be Oliver,' Nick said, with a grimace.

The thought that it might be had me answer. Not Oliver though, but Paolo. I'd left him my number in case he came across anything new.

'Grace, how are you?' He didn't wait for a response. 'Sorry to interrupt whatever you're doing, but I've had an idea.

'Yes?'

'The Guild of Architects. They are in Bedford Square.'

'I know. But I doubt they have archives that early.'

'I asked my colleague and she says they were founded in 1850, and that's just within your date. It might be worth a try.'

'It might be,' I agreed, though I'd no intention of trying, 'and thank you, Paolo.'

'No problem.' He was sounding less Italian all the time.

'Who was that?' Nick was leaning forward. He'd heard enough of the conversation to be fired by the chance of keeping the quest alive.

'Paolo Tirelli. He works at the V and A. He mentioned archives held by the Guild of Architects.'

'Great idea. So what are we waiting for?' He gulped down the rest of his coffee and was nearly to the door before I'd managed to snatch up my bag.

'Hang on, Nick. I haven't the time. I must get to Hoxton.'

We were standing on the pavement, and I was poised for flight. Suddenly he put both hands on my arms and pulled me towards him.

'I need you,' he said urgently. 'I want you to be there if I discover anything.'

I found myself drawn into his gaze. Once again I looked at him for just a little too long and felt embarrassment seeping through me.

'It's okay,' he said soothingly, 'I like looking at you, too.'

Then he was smiling. 'On a purely practical level, they won't let me within an inch of their archive. With your uni credentials, we should manage it.'

I fought against going. 'Don't you have some kind of paperwork to show you're a researcher?'

'I've got a press card from *Art Matters,* but it's a bit out of date. They probably don't like journalists, anyway.'

'No, they probably don't.'

'Come with me, please!' And he smiled down at me. What was it about those eyes that made me such a pushover?

'I'll give you an hour,' I said, knowing full well I'd be lucky to be finished by lunchtime.

# Chapter Nine

The elderly receptionist at Bedford Square was courtesy itself. He took only the most cursory glance at my university reader's card before leading us down to a basement lined from floor to ceiling with aluminium shelves. From these he abstracted three very substantial cardboard boxes, each marked 1850–1860 in bold, black ink, then ceremoniously handed us two pairs of clean white gloves.

'You'll be all right if I leave you?' His smooth, pink face shaped itself to a gentle enquiry. 'You know what you're after. I'll look in on you in about an hour.'.

When he'd disappeared up the stairs, I dived into the first box. 'I think that was a warning we shouldn't take too long.'

Nick gave a shrug. 'Let's hope not.'

But over the next hour we toiled through every one of the three boxes, all of them crammed with files. Papers were stacked, fell into disarray and then were painstakingly stacked again. The Guild had kept vast numbers of documents: proposals for projects, lengthy correspondence, roughly sketched designs, detailed plans. It was a treasure chest of mid-Victorian architecture, but not it seemed, our treasure chest. The discovery of one or two projects instigated by de Vere and Partners temporarily heartened our search, but they turned out to be of no interest. It was Nick who first came across Royde's name.

We had been labouring for what seemed an age when he jumped to his feet. 'Royde, I've found him!'

I caught some of his excitement and moved quickly over to the section of table he'd been working on. I picked up the file and my excitement died almost immediately. It contained copies of Royde's plans for the Carlyon chapel, meticulously preserved between sheets of pristine tissue. Along with the chapel plans, there were a number of other projects the architect had worked on during the rest of the decade. But of the Great Exhibition, there was not a trace. Nick slumped in his chair, his enthusiasm vanquished by this new setback. I carried on mechanically sifting through the few papers that remained. I knew what the result would be.

Promptly on the hour our guide arrived to escort us back to reception. 'Any luck?'

I shook my head. 'I'm afraid not. There are plans of Royde's projects in the 1850s, but they're not the ones we need.'

'Then they probably don't exist,' he said presciently. 'Royde was a major architect and we would have copies of all of his papers.'

'De Vere was the other name we were looking for,' Nick put in, as though throwing his last dice. 'But there's nothing very useful on him either, not here and not on the net.'

Our escort came to a halt. He looked a trifle puzzled, his furrowed brow at odds with the smooth pink cheeks. 'That seems a little strange. We don't worry too much about the internet, but there should certainly be comprehensive paper records. Mr Daniel de Vere was a famous name at the Guild.'

My ears pricked. 'Really?'

'Indeed, yes. If you have a minute, I would like to show you something.'

Nick and I looked at each other. We had a minute, more than a minute if it gave us another clue. We followed the pinstripe trousers up the basement steps and along a thickly carpeted corridor to the room at the very end. Its double doors were massive and made of polished mahogany. Our escort flung them wide and ushered us in. It was perfectly quiet, perfectly still. Not even a distant hum of London traffic. The room was beautifully proportioned with large rectangular windows overlooking a garden filled with May colour. But my attention fixed on the roll of honour set in the middle of the farthest wall. A mahogany wood scroll engraved with a list of names in gold lettering, at whose head appeared Mr Daniel de Vere.

'Our first President,' our new friend declared proudly, 'a founding member of the Guild.' Nick's mobile face was registering disappointment even as my pulse was quickening.

'Mr de Vere must have been a very important figure over a number of years,' I suggested.

'Naturally. As I said, he helped to found the Guild, but he was also instrumental in mentoring many excellent young Victorian architects. He set up an Academy at the lower end of Great Russell Street and after about 1860 left the running of the partnership to his cousin, Mr Joshua de Vere. He wanted to concentrate on teaching — he considered it the most important work he could do.

I was thinking hard. 'So he's likely to be the subject of at least one biography.' It was an avenue I hadn't thought of travelling, but it could prove fruitful.

Our guide smiled benignly. 'Three, in fact. Two contemporary accounts and one I think written in the 1960s. They're almost certainly out of print, but we have copies of all three in our library.'

'Would it be possible to borrow them?' I switched on my most fetching smile, hoping the green eyes would work their charm. They did — up to a point.

'I'm afraid you wouldn't be able to take them off the premises, but if you wish to read them here, then I'm sure that will be in order.'

'It would be wonderful,' I enthused. 'May we use this room?'

The green eyes were still doing their stuff and he smiled back. 'That won't be a problem. I'll fetch them for you.'

He had hardly closed the door behind him when Nick exploded. 'You must be mad! Three biographies and read them here!'

'Yes, and you're reading two of them.'

He seemed to be making strange spluttering sounds, but I took no notice. So far he had drifted through the enquiry in the hope of gaining a sizeable fee without too much effort. But it was no longer simply a question of getting the Royde Society to pay up. Nick had been the one who'd tempted me into this search and now I was caught in its web. We both were. It was time he did some hard work. I was determined we would skim those biographies until we had exhausted their every last word. We had drawn a blank at Great Russell Street and a blank in Red Lion Square, but I knew there had to be more. There was something missing beyond mere plans; something waiting to be found.

* * *

'It's Dorset!' Nick was suddenly a dervish, whirling crazily around the room. 'He came from Dorset!'

I craned my neck to get a glimpse of the page he was flapping wildly in the air. 'Slow down. Let me see.'

I felt piqued he had been the one to find something, if indeed he had. He'd skimmed through the first biography rather too swiftly and then immediately pounced on the one book that was left.

'Here, here, look.' He came to settle at my elbow. 'The author quotes a letter from some architects in Dorchester and they're praising Royde to the skies.'

'What exactly does the writer say?'

I was dubious. We'd already had too many false starts, but Nick's excitement fairly crackled through the quiet room.

'He's fulsome about Daniel de Vere — argues he was a top man in encouraging young talent and Lucas Royde is his star illustration. According to the author, de Vere gave Royde his first break and started the guy on his path to becoming the big name in Victorian architecture.'

'And the letter?'

'It's a reference, pretty sycophantic stuff, too. Listen to this,' and he assumed a suitably fawning voice.

*…We have no hesitation in recommending Mr Lucas Royde to your employment. Mr Royde came to us as an apprentice in January, 1841. He had received an excellent education at Dorchester Grammar School, with added tuition in Latin and Greek, but had decided that he would not proceed to the university. At the age of sixteen, he felt himself ready to train for a profession. Over the next six*

*years, Mr Royde showed himself to be an extremely apt
pupil, demonstrating a skill, creativity and originality that
eventually surpassed anything that existed within our
offices. He was at that time destined for a position in a great
London practice such as your own, but on the receipt of an
unexpected legacy Mr Royde took himself to the Italian
states in order to develop further his exceptional talent. We
know that you will find him industrious, enthusiastic and
an enormous asset to your business....*

The ponderous phrases sat oddly with Nick's faded tee
shirt and frayed jeans, but for a moment I was transported
back to that Victorian office and Daniel de Vere reading the
response to his enquiry. He must have been intrigued by a
young man with such evident potential. Royde had been
working for himself when he designed the Carlyon chapel,
I knew, so if de Vere had indeed provided him with a start,
the young man must have designed something important
while working at the practice. Was that something a design
for an Exhibition space at the Crystal Palace and if so, how
did those plans disappear and where did they disappear to?

'What are you thinking?' Nick was studying me closely.

'That East Anglia doesn't look such a good bet.'

'Okay, I got it wrong. But we've solid evidence now. Let's
go.'

'Go where?'

'Dorchester!'

He said it as though I must be missing a brain cell or two
if I couldn't see the necessity and, when I remained silent,
his voice took on the slightly coercive tone I'd heard before.
It didn't seem to fit the easygoing character I had given him.

'This firm that Royde was apprenticed to, Poorgrass and

Fray — get that name — had an address in Dorchester — number forty-four Orchard Street, it's right here — so what are we waiting for?' He was back in his seat now, his hands tapping the table.

'The idea is as crazy as going to Norfolk. What do you expect to find at the address after all these years? Another dry cleaners?'

'Even if that's the case, there must be something in the rest of the town that will give us clues about Royde's early career. The local-boy-made-good angle. There's bound to be a museum or local history centre.'

'Dorset County Museum, but honestly, what are they likely to have?'

The expression on his face was mulish. He wasn't going to listen to common sense; he was going to Dorchester.

'Till I get there, I've no idea what I'll find. But if there is anything, *I* want to find it.' He looked at me across the table. 'I thought you did, too.'

I thought I did as well, but apart from the unlikelihood of discovering anything new in Dorset, a vague fear, formless and imprecise, was holding me back. I sensed an abyss opening beneath my feet, where just one step forward would topple me over the edge. I couldn't properly explain the feeling to Nick, or indeed to myself, so instead I was dismissive.

'I haven't the time to go careering around the West Country. I've an exhibition to organise at the other end of England.'

'But you don't have to go to Newcastle right away, do you? At least it didn't sound like that. Isn't everything already organised at this end?'

I glared at him, and he lifted his hand in a mock shield.

'Don't get touchy. I couldn't help overhearing your row with Oliver last night.'

'Overhearing? Eavesdropping, don't you mean?'

'If it makes you happy. But will you come?'

'Definitely not, and if you've any sense, you won't waste more time on a pointless search.'

'So what do you suggest I do?'

'Try looking for work — I imagine the Royde Society cheque will disappear as quickly as all the others.

'You really know how to put a man down, don't you, Grace?'

If I did, I didn't seem to have succeeded. He was gathering the books together, ready to return them to our helpful host, and smiling happily to himself.

We walked to the underground station without speaking. I didn't for one minute think he would find anything in Dorchester. Hours ago, I'd come to the conclusion that nothing about this search was likely to enhance my reputation, but I still felt envious of the journey he was planning. There were ends left untied and I didn't like that. I was sure, too, there was a discovery to be made, even if it wasn't in Dorchester. But in the next few days Oliver was certain to set a date for the Gorski paintings to go north, and I had to be around. It could be as soon as tomorrow for all I knew.

We hadn't been in touch since last night's tense standoff, and I was getting anxious. He hadn't behaved well, but neither had I. In retrospect, I could understand his outburst: he'd been tired and frustrated by the difficulties of the day, and I had shown him little sympathy. We needed to clear the air, needed to restore harmony, and it would help if we worked together on the new exhibition. Going off to the West Country most certainly would not.

In the ticket hall, Nick stopped at the barrier. 'Are you off to the gallery?'

I looked at my watch and saw that it was past three. 'It's hardly worth it now. You've managed to waste my entire day.'

'Or helped you come up with something amazing! If I eventually find the plans, I'll let you claim first rights to what will be the biggest scoop for years.'

'I don't write commercial articles.'

Nick pulled a face. 'Naturally not, Doctor, so you can write another thesis instead.'

'There won't be a thesis to write. There won't be an article. You won't find anything.'

Now I sounded sour and was desperate to get away. His untiring enthusiasm was making me feel old and weary.

'Oh ye of…,' he said, waving a cheerful hand at me, and disappeared down the escalator.

# Chapter Ten

*London, early February 1851*

The following Thursday Lucas left Great Russell Street promptly at half past one in the afternoon. The Renville house lay only a short walk away, but he needed time to compose himself before the meeting with Alessia. It had been dominating his thoughts for days; *she* had been dominating his thoughts. He had felt her presence constantly: the soft glance of liquid brown eyes, the rustle of blue silk, the faint trace in the air of what he now realised was jasmine. Each time he reached for his pencil to map out sketches for the Renville pavilion, she had been there following every line he drew. It had been difficult to concentrate on the task, but by dint of spending every waking minute on the designs, he had come armed today with a small sheaf of drawings.

The more he thought of her, the more he knew the Renville space must be a shrine of some kind, almost a secret arbour. He had decided on the thinnest of marble pillars to enclose the space and sketched them wrapped in serpents of shimmering silk. The pillars supported an undulating roof and to reflect the beauty beneath, he lined it with glass. Swathes of the finest gauze followed the line of the roof and acted as a canopy over the central feature, which in his mind's eye took the form of a bed. A large, circular bed.

But he was not foolhardy and knew that if Edward Renville scented even a hint of immorality, his dismissal from the project would be instant. He guessed, too, that such a daring statement would not please Alessia either. Instead he compromised on a love seat, its cushions covered in rich silks. The exquisite tiles, whose design until now had occupied every hour of his free time, would be cast in gentler hues, from the palest oyster to the deepest royal purple, and strewn between the fragile pillars.

As he walked, he went over the plans in his mind, and for the hundredth time heard himself explain them. He decided that he sounded confident and professional and could only pray that when he met her again, he would not be struck dumb as he had in de Vere's office.

Prospect Place proved to be a small cul-de-sac and the house, when he reached it, fulfilled his expectation of a prosperous, middle-class residence but one that stood in the midst of a row of grander houses which, like his own in Red Lion Square, had suffered the indignity of being divided into smaller lodgings. He opened an impressively solid iron gate and walked up the short path to Wisteria Lodge. The bay windows were hung with thick curtains and behind them a further layer of net. The doorway had been refashioned into a mediaeval arch and the front entrance was a massive brass-studded ebony door. It was frighteningly reminiscent of a fortified castle. He sounded the knocker.

A parlour maid ushered him through a tiled hall into a drawing room that looked on to the street. It might have been a light and airy space but for the heavy curtains and overstuffed furniture. A cast iron fireplace and a large expanse of dark-stained wood swallowed whatever breath the room possessed. The sole saving grace, Lucas thought, was the delicate chandelier that hung from the centre of the ceiling, its glass droplets swaying gently even in the still air.

He placed the papers he had prepared on a small marble table and waited, hat turning in his hands. The clock ticked the minutes away. When the quarter struck, he began to wonder if he should leave. His presence might not after all be welcome today, but he could hardly let himself out of the house, and the maid had disappeared below stairs. He glanced at the servants' bell but his courage failed and he remained immobile.

At last sounds from the upper floor reached him, a creaking on the stairs, and then he was facing not Alessia, but a black-clothed matron of some sixty years. His surprise told and she looked at him severely.

'Mr Royde, I imagine.' Hand outstretched, her advance was brisk, setting the rows of jet beads adorning her breast into an angry fuss. 'I am Florence Renville. I believe you have met my son, Edward.'

He gathered his wits. 'Indeed, yes. I am most pleased to meet you, Mrs Renville. Mr Renville asked me to call today with initial plans for the pavilion he wishes to build for the Great Exhibition.'

She sniffed. 'I cannot imagine why he wishes to exhibit. The business is extremely successful and has no need to advertise.'

Her words were almost a complete echo of her son's. Mother and son were evidently in accord and he wondered if, unknown to him, plans for the Exhibition had been rejected on her advice. She spoke with an undoubted air of authority. If that were so, all his labour had been futile, his hours wasted. Even worse, he would not see Alessia.

'Take a seat, Mr Royde.' She indicated one of the over-stuffed chairs that guarded the fireplace. 'My daughter-in-law will be with us shortly.'

The hand that had been squeezing his heart stopped.

'I am looking forward to presenting my initial ideas to Mrs Renville,' he managed, and gestured towards the table and the papers he had brought.

'Mrs Renville will no doubt have her own ideas,' the older woman said repressively. Then, unable to subdue her irritation, she continued, 'Though goodness knows why she needs further occupation with a household and two young children to manage.'

As if on cue, two small girls dressed in identical white cotton outfits stood shyly in the doorway and behind them, Alessia Renville. Their mother urged them gently forward to make their curtsies.

'Mr Royde, please forgive my unpunctuality. We have had a small schoolroom problem,' and she smiled con-spiratorially down at the children, 'but all is resolved now. May I introduce my daughters to you?' She pushed the girls towards Lucas as she spoke.

'This is Florence.' Lucas solemnly shook hands with the older girl. 'And this is Georgina.' The smaller child gave a lopsided grin that broke the formality of the moment.

'Now, girls,' Alessia said quietly, 'you must return to Miss Timms, and this time mind her well.'

The children turned with some reluctance towards the door where their mother waited. One by one, she kissed them lightly on the top of the head and watched them out of sight, their bunched skirts and ruffled pantaloons disappearing swiftly up the stairs.

'Can I offer you some refreshment, Mr Royde?' she asked, turning towards him.

Before he had the chance to decline, her mother-in-law said sharply, 'Mr Royde is a busy man, Alessia. He has brought sketches for you to see. I would suggest you view them immediately and allow him to return to his office.'

Florence Renville lowered herself heavily onto the brocaded sofa and fixed them both with an unwavering glance. It was clear she intended to remain until he had left the house. Alessia blushed at her mother-in-law's lack of courtesy, but responded in her usual soft manner. 'Naturally, Mr Royde, I understand you have many calls on your time. We will set to business — and thank you for producing plans so quickly.'

He jumped to his feet and retrieved the papers. When he passed them to her, he noticed her hand shook a little. Hardly surprising, he thought. Between her husband and his mother she must lead an unenviable life. She spent some minutes leafing through the sketches, occasionally holding one up for a closer view, once or twice turning a sheet this way and that.

At last she turned to him, her smile warm and inviting. 'Perhaps you could describe to me exactly what you intend.'

'Surely the plans are clear enough,' the elder Mrs Renville interjected.

'They are beautifully drawn, Mama, but I would still like to hear Mr Royde spell out his vision.' Her voice was surprisingly firm.

The older woman tutted impatiently, but Lucas went to

stand beside Alessia's chair and began to go through each image in turn. He tried to keep his eyes on the drawings, but could not stop them feasting occasionally on the dark glint of her curls so close to his face or the shapely hand turning the pages. He cleared his throat and began the speech he had prepared.

'The essence of the plan, Mrs Renville, lies in our not having a solid construction. As you can see, one side of the display space will be made entirely of glass — this is the outer wall of the Exhibition Hall — while the other three sides consist of closely positioned marble pillars. These would be an echo of the iron pillars with which the Exhibition Hall itself is being built. I believe they are so slim that one can put one's hands around them.

'I wanted to give the sense of a piazza and also a taste perhaps of historic Rome. The pillars would be narrow and would have Renville silks wound around them. Their marble would be carved top and bottom with a relief displaying aspects of the company's business. Perhaps , too, the motifs that pattern many of the silks?'

She said nothing, but he sensed the warmth of her interest and was encouraged to continue. 'We might also consider a maritime theme to reinforce the notion of materials so special they must be shipped from a foreign land. You will see, too, that the roof is undulating — here, this image should show that more clearly — and lined with mirrors to reflect back the colours and patterns of the silks. The roof is an innovation. Decidedly modern, I feel. I see it as a counterpoint to the historic, an expression of a more contemporary Italy. What do you think?'

'I think I will have to depend on your judgement, Mr Royde. It is many years since I lived in my country.'

'You never visit?'

'No,' she said slowly. 'I have no reason to return.'

The sadness in her voice fingered him with her hurt and he went on hurriedly, 'My idea, you see, is to present a fusion of the old and the new, to present the Renville silks as part of a legacy of style and beauty, but one that is still relevant to the modern world.'

'Italy is a most beautiful country, do you not think, Mr Royde?'

'I do. I lived there for only two years, but it stole away my heart — and very easily.'

Their eyes, when they met, were warm with shared pleasure.

'The plans, Mr Royde.' It was Florence Renville. 'I think you have forgotten the plans.'

'The plans, yes. Let us continue.' His voice was only a little unsteady.

Alessia bent her head once more over the sketches, the earlier light extinguished from her face. She was silent for a considerable while; it seemed she was concentrating intently on one particular page.

'Mr Royde, forgive me, but I cannot understand this drawing. What is this?'

She was pointing to the love seat and Lucas could only thank heaven that he had not dared the bed. Florence Renville had become steadily more antagonistic as he had expounded his ideas, her expression showing clearly the affront she felt at the pagan nature of his suggestions.

'That is a… bench,' he finished lamely.

'A bench?'

'I thought we might cover it in silk. Then scatter along its length soft cushions and bolsters that would display yet more samples from the Renville range.'

'Yes,' she said a little uncertainly. 'But do you not think it is a little… tame?'

'Tame!' Her mother-in-law exploded once more into life. 'Tame! In my opinion the whole thing is decidedly unchristian. It *needs* taming.'

'Mama, surely not. It is a beautiful design. And, of course, the bench will be fine, Mr Royde. It's only that the rest of the design is so…'

'Immoral.'

'Mama!'

'I shall speak with Edward,' the older Mrs Renville announced imperiously. 'In the meanwhile, Mr Royde, I am sure you must be due back at your office. I would ask you to do nothing further with the plans.'

Alessia's lovely face flushed pink and her hands began a compulsive smoothing of her voluminous skirts. Lucas felt her agitation as his own. He would like to have struck down the stiff black satin opposite, beads and all.

Instead, he turned to the matriarch and said smoothly, 'Thank you for your hospitality, Mrs Renville. I hold myself in readiness for your son's instructions. No doubt Mrs Alessia Renville will wish to speak to him also.'

The older woman glared. She would not easily relinquish her authority, he realised, but he was confident that Edward Renville would listen to what his wife had to say. And Alessia had liked his plans. All except the bench. If he could have told her it was a love seat, she would have delighted in it, he was sure. But there had been no chance with her mother-in-law standing censor.

The maid ushered him out of the house and he started a slow walk back to Great Russell Street. The meeting had given him much to ponder. His brief glimpse of the Renville household suggested only too clearly that the older woman wielded considerable power at Prospect Place. Remembering Alessia's brave attempt to champion his ideas against such formidable opposition, his heart reached out to her. If they were to work on these plans together and without interference, he would have to find a way of seeing her alone.

# Chapter Eleven

The chance came sooner than he thought. The week that followed his visit to Prospect Place was immensely busy, with a rush of work deluging the practice and keeping every one of the assistants fully occupied. Each day brought requests from de Vere that they undertake new consultations, research new materials, refashion existing plans. And from the neighbouring office came a welter of yellow sheets heralding queries from the draughtsmen on submissions that were unclear or that needed further work before they could begin final drawings. But even as task followed task in quick succession, Lucas refused to lose sight of the Renville design.

His mind continually replayed his conversation with Alessia. She had welcomed his plans, loved the notion of classical pillars, the swathes of luxurious silk, the sense of magical space. He was exhilarated: it would be a true bower, with Alessia at its centre. In his mind's eye, she would not be dressed in the stiff brocades and satins of Victorian England, but in the soft gauzes of a hotter clime, gauzes that clung, curving and tangling to her form. This tantalising vision kept him company through dreary days and into the night. It was well that his work at de Vere's, despite its bustle, hardly stretched him.

At home, his precious portfolio began to suffer. Every evening, after a meagre supper, he would set himself to work and every evening he would find himself, pencil in hand, the paper blank, but shimmering before him the image of a beautiful face. Minutes later, even hours later, he would wake and realise he had not drawn a single line. He tried scolding himself severely. Had he not sworn to concentrate entirely on his work, to put aside romantic dalliance? Did he not remember to his cost the perils of allowing himself to wander that path?

He had only to recall Marguerite. She had known what she was doing; she was a seasoned player and Lucas had provided a pleasurable interlude. As companion to an exacting and difficult contessa, Marguerite had welcomed the liaison with Lucas, a break from the tedium of provincial Lombardy. But it had only ever been an interlude for her. She was betrothed to a Frenchman, someone, Lucas had learned, quite senior in the diplomatic service, and she was merely waiting out the months until marriage freed her from the dowager's demands.

Marguerite had been well versed in dalliance but he had been a novice, and had tumbled into uncritical love with her. When it became clear he was only the means to an end, his ardour had cooled, and he had taken what was on offer and asked for no more.

The experience had strengthened a nascent cynicism in him. Worse, it had undermined his confidence that he could judge well. If he had been so easily swayed by one woman, what might he not be with the next? And here was the next. Except that Alessia Renville could never be just the next woman. She was a queen, an empress. Her presence thrilled him and made him want to do great deeds for her. She was a fairy tale come true. And she was married. He might weave dreams around her, but he had always to come back to that fact. And it was one he needed to remember.

But it was nowhere in his mind when his next meeting with Alessia came upon him unexpectedly. A week after his visit to the Renville house, he and Fontenoy had left the office at noon to visit the market in Bury Street. For the past week they had eaten lunch at their desks, but now the pace of work had slackened a little, they decided on a brief saunter. Friday was the first day of a two-day market and provided an excellent opportunity to buy fresh fruit and vegetables at a reasonable price, and for Lucas to supplement the frugal diet deemed sufficient by the matron who ran the lodging house at Red Lion Square.

They had inspected a couple of stalls and were moving on to a third before deciding on their purchases, when Fontenoy inadvertently knocked into a young woman walking in the opposite direction. He apologised profusely, even more so when he realised she was a most attractive young woman. She rescued the parasol and parcels wrenched from her hand by the impact and made haste to reassure him.

'There is no cause for concern, sir.' She smiled gently up at him. 'A slight accident only — and no wonder. The market is so crowded this morning, it is a miracle we can move at all.'

Fontenoy appeared anxious to linger and she repeated her words, this time a little more firmly. 'Please do not be concerned.'

When he still made no move, she was forced to add, 'I believe you will lose sight of your companion if you do not join him immediately.'

Lucas had walked on, heedless of the small affray. She looked after him as she spoke, and her voice faltered a little. 'Is that the gentleman who accompanies you?' She indicated with her parasol the sombre black of Lucas's frock coat, even now disappearing into the crowd.

'Yes, do you know him?' Fontenoy's enquiry was eager. There might be an intriguing story here awaiting discovery.

'Is that not Mr Royde, Mr Lucas Royde of de Vere and Partners?'

'The very same.'

A slight flush had crept into Alessia's face, but her voice was as calm as ever. 'Mr Royde is creating a design for my husband's business.' She saw Fontenoy's mystified expression and elaborated. 'A display space for the Great Exhibition.'

'Ah yes,' he caught on quickly. 'Did you not visit our offices a short while ago?'

'Indeed I did, Mr…?'

'Fontenoy. At your service, ma'am.'

She inclined her head a little. 'Yes, Mr Fontenoy, we visited de Vere's and commissioned Mr Royde to work for us.'

By this time Lucas had realised he had lost his companion. He stopped and retraced his steps. The sight of Alessia Renville in animated conversation with Fontenoy affected him curiously. There was a ripple of sheer joy at seeing her, but a stab of annoyance that she should sully herself by talking with such a man. He reached their side very quickly.

'Mrs Renville.' He doffed his hat as he spoke. 'How good to see you again. I hope you will be pleased to hear your design is near completion. And that I have followed your advice.'

'It was hardly advice, Mr Royde,' she responded gaily. 'If my memory is correct, my attempts to contribute were ruled unacceptable.' Her eyes were sparkling with inner amusement, and he knew she was remembering the elder Mrs Renville's angry repudiation of plans she deemed pagan.

'*I* did not rule them unacceptable, Mrs Renville. I have tried to incorporate your sentiments within the new drawings and am hopeful you will no longer consider the project too tame.'

'I should not have said that,' she confessed, a lingering smile lighting her face.

Fontenoy was watching them thoughtfully. She might be a married woman, but...

'I am very glad you ventured your thoughts,' Lucas was saying, 'for they confirmed quite decisively my own.'

There was a momentary silence as they felt the pleasure of mutual agreement, and then she said a little shyly, 'When may I see the new plans?'

'Whenever is convenient. I have them with me.'

'With you?' Fontenoy was surprised into speaking.

'Yes.' Lucas flushed a little. 'I carry them with me in case I should think of any additions or alterations.'

He knew that he carried them as a small reminder of the woman who stood an arm's length from him, looking in ruby-red velvet as though she had stepped from an artist's study of winter.

'Perhaps you would like to show them to me now?'

For an instant he was bemused, and seeing this she made haste to retract her invitation. 'Of course, you gentlemen must lack the time,' she said quickly, looking from one to the other. 'How stupid of me! But if you had not to return to your office immediately, you would be most welcome to take tea at Prospect Place. The house is very close.'

It was close and he wanted to be there. Fontenoy helped him on his way.

'You go, Royde, by all means and I'll let DV know where you are. He will be pleased the project is progressing so well.' He tried hard to keep a snigger from his voice, but failed.

Lucas had no wish to hand him a victory, but his need to be with Alessia Renville was overwhelming. She was looking at him expectantly. 'Will that be convenient, Mr Royde?'

'Quite convenient, Mrs Renville.'

'I am so glad. I am most eager to go through the plans once more with you. I have thought of one or two slight changes that may be beneficial.'

In a moment they had bid Fontenoy goodbye and turned to walk away in the opposite direction. Lucas's colleague watched them go and gave a long, low whistle. Things might soon be getting very interesting at de Vere and Partners.

# Chapter Twelve

The journey to Wisteria Lodge was accomplished in ten minutes and filled with quiet talk on the most general of topics: the inclement weather of late, the hope for an early spring, the state of the silk trade. The parlour maid Lucas had seen on his previous visit opened the front door to them.

'Thank you, Martha.' Alessia handed parasol, parcels and velvet cloak to the waiting girl and led him to the rear of the house, passing on the way the closed door of their earlier drab meeting place.

The room they entered now was entirely different. It was largely uncluttered and the furniture it held was delicately constructed, the chairs covered in straw silk and the carpet a faded forest green. A large rococo framed mirror and an elegant round table engraved with delicate marquetry seemed to be the only overt ornamentation. Soft gauze curtains hung at the long windows, and beyond Lucas could see an attractive garden that in the summer would be ablaze with colour.

His face must have registered surprise. 'This room is my particular haven, Mr Royde. We keep the drawing room for strictly formal occasions, and I do not feel this is one such.'

He was returning her smile with an equal warmth, when Martha came in and noisily arranged teapot and china. Her disapproval was evident. She must, he thought, have been well trained by the elder Mrs Renville.

'Do you take milk with your tea?' Alessia asked, when the maid had once more disappeared.

'No, thank you. But your mother-in-law?'

'She is no longer with us.'

Alessia crossed the room and handed him a cup and saucer. Bone china, he noted, and the latest of Wedgwood's expensive designs.

'The elder Mrs Renville does not live with you?' he hazarded.

'She visited for Christmas. She lives in St Albans and returned there a few days ago. My daughters have travelled with her; they are to stay with their grandmother for several weeks.'

He hoped the relief did not show too plainly on his face. As a distraction, he began searching in his inner pocket for the plans, readying himself to go through them, page by page. But before he could begin, she had crossed the room again and taken a seat beside him on the couch. He could not take his eyes from her face; a face whose beauty wore the lustre of finest crystal. He felt as gauche as a schoolboy and could only hope that his manner did not betray him.

'Though much of the design remains the same,' he began, 'I have tried to think more boldly. I believe I've already shown you a drawing of the roof — I would like to keep the same rolling shape and the same mirrored glass. It should reflect the potpourri of colours that will be crammed into what in fact is a small space.'

She nodded happily. 'I love the design of the roof — it

flows wonderfully and is quite different. Using mirrors is perhaps even a little daring!'

'Daring is what we need to be,' he agreed, 'to make people take notice. We want them to pause, not pass by. Hopefully we can entice them to enter the pavilion.'

'I imagine there will be many other exhibitors.'

'That is true. I had not previously given much attention to the event, but since your husband placed his commission with de Vere's, I have been doing a little research. The Exhibition Hall will be vast — some hundred thousand square feet — and will cover every kind of manufacture and technical innovation.'

'I saw a sketch of the Exhibition Hall in *The Daily News*. It seemed for all the world like a very large greenhouse.'

'I believe that is what it is. Joseph Paxton designed it. He was inspired by the plans he drew up some years ago for the Duke of Devonshire, and they were indeed for a greenhouse! But there I think the similarity ends. This will be a vast space, tall enough to encompass living trees, and large enough to accommodate over a hundred thousand exhibits from all over the world.'

'Which is why we must do something a little different?'

'Exactly.' He shuffled the papers into a neat pile. 'There is no defined entrance — the space between each pillar makes the pavilion accessible from different directions. Hopefully it will tempt people to stop and puzzle out the structure. And then entice them in. Once they are inside, they must feel cocooned in a magical sphere.'

'The roof will be important for that magic, I think.'

'The roof will be key. I would like to use swathes of fine tulle.' He gestured to her window coverings. 'Something like those curtains, to follow the line of the roof and drape from one side to the other.'

'A canopy.'

'That's it.'

'But a canopy over a bench?'

'I have ideas other than a bench, but I fear Mrs Renville senior would not approve.'

She caught her bottom lip between her teeth, and his heart turned over at the small intimate gesture.

'Mrs Florence Renville will not be here to judge, and Edward has given me the authority to decide. So tell me, please.'

'I thought,' he said slowly, 'a love seat filled with cushions made from Renville silks.'

He watched her closely, but she appeared unfazed. She was thinking hard. 'But then only people coming from one direction would see the seat in its entirety. Could we have two? Or perhaps a circular seat?'

Lucas tried to appear as though the suggestion was completely novel and he was giving it serious consideration for the first time. 'Why not?'

'With strands of the finest gauze drifting from each of the four corners and meeting at a central point above,' she went on eagerly. 'Just like the Arabian Nights.'

She had read his mind and his pulse raced at the realisation of how much they thought and felt alike.

'More like the Italian Nights,' he amended incautiously and saw her blush.

Hurriedly, he resumed his commentary. 'I thought also that between the pillars we might have a scattering of tiles, designed to chime with the gauzes and silks in shape and colour.'

'At the moment, the pillars stand alone and they create a

wonderful spaciousness. Would not tiles mar this?'

A whisper of dejection murmured through the air, and she seemed to sense immediately the disappointment her words had created. 'But if you think they would enhance the display, Mr Royde, by all means include them.'

He sat in silence for a moment. 'No, you are quite right. They would add nothing; on the contrary, they would detract.'

'Is it important to you?' she queried. 'To use decorative tiles?'

'It is a small personal endeavour only.'

'Yes?' She invited him to go on.

'I have been designing a collection. A vanity project no more.'

'Do you have your drawings with you? I would very much like to see them.'

'My portfolio is at my lodgings.'

'Then please bring it the next time we meet. I am sure the designs will be very new and very beautiful.'

He could not really believe she would be interested. It was her natural politeness speaking, but when she continued to question, he was happy to respond.

'Did you derive your ideas from your stay in the Italian states?'

'I did — the colours in particular, the way they blend and contrast. My earliest designs used a range of Tuscan reds.'

'You were in Tuscany?'

'Not so far away. Verona. Do you know the town?'

She gave a little gasp and her hand flew to her mouth.

'It was my birthplace. We lived in via Forti.'

'And for two years I lived in via Cappello, a stone's throw away!'

Her face was suddenly alight. 'How wonderful. Tell me, Mr Royde, have things changed very much?'

'It's difficult to say since I have known the place only recently.'

'Naturally. But the bridges? The arena?'

'All still there,' he confirmed.

'And the opera is still performed in the amphitheatre? On summer nights we could hear the singing over half the town. I wanted so much to see a performance, but I was too young, my grandmother said. When you are older, she promised…. But I never visited.'

'Then you must return to Verona at the first possible opportunity and book the very best seats.'

Her face shadowed. 'It is unlikely I shall ever return.'

'Your parents are no longer there?' He hardly knew her, yet it felt the most natural thing in the world to enquire of her family.

'My mother died many years ago, in childbirth, and my father is an Englishman. He travelled always between England and Lombardy for his business and met my mother on one of his visits. When they married they settled in Verona, and when my mother died, my grandmother came to live with us.'

'I am sorry to hear of your mother's death.'

'I was a young child, only seven years old. I hardly remember her.'

'And your grandmother?'

'She also has left this world. At the time of her death, my father had remarried and was living in Cambridgeshire, so I came to England to stay with him and his wife.'

She wore an uncomfortably bleak expression, and he dared not ask more. It could not have been easy at such a young age to give up her home for a foreign country. Not easy to cope with a new stepmother.

'And why did *you* return to England, Mr Royde?'

He found himself telling her of his plans for the future, telling her how the move to London had signalled a new beginning, a chance to gain recognition for his work, a chance to shine in the first architectural circles.

She listened attentively, hands lying quietly in her lap, and when she spoke, her voice was filled with admiration. 'You deserve the greatest respect, for it is clear you have a deep love for Italy and yet you tore yourself away in order to follow your dream.'

She beamed at him and he had the grace to feel a fraud. His work at de Vere's could hardly be classed as following his dream.

'This design will be your very first step to success,' she continued, 'but only the first. There will be many others, I am quite sure.'

'You are most kind. I hope to create a structure that will be truly worthy of the Renville silks. Mr Renville assures me they are the very best in the world.'

The mention of her husband seemed to dampen her spirits, but she regained her gentle smile to hold out her hand in farewell. He took it in a firm grasp. It was small and smooth. He felt the individual fingers lying in his palm and a deep tenderness washed over him. He longed to stroke those fingers one by one, but instead shook her hand in a business-like manner. Then somehow, unbidden, she raised her fingers to his lips, and he touched them lightly with his mouth. They stood silently for a moment, his blue eyes half-closed in pleasure.

'Shall we meet in three weeks? Will that give you sufficient time?'

He snapped out of his reverie. 'Three weeks today,' he confirmed, wishing only that it could be sooner. 'By then I will have worked these drawings into a finished state, and you will be able to judge how well you like them.'

She rang the bell and Martha came quickly to escort him from the house. The look on the maid's face as she watched him walk to the front gate clearly proclaimed him an unwelcome visitor. He shrugged off the disapproval, shrugged off the small warning voices that struggled to be heard. The simple pieties of his Dorset upbringing and the wreckage of a malign love affair were neither of them sufficient to restrain him. Three weeks and he would be at Wisteria Lodge again. Twenty-one days and he would see Alessia once more. How could that possibly harm?

# Chapter Thirteen

I found Nick Heysham infuriating, but I was sorry we'd parted at odds. I wanted to blame him for being unreasonable in expecting me to travel to Dorchester at a moment's notice, but really I was cross with myself. Deep down, I knew it was what I wanted to do — but didn't have the courage.

I needn't have worried I'd hurt his sensitivities, though. He rang as I walked up the hill to Lyndurst Villas and I could only be glad I hadn't yet reached home. Oliver was unlikely to be there, but I didn't want to chance it. Another call from Nick Heysham would mean another unpleasant conversation.

'Just thought I'd update my partner,' he began. I sighed inwardly, and wondered why he persisted in the fiction we were in this together, especially as I was about to put a very large distance between us.

'I'm catching the 15.45 tomorrow from Waterloo. It's direct to Dorchester. If you fancy a sojourn on the Dorset Riviera, you know what to do.'

'Dorchester isn't on the coast,' I found myself snapping, 'and no, I don't.'

I rang off abruptly. Nick seemed to have the gift of riling me without ever having to exert much effort. I supposed I shouldn't be surprised. The truth was that he was as free as a bird and I wasn't.

As I let myself into the hall, I tripped over Oliver's leather safari bag, while above I could hear someone moving around in the bedroom. Startled, I climbed the stairs two at a time. An open case lay on the bed and Oliver was busily folding shirts into it. He looked up as I appeared in the doorway.

'Ah, Grace, I'm glad you're here. It saves me leaving a complicated message.'

'And what would that be? Why the packing?'

'I'm off to Newcastle.'

'Now?'

'That's right. I think I told you the exhibition was a rush job.' His voice was smooth, but there was a distinct edge to it.

'Not this rushed, surely.'

'I'm not entirely happy with the arrangements — I told you that, too, I believe — and I need to be on the spot to troubleshoot.'

The idea of Oliver troubleshooting made me smile. He was an excellent communicator, an accomplished networker, but troubleshooting? He'd always been amazingly deft at avoiding it. It was fortunate he was bent over his suitcase at that moment and didn't notice my grimace.

'I see.'

I didn't, of course. I couldn't understand the haste unless it was Oliver's way of making sure I understood how badly I'd let him down, but I decided to be conciliatory. Thank goodness I'd not been tempted to go to Dorset. It looked as though tomorrow I'd be travelling in the opposite direction.

'And when exactly should I arrive?'

'No hurry. Come when it suits.' His tone was indifferent.

I gaped at him. Was this the man who only yesterday was berating me for not being around when needed?

'Twenty-four hours ago you were crying on my shoulder, bemoaning the fact that Sue was a useless organiser and I was indispensable. So what's happened to change that?'

He straightened up, but his eyes didn't quite meet mine, and before he could answer the doorbell rang. The sound had a curious effect on him. His limbs jerked themselves into a scramble for the door, as though he were a clockwork toy that had been wound and just released. It might have been comical if I had been in the mood to laugh.

'Stay there,' I muttered. 'I'll go.'

The face that looked at me across the threshold was young and pretty. Very pretty. Tousled blonde curls, slim figure, a smile as wide as the Thames estuary. But good teeth, I noted.

'Yes?' I wasn't exactly welcoming.

'This is Professor Brooke's house?' Her voice said she was nervous but undaunted.

'It is. How can I help?' I didn't sound too helpful.

She looked at my face and then turned away. 'Professor Brooke has asked me—.'

She broke off and a relieved smile flooded the soft curves of her face. Oliver had arrived behind me, unheard.

'Rebecca, how lovely to see you, my dear.' Oliver's voice was honey. I could see her shoulders relax even as he spoke. 'I shan't be more than a few minutes. Do wait in the car. The door is open.'

I hadn't noticed the Mercedes as I'd walked home. It was parked a little farther up the road, and she turned immediately towards it, evidently glad to be away from an awkward encounter.

'Why didn't you introduce me?'

'I hardly thought it worthwhile. We'll be gone almost immediately.'

'To Newcastle?'

'Where else?' He sounded irritated by my questions and eager to brush the matter to one side. 'Rebecca has been an enormous asset to the gallery during the last few days and has volunteered to come with me to Newcastle and help out.'

I bet she has, I thought. 'And who is Rebecca?'

'She is a student on work experience. Setting up a new exhibition will be excellent practice for her.' His face wore a satisfied smile.

'And what else?'

'I don't understand.'

'I think you do. A student? Work experience? Does that ring any bells for you? It certainly does for me.'

'Now you're being ridiculous. Rebecca is barely out of her teens, little older than my own daughter.'

'Something of an exaggeration. Kezia is twelve.'

'Still, it would hardly be a suitable liaison,' he joked rather too heavily, his eyes once again refusing to meet mine. 'You are my partner, you know that.'

'Yes, of course. I remember. You can't do without me, can you?'

He was forcing several pairs of socks around the edges of the case with ill-tempered, jabbing motions.

'I've no wish to quarrel with you. I needed all the help I could get yesterday, and Rebecca did her very best. She is keen to see the project through and since you've shown little enthusiasm for the job, I felt justified in asking her to accompany me.'

'Little enthusiasm? My crime was to be busy elsewhere for the one day when you needed me.'

His fingers began to pull at his beard in short, sharp tugs. 'Precisely. As my assistant, I should be able to call on you at any time and have your support. It was highly inconvenient you were unavailable, as I think I made plain.'

Had he always been this pompous and I hadn't noticed? 'Indeed you did, but it's not an assistant you need, Oliver — it's a handmaiden.'

He refused to respond, his lips closing tightly on themselves, and my anger broke loose. 'So Rebecca is the new bond servant. I can see why she has to be so very young — easily impressed, easily controlled — but why so very blonde?'

'Now you are being offensive.'

'If so, I think I'm justified. I seem to have hit the situation pretty much on the nail. So why don't you come clean?'

With a huff, he pulled himself up to his full height. 'You have a vulgar mind, Grace, I regret to say.'

Abandoning the last few shirts on the bed, he clicked the suitcase catches angrily into place, then strode to the door. I made no attempt to stop him. At the top of the staircase, he paused and said calmly enough, 'When you are yourself again, I hope you will consider making the journey to Newcastle. Let me know your train and I'll meet you.'

The front door banged, and I sat down on the bed with a thump. I found myself shaking and wondered why; I should be getting used to fighting with Oliver. But conflict makes me ill and I had been the one to do the fighting. Throughout he'd remained above the fray, measured and dignified. It was seeing the girl that had stirred me to anger and made me careless of the damage I might cause.

But that wasn't really true, was it? I had become careless weeks ago. Oliver was right: I had lost enthusiasm, and not just for the work. A lurking disenchantment had suddenly assumed a sharp focus. Oliver and I never quarrelled, but twice in as many days we had — and badly.

I hadn't forfeited his good opinion entirely since he seemed willing to believe I had run temporarily mad. He was still holding the door open for me, but only just. It was down to me whether or not I chose to walk back. He had been good to me. He had cared for me, paid for me, given me a comfortable home — a very comfortable home, I amended, looking around me. And in exchange I'd given companionship, friendship, even a tepid love, but also my freedom. That was the most frightening thought, and I could no longer avoid the truth.

I had sacrificed freedom: Oliver had always to know where I was and what I was doing; he had to have first call on my time and my attention. Outside this house, I had little life. Friends were absent. Not that I'd ever had many, a few acquaintances from my student days, but they had disappeared soon after I'd moved into Lyndhurst Villas. He had gently persuaded me to let them go. They weren't up to my weight, he'd said; I was worthy of more interesting company, or rather company he considered interesting. My life was lived on his terms and until now I had been happy to accept them.

If I chose not to walk back through that door, if I walked the other way, what then? Nine years of my life wasted. Nine years in which I'd convinced myself that being Oliver's helpmate was what I wanted. It had been an easy life, and I'd been happy for much of it. He could be charming, an interesting and intelligent man, who was going places. I'd wanted to go there with him, and I had. But I didn't like where I'd arrived. That was the nub of it.

I walked downstairs and for some reason remembered Mr Merrick. Perhaps, very faintly, he represented a new beginning, the first infant steps to independence. Whatever the reason, he deserved a phone call, even a belated one.

'I'm afraid I've found out little more than you already know,' I began.

'The building was a school?'

'Definitely a school. It was called the Raine Foundation—Raine Street was where it first began. Originally the school in Silver Street housed only boys. The section of the building you're hoping to make your home was an addition, built in 1845.'

'To accommodate more pupils?'

'To accommodate female pupils for the first time. They were there until the 1880s when the entire school left Silver Street to move to different premises. Over the years the school kept moving, though always within the East End.'

He was quiet at the other end of the line and I felt that in some way I should be apologising. 'What I've found isn't likely to solve your ghost problems, I'm afraid.'

'No,' he said slowly. 'But do you think there's more to discover?'

'There may be.' I was sounding reluctant.

'Then discover it if you can, Dr Latimer.'

'I'll try.'

My promise was half-hearted. At any other time I might have been glad to dig deeper, but chasing ghosts hardly chimed with my present mood. I wasn't entirely sure what my mood was, but I poured myself a glass of Oliver's very best red and sat down to think.

That bright, fresh-faced young woman, Rebecca, was she to be the new Grace? Of course, she might simply be another of the many women who flocked around Oliver in starry-eyed appreciation. His groupies, I used to tease him. He was an eminent man, as much at home in front of a television camera as in the lecture hall, and for years he'd attracted a score of distant worshippers. But they had never been sufficient for him: it was meticulous attention he needed and was no longer getting. Rebecca would make my perfect substitute.

My first reaction at being supplanted had been anger, but that had quickly passed and when I thought through my feelings, I was surprised at what I found. I should be riven with jealousy, but I wasn't, or only mildly so — rather, I was curious as to what might happen in Newcastle. Tomorrow I could buy a train ticket and see for myself.

# Chapter Fourteen

**W**hen the alarm shrilled me awake the following morning, I wondered why on earth I had set it to ring. Before I'd dropped into an uneasy sleep last night, I had decided I wouldn't chase after Oliver, but would see him on his return. And I wouldn't be going to Dorchester either. Why make a pointless journey? As though in answer, a pair of deep-blue eyes smiled out at me. But I couldn't risk it, I decided. If I went, Oliver would never forgive me, and I would have jettisoned for good the security I'd been chasing all my life.

I hadn't slept well. The fight with Oliver had disturbed me more than I realised, and I had no idea what would happen when we saw each other again. Hopefully, whatever confrontation lay in store would be over quickly, and I'd be allowed to sink back once more into the restful drift I knew so well.

But is that what I wanted? I felt bored, not restful, and it had been fortuitous that a Victorian mystery had landed in my lap, and for a few hours at least, had energised me. A mystery that in all probability was bogus. But yesterday I'd felt certain there was more to be discovered. So was it worth making another attempt to crack the Royde enigma while Nick was trundling his way to Dorchester?

I rummaged in my handbag and found my phone. I had meant to check the photograph when I got home last night, but with all the aggravation, I'd forgotten. The beautiful poster I'd found at the V and A had, alongside the name of de Vere, that of the silk importer. I hadn't been able to read the name and had taken a surreptitious photograph, hoping that with the professional magnifying glass I kept at home, it would become clear. I hovered the glass over the surface, but the wording remained indistinct, and my eyes quickly began to feel the strain. I thought I could decipher an *l* and maybe the first letter was a capital *B* or an *R*. I switched on my laptop. It was a very long shot and was probably why I hadn't thought of it before, but it was possible the exhibitors were mentioned in one or two of the newspaper articles written at the time.

I logged into the British Library and prepared for a few hours of hard work. From 1850 onwards, the Great Exhibition had been a constant topic of debate in the papers, weekly and local papers as well as the dailies. I was familiar with a fair number of the articles, but certainly not all. I started in April 1851, a month before the opening, and found twenty-five items in the *Morning Chronicle* alone. Then on to the *Daily News*, where on April 19 I struck a little gold: a final list of exhibitors along with a brief mention of what they would be showing. Among those listed were importers of various kinds of materials and I looked hard for any *B*s or *R*s specialising in silks and situated in central London.

It took me an age, but I could find only three: a Barnham and a Belotti both with offices in Baker Street in the West End and a Renville in Onslow Street in the City. I glanced through the accompanying articles and spent a long time trawling several other dailies, but there was no further mention of the three names. Not a breakthrough then, but if Nick contacted me again, I could pass on the information.

By now, it was long past lunchtime, and I wandered into the kitchen and stood staring down the hill towards Archway. I didn't feel at all hungry. The chase had been a temporary respite from my difficulties, but anxiety was flooding back. I was at a crossroads, it seemed, one I had been approaching for some time, but now I'd actually arrived I hadn't a clue which direction to take.

The clock struck three. Nick would be on his way to Paddington. I reassured myself there was absolutely nothing to find in Dorchester. It was a crazy journey made by a crazy man. A man with no money, no prospects, I reminded myself. A man with the bluest eyes I had ever seen.

I began to make tea, hardly conscious of what I was doing, while I listened to the ticking of the clock marking off the seconds. It was five minutes past three and his train would be leaving in just forty minutes. If I were going for that train, I needed to move. But I wasn't. I was staying here in Hampstead and waiting for Oliver to come back with tales of a northern triumph. We would kiss and make up. Rebecca would be consigned to history or to the bowels of the Papillon gallery. All would be well. Life would go on as before.

I turned the kettle off and ran into the bedroom. In ten minutes I had showered, dressed and slung whatever clothes I could find into my old student bag, and was on my way to the underground. It would be far quicker than any taxi, and speed was crucial since I would be very lucky to make that train. But today the Circle Line into Paddington, notorious for delays, was behaving itself. I was going to be lucky or maybe unlucky. It's strange that one's whole life can be shaped by a simple thing like catching or not catching a train. If I had missed the 3.45 to Dorchester, I'd have returned to Lyndhurst Villas and unpacked my bag for good.

A platform guard heaved me through the door of the last carriage as the baton for departure went down. I stumbled over assorted bags, briefcases, into somebody's newspaper, and finally arrived upright in the aisle. Smiling apologies, I tried to straighten my unruly hair. I'd managed only a partial dry, and my reflection in the carriage window showed a slightly mad halo sitting atop my head. The man whose newspaper I had trampled looked alarmed at the sight. Still smiling, I moved on. It was a long train, and heaving the rucksack with me, I realised that thirty was not the new twenty after all. The bag felt heavier than I could ever remember. I was two-thirds of the way down the train before I found him.

He was reading, which came as a shock. Somehow I hadn't seen Nick as a reader — and a reader of Dostoevsky, to boot. That was interesting. All those tortured family relationships reminded me how he'd spoken of his own family.

As soon as he became aware of me teetering unsafely above him, he bounded to his feet. 'Grace! How great to see you!'

My rucksack was hoisted on to the rack with annoyingly little effort, and with a good deal more effort I managed to squeeze myself into the seat opposite, beside someone who might have benefited from Oliver's Spartan diet.

Nick smiled encouragingly across at me, but neither of us spoke. Instead, we fixed our glance determinedly on the view from the window as the outer suburbs of London slipped past. I knew he was desperate to ask me the all-important question, but unusually for him he hesitated. In the end, he did it as delicately as Nick ever could.

'So, the Newcastle exhibition?'

'It turns out Oliver doesn't need me after all,' I said airily. 'It means I have a few days free — I thought I'd go mad and risk the journey.'

'That's great,' he repeated, his voice awash with unasked questions. But if he was tempted to probe further, the arrival of the refreshment trolley stopped him.

'Can I get you something?'

'A coffee and a bun,' I said recklessly. His eyebrows rose in surprise.

'No breakfast, no lunch.'

The apricot Danish was quite the most delicious thing I had tasted for years. I suppose all forbidden things taste that way. Whatever the truth, I felt a great deal better after I'd wolfed it down and despatched a very large mug of coffee.

We were an hour into the journey and the man beside me was snoring heavily. It was a good time to start discussing tactics. Nick was immediately brimming with enthusiasm.

'I thought I'd start with the address we've got — Poorgrass and Fray's. I looked up Orchard Street last night and found it on the town plan, but no indication of who owns the house now. If there had been postcodes in the 1850s... but we'll have to wait until we're standing outside number forty-four.'

I managed a faint smile. 'It might belong to the descendants of Poorgrass and Fray.'

'Wouldn't that be something! But you don't believe that's likely?'

'Afraid not. Still, as long as it's not another dry cleaners, I can cope with the disappointment.'

'Perhaps we should give the street a miss,' he mused,

'and go first to the County Museum. They might field a local guru who could tell us a lot more than we'll discover just looking at a building.'

'Perhaps we should go first to where we're staying.' I was remembering the heavy bag on the rack above.

'Okay. It shouldn't be too difficult to get lodgings.'

I never imagined that people's mouths could fall open, but I'm sure mine did. I was used to having trips planned down to the smallest detail, and the thought of arriving in a strange town without a place to stay momentarily stunned me.

'You mean you haven't booked anything?'

'What time have I had?'

'Last night, perhaps?'

His blue eyes lost their warmth and held a decidedly flinty expression. 'You're a little too demanding, your lady-ship. I found the train, bought my ticket, downloaded a town plan. What have you contributed?'

'I didn't know I was coming,' I said, and then wished I hadn't. But luckily he spared me the interrogation of why exactly I'd changed my mind, and to make sure I said nothing I lay back in my seat and closed my eyes.

His conviction that it would be easy to find accommodation was dashed after a fruitless search on our mobiles and two hours trawling the byways of Dorchester. This was a county town in the middle of prime tourist country, and it was, I pointed out, the half-term holiday for most schools.

'How was I to know that?'

'I knew it,' I said a trifle tartly.

'Then don't keep these good things to yourself.' He turned off down yet another side street, his shoulders moodily hunched.

It didn't look promising, and my bag was now dragging on the floor. I was weary and wishing I had never come. Halfway down the road, he stopped outside a dusty window, its paintwork crumbling, and displaying a yellowing, lop-sided sign. 'Vacancies', it read.

'You must be joking!'

'Then you find somewhere to sleep. I'm staying here if they've got a room.'

There was no bell and he lifted the door knocker. The noise echoed down the hall, but there was no sound of feet approaching. He lifted the knocker again and suddenly the door flew open. A middle-aged woman with a stained pin-afore tied around her ample waist stood on the threshold, looking none too friendly.

'I've only the one room left,' she said with a martial look in her eye. 'So if doesn't suit, you'll have to go elsewhere.'

Disappointed callers were evidently a regular feature of her life, and I wasn't surprised. I was quite sure the room wouldn't suit and sharing with Nick Heysham was the last thing I wanted, but I found myself unwillingly following him inside. It was no more appetising than the exterior. In a sad crocodile we made our way up the creaking staircase towards a room at the far end of the passage.

'The bathroom's on the left.' She waved her hand at the small, murky space we were passing. I've travelled back to the 1950s, I thought — or what I imagined the 1950s were like.

'Here,' and she opened the door wide so we could all squeeze into the one vacant room. It was brown like the rest of the house and, like the rest of the house, not overly clean.

'Well?' Her arms were held across her body and her chin

jutted dangerously.

'We'll take it for two nights,' Nick said.

I waited until she'd left before I asked coldly, 'There's only one bed, or hadn't you noticed?'

'I'd noticed. I'll sleep on the floor.'

I hadn't imagined him as a knight errant. 'Where precisely?'

'Anywhere.'

'There's no space on the floor.'

'Then we'll both sleep in the bed, and you can put a blanket down the middle in case you touch me by mistake.'

His tone was acid, and I didn't blame him. But I was feeling sore myself, mostly for having come on this stupid safari. I couldn't imagine now why I'd done so. I had risked losing Oliver and for what? This truly horrible house with its sagging bed and its dubious bathroom, and a man who was wholly unfazed by finding himself here.

'Hey, lighten up.' He was wearing a let's-make-the-best-of-it face. 'We'll go and find a meal. Nothing seems as bad after food.'

He was wrong. The food was on a par with the room and not even copious amounts of cheap wine could make it better. After we had sat in silence for a good ten minutes, he said, 'You know, you can be a real prima donna, Grace.'

'Because I prefer to sleep in a comfortable room and eat a meal without ingesting a month's fat?'

'If you feel so bad, why did you come?'

'Right now, I can't recall.'

'I'll tell you, then. You came because you had another fight with Oliver. Working with him in Newcastle was out of the question and you had a few days to fill. Perhaps you figured it might also annoy him, even make him jealous, knowing you were with me.'

'Hardly. Why on earth would Oliver be jealous?'

'I haven't a clue,' he said grimly, and got up to go.

The night was every bit as uncomfortable as I'd expected. There was no blanket to partition the bed and we both lay as near to the edges of the mattress as we could, clinging to our individual precipices. Each time I began to doze, I found myself slipping. Seemingly, Nick was having the same problem, and every so often we would touch and then hastily regain our rocky crag, bodies stiff with tension, until we dozed again and repeated the whole sorry performance.

At one point during that endless night, I heard the grandfather clock in the hall strike three discordant chimes. I clung to the sound as though it were a lifeline back to a familiar world, but when the last tinny echo faded, I knew myself abandoned.

# Chapter Fifteen

We ate the small bowl of cornflakes and the one slice of toast in silence. I could see Nick had slept about as well as I had. The blue eyes had lost their sparkle, and he wore dark smudges beneath. He ate the miniscule breakfast in less than five minutes and looked around hopelessly for more. Our formidable landlady stood in the hall watching our every swallow. Any minute her foot would start tapping. We didn't linger and were out in the street where she wanted us by nine o'clock.

Once outside, Nick trudged ahead and I followed. He was upset and I'd been the one to upset him. Last night I'd dismissed the idea he might rival Oliver in my affections, and he hadn't liked that one little bit. I didn't want to think why it had made him angry, but it had been an unlucky remark. His usual cheerful manner had disappeared entirely. I wasn't used to seeing him like this, and somehow the morning felt chillier than it should have done on a bright June day.

'Where are we going?' I asked, when it was clear he'd no intention of speaking.

'*I'm* going to the address I've got—the offices where Poorgrass and Fray hung out. But feel free to do your own thing—get a decent breakfast, indulge in some retail therapy, catch a train back to Waterloo.'

'Why don't we both get a decent breakfast?'

'Because I can barely afford to pay that gorgon her miserable mite as it is. I certainly don't have money for another meal.'

We had stopped at traffic lights, and for the first time that morning I managed to make eye contact with him.

'Then let me pay — for being a prima donna.'

He stopped suddenly at the entrance to a greengrocer's shop, and I nearly cannoned into a pyramid of oranges, balanced precariously on one of the open-air stalls.

'I can't punish you for what comes naturally, can I?'

'A hot bacon roll?' I tempted. 'Fruit yoghurt? Lashings of coffee?'

For the first time that morning, his face broke into one of those irrepressible grins. I hadn't realised till then how much I'd missed them.

'The roll and coffee will do fine.'

It didn't take us too long to find a café that fitted the bill. I swear Nick had a nose that could sniff out carbohydrates wherever they were hiding. The coffee helped to dissolve any surviving strain, and two cups in we had relaxed sufficiently to discuss the day ahead. Orchard Street was a few minutes' walk away, and we decided to check first whether the present day occupants of offices that had once housed Poorgrass and Fray could offer any help. Depending on our success — or lack of it — we would move on to the County Museum and ask to see their archive. I knew my uni card would gain us access to any relevant papers. After that, if we'd still not found any leads, we might be reduced to asking at random, targeting the older inhabitants of Dorchester. I wasn't looking forward to this final slice of the Heysham plan and hoped we might never have to put the idea into practice.

* * *

Even before we stood in front of number forty-four, we'd spotted the blue plaque. At least we had the right place, and I couldn't stop myself feeling just the slightest tremor of excitement. It still housed an architects' practice, too, although one with a completely different name. The girl on the reception desk stopped her phone conversation to smile vaguely in our direction.

'I wonder if we might speak to someone about Lucas Royde.' I felt a little foolish asking.

'Sorry, but we don't have a Mr Royde here,' the girl sang out, ready to make a swift return to the telephone.

'No, we know you don't, but you do have a plaque on your wall engraved with his name. We wondered if there was someone — one of the partners perhaps — who might be able to tell us something about the man.'

She looked nonplussed and then said slowly, as though addressing an alien being, 'Mr Hammond is in this morning. He's an architect.'

'Mr Hammond will do fine if he can spare a few minutes.'

He could — and more than a few minutes. Roger Hammond was a jovial man with time on his hands. He was delighted to welcome us into his comfortable office, ordering refreshments on the way. By now we were almost floating on a sea of coffee, but we tried to look suitably grateful.

'Lucas Royde?' He rocked backwards against expensive cream leather. 'I see you've spotted the plaque. No relation of course to the existing partners, but an architect we're proud to have succeeded in the same offices.'

'Royde was famous in his time?' Nick had gone down the route of pretending ignorance. It was a good decision.

'Very famous, probably the most celebrated of all Victorian architects.'

'What did he design — would we know any of his buildings?'

'You might, if you're from London. You are? There's a splendid church in Shoreditch — in Hoxton Road or Hoxton Street?'

For the last ten years I must have passed very near this church, but never realised the connection.

'Was the church his first commission?'

I was continuing with Nick's naivety and was rewarded by an expansive beam. I was Mr Hammond's kind of audience.

'No, it's an example of his more mature work. I have a feeling his first work was a chapel for some aristocrat. Yes... that's right.' He was remembering his past studies, too. 'It was quite different from anything that had gone before and caused a storm. Of praise, I hasten to add.'

I decided to go straight to the vital question. 'I expect he was involved with the Great Exhibition,' I said innocently. 'Such a famous architect must have been commissioned to produce something for it.'

'Now there you have me. The Exhibition was 1851? I'm pretty sure Royde did most of his work after that date.'

Nick was getting restless with a conversation that appeared to be going nowhere, fidgeting this way and that in his chair; either that or the coffee was making him twitch. His interruption verged on the curt when our host began to recite a list of the Royde triumphs he remembered.

'I don't suppose you still have any of Royde's plans here.'

Mr Hammond laughed uproariously as though Nick had told the joke of the year. 'I doubt we ever had anything, and if we had, it would have disappeared forty years ago.'

'Why forty?'

He leaned towards me with a conspiratorial air. 'A fire!' Then warming to his theme, 'You could see the blaze from Maiden Hill two miles out of town. The rear storage area had to be completely rebuilt. I designed it, I was a very young man then and it was my first job.' He must be older than he looked. Having a happy nature certainly kept you young. 'Would you like to see it?'

'No,' I said rather too definitely. 'You've been most kind, Mr Hammond, but we mustn't trespass on your time any longer. Thank you so much for the coffee and talk.'

We had almost reached the street when we heard him calling after us.

'Quick,' Nick breathed, 'run for it.'

Mr Hammond's plump figure moved with surprising agility and in a few minutes he had caught us up. 'If you're really interested in Royde, you could talk to Mr Fawley. I'm not a great one for local history, but he knows just about all there is to know about Dorchester.'

We stopped on the spot. 'Mr Fawley?'

'That's right. He works at the County Museum.'

We thanked him profusely again, only this time it was sincere. We'd planned to visit the museum, but we now had the name of someone, according to Mr Hammond, who would know anything there was to know. We walked quickly, turning into the High Street outside a black and white Tudor building. A pub sign depicting a cloaked and bewigged figure creaked in the breeze.

'That must be Judge Jeffreys.' I pointed at the grim face

swinging above our heads. 'He must have lodged in this house when he came to Dorchester — for the trials of men who took part in the Monmouth Rebellion.'

Nick looked impatient. 'Thank you for the history lesson. How about we stick to architecture?'

'It was called the Bloody Assize,' I teased.

He grabbed my arm and hurried me along the pavement. He was high on anticipation and Judge Jeffreys was an unnecessary distraction, but when we reached the museum, his hopes were dashed. Mr Fawley wasn't in. Today he was working from home.

'Are you able to give us a contact number?' I sounded professional, but to no avail.

The assistant looked shocked. 'I couldn't do that.'

'Could you perhaps ring him for us?'

Her face remained in shock mode. 'Mr Fawley doesn't take office calls when he's working at home — not unless it's an emergency.'

She saw our faces fall to somewhere around our knees and said more kindly, 'You could try again this afternoon. He said he might pop in for a few hours. You never know, you might catch him.'

'*Might* catch him,' Nick repeated, once we were out on the pavement again. 'I'm beginning to think you were right. This is a wild goose chase.'

'Hey, it's not like you to give up. It could be worth our while to come back. If we hang around the museum long enough, the receptionist might get fed up and decide we are an emergency after all!'

'Sorry. My turn to be a prima donna now.' He grinned and his blue eyes were alight with laughter. 'It's the carbohydrates, you know.'

'What is?'

'Losing heart. I'm starving again, and I can't operate on less than three thousand calories a day.'

I sighed. Too much time spent with Nick Heysham and I would be as wide as I was tall. 'Okay, we'll find somewhere to eat, but it's got to have salad on the menu.'

Halfway through a very large plate of lasagne, he suddenly stopped eating and fixed me with a penetrating look. 'So where is Oliver?'

I was caught on the hop and answered before I thought. 'Newcastle.'

'Without you?'

'As you see.'

'I thought you were essential to his comfort.'

'I thought so, too.' I must have sounded sad because he reached out and squeezed my hand.

'We'll be back in London tomorrow. You could always get a train there.'

'I could, but I won't. He assures me I needn't worry over arrangements at the Newcastle gallery. He has a new assistant to help him.'

'And she is… I take it, it is a she?'

'Oh yes, it's a she. Rebecca. She's on work experience.'

'Blonde and petite?'

'How did you know?'

He smiled compassionately. 'Have a think.'

'They don't have that kind of relationship.' I knew he wouldn't believe me, but pride required me to say it.

'Who says they don't?'

'Oliver says.'

'I rest my case.'

'When I accused him of behaving badly, he told me I had

a vulgar mind.'

'He would, wouldn't he? No man likes to get caught out and I guess he was.'

I thought about Rebecca standing at the door. Oliver hadn't expected me home so early. He had told the girl to come to the house on the assumption I wouldn't be there. He would have left me a note saying he'd had to go earlier than expected and not to worry about making the journey myself. I could see it all now.

My silence seemed to make Nick uncomfortable. 'It's probably one of those middle-aged flings,' he said. 'Over in a trice. He'll be back in a few days, begging your forgiveness.'

'Middle-aged?' The description was annoying.

'How old is Oliver?'

'Forty-five.'

'There you are. Classic case of the male menopause. How long have you known him?'

'Nine years.' It was beginning to feel like an interrogation.

'A lot can happen in nine years, sweet Grace. He's not going to stay the same and neither are you.'

'What are you trying to say? That we should call it a day?'

'I'm just pointing out that people change and the reasons for the way they behave change, too. Why did you hook up with him in the first place?'

'I didn't hook up with him, as you put it. Not initially. He'd just gone through a messy divorce and wasn't looking for commitment.'

'And you. Were you looking for commitment?'

I didn't answer. I remembered the twenty-year-old I had been, shy, lonely, already bruised by life. If I were honest, I *had* been looking for commitment or at least a safe haven.

And Oliver had provided it. Nick was looking quizzical.

'Oliver gave me what I wanted at the time.'

'And now?'

I couldn't answer. I wasn't sure any longer what I wanted. I must have looked confused because he said easily, 'Like I say, times change, people change. No dishonour in that.'

I swallowed the rest of my elderflower and went to pay. Right now, I didn't want to think of Oliver and what might be happening between us. It was worth the expense of funding Nick to keep him happy and away from a subject I'd no wish to discuss. We made our way back to the museum without much real hope of seeing the man we sought, but a different receptionist nodded her head when we asked for the local historian.

'Mr Fawley? You're in luck. He's just got in. I'll go and see if he can spare you a few minutes.'

# Chapter Sixteen

I felt a surge of excitement that was completely irrational. I couldn't explain it, couldn't explain why this figure from the past had become so compelling. Nick's foot was beating time on the polished wood floor, a sure sign, as I'd come to recognise, that he was excited, too. Mr Fawley could prove our saviour.

He didn't, as it turned out. At least not obviously so, since he knew little more of Royde's architectural career than we had managed to piece together for ourselves. Royde was from a poor family, one of six siblings born and bred on a local farm, but a man who had risen to become one of the most celebrated sons of Dorchester. Excitement drained away as he told us what we already knew. But we were riding a roller coaster of emotions and his next words sent our spirits soaring.

'There is one person who might possibly help you. I'm not entirely sure, but she's certainly worth a try.'

'Who?' we chorused.

He smiled at our eagerness, but was not to be rushed. 'I'm sure I have the lady's details here.'

He began to trawl the contents of his battered desk. Handfuls of dog-eared papers slowly emerged, accompanied by regular puffs of dust. Nick and I exchanged a glance. I knew we both longed to grab him by the neck and shake him hard until he told us the magic name.

'Ah, here it is,' he said at last, brandishing a small slip of crumpled paper. 'Mrs Gardiner. Mellstock Close. I'll give her a ring.'

And he did. Before we knew it, he had made an appointment for us to see our new friend at ten the next morning.

'She would have seen you today, but Hector has to go to the vets.'

'Hector?' Clearly agitated by the delay, Nick was tugging at his hair. The image of Oliver and his beard flashed through my mind. How strange — surely there couldn't be two more different people?

'Hector is the cockerel. Most important to get him right, you know.'

I took his word for it, though Nick was finding it difficult to contain himself. 'Who is Mrs Gardiner? I mean what connection does she have to Lucas Royde?'

Our mentor smiled sadly. 'Only a distant one, I fear, but if there is anything useful to find, she will have it. Her godmother was the daughter of a friend of Lucas Royde's only sister.'

'That's pretty distant.' I was unable to keep the disappointment from my voice, unsure now if it was worth visiting Mrs Gardiner, not to mention a sick Hector.

'True.' Mr Fawley's head was nodding in vigorous agreement. 'However, I have had some conversation before with the lady, and it appears she has a number of keepsakes, including papers — from the way she described it, I would say a cache of papers — that she inherited from her godmother. That was some thirty years ago.'

'I don't suppose you know what's in those papers, Mr Fawley?' I asked the question without any real hope.

'I'm afraid not, but I wish you good luck on your mission.'

We thanked him for his time and made our way to the exit, wandering disconsolately along the gallery we had walked earlier, and passing an impressive collection of statuary with barely a glance. It was unlikely anything handed down through godmothers, friends and sisters, would be of use to us. It was too distant a chain. But it was the only lead we had, and we decided in the most positive mood we could muster, to keep the appointment but make a dash to the station immediately afterwards and catch the first train back to London.

It was late afternoon and neither of us had the heart to face our miserable lodgings just yet. We walked back along Orchard Street, and this time carried on to its very end where I'd noticed a tree-lined walk. It was an attractive place in which to stroll. The sun was still quite high in the sky and its warm rays filtered through foliage that had not yet lost its spring freshness. For a long time we walked without speaking, both of us in low spirits.

'We shouldn't feel too bad.' I decided to try for the positive. 'Mrs Gardiner might come up trumps and, if not, we can state pretty definitely that plans earlier than the Carlyon chapel don't exist.'

'I guess so,' he conceded bleakly. 'I'll get my cheque come what may, but I'm sorry I've wasted *your* time. You've a right to bawl me out.'

'I won't be doing that. I didn't have to come, and at least I've seen the town where Royde grew up.'

'It's not enough.'

I could see Nick was becoming more morose by the

second. His was a mercurial nature, but even so his disappointment seemed extreme.

'I really wanted to find something,' he offered, kicking a stray stone along the paving. 'I felt sure there *was* something.'

'I felt it, too.'

'And if I had, if *we* had,' he corrected himself, 'that would have been some story, wouldn't it?'

'And freelancers need stories.' I was sympathetic.

'It's not that I haven't plenty to write. I've several leads already waiting to be followed up.'

'Why so gloomy then?'

He looked a little self-conscious. 'I guess I wanted to make a splash.'

'In what way?'

'It would be good to be special — the man who found Lucas Royde's first commission!'

'And that's important?' I had a suspicion why, but I wanted to hear it from him.

'I told you about my successful family, didn't I?'

'You also told me you didn't much care for them.'

'Whether or not I do is unimportant. It doesn't stop them making me feel this high.' And his fingers narrowed to an inch gap. 'It would have been great to make them eat their words just once in my life.'

'Which were? The words, I mean.'

'That I'd never make anything of myself. That I was a drifter, a piece of flotsam — or is it jetsam? I've never been sure.'

We had stopped at the entrance to pretty gardens, but he made no move to walk on. In the distance, I could see the cascade of a fountain silhouetted against the sweep of June colour.

'You don't have to value the same kind of success as they do.' I hoped he wouldn't take offence at the small homily. 'If they can't see what you do is worthwhile, it's their problem, not yours.'

'That's counsellor-speak. You know it doesn't work like that in real life. It's status — and money — that's valued.' He kicked another stone, this time into the well-trimmed hedge. 'How supportive is *your* family?'

'I only have a sister.'

'And you don't speak to her, which rather proves my point.'

I could say nothing and turned to retrace our steps. It was time in any case to head back to the grim room and the even grimmer bathroom, but by dint of promising ourselves a decent meal that evening, we somehow managed to ignore the worst of our surroundings. On the dot of six o'clock we had showered and dressed in whatever finery we could manage and were ready to escape its four walls again.

Nick had for once ditched his endless supply of tee shirts and was wearing a pale blue shirt that did amazing things for his eyes. He looked his most attractive, and I was pleased to be walking beside him. I hoped I looked as good. The bathroom mirror, more tarnish than glass, was an unreliable friend, and when I wriggled into the skinny emerald shift and matching heels, I could only hope they would work as well as they usually did. A slick of lipstick and a quick brush through my hair and I was done.

Nick gave a low whistle. 'No one looking like that should ever emerge from a place looking like this.' He gestured derisively at stained plasterwork that would need an industrial solvent to burn it clean.

* * *

It didn't take us long to find a welcoming wine bar, with soft lights and even softer music, and we settled down for some serious drinking. I guess we hoped it might make the disappointments of the day less raw. We were well down the second bottle of wine, and had argued our way through the works of several artists and their respective merits, before Nick's appetite kicked in.

'We should find somewhere to eat, somewhere decent. And no salad.'

'Okay, but no bacon rolls either.'

'It's a deal. I saw a smart-looking place in a courtyard off Orchard Street. We could give it a try.'

'Let's finish the wine first.'

'Should you?'

My head was spinning slightly, but his words were too strongly reminiscent of Oliver. This was the second time today I'd been reminded of what I'd left behind, and it jarred.

'Yes,' I said belligerently. 'I should.'

His expression remained calm, appraising even. I imagined he was weighing up whether to make an issue of it, but he said nothing and I raised a defiant glass. I'd taken only the smallest sip when out of the blue, he asked, 'What is your sister's name?'

'Verity.' I blurted the word, shocked at what felt like an attack. If there was someone I didn't want to think about, it was Verity.

'Verity and Grace,' he mused. 'Someone had a sense of humour.'

The wine no longer looked so inviting and I stood up

abruptly. 'You wanted to go to the best restaurant in town?'

'Only if you're paying.'

'Who else?'

I led the way to Orchard Street, thankful he seemed to have lost interest in my family. But when our dessert plates had been cleared and we were sitting over a second cup of coffee, it was evident he was not going to let the topic go. I didn't understand his persistence. What possible interest could these people have for him? It seemed my reluctance to discuss the past was enough to make him want to worry his way into it.

As so often, his words came as a jolt. 'So why don't you speak to Verity?'

'It's simple — we don't get on.' I was prevaricating, but it would have to be enough.

It wasn't. 'Not many siblings do, but cutting them out of your life completely is pretty extreme.'

'My sister is eight years older than me and we were never friends.'

He looked sceptical and I rushed on. 'Our parents were killed in a car crash when I was only ten. Verity was on the brink of going to uni and she gave up the chance in order to look after me. I don't think I was very grateful. I missed mum and dad and felt guilty they'd died. I couldn't have been an easy child and we were always having arguments.'

'Why did you feel guilty when your parents died?'

Another can of worms, but easy enough to answer. I had been asking myself the same question for ever. I felt guilty because I was to blame. I was the one who'd set in motion the whole terrible event. But twenty years had passed and I could speak of it calmly.

'My parents had been quarrelling, and they were still

quarrelling when they got into the car. My father drove off as though every demon of hell was in pursuit.'

'And the quarrel was over you?' I had to hand it to Nick, he was perceptive.

'It was stupid.'

'It usually is.' He looked questioningly at me, and I couldn't see the harm in telling him what I could remember.

'I'd wanted to go on a sleepover at one of my very best friends' and my mother had said I couldn't. So I asked my father and he said yes.'

'Because you could always wheedle what you wanted out of your father? Don't worry, I know the score. I've a sister of my own, remember.'

'My mother was furious — but at him, not me. She said he was always undermining her authority and then...'

I didn't know if I wanted to tell this story after all, but Nick was waiting.

'Then she said that the only reason he encouraged me to go to Bella's house was so he could see more of Bella's mother. That he was having an affair with her.'

'And was he?'

'How would I know? I was ten years old and not even sure what an affair was. My father was very angry and denied it. He'de'dHHH been drinking heavily. Then he said that he and my mother had been invited to the Langhams' party, so they should go. Bella's parents would be there, too, now there was no sleepover, and my mother would have the opportunity of telling her tales directly to Bella's father.'

'Ouch.'

'It was more than ouch. The police found their car upside down in a ditch about five miles along the road. It had caught fire on impact and was still smouldering.'

'That's an ugly story.'

'Yes,' I agreed in a small voice. It still had the power to haunt me.

'But no way was it your fault.'

'Children always think the bad things that happen in their family are their fault.'

'But not thirty-year-olds.'

'Hey, wash your mouth out. I'm not thirty for at least three months.'

* * *

We walked back along the quiet streets hand in hand; I felt warm inside and strangely mellow. For the first time in years I had relived that dreadful experience, and it helped that Nick had been with me. When we got to the room, I pulled open the curtains and let the moon shine in. The room looked better like that. I opened the window and the cool night breeze flooded through, wafting the jasmine perfume I'd been wearing into every one of the four corners. We undressed silently, not bothering with the one-in-the-bathroom, one-in-the-bedroom routine we had adopted the night before. We slipped into bed and let ourselves roll into the centre, bodies touching. He reached for my hand and held it tightly.

'Don't let anyone tell you you're to blame for the ills of the world — your parents, your sister, Oliver. That's not a line you should fall for. Fight it. Sometimes you need to fight — if the cause is good.'

'Thank you, Che.'

He laughed softly. 'I'm the last one to give advice — I do nothing *but* fight.'

'A small chip on your shoulder perhaps?'

'You've noticed.'

'Slightly, but it's not that obvious — the way you're flippant about everything perhaps, the way you dress. The tee shirts, for instance. I don't imagine your family would go a bundle on them, although they could be worse.'

'They could. I haven't yet worn SIZE MATTERS.'

'Please don't.'

'I won't, I promise. You're a calming influence. We should get together more often.'

I could feel his body warm and strong beside me, and then his arms were cradling me and I lifted my face for the kiss I knew I had wanted since I first met him. His mouth tasted of the best Beaujolais mixed with peppermint. It was a tender kiss, so tender it made me want to cry. I stroked his hair, still soft from the shower, and he kissed me again much less tenderly. His hands were on my body and I liked it; his kisses were hard and insistent and I liked them, too.

The bright silver of moonlight illuminated our bodies, hiding from sight the ancient bed and dilapidated furniture. His lips grazed my stomach and arrowed downward. A sharp burst of pleasure shot through me, and I heard myself gasp with delight. It had been a long time since that had happened. We began exploring as though our lives depended on it, rapidly, greedily, snatching at every moment of pleasure. He looked down at me for one arrested moment and then before we had time to consider consequences, I grabbed him by the shoulders and brought him down on me. There was only one thing I wanted and that was him, all of him.

# Chapter Seventeen

It's amazing how much difference a day can make, or rather a night. I had come on this trip against my better judgement, but if I'm honest partly to play truant and annoy Oliver. Nick had been right when he said I was in Dorchester because of a quarrel. In fact, he'd been right about a lot of things. I *was* scared of life, but tried to clothe my fear in a shiny dress: I was an agreeable woman, an amiable companion, who kept her head down and stayed far from conflict. Who wouldn't like me? Who would ever blame me?

That was the heart of it. Ever since my parents died, I had been blaming myself — for causing their deaths, for losing Verity her chance of happiness, for giving up on my own. Yet at the same time I'd waged an inner battle to resist blame, to reject its claims as unjust. My claws, as Nick had so expertly diagnosed, had always been there and just maybe they were starting to unsheathe.

It took only a few minutes to pack our bags the next morning and flee the aptly named Crook Lodge before the hall clock sounded its nine wavering chimes. We passed an empty breakfast room, glad to give its home comforts a miss, and went straight towards the bacon rolls. Nick was looking bright-eyed and sprightly, but apart from a swift kiss on the lips, he made no reference to what had happened between us. We instinctively fell into holding hands as we walked to the café, where over a good deal of black coffee we puzzled our way round a plan of Dorchester, tracing a route to Fordington and Mellstock Close.

The district of Fordington lay beside the river on the southern outskirts of the town, an area that not so long ago would have been countryside, and Diggory Cottage, when we found it, still looked much as I imagined it had two centuries ago. It was set back from the road with a long, narrow front garden leading to a white-painted porch. From the rear of the house came the contented cluck of chickens; Hector must be back, alive and well.

Mrs Gardiner came to the door, with a cat under one arm and a dog frisking around her ankles. Two other cats made for the stairs as they glimpsed the strangers on their threshold. The cottage had all the appearance of an animal refuge and Mrs Gardiner of a live-in attendant. Long strands of grey hair escaped what I thought must be a bun at the back of her head and the dress she wore bore all the signs of long cohabitation with an assortment of creatures. But her smile was pure joy.

'Come in, my dears. How nice of you to call. Mr Fawley — such a pleasant gentleman — said you would come by. I would have made a cake, but it seemed a little early in the day to be eating sweet things and then there was Hector to see to. Yesterday was a bit of a mess.'

I imagined every day was a bit of a mess for Mrs Gardiner, but we thanked her politely and followed her into the sitting room. She waved us to take a seat, and we gingerly lowered ourselves into chairs patched with wisps of fur. They had a tendency to sag to one side so that when the three of us looked across at each other, it was as if we were aboard the deck of a listing ship.

We declined the offer of tea and went straight to the point. Mr Fawley had mentioned papers that originally belonged to Lucas Royde. She nodded enthusiastically and I hoped she would go to find them, but she was as garrulous as Mr Hammond. She wanted to talk so we let her. It was possible we might even learn something.

'I inherited the papers from my godmother, you know, Miss Flora Hannington. She left them to me because she had no children of her own. Well, of course she wouldn't have, being a spinster lady. And she herself was an only child and was left the papers by her mother, Henrietta Hannington.'

She noticed our puzzled looks. 'You're wondering what the Hanningtons have to do with Mr Lucas Royde. The fact is that Henrietta was a great friend of Mr Royde's young sister, Mary. His only sister, in fact. He left his personal possessions to Mary. All of his brothers were dead by then. Mr Royde lived to a very good age, for those days at least. Eighty-two.'

'He had no children of his own?' The biographies we'd read had avoided or been uninterested in the great man's personal life.

'My dear, no! He never married. Strange, isn't it? One thinks of the Victorians as being particularly prolific in making families, but Mr Royde seems to have decided early in life to stay single.'

'And his brothers?'

'I believe three of them married and had children and a fourth died very young — not that unusual at the time, unfortunately.'

'So Lucas Royde had nephews and nieces?'

'Yes, quite a number. But he was particularly fond of his

sister, or so it's said. She was some sixteen years younger than him, but often that kind of friendship springs up within a family. He must have decided she would be the best caretaker for his most personal possessions.'

'And when Mary died, she didn't think to leave them to her brothers' children?'

'I don't know why not. My godmother told me that her mother, Henrietta, always maintained that she and Mary were the greatest devotees of Mr Royde's work, and that Mary felt she could do no better than leave his personal effects to a friend who was bound to treasure them.'

'That's interesting, isn't it, Nick?'

I could see his eyes had been on the brink of closing and he was perilously near to falling asleep. It had been an energetic night. He jerked his head up and beamed vacantly. I turned to our hostess with what I hoped was a slightly more lively smile.

'Would it be possible for us to see them, I wonder?'

'But of course, my dear, I have everything right here. When I knew of your interest, I made sure to start searching as soon as I got Hector home yesterday. It took a while to locate my godmother's stuff, but I've brought down what I think you'll find most interesting.' She waved her hand at a table that sat beneath one of the cottage's small-paned windows.

Nick, who had so far contributed nothing to the conversation, was out of his chair and at the table before I could blink. Then he remembered his manners. 'Perhaps you could take us through what you found,' he suggested.

Mrs Gardiner exuded pride. She picked up several battered leather-bound books and started to leaf her way through first one and then the other. 'These are photograph albums. I believe the pictures are all of the Royde family — many of them of recent generations, but there are a few of Lucas. Well, one is an engraving. See here.'

She held up the book for us. It was a very early image; the figure depicted seemed to be barely out of his teens. Something of his youth and innocence had been caught by the delicate engraving, but in truth he could have been any very young man on the point of starting out in life.

'These, though,' and she shuffled through more of the old pages, sending clouds of paper dust into the air, 'these are photographs of his immediate family, I believe. Naturally, they are of a later date than the engraving — photography was only then in its infancy.'

Most of the photographs were of different groups of family members and had been taken standing under trees in what looked like an orchard, sitting on a stone-flagged terrace in the summer sun or posing against a backdrop of a garden bursting with produce. It looked a homely existence, comfortable without ever being easy. The family seemed to enjoy being together. It was strange there was no sign of Lucas in any of the photographs — some of them at least must have been taken in his lifetime.

There was just one other of him, taken — or rather posed — in a photographer's studio. He would have been a well-established architect by then. He was standing stiffly, almost to attention, and the photographer had arranged the backdrop to illuminate him. He wore a dark cutaway jacket, a white shirt with a slightly winged collar and a glossy black cravat. Almost a study in *chiaroscuro*. He was clean shaven and his hair parted very precisely, high on the right side. It was a good-looking face, very good looking: wide, clear eyes, straight nose and a sensitive mouth.

I looked at the face for a long time and began to realise that though his eyes met the camera head-on, they were in reality looking elsewhere. Where I didn't know, but my impression was of a man a little worn, haunted even, as though he had known a difficult life. That was hardly likely. Royde had made his name early on, he had been a precocious talent, and riches and good living must have flowed abundantly. Whatever troubles he'd had, they could have been nothing that money could cure.

I tried to murmur suitable approval as one photograph followed another, but I could see there was nothing of real interest to us. Nick had relapsed into silence, his earlier enthusiasm replaced by indifference. Or so I thought. But when I glanced across at him, I saw him looking at me thoughtfully, even lovingly. I felt myself blush. I'd assumed he would dismiss last night as one of those things that happen occasionally when two people are away from home and a little drunk. It hadn't felt that way, but I've never been one to take anyone's feelings for granted. How could I be, when the people closest to me had proved so unpredictable?

I must have been sounding increasingly fatigued because he decided we had suffered enough. He smiled persuasively at our hostess. 'These photographs are really interesting, Mrs Gardiner — seeing Lucas Royde in the flesh, as it were. But I wonder, do you have any actual papers among the stuff you inherited?'

'My dear, yes, plenty of papers.' We sat up, a little invigorated. 'But there's one other thing you might like to see first.' We slumped back again.

'It's this. A most beautiful necklace. I have no idea why it was among the photographs, but I think it must be valuable.' She opened the small box that had been sitting amid the albums.

Highly valuable, I guessed, when she held up three stunning strands of lapis lazuli weaved into a glowing crescent. I took the proffered jewellery and nestled it in my palm. My hand instinctively closed over it and for a moment I felt the most powerful connection. The necklace was quite beautiful, of course, yet there was something else making me reluctant to let it go. But then I saw Nick looking at his watch and went to replace the necklace in the box, loosening a small piece of cloth as I did so. Instantly, I was aware of the scent. I put the faded velvet to my nose and sniffed. It was a perfume I knew well.

'Jasmine,' Mrs Gardiner said complacently. 'The scent was as popular in Victorian times as it is today.'

'The necklace dates from then?'

'Almost certainly. I found it in a paper bag, would you believe, wrapped tightly in that piece of material. Then I rooted around for a box to put it in. I thought I should. I am right, my dear, it is valuable?'

'I'm sure it is, Mrs Gardiner, so guard it well. But the papers…'

'There, I'd quite forgotten. Give me a minute and I'll find exactly what you want.'

She trotted towards the staircase and we soon heard her footsteps creaking overhead. Neither of us really believed she would produce anything significant, but a few minutes later she was staggering into the sitting room with a large pile of manilla envelopes and spilling their contents at random.

'Here we are. Enough papers for you?' She sounded triumphant.

We started searching while she busied herself in the kitchen, determined we wouldn't leave before we'd taken some Dorset sustenance. For the most part, the envelopes were filled with old letters and postcards, dating from the final years of the nineteenth century and sent by family members to each other. Again, there was no evident connection to Lucas Royde. A few recipes popped up here and there, interesting enough to make a non-cook stop and read, until I felt Nick's reproving eye on me.

I plodded on — more letters, notices of village events, a few keepsakes, dried flowers, ribbons, small badges, and a few tattered theatre posters at the bottom of the pile. Out of curiosity, I scooped them up, wondering what kind of theatre Dorchester would have boasted at the time. But they turned out to be from much further afield, from London. I felt the old familiar stir of excitement and waved one at Nick.

He didn't spark, and I decided to make him. 'These must have belonged to Royde himself. I can't imagine another member of the family visiting a London theatre.'

My excitement slid off him. 'Another dead end,' he opined.

'I guess so…' My voice trailed off while I studied the poster. It was slightly torn around its edgtes and seemed to be the oldest. The Adelphi had produced it to advertise a play called *The School for Tigers,* staged at the theatre in March of 1851. The date was bang-on.

'March 1851.' I waved the poster at him again, and my voice was a little croaky.

'Interesting, but where does it get us?'

I turned the poster over and stared fixedly, trying to decipher the old-fashioned writing, and hardly believing what I was seeing.

Nick looked curiously at me. 'Your eyes are like head-lamps.'

'You bet! There's a note on the back. A scrawled note — he seems to have written it in haste.'

'So?'

'It reads,' and I took a breath, 'it reads, "Meet A, Onslow Street."'

I jumped to my feet and launched myself at him, hugging him so tightly he was in serious danger of suffocating. 'Onslow Street, Nick. There were offices in that road belonging to a silk importer, an Edward Renville, who paid for a display space in the Exhibition Hall of the Crystal Palace. We've got our connection at last!'

'That's great.' He didn't sound as enthralled as I thought he should. 'But how much further does it get us, Grace? Who on earth is A?'

I refused to be daunted. 'Who indeed?'

# Chapter Eighteen

*London, March 1851.*

Lucas Royde stood on the threshold of five Onslow Street and adjusted his cravat. This was not what he had been hoping for, even dreaming of. For the last few weeks he'd pictured himself returning to Wisteria Lodge and meeting Alessia alone, taking tea with her once more in the beautiful room overlooking the garden, talking together, exchanging confidences even. But the message from Edward Renville had been unequivocal: he understood that designs for the Renville pavilion were now complete and he wished to see them as soon as possible.

Delighted that an unsatisfactory commission was nearing its close, Daniel de Vere had graciously indicated Lucas might take a few hours away from the office to attend on Mr Renville at his place of business. He had hurried Lucas from Great Russell Street, allowing him only to gather final drawings, before bundling him unceremoniously into a passing hansom. DV, it seemed, had plans for his talented young recruit and was anxious to wash his hands of a difficult and none too lucrative client.

The new commission, Lucas gathered, involved yet another ancient church marked for Gothic renewal. The task would extend his professional expertise, but he felt little enthusiasm for it. He wanted no other commission, least of all one that led to a vandalism he detested. He wished to stay just where he was, dig in his heels and refuse to move. He was willing to design the Renville space over and over again, as long as it kept him close to Alessia. His hope today was that she would be waiting for him behind the front door of number five.

A grey-haired clerk, his trousers shiny from long wear, opened the door and bowed Lucas in. He had imagined the Renville offices as dark, sombre, overpowering, like the man who owned them. Overpowering they were, but it was their sheer opulence that came as a shock. Wisteria Lodge, though a substantial dwelling, was modest in appearance. It was his workplace into which Edward Renville had poured every particle of pride. Sumptuous velvet hung at the windows, beneath his feet a carpet so thick it felt as though Lucas walked upon air, and scattered lavishly around a room designed to receive and impress visitors, a host of valuable antiques.

The clerk did some more bowing and Lucas found himself in the great man's office. It was similarly furnished, and he was waved into an expensive chair of black Jacobean oak. There was no sign of Alessia and his mood plummeted. Edward Renville accorded him only the smallest of bows before he retreated with the designs to a desk so imposing it stretched almost from one wall to another.

There was silence while Lucas awaited his sponsor's judgement. A solid gold Georgian timepiece ticked loudly in the background while Renville shuffled papers back and forth, studying one sheet at a time, but giving no indication of his thoughts. A very small hope sprang up in Lucas that the man was dissatisfied, not sufficiently to cancel the whole project, but enough to necessitate his return to Prospect Place for another consultation with the woman whose image had for weeks filled his every waking moment. After what seemed an age, and which Lucas later calculated to be at least fifteen silent minutes, Edward Renville sniffed loudly.

'It will do.'

The grudging acceptance was irksome and Lucas decided to irritate, returning to the question he had first asked days ago. 'The Exhibition Hall will be enormous. What is the precise location for the Renville display?' He deliberately omitted the customary 'sir.'

Edward Renville's face duly registered annoyance. He had already made it clear such trivial matters were not his concern. 'Upstairs.'

The answer was as grudging as his acceptance of the plans, but at least Lucas had forced him to answer. A small victory in a war that only Renville could win.

But then something miraculous happened. 'You will need to see the location before these plans are realised. You may need to make adjustments to take account of the venue. Take Mrs Renville with you. It must be perfect.'

How could it not be, thought Lucas, with perfection overseeing the project? His heart was hammering so loudly he was sure Renville must hear it. He took a deep breath and tried to recover his poise.

Leaning forward on the uncomfortable wooden chair, he spoke with the first genuine enthusiasm he had felt that afternoon. 'It would be helpful to view the materials you have in mind for the display.'

'I have nothing particular in mind. All Renville materials are of the highest quality. It matters not which you choose — each will prove an excellent ambassador.'

When he spoke of his business, Edward Renville's pomposity excelled itself; the enterprise appeared to be his whole life. What about Alessia, Lucas thought savagely, how does she fit into this narrow little world? And her daughters? What does their father think of them — the fact that his only children are girls? The youngest, Georgina, must be at least six years old and further additions to the family seemed unlikely. But producing a male heir would be paramount since Renville and Daughter was unimaginable.

Edward Renville got up and moved in a stately fashion to the door. 'Follow me, Mr Reed.'

'Royde.'

'Follow me.'

He led Lucas along a richly panelled hallway and through a door at the back of the building. Outside, they followed a paved pathway towards a vast structure of galvanised iron. There was far more space behind the house than Lucas had imagined. It appeared Renville had bought up the gardens of his neighbours to the left and right of number five, and erected one of the ugliest warehouses Lucas had ever seen. The contrast with the overblown luxury they had left behind was comic.

Renville threw open the door, and Lucas was confronted with mile after mile of racking, filled to overflowing with bolts of every kind and colour of material. Silks, gauzes, satins, taffetas and tulles blazed forth, their radiance disconnecting them from the drab space in which they sat, as though the markets of southern Europe and the bazaars of the East had taken flight together and by mistake had come to rest in an alien land. They shared no bond with the glaring light of gas above or the rough ground beneath, but shimmered intangibly in a sphere of their own. Even their smell marked difference. Warm spice and tangy citrus wafted by Lucas as he passed along their rows. He felt immediately at home, and unthinking, was encouraged to speak.

'We had in mind a primary scheme of pinks, lilacs, perhaps a darker fuchsia on occasion.'

Renville sniffed. It seemed to be his chosen mode of communication for those with whom he had no wish to communicate.

'You might prefer a bolder scheme — scarlets, deep purples, indigos?' Lucas hazarded.

The thin, clipped tones of his host put him right. 'I have no interest in colour, Mr Reed. That is your province. Choose what you wish. Dearlove will assist you.'

A small, bald-headed man had appeared from the shadows. He was dressed in light brown overalls and wielded an enormous pair of scissors. While Lucas was nodding a greeting, Renville abruptly turned tail and without a word, disappeared back to his empire. Mr Dearlove looked meekly at Lucas and waggled his shears in preparation.

Lucas took another long walk around the racks. They presented a bewildering array of possibilities, but keeping Alessia's beautiful face firmly in sight, he decided on the choices she would make. He managed eventually to whittle his requirements down to five silks and three gauzes, and Mr Dearlove set to work with a will, expertly slicing numerous lengths from each of the bolts indicated. Then he trussed them in brown paper and string and handed them over, all without speaking a word. Lucas made his way back through the heavy luxury of the main building and out of the front door. The materials were surprisingly heavy, and he felt it a great good fortune that the hansom was still waiting. And that de Vere's was paying.

'Great Russell Street?' the jarvey asked.

'Yes — no.' An idea had sprung unbidden into his mind. Why not? He had the materials; he had the cab.

'Prospect Place,' he commanded.

* * *

There was little traffic on the roads, and he was there in a matter of minutes. The hansom drove away, leaving him by the roadside, the brown paper parcel at his feet. Nothing stirred and once the cab had turned the corner, the road returned to silence. Bathed in the weak sun of early spring, the house gave all the appearance of being abandoned. He should not have come. It was a foolish idea, but he had so desperately wanted to see her, to rescue something of the day, something of the dream. He grasped the brass lion head and knocked loudly, but without much hope of being heard.

A maid answered almost straight away, not the disapproving Martha, but a younger girl, pert and black-eyed. A merry girl who smiled expectantly at him and said, yes, her mistress was in but not in the house.

'In her studio,' she explained.

He remembered Edward Renville speaking of his wife as a painter, remembered, too, the scathing thoughts he had had at the time. He felt a little ashamed, yet even now found it difficult to take seriously the idea of Alessia as a dedicated artist. He was a professional, she was an amateur, and there was a chasm between them. But a studio sounded serious

146

enough and he was intrigued.

'Where is this studio?'

'In the garden, sir. You can't see it from the house,' the maid added helpfully. 'It's tucked away in a corner past the shrubbery.'

He followed her to the rear of the house and into the beautiful room where several long weeks ago he had sat talking the minutes away with Alessia.

'Through there, sir, and turn right.' She indicated the long french windows.

He walked through the double doors that gave on to the garden and turned right through a small shrubbery. He could see now that the garden was an L-shape and the studio, a wooden building painted green to blend with its setting, sat at the foot of the letter. In fact, the building was constructed as much of glass as of wood, one whole wall being entirely of glass and the roof above sporting not one but three skylights. The studio would catch the sun most of the day and the light would change from morning to afternoon to evening. It was a clever choice and Lucas was glad for her. He had the sense she had little she could call her own.

He rounded the last cluster of shrubs and saw her immediately. She was dressed in a spattered smock and seated at an easel, leaning forward into her painting, her brow furrowed, her whole body tensed in concentration. The energy, the containment, reminded him strongly of his own attempts to tame imagination onto paper.

His footsteps crunched across the grass, still frosty from the cold of the night, and she looked up at the sound. Her expression registered surprise but then a smile dawned, illuminating her face, lighting her whole body, breaking through the glass wall and sweeping towards him in a ball of warm pleasure. She opened the door and held out her arms, but only to help him with the awkward parcel, now sliding from his grasp.

'I had no idea you had a studio, Mrs Renville.'

'As you see, Mr Royde. It is my one indulgence.'

'Why so? You are evidently hard at work — and I have interrupted you.'

'I cannot claim to work, I fear. It is more that I daub.'

Her dark hair was loose and curling to her shoulders, stray tendrils framing her lovely face. He felt an overpowering need to reach out and touch, but instead he looked away from her and towards her picture.

'May I see?'

He moved a little closer to the easel. Her face showed plainly she was embarrassed at his scrutiny, but she did nothing to prevent him.

'It is of Lombardy,' she explained. 'From memory.'

'It is good, really good.' And his voice expressed conviction. He had been worried it would be an amateur botch, but the painting of a piazza in Verona, its pigeons scattering in the wake of a delivery boy's bicycle, was true. More than true — haunting in its remembered love. 'Are you professionally trained?'

Her smile was one of reminiscence. 'For some years a painter stayed with us at my grandmother's house, but nothing more. He was well thought of, I believe. As a child I found him a genius. He encouraged me to paint — he helped me greatly.'

Lucas felt a sharp sting. 'Is he still in Verona? Do you correspond?'

'Alas, no. He died a few years before my grandmother.'

The surge of jealousy died as quickly as it had appeared.

'And do you paint every day?' He looked around the room. A number of canvases were stacked against its rear wall, but there was little evidence of constant endeavour.

'I paint when I can,' she said simply.

'When your daughters are not at home,' he suggested.

'When Edward does not need me.'

The jealousy was in danger of return. 'I have just visited Onslow Street,' he said almost casually. 'Your husband wished to see the final designs. I had thought you would be there. We had an appointment to meet.'

She brushed his reminder aside. 'And does Mr Renville approve the plans?'

'I believe so, though his actual words did not suggest strong endorsement.'

'My husband is not the most effusive of men,' she conceded, 'but he would have told you if he had not liked what he saw.'

'I hope so. He certainly considered them well. At one point I began to wonder if he wished to go ahead with the Exhibition space.'

'I am sure he does. He is very proud of his business and wants others to share his pride.'

Her championship caused him a swirling irritation. 'That is hardly to be wondered at,' he agreed duplicitously. 'He has built a most successful business.'

'And from virtually nothing, Mr Royde. When his father died, Edward and his mother were left almost penniless.'

'Even more admirable,' he heard himself enthusing. 'It takes talent as well as capital to achieve such success.'

But he wondered where Renville had found the considerable sum of money on which to base that success. He had his suspicions, but dared not pursue the subject. Instead, he began to open the package of materials.

'I should be glad of your opinion on my initial choice of colours.'

She took time to examine each sample, taking them one by one to bright daylight and then moving back to the furthest recesses of the room where a paraffin lamp burned dimly.

'They are completely right,' she pronounced. 'You have chosen well.'

'Would they have been your choice, too?' His voice had softened and the simple question assumed a strange intimacy.

She flushed but looked directly into his eyes, soft brown meeting warm blue. 'They are exactly what I would have chosen.' Then a little hastily, 'I only hope they will suit the space we have been allocated.'

'In their raw form, the Exhibition spaces are likely to be identical. These colours, these textures, should attract attention without imposing their presence too loudly.'

'You have not seen the precise location then?'

'Not yet, but I need to. Your husband was keen that you also view it, and I have called today to ask if you would care to accompany me.' That was at least partly true.

'I would like it very much.'

'Shall we say next Monday? If it is convenient to you, I will call at ten in the morning.'

'It will suit perfectly. Edward leaves for his office well before nine, and I will not be needed after that time.'

Lucas was already tired of Edward Renville's demands and his annoyance only increased when she said in a new and doubtful tone, 'I am not sure now that Edward will like the materials we have chosen. He may prefer a bolder, more robust scheme.'

'Your husband was happy to entrust the choice of colours to us, and I think we have chosen well. Did we not envisage this space as wholly feminine?'

She looked a little downhearted. Her husband's approval seemed depressingly important and he was driven to say, 'It *is* the right choice. Forgive me, Mrs Renville, but your husband has little of the feminine about him.'

She smiled. 'No, indeed. That is not an adjective I would ever apply to Edward. But you must not think him harsh.'

Lucas could not prevent his scepticism showing and she continued a little awkwardly, 'He can sometimes appear so, but that is because he cares greatly for his business and for his family.'

'I am sure that is true.' His tone suggested quite other, and she appeared to redouble her efforts to convince him.

'He loves his daughters.'

'And you?' he found himself asking.

She looked shocked. 'Naturally, I am his wife.'

How had they got to this? He must be mad to speak so to her. Yet he knew what impelled him. He knew the loneliness in her, the lack of love she could not admit. His heart had spoken plainly to hers from the day they met. It was what drove him constantly to seek her out, to hold close the image of her night and day, to feel the thrill, the leaping pulse, whenever they met.

They were standing close to each other, a mere hand's touch away. Her eyes were worried, but there was something else in their depths, a feeling she could not quite conceal. A lock of hair had come loose and fell across her forehead. Without a thought, he reached across and gently pushed the lock back into place. She stood without moving and his fingers traced a line from her hair down her cheek to her neck. His hand slid behind her head resting in the softness of her curls. He felt her tremble slightly and he was far from steady himself.

Slowly he brought her closer, his face bending towards hers. His lips were brushing against her forehead, her cheek, and then her mouth. Her lips parted slightly, and he fastened his mouth to hers. He felt her body melt and cling. The kiss was long and deep and a wild joy raged through him. He wanted more and more. But she had sprung apart, breathless, her cheeks burning and her hands frantically smoothing her hair into some kind of order.

'Thank you for showing me the materials, Mr Royde,' she managed finally, her voice hollow and strained. 'You must excuse me now, I have much to do. Hetty will see you from the house.'

She opened the door of the studio, and he could do nothing but bow stiffly and walk through it. The door closed behind him before he had taken two steps along the pathway. He had ruined whatever friendship they had. He had ruined any chance of ever seeing her again. How could he have been so utterly imprudent?

# Chapter Nineteen

**H**e returned to Great Russell Street in the blackest of moods. He wanted to kick himself and very hard.

'And how was the delectable Alessia?' Fontenoy's jibe roused fury in him, but he would not give the man the satisfaction of knowing he had scored a hit.

'Mrs Renville is well. You will be pleased to know that both she and her husband have today approved the final plans. I believe I am shortly to work on a different and much larger commission.'

He was glad of the man's evident disappointment. A different project was unlikely to provide Fontenoy with anywhere near the same excitement. And a different project intimated that Lucas was climbing the architectural ladder and leaving his meddlesome colleague behind. Fontenoy was not to know that in destroying any chance of seeing Alessia Renville again, Lucas had reduced his world to ashes.

Try as he might, he could not free his mind. He was used to carrying her close to his heart, but now sweet remembrance intermingled with memories of their last catastrophic meeting. How could he have allowed himself to break the unspoken rules of their relationship, to step across that invisible marker both knew and silently acknowledged?

Was it the informality of her appearance, the unconventional setting, the shared passion of two artists? He had no idea, only that he could not have stopped himself from kissing her.

She had tasted sublime, but she was not his to taste and she had been swift to remind him. If she told her husband of his encroachment, he could look forward to instant dismissal, not just from the Exhibition project but from de Vere's itself. Would that be such a blow? Of late, he had neglected his portfolio shamefully, and leaving the practice would mean the time to create. But it would also mean a drastic loss of income, and after two years' study in the Italian states, his inheritance had dwindled to almost nothing.

And what if knowledge of the incident spread in some way, became gossip, distorted and exaggerated? His reputation would be wrecked. He could forget any chance he might have of establishing his own London practice. But it would not happen. Alessia would say nothing. She was angry with him, but she would not risk his whole future. He trusted her, loved her — passionately, deeply — in a way of which Renville was wholly incapable. Life was wretchedly unfair.

'Royde?' De Vere had emerged silently from his office. 'May I have a moment of your time, please?'

Lucas wondered what was coming. Daniel de Vere was looking particularly smart, a stylish crimson waistcoat and matching cravat lightening the professional black. Whatever mission had engaged his principal that morning, it had been important. He followed him to the inner sanctum and before he had quite closed the door, de Vere had begun speaking again. It was as near eager as

Lucas had ever seen him.

'Today, Royde, I have been consulted by a well-connected gentleman. Very well connected. The Earl of Carlyon no less.' He paused to allow the name to percolate his junior's consciousness. 'You may know that he is the owner of a large estate in Norfolk.' Lucas did not, but thought it best to adopt an expression of mild interest. 'Lord Carlyon is wishful to undertake some renovation on his estate, in particular the family chapel.'

So this was the new commission, the Gothic renovation he had been anticipating. It was possible Carlyon was an important man, a man well to the fore of public affairs, and if Lucas had to vandalise beauty, it would be as well to do so in the service of someone who might prove helpful to his future.

Unusually, de Vere did not immediately take a seat behind his fortress desk, but remained facing Lucas. He steepled his fingers, as though intending to measure his words. When they came, they were as always delivered in a calm, even tone.

'You may wonder why I have seen fit to involve you in such a prestigious project.'

Lucas's pride rejected the implication. However junior in the hierarchy of de Vere's, he knew himself to be their most skilled and creative architect.

'I have seen how well you have worked in the few months you have been with us, and how well you have managed a client who, I must confess, has not been easy. Within the last hour, Mr Renville has sent a message to say that he is completely satisfied with your design.'

Was that Alessia's doing, he wondered — her way of reassuring him that his lapse of good manners would not damage his career?

De Vere was smiling benignly. 'You deserve to work on something substantial and the Carlyon chapel will give you the opportunity.'

'Thank you for your trust in me, Mr de Vere,' he murmured. Was that sycophantic enough? 'Did Lord Carlyon have any particular style in mind?' There was a vain hope that he might, after all, be given a blank sheet.

'He is very open to suggestions and that is always beneficial. I think myself he would be happy with a remodelling in the Gothic style. He seems a gentleman who would wish to keep up with current fashion.'

Lucas smiled and executed a respectful bow. The phrase 'open to suggestions' hovered before him. If he could employ quiet persuasion, the new Carlyon chapel might emerge as far from Gothic as possible, particularly if his design for the Great Exhibition was well received. It would give him the influence he needed to persuade Lord Carlyon that Gothic was outdated, and that his own ideas were at the forefront of new architecture. The Norfolk commission might have come at the perfect time. It might prove to be the very springboard he needed to help him into his own practice. If he could influence the client to assign him the work privately, rather than through de Vere's... That would be disloyal, but a man intent on going places cannot let loyalty get in his way.

\* \* \*

Monday morning came too quickly. He awoke at six o'clock and lay staring at the mottled ceiling. The question that for days had hung so heavily on him remained unresolved. Should he try to keep the appointment with Alessia or accept that her farewell had been irrevocable? He lay motionless in bed for a long time until the rattles and bangs of his fellow lodgers beginning their separate days grew too loud to ignore. He had to decide. What if she was waiting for him at Prospect Place and he did not arrive? What would she think? And if her husband knew of their appointment, how could he explain his failure to keep it?

When he thought more, he was convinced that Edward Renville would know. He had been keen his wife should view the exact location of the firm's pavilion and he would be sure to question her. Lucas would have to go to Wisteria Lodge. If she denied herself when he called at the house, he would have his answer. And if she agreed to see him, he would risk her wrath. He could only hope her anger had since dissipated. It was an anger, he thought, directed as much at herself as at him. She had responded to his love-making, opened her mouth to his, fused her body with his. But he must never again think of such things. If he escorted her to Hyde Park, it must be as a client.

He dressed slowly and with care, choosing from his small wardrobe the most muted shade of cravat and waistcoat he possessed. Then walked to and fro to the small mirror that hung askew on the back of the door, to check and recheck his appearance. On a last trip to the mirror, he noticed the reflection of his portfolio, languishing in the opposite corner. Every time his eyes had rested on it in recent weeks, he had felt guilty. Creativity had been neglected so that he might devote himself entirely to Alessia Renville. And look what had happened.

But perhaps the portfolio could help him on this most difficult of days. She had expressed interest in seeing it — could it be the means of diffusing any discord that lingered?

It was Martha who opened the door, her face assuming her customary disapproval as soon as she recognised the visitor. She left him standing in the hall while she went to find her mistress. Evidently Alessia had made no firm plans to accompany him.

The sound of light steps on the stairs made his heart jump furiously. When she came into view, he saw she was wearing a plain gown of corded Italian silk, which despite its simplicity did nothing to hide the voluptuous figure beneath.

'Mr Royde.' She came forward and shook hands. Her voice was studiedly neutral. 'I must apologise for Martha's shortcomings in leaving you standing here. Please come into the drawing room.'

He said nothing and followed her into the joyless space. There was to be no garden room for him this morning, he reflected wryly, only this drab overstuffed chamber with shades of the older Mrs Renville crouching in every corner.

'I should have sent a message, Mr Royde. I regret I will not have the time to visit Hyde Park. However, my husband is sure to take me in the next few days and I will communicate through him any further ideas I have.'

So stiff, so formal. She was hardly the same woman. He took a breath and tried to match her formality.

'That will be most helpful, Mrs Renville. I came this morning merely to ascertain your wishes and also to show you these.'

He drew his portfolio from the battered leather bag that had done him service since he first left Dorset, and extracted a small number of sheets. He was careful to choose his most recent illustrations, those most redolent of her home region. 'I believe you expressed a desire to view my designs for decorative tiles.'

She was clearly surprised. This was something she had not expected. But she was also intrigued. He went on as smoothly as he could. 'Naturally I would not wish to interrupt your morning, but if you would care to look through them at a more convenient time, I am happy to leave them with you. A servant, perhaps, could be entrusted to return them to Mr de Vere's office.'

She had begun slowly to leaf through the pages as he was talking. 'These are from your portfolio?'

'They are. I was wondering if you thought any might suit the design we have agreed.'

He made sure the 'we' was there. She leafed through a few more sheets, clearly engrossed. He waited without speaking, watching her every fleeting expression. At last, she looked up.

'These are wonderful.' She was suddenly animated and the stiffness dissolved. 'They remind me of Verona. They are the colours of Lombardy.'

'I fear they may not be entirely right for the Renville pavilion, but I am happy that you like them.'

His look was anxious. He no longer cared if his tiles were used or not, but he wanted that she speak to him, respond to him, stay with him.

'I cannot be sure, Mr Royde.' The familiar furrow appeared on her brow. 'I would need to see them *in situ* and with the materials we have selected.'

That glorious 'we' was back. 'I am on my way now to Hyde Park with the materials — I have a hansom waiting outside. I will do my best to judge correctly whether or not to use the tiles.'

She walked to the window and looked out. The horse was

shaking its head impatiently and the jarvey yawning into his hands. She turned round to Lucas, her face wearing an unreadable expression. He hoped it might mean she was reconsidering and decided to take a chance.

'If you *could* spare a short while — we could be there and back within the hour — I would welcome your views. I need an impartial opinion.'

For a moment she looked torn. 'I am not sure I can claim to be impartial.' Then quite suddenly, she decided. 'But I will come. For just an hour.' And she rang the bell.

'Please fetch my cloak, Martha, and make sure Cook has luncheon ready for noon. I shall be returned well before then.'

Martha's expression gave nothing away, but the sharp slap of her footsteps as she disappeared to find the cloak expressed her displeasure.

An hour was all he needed. An hour to have her near, to feel her body close, to feel her soul walk with his. His heart's familiar thud had begun once more, but he knew he must be vigilant, watch his every word, his every movement, for nothing now must mar their time together.

# Chapter Twenty

He was mindful to seat himself in the far corner of the hansom and allow her as much space as possible. It was enough to share the same seat, to smell again the faint perfume of jasmine, to steal gazes at the shapely, erect figure beside him. He noticed that today her hair was fastened behind her neck in an intricate coil but several stray curls had escaped, soft wisps he longed to seize and wind around his finger.

'Are you still very busy at de Vere's?' she asked politely. It was an attempt to break the uncomfortable silence building between them; he wondered if she was feeling the same irresistible urge to touch.

'We are, Mrs Renville,' he replied, equally polite. 'Mr de Vere has intimated that he wishes me to lead a new and substantial project once my work on the Exhibition is complete.'

They fell back into silence again. Her eyes were downcast, studying with intensity the embossed pattern on her long kid gloves, and he hoped she felt a little sadness that their association was nearing its end.

'And how are your children?' He needed to keep talking and make this visit unexceptional, as though they had never exchanged more than a formal handshake.

'They are well, thank you. They will be returning home shortly.'

'You must have missed their young presence.'

'I have. They are very precious to me.' Her voice was unusually heightened.

'They are beautiful young girls. You are very lucky.' He did not know what else to say.

'So I tell myself every day. God has been good in giving me my two darlings.'

There was something not quite right. Her tone was too solemn for what had merely been a courteous enquiry. He half turned, trying to snatch a glimpse of her face, and saw a small trickle of a tear making its way slowly down one cheek.

'I am so sorry, Mrs Renville.' He blurted the words, thoroughly discomposed. 'I had no intention of causing you upset.'

With a visible effort, she pulled herself together and wiped away the tear. 'Of course you had not. I am being foolish, but you see…' and in a sudden, astonishing breach of her privacy, she rushed out, 'I have recently been told that I am unable to have more children.'

He was shocked but also gladdened, not only because she would bear no more of Renville's children, but because she had confided in him. Something so private, so personal. His physical closeness had made her emotional and in turn she had made him her confidante.

'Your daughters, then, must be even more precious to you both.' It was all he could offer.

'They are.' She began to pleat the silk of her dress, fold by fold. Her continuing agitation was clear. 'Edward loves his children dearly,' she asserted, and then in a voice that was hardly audible, 'but a son to continue the business would have been a blessing.'

He said no more. She had been surprisingly candid and he was appreciative of her trust. But he had no wish to probe the marriage, though her inability to provide Edward Renville with a son went some way towards explaining the man's coldness towards his wife.

The carriage had reached Hyde Park and was making its way through the partly completed south entrance. 'This must be the Prince of Wales Gate,' Lucas decided. 'I believe it is to be the main entrance for the Exhibition and should be finished in the near future — the road, too, I trust.'

They were travelling along a heavily rutted track and being bounced from one side of the cab to the other. He longed to have the right to reach out and hold his delicate companion safe from injury. But he did not have the right and remembering his earlier trespass, he stayed his hand.

'Just look, Mr Royde.'

She was clinging to one of the hansom's creaking doors and almost leaning out of its window in her eagerness. Her eyes shone.

'Just look at that,' she repeated.

He did look. This was his first visit to the Exhibition Hall and though he had seen plans of Paxton's design and read any number of newspaper descriptions, nothing had prepared him for the sheer scale of the giant glass structure. No wonder commentators talked about the building being six times the size of St Paul's.

At one side of the entrance he saw an enormous store of prefabricated cast iron units waiting to be welded together on site. On the other side, thousands of huge glass panes were stacked, ready to hang on the iron framework. No wonder the building was being erected at such incredible speed. The design was brilliant in its simplicity.

Lucas helped his companion down from the cab and turned to pay the driver. A shaft of sunlight momentarily burst through the lowering March sky and illuminated the zigzag layers of glass sheeting already in place. Beside him, he felt Alessia draw a wondering breath.

'It is like a giant concertina,' she said, looking about her and wrinkling her brow in a way he had come to love, 'but made of diamonds.'

Even half-covered in scaffolding and with the noise of the workmen's hammers and saws pounding in their ears, the Exhibition Hall was magical. 'It is magnificent,' he agreed. 'I can understand now why *Punch* has named it the Crystal Palace!'

A team of horses pulling a Pickford's van with yet another consignment of iron columns drew up close to where they were standing, and he took the opportunity to suggest they walk inside the building.

'I remember you said it was large, but I had no idea just how large,' she confessed.

'Nor me. I read somewhere that Paxton has made it exactly 1,851 feet long in homage to the year, but even for an architect that figure is difficult to visualise.'

They had walked only a few paces when a bank of turn-stiles stopped their progress. Lucas sidestepped to a small wicket gate and held it open.

'Come this way, Mrs Renville. As exhibitors, we may pass freely.'

'But have people already visited? I had not expected that.'

'They have been turning up since last September, I

believe, to check on progress. But since the exhibits started to arrive, members of the public have been banned.'

Once in the Hall itself, they paused to take stock. The glass roof rose two storeys above them, but a cross passage or transept provided an arch even higher, to skim the top branches of three majestic elm trees. A large semicircular clock a few feet away had been designed to blend with the curved glass roof and beyond the clock, a glass fountain shaped like an immense crystal chandelier stood waiting for the waters to flow. For a long while the pair stood side by side, slowly adjusting to the monumental scale of their surroundings.

'I am so glad they did not destroy the trees,' Alessia said finally.

'They would not have wished to add to criticism of the building by doing so, I imagine. There has been much disquiet that so much glass is likely to shatter in hail, or be blown away by high winds.'

'But the building is safe?'

'As houses — literally. They have had soldiers marching and running and jumping together across the galleries above and nothing has moved, cracked or otherwise failed. We shall be quite safe.'

They walked along the wide, middle passage. This central walkway looked almost a church nave, Lucas thought, the large rooms on either side a line of pews radiating outwards. At the centre point of the passage a double spiral staircase led to the second floor, and they made their way up. This storey was narrower with a single row of rooms and balconies running along one side of the building.

'Are you disappointed?' He had been studying his companion's expression.

'A little. The ground floor appears so grand and it has that elegant clock and the splendid fountain. When you mount the stairs, perhaps you are expecting more of the same and instead it is... a little less imposing,' she finished on a deflated note.

He glanced around at what was still no more than a row of empty spaces, demarcated by either cloth or wood walls. 'I have to agree it hardly sends the pulse racing. But we must remember it is still unfinished. And the Exhibition is over-subscribed — we should be in good company. I understand this upper gallery will house the smaller objects.'

He guessed that Renville had paid a very large sum for the privilege of renting this drab area. No doubt he had had to twist a few eminent arms as well, since he had been a late convert to the idea of displaying his wares.

'Look up, Mrs Renville.' He hoped to console her. 'Is that not a sight worth seeing?'

Together they looked towards the ceiling and followed the iron and glass walls soaring ever higher and then curving inwards to meet at the apex of the arched transept. 'If the passage below us is the cathedral's nave, this is its dome.'

The Renville space was found without difficulty. It was well-positioned near to the middle of the building and its walls were made of cloth rather than wood.

'That will help.' Lucas walked slowly around the space. 'We will not have to destroy too much before we can build again. And these pillars —,' he pointed to the few cast iron columns already in place as supports, '— they are indeed so slim that my hands reach around them. They will not quarrel with our marble.'

'Might we be able to use them for our display?'

'That would certainly make the building a part of the Renville space, rather than the other way round.'

He pulled out a roll of papers from the battered satchel and spread them on the floor. Together they began to mark out the area, adjusting the plans slightly here and there to take account of its shape and dimensions. Alessia came to rest at the centre of the pavilion. 'This is where we should have the… bench.' She blushed brightly, unable to give the seat its true name.

To allow her to recover, Lucas made himself busy unpacking the parcel of materials. 'We have a range of colours from which to choose.' He was stacking the bolts of silk and gauze to one side. 'I wonder if we should saturate the space in one dominant hue, gauzes and all — that would gain impact — or whether we should go for a softer, more diffuse spectrum.'

'I'm not sure. Perhaps we should first decide on the position of the pillars.'

She was thinking hard and had forgotten her earlier embarrassment. Soon she was moving around the space, marking out the location of each marble column and then moving different coloured silks between them — planning, deciding and then replanning, until she had in her mind exactly how the room should look. Lucas did not interrupt. He was happy simply to watch her and know that she was happy, too. By the time she had finished, her face was flushed and her eyes sparkling.

'Should we repair to the tea room?' he asked. 'I believe something temporary has been established on the floor below. Then I can make a note of the modifications we have agreed.'

'I am sorry this gives you more work after your plans have been so meticulous.' She looked regretful.

'They are architect's drawings only. The design we now have will be what we need for the workmen — theory made practice.'

She was smiling again and it felt to him as though the sun would never leave the world. He wanted this day to continue forever. On their way down the staircase, he suggested that before they reward themselves with tea, they take a look at some of the exhibits already on display. Anything, he thought, to keep her with me just a little longer.

They walked towards the western end of the building where displays from Britain and her colonies were to be accommodated. At the very beginning of the section, a mediaeval court had already been constructed. Its walls were made of guilded wood and hung with paintings and stained glass. A few items of ornately carved furniture had begun to fill the space. On the other side of the passage was the Canada room, exhibiting sleighs, canoes of birch bark and Indian feather bonnets. Then the India room, for the moment quite sparse and containing only a howdah with its elephant cloth, and an imposing but empty cabinet right in the middle of the room.

'I wonder…' she began.

'The Koh-i-noor diamond? I believe this is the cabinet that will house the jewel.'

'How marvellous to see it at such close quarters! The first day of May cannot come soon enough.' But not for me, he thought sadly. It will be the very last time I see her.

'Tell me about the new project you are to work on.'

They had settled themselves at a table in the small café, and all thought of returning to Prospect Place within the hour had vanished from both their minds.

'Unfortunately it is a church doomed to become Gothic.'

'You sound unhappy with the commission.'

'I should be happy. Or at least I should feel flattered. It is an important chapel and so an important job. But I hate to see beautiful old buildings desecrated in the name of fashion.'

'Can you not request Mr de Vere to work on something other?'

'I am a junior architect, Mrs Renville. I am not able to make requests of my principal.'

'But you are a very talented man and Mr de Vere must be gratified to have your services.'

'I am one among many,' he said ruefully. 'But one day… one day I shall have my own practice and choose my own commissions.'

'I hope that day will come soon for you.'

'I hope so, too, but I must be realistic. It takes a substantial sum of money to set up a practice and I have already spent whatever I had on studying abroad.'

'It was well spent, I am sure.'

'It was, but it cannot be spent again. It was an inheritance from my godfather,' he confided, seeing the sympathy in her face. 'I was fortunate, but I cannot hope to inherit more.'

'And your parents?'

'I cannot look to them for help. My father is a tenant farmer eking out a small living and with six children to provide for. Two of my younger brothers have found work on the land, though I never had aptitude for it. My mother scrimped for years to buy an education for me — Latin and Greek extra! — and then to buy my apprenticeship with a local architect. Everything I have, everything I am, I owe to her.'

'It seems to me you have already repaid much with your

evident love for her.'

'But I want to repay materially. When I become rich and famous, I will spend every last penny to make her comfortable.'

'*When*, not if?' she teased.

'When,' he said firmly.

The cab was still waiting when they emerged from the glass palace, and within thirty minutes they were standing outside the studded front door of Wisteria Lodge.

'The men will begin work on the pavilion next week,' Lucas told her. 'When all is ready, you might wish to visit again and confirm you are completely happy with the result.' His stomach tightened at the thought she might ask him to finish the work by himself.

He raised his gaze and a pair of dark brown eyes looked back at him. They carried a softness he could not ignore. 'I think that a very sensible suggestion, Mr Royde.'

'Lunch is ready, ma'am.' The maid's disagreeable face appeared at Alessia's shoulder. 'It's been ready for the last hour — as you requested.' Her accusatory tone was accompanied by a determined scowl.

'Thank you, Martha. I will come in a moment.'

He waited until the maid had reluctantly withdrawn before saying, 'I will send you news when the pavilion is finished. Then we can agree a convenient time for you to visit.'

'Thank you, you are most kind.'

He stepped towards her, bowing his head and lightly kissing her hand. 'It is my pleasure, Mrs Renville.'

There were no truer words. The door shut behind her and he dismissed the cab, deciding to return to Great Russell Street on foot. A walk would give him time to think, although there was little to think about. Everything was only too clear. She might like him — greatly. She might like to be with him; they had just enjoyed three magnificent hours together. But he was simply the architect employed by her husband and nothing more. In honesty, he could be nothing more. He had overreached himself before and frightened her badly. A married woman was allowed no foibles. She belonged to her husband, body and soul, and Alessia knew that well. She might not be happy, he knew in his heart she was not, but she had made her choice and she was living with it. He wondered, though, just how much of a choice it had been.

# Chapter Twenty-One

**N**ick ran his fingers down my spine in an exploratory gesture. The metallic tick of the bedside clock sounded in my ear, and I raised myself onto one elbow to squint at its dial. The sodium glare of street lights penetrated the room's thin curtains and I could easily make out the hands. They showed ten minutes to four, well before dawn. I gave a small sigh of protest, but it did nothing to deflect him, so I turned over and made ready to enjoy what was on offer. I hadn't known what to expect after our night in Dorchester, but he'd turned out to be a surprisingly expert lover. Fun, too, and we had spent most of the three days since our return in bed. It made a happy change from Oliver's punctilious schedule, and I'd begun to embrace Nick's chaotic lifestyle with worrying ease.

When we'd arrived back at Waterloo, he had accompanied me to Lyndhurst Villas. I hadn't expected that, but I was glad to have him with me. The house was empty and echoing, and for the first time in years I didn't feel at home.

'I can't stay here,' I said.

'Why do you think I came back with you? Pack a bag and stay at my place.'

I hadn't been at all sure. If I went to his flat, I'd be

burning my boats, opting for one man over another. Or would I? I could stay with Nick as a friend, as long as I made that clear. Oliver was in Newcastle and would be there for at least another two or three days. Perhaps that was all I needed to clear my mind. I grabbed clean clothes from one of the capacious wardrobes Oliver favoured and then went to the small room that functioned as my office, packing my laptop, books, my copy of Kelly, a few papers — even to me it seemed I was planning to stay longer than a few days.

Nick's flat turned out to be every bit as grim as he'd described. It was in a small, grubby side street a few minutes from Kings Cross. In daylight the area was hardly salubrious, but by the time we passed the station, the ladies of the night were already doing good business. His rooms, all two of them, were in the basement of a dreary Victorian terrace. Even on a fine June evening they were lacking in natural light, and the very few pieces of furniture Nick possessed were lit by a harsh neon glow. Their air of moth-eaten dilapidation suggested they might well have fallen from a passing skip. I tried not to advertise my sinking spirits, but the contrast with Lyndhurst Villas was too stark to ignore.

'I did warn you,' he said, and shrugged. Nick's shoulders were as expressive as most people's faces. 'But you're welcome to crash for a few days.'

At least he wasn't suggesting I move in permanently, and then to gladden my heart further he added, 'I'll sleep on the couch. There are clean sheets somewhere for the bed.'

Our relationship was being tactfully defined, and I was grateful. Thetford Road was hardly a home-from-home, but it would offer me a perch until I regained my bearings. No doubt I would soon be fluttering back to Hampstead. That was evidently what Nick assumed; he wasn't setting any store by what had happened in Dorset.

He busied himself cooking us an evening meal while I searched out the sheets he had spoken of. They turned up in one of the kitchen cupboards, but they were clean as he'd promised and by the time I had wrestled with making a bed hemmed in by three walls, he had produced a decent Bolognese from the store cupboard. I was seriously impressed. It was a great deal more than I could do.

But did I really believe I could live here as a friend? It was naïve in the extreme, hardly worthy of a woman nearing thirty. Entombed in my large and lumpy bed that night, I could hear him in the next room, thrashing around on what I judged the hardest couch in London. Whether it was sympathy for his plight or self-pity at being abandoned to a horribly empty bed, I don't know. But two hours into a night of wakefulness, alert to every small sound while trying to pretend heavy sleep, I gave in. The door opened and Nick swayed hazily on the threshold.

'I don't suppose you'd like to share? My back is in at least six pieces.' He was trying to sound winning, but he needn't have bothered. I was already a fair way to being a pushover.

'We could always find a spare pillow to divvy up the bed.'

I threw back the coverlet. 'No pillow.'

'Thanks,' he said and fell in on top of me.

It felt good to have him close again, and we didn't waste much time rediscovering each other. It was a pity we seemed destined to love in the most dismal surroundings, but somehow it didn't matter. I fell asleep in his arms.

That first night set the pattern, and now I was used to being woken half way through the night, to eat, sleep or love, as the mood took us. I could have happily continued the lotus life indefinitely but for the fact that I was running out of clean clothes, and the launderette Nick patronised was a two-mile walk away. Far better to brave Lyndhurst Villas again and pack a couple of suitcases.

But come the morning, it didn't seem so simple and I put off making the decision to go. How better to prevaricate than by ringing Paolo Tirelli to tell him what we'd found in Dorset. He sounded intrigued.

'So… you think this person, this A, might have been involved in the plans you look for?'

'He could have been. Royde's meeting with him is around the right date. Of course, they could have met to discuss something personal, nothing to do with Royde's professional life. The note was on the back of a theatre programme, so it's more than likely.'

'No, no, Grace. You must believe this clue is the one you need. But can I do anything to help?'

'Not right now, but later perhaps.'

'That will be good. And will you promise to have coffee with me one morning?'

I promised, surprised by the warmth in his voice. After I'd rung off, I prevaricated a little more by checking the emails I'd been ignoring for days. I was glad I had because alongside the usual dross, there was a message sporting a bright red exclamation mark. It was from Leo Merrick. He was desperate. It was not only his wife now who felt a malevolent presence on site, but the builders who were working there. They were threatening to walk away from the job if the strange activities didn't cease. What these were he didn't specify. It was evident though that he was taking it seriously. Mrs Merrick might be dismissed as fanciful, but a clutch of brawny builders was another matter.

I felt like telling him to call in the local priest, but instead

I checked out the school again. I had promised to do that days ago, but the Dorset trip had pushed it from my mind. The Raine Foundation School still existed, albeit under a different name. It had moved around the East End over the last century and a half, but its records had been preserved from a long way back. It wasn't difficult to call up those relating to the 1845 wing; they were more or less complete and had been uploaded into the school's archives, courtesy of a lottery grant. I sent silent thanks to Camelot. There was a good deal of information that was of little interest: building specifications, architectural plans, budget details. I was looking for something more personal, and I found it when I alighted on a roll call of teachers who had been in charge of the girls' school.

Leo Merrick seemed relieved to hear my voice. 'I'm not sure you can do anything with the information I've found,' I cautioned.

'Anything has to be better than nothing. Can you come?'

'Come where?'

'To Silver Street. The schoolhouse. Can you meet me there? I think it's important you see the place. I'll bring my wife and you can tell us both what you've discovered. She'll know then I'm not trying to pull the wool over her eyes.'

It was an unusual request and I hesitated. 'I could, I suppose, but I should really be somewhere else this morning.' I should, but I didn't want to be.

'It would take less than an hour of your time, and I'm happy to pay whatever fee you feel is appropriate. Things have got quite bad, you know.'

I assumed he meant between him and his wife. The pressure was subtle, but to be honest, it suited me to sidestep what I wasn't ready to face.

'I'll be there by eleven.'

'Thank you. Thank you, Dr Latimer.' He sounded genuinely grateful, though heaven knows there was little to tell and what there was, was unlikely to make much difference to Mrs Merrick's fear of the place. But I was keeping my client happy and that was the name of the game.

* * *

I reached Silver Street before the Merricks, and the tarpaulins flapping in the wind led me straight to the schoolroom. Apart from an ineffectual attempt to shelter the part of the roof that had been opened to the sky, it was obvious the builders had abandoned the site without securing it. I was able to open the heavy front door and wander into the narrow vestibule. This was where the girls would have hung their coats and capes and left their galoshes on inclement days.

I should have waited for the Merricks here, but I didn't. I was being nudged to explore. Another door faced me; I pushed it ajar and was drawn into a wide, open space. I imagined the schoolroom had stayed much the same as when the last child closed the lid of her desk.

I walked across the scratched tiled floor towards the dais that stood at the very end of the room. Remarkably it still boasted a desk, placed in a position of authority. This was where the teacher would have sat, cane no doubt by his or her side. It was when I approached the raised wooden structure that I felt the prickling. A definite prickling of the skin that started at my scalp and inched downwards to my feet. Then my chest began to feel tight and my breath to come less easily. This is absurd, I thought. I was in an empty room, a space that was entirely innocuous. Was I allowing Leo

Merrick's tale of unquiet spirits to get to me?

I was at the dais and starting up the steps to the desk when I stumbled. My legs felt suddenly heavy, so heavy I could hardly drag one foot in front of the other. It was as though an invisible force had me in its grip, a force I wasn't able to control. Somehow I managed to clamber onto the dais and collapse into a seat. The prickling had ceased but my chest was still tight, encased in a band of steel. I sat staring down at the desk top for what seemed an age, until its grimy ridges began to flow one into another in a mad criss-cross dance. When my pulse gradually steadied, I dared to look around. I had been fearful at what I might see, but all I gazed on was emptiness. Light from the tall, arched windows fell crookedly across the floor, casting the corners of the room into shadow. But nothing moved, nothing breathed.

I should have walked back to the vestibule then, but instead I lifted the desk lid. What made me do it, I have no idea, only that in that instant I knew I had to. The desk was empty. Except for the scent. It was a scent that was very familiar and for a moment it caught in my throat. Then common sense returned, and I lifted the lid a little farther and glimpsed a patch of white. Scrabbling in the deep well of the desk I brought out a linen handkerchief and put it to my nose. The perfume was unmistakeable — jasmine. I shook the handkerchief out and looked at it closely. Patched with a century's dirt, it must have been tucked at the very back of the desk. One corner held a small, embroidered initial. When I saw what it was, my heart gave a sharp jolt. It was the letter A.

'Dr Latimer? Thank you so much for coming.'

Leo Merrick had walked through the inner door without my hearing a footstep. I had been too occupied, too overwhelmed by the coincidence.

'It's a splendid specimen, isn't it?' He gestured towards the desk. 'Original I believe. It must have belonged to the last person to teach in this room.'

I nodded mechanically. My mind was all over the place. I looked around for Mrs Merrick, but he appeared to be on his own. 'Your wife?'

He seemed embarrassed. 'She's not coming, I'm afraid. I couldn't persuade her here, not even to see you, but I've promised to make a faithful report.'

'As I told you, there's very little *to* report.'

He looked disappointed. 'I was hoping there might be more. With your coming here, I mean. I thought it might jog your mind, help you make connections.'

I wasn't sure what he meant. The only connections I had made — jasmine and the letter A — were with Royde's story, and had absolutely nothing to do with the problems Leo Merrick was experiencing.

'So tell me the little you know.'

'This part of the site was the girls' school,' I began, 'but you know that already. I imagine the oldest section where the boys were educated, is derelict.'

He nodded. 'What was left of it was dangerous, and had to be completely demolished.'

'As I said, the entire school moved from here at the end of the century, and continued to move from site to site before settling in its present location.'

He nodded again, and I felt his solid presence bring calm into the room. I could move and breathe without effort now.

'But while the school was here in Silver Street,' I went on, 'there seems to be something odd about the teachers who were in charge. At least according to the records I've seen.

'Go on.'

'Their names are listed meticulously right up until 1883. That's when the school moved. Each headmistress of the girls' section appears to have stayed in post for around three to five years. Presumably at that point they either married or moved to another school.'

'I'm afraid I have to say, so what?'

'What's interesting is that initially those heading the school *were* all mistresses — there are five different sets of female names — but after 1863, the teacher appointed was male, and the Board of Governors continued to appoint a man to lead the school until it moved to its new location. A total of twenty years.'

'You think there's something significant in the shift from women to men?'

'It was pretty sudden and unusual, too. At the time, school teaching was not a particularly respected profession for men, and heading a girls' school would have been even less attractive. The Board wouldn't have found it easy to hire male head teachers. But despite the difficulties, they did. Something could have occurred in 1863 to precipitate their decision.'

'What, for instance?'

I shook my head. 'I have no idea. But the last female name on the list might offer a clue. It's doubly interesting — literally so — not one woman but two were in charge in that final female year, and they stayed for a mere nine months.'

'Do you know anything else about them?'

'Only that their name was Villiers, the Misses F and G Villiers. They may have been a sister act. One that went wrong?'

'Can you find out?'

'Quite possibly, but I don't honestly see what use it will

be to you.'

'Dr Latimer, I have a wife on the edge of a nervous breakdown. She thinks she is going mad. I have builders ready to pull out of the project completely, and the whole thing is costing me an arm and a leg. I know I'm clutching at straws, but if I can give them any kind of explanation, it might help. You've made a start.'

'And that's where it could end,' I warned, 'but you're the client. If you want me to continue, I will.'

'I do. Very much.'

By now we were back in the vestibule and for the first time I felt able to smile. 'I'll contact you as soon as I can, Mr Merrick.'

I hope I sounded more professional than I felt. The experience in the schoolroom had shaken me, and I was tempted to make a dash back to the flat and normality. But Nick would want to know how the meeting had gone and I felt the less I talked about it, the better I would be. I would go to Lyndhurst Villas after all. If I could brave the paranormal, I could brave Hampstead. Nick had volunteered to come with me, but I thought it best to go alone, just in case Oliver had returned from Newcastle.

# Chapter Twenty-Two

**A**nd he had. I had barely turned the key in the lock when he appeared at my side, his skin an odd shade of pink and the usually calm lines of his face distorted by suppressed anger. I hadn't expected to be welcomed joyously, but his reaction took me aback. I speculated, foolishly as it turned out, that somehow he had found out about Nick and this was jealousy in action. I soon learnt otherwise.

'Where have you been?' were his first words. No greeting, no pleasantries.

Despite the enormous effort he was making to control his temper, his tone was querulous. We seemed almost to have travelled back in time, to continue the dispute of days ago. There was a difference though: I wasn't the same person. Then I had reacted stormily to his departure with Rebecca. I had been upset by his abandonment and angered that a young girl was threatening to displace me. Now, though, I was thinking dispassionately, and decided I didn't like his attitude one little bit.

'Does it matter where I've been? You were happy enough to disappear to Newcastle for days. Presumably I'm as free as you to go where I wish.'

'*I* went on a business trip,' he said, with heavy emphasis.

'Are you saying your journey was as essential?'

I couldn't say that, so I said nothing.

'Exactly. As I thought.' A note of triumph had replaced the anger. Then a sad shake of the head. 'I don't understand what's got into you lately, Grace. You seem determined to upset me.'

'That certainly isn't my intention.'

'Perhaps not, but that's how it appears. We're partners — we work together as well as live together, and I depend on you to assume certain responsibilities. These days you seem to make a habit of ignoring them. It's disappointing.'

He tugged fiercely at his beard. He was the college principal and I the head girl who had not lived up to expectations.

'And what responsibilities would they be?'

I had little interest in learning. I thought he was sure to start droning on about the exhibition again and how much trouble my truancy had caused.

'Kezia,' he said.

It was totally unexpected, and for some reason the single word struck me as comic and I began to laugh. That made him explode. If he had been angry before, he was incandescent now.

'You find it amusing that you completely ignored a young girl's birthday to go gallivanting I-know-not-where on some pointless whim, presumably just to spite me.'

The latter held some truth, but I wouldn't admit to it. Instead I challenged his preposterous suggestion that somehow I was accountable for his daughter's happiness.

'Kezia is your child,' I reminded him. 'It's *you* who has forgotten her birthday.'

'I did not forget, but I was quite unable to do anything about it. I was away working.'

'So you have said. But people do manage to juggle work and family, Oliver. You might even be successful if you gave it a try.'

'Naturally, I would not have gone to Newcastle if I'd had an inkling that you would let her, me, down so badly. Every year for the last — nine, is it? — you've arranged a suitable present and attended her birthday party. I depended on you to do the same this year.'

'Why?' I felt incensed. '*You're* her parent, not me. Let's be honest'— and I was suddenly filled with a burning desire to be honest, to utter the words I'd smothered over the years — 'I doubt if you even know how old she is. You're simply not interested in your daughter and never have been.'

'That's a lie.' The pink tinge had darkened to an unsightly red.

'I think not. Interesting yourself in Kezia's life would involve a degree of selflessness.'

'How dare you speak so! You are in no position to judge my relationship with my child.'

'On the contrary. Over the years I've visited Kezia in your stead, gone to her parties for you, chosen her presents, even taken her on shopping trips you promised but couldn't quite make. I'm more than capable of judging your adequacy or otherwise as a father. Forgetting her birthday — and don't bother to protest, you've only just remembered it — is *your* fault. Not mine.'

'You are my personal assistant. It was your job to remember.'

His refusal to accept any blame was wilful. I'd thought I knew Oliver, knew him and accepted him warts and all, but I had never felt more disenchanted.

'It wasn't my job,' I repeated wearily, 'but I'm not going

to argue.'

'Good.' His tone was brisk. 'There seems little point, now that it's too late to rectify. But it mustn't happen again, Grace. Lately we seem to have got our wires crossed. In future, we must make sure we work more closely together and you're clearer about what needs to be done.'

A tentative smile crept across his face and he breathed out forcefully, seeming to blow away the problems of the past. I hated to ruin his moment of satisfaction, but I was going to.

'I don't think so.'

'What do you mean?' His eyes narrowed as though I was about to play a trick on him, which I suppose in some ways I was.

'I'm resigning, Oliver. I don't wish to be your assistant. You can take your job back.' He was looking shocked, but I ploughed on. 'And your house. And your sponsorship.'

There, I had done it, finally jumped free. He didn't move, didn't speak. He had begun to resemble a stuffed exhibit in a museum. I decided against staying to pack suitcases.

'I'll take a few things today and clear my belongings next week.' I pushed past his immobile figure to climb the stairs.

The bedroom looked different, somehow alien, as though I had never slept there. But my clothes still hung from the rails, my shoes were tucked neatly beneath the dresser and my potions and creams nestled on the bathroom shelf. I had slept here, but I no longer did. I had burned my boats.

* * *

I walked down the hill in a daze. I guess I was making for Nick's flat, but I wasn't entirely sure. I just needed to keep moving. Down the hill and towards the centre of London, shimmering in the distance. I passed underground stations, passed bus stops, but kept walking. I needed the journey back to Thetford Road to take a long time. I felt too upset to return immediately, upset but also relieved. I had just thrown away nine years of my life and that was distressing, but it was also inevitable.

The business about Kezia had been absurd, a symptom of all that was wrong between Oliver and myself. For years I had travelled smoothly, comfortable day following comfortable day, but only because I had been quiescent. If I'd voiced any hint of challenge, trouble would have ensued. Oliver had to be in control, and I'd accepted that as a price worth paying — but no longer. For all his kindness and generosity, he couldn't be happy with a free-thinking partner, and since meeting Nick I had shown independence to an alarming degree.

Nick was so very different — easygoing, spontaneous, almost careless in his attitude to life. He had blown a refreshing breeze through my world, but from the first hello, he had been pushing at an open door. I'd been ready for change and he had been the catalyst.

I felt sad and scared. Sad that I had left Oliver with unkind words; he had looked dumbfounded as I'd walked out of the door. And scared because I had thrown away for ever my hard-won security. But I'd had no choice. I had been living behind a sheet of glass, I could see that now, living a life but never truly in it. And despite very real forebodings, I knew I must walk through that glass and hope to find myself on the other side.

\* \* \*

By the time I reached Thetford Road, I had blisters on my

feet and my legs felt woolly and disjointed. I wasn't used to walking any distance and kitten heels were hardly the most suitable footwear. The small haversack I carried had begun to feel as heavy as a cabin trunk. I couldn't imagine I would ever feel grateful to be descending the dingy stairs to Nick's basement, but I found I was.

He was sitting on the floor of the main room, surrounded by a scatter of art catalogues, and with the remains of breakfast congealing beside him. He had been busily sifting through one catalogue after another, marking pages, scribbling notes, but he looked up as he heard my step.

'Hi Grace, I think I may have an idea for —.' He saw my face and broke off. 'What's up?'

I slumped down into one of the bedraggled armchairs, dropping my bag onto the floor. He was on his feet and at my side in an instant. 'Was Oliver there? Is that what it is?'

I nodded, and the stupid tears began to fall. He put his arms around me and soothed as though I were a child. When I had snivelled to a halt, he went into the tiny alcove that masqueraded as a kitchen and made two large mugs of tea. I saw him ladle spoonfuls of sugar in mine. Usually, I can't drink sweet tea, but this morning it was just what I needed.

'So tell me,' he said, sitting at my feet and slowly sipping from his mug.

'We had a row.'

'Why are you so upset?'

'Why wouldn't I be?' I felt nettled. He seemed to assume I was dead to normal feelings.

'It's not exactly the first row you've had. I thought you'd be accustomed to the yelling by now. Ever since we met, you've been at odds with Oliver.'

'There was no yelling,' I answered a trifle sullenly.

But he was right, of course, and I tried to explain. 'It was over such a stupid thing. His daughter had her birthday while we were in Dorset and Oliver blamed me for not being there. I should have bought a present and gone to the party.'

'While he was in Newcastle? Makes sense.'

'It's ridiculous, I know. He's never taken an interest in Kezia since the divorce. And if you believe her mother, not much when they were married. Oliver and children don't really gel.'

'So the two of you never talked babies?'

The question took me aback.

'You shouldn't look surprised — you were together nine years. It's not unreasonable for the topic to have come up.'

'I suppose not,' I conceded. 'But knowing Oliver wasn't a fan of small people meant I never raised the subject.'

'What about you? Didn't what you want come into it?'

'I've no burning wish to populate the world,' I said airily. But then I realised I'd never examined my feelings too closely. It hadn't been worth it, knowing Oliver's likely reaction.

'And the problem over Kezia did for you both?'

'In a manner of speaking. The whole thing was ludicrous. Kezia was the small straw, I guess, the death knell.'

'Wild mix of metaphors.'

'It's how it felt. Oliver wouldn't compromise — all he would say was I should have stayed in London because it was my job.'

'So how did you leave things?'

'I left him. I resigned. I don't have a job. At least not *that* job.'

Nick didn't reply straightaway, which surprised me. I had

188

expected him to rush in with sympathy and hearty words. When he spoke at last, his tone was just this side of peevish.

'What will you do?' He must have seen my dismayed expression because he added quickly, 'You're welcome to stay here as long as you like.'

It wasn't quite quick enough: in a few minutes, it seemed, I had been demoted to an unwanted lodger. I'd never had any intention of staying too long. I suppose I'd thought Oliver and I would eventually patch up our differences, and then Nick and I would say a friendly farewell. The flat had only ever been a temporary reprieve, but Nick's lack of enthusiasm decided me to leave as quickly as I could. As soon as I found new work and a place to stay.

He tried again, and this time the sounds were a little more encouraging. 'Let's give it a go, you're staying here — you never know, we might enjoy it. Then if we both wanted to, we could opt for permanent.'

Did I want to? I hardly knew. But I did know that right now I had little alternative but to stay. 'Thanks, that would be good.' I hoped I sounded suitably grateful, and then wondered why. Hadn't I just escaped years of gratitude?

There was another lengthy pause and it was evident Nick was thinking hard. 'I suppose it's unlikely Oliver will keep you on as his assistant? I mean, despite the personal stuff.'

I couldn't quite believe he was asking the question. 'I have no idea,' I said sharply, 'and I'm not about to find out. I've no intention of ever returning to Oliver.'

'Fine. I can see that.' He ruffled his hair and despite my annoyance, the gesture was endearing. 'But things are going to be tight. I don't have a job either, remember.'

'I do remember and I won't be sitting around hoping something comes my way. First thing tomorrow, I'll be out looking.'

He seemed relieved. That was another surprise. I hadn't thought anything worried him greatly, least of all money.

He stood up and put his arms around me, dragging me from the chair and pulling me close.

'Don't fret, we'll get through. Have I told you how delighted I am you've split with him?' He kissed both my cheeks and then my lips.

'Not exactly.'

'Well, I'm telling you now.' And his kiss hardened. I tried to kiss him back, but I felt too miserable.

'I'm sorry, Nick. It's been a difficult morning.'

He smoothed my crazy curls into some kind of shape. 'I can imagine. But it's over and the future is bright.'

'It is?'

He laughed aloud. 'Sure it is. We're going to knock this Royde investigation on the head and claim our rightful prize. That means a nice large cheque and by the time we've spent it, we should both be gainfully employed.'

It was a good enough plan. He'd mentioned already he had a store of ideas for his freelance work, and he'd been about to share one possibility when I dissolved into sobs.

'Sorry, I hijacked the conversation. What are you planning to write?'

He glanced at the catalogues piled high on the carpet. 'It's a pretty vague notion at present, but I think it will run. On second thoughts, though, I should probably put it to one side and concentrate on Royde. That means certain money.'

He let go of me and started searching the accumulated litter beneath the small gate-legged table that functioned as his desk. After a few minutes of tossing papers aside, he pulled out a large black object.

'Let's get on with the research.'

'Now?' For the moment I had lost interest in the Royde story — my own felt too important — but I knew we couldn't afford to let the investigation slip.

'Why not? We've still got to figure out this mysterious A.'

I thought of the handkerchief I had picked up this morning and the discomfort I'd felt in that schoolroom. It had been an uncanny coincidence, that was all, and I needed to forget it.

'It will be complete guess work,' I said.

'Are you willing to hazard one?'

'I've been thinking that perhaps A is an employee, someone working at Renville's office. He could have been deputed by his boss to oversee the design — Renville himself might be too busy. It would be important for the company to get the Exhibition space right. Lucas Royde could have made an appointment to see this man at Renville's office to discuss progress.'

'If you're right, A is an important person. I knew he was. I said so on the train.'

Nick's calm superiority was annoying. 'I was the one who found the note,' I reminded him, 'when you were unexcited.'

'Well, I'm excited now. Let's assume he's an employee — where do we start?'

'If A were being trusted to oversee such an important project, he must have been a valued member of staff.'

'So…?'

'If he were an older man with a decent salary, he would have rented a property and without his name, we have no way of tracing him. But if he was young and single and a rising star, he might have lodged with his employer. It was common for proprietors to house one or two of their employees if they had room. We should go census search-ing again — it could be worth a shot.'

Nick looked blank. 'To find Edward Renville's home address,' I explained. 'It's possible A lodged with him and if we find him listed at that address, we'll have his name and age and we can go from there. If not, it's another dead end.'

'Let's get cracking and then we can wrap up this investi-gation for good.' He had started to bounce very slightly.

'Tomorrow maybe.'

I felt weary and worn. The morning's upheaval had taken its toll. I could have easily tucked myself into the chair, moth-eaten or not, and dozed the afternoon away. But Nick was on to it in a flash.

'Why not now?'

'Aren't you tired?' I was still suffering from waking in the early hours and I hoped he was, too.

'What's to be tired about? We'll use two computers and if we narrow it to the four districts I searched to find Royde, it shouldn't take too long.'

'Edward Renville might have lived in the City,' I warned. 'Near his workplace.'

'Then why did he employ a firm of architects based in Holborn?'

'Because there weren't too many architects in the City?'

Nick naturally had an answer. 'He could have found one in the West End — I'm sure there were plenty there. No, I think he went to de Vere's because it was well known and because it was on his doorstep.'

I must have looked unconvinced. He came up to me and wound one of my curls round his finger, letting it unravel slowly. He did it again, and I felt a wave of tenderness seep through me.

'Okay,' I agreed. 'We can try, but if we don't hit gold with Bloomsbury or Holborn then we give it up. For today at least.'

'It's a deal,' he said, then turned on one of the most battered computers I had ever seen.

He saw my expression. 'Salvation Army reject,' he said cheerfully.

# Chapter Twenty-Three

Reject or not, it worked, and it was Nick who found the Renvilles. There he was: Edward Renville, aged forty-five, importer, and living at Wisteria Lodge, Prospect Place, in the borough of Holborn, a short distance from Great Russell Street. There were two children living in the house, girls aged eight and six, named Florence and Georgina. But no lodger.

'No lodger,' Nick said excitedly, '*but* there was an 'A' at Wisteria Lodge. A wife, Alessia Renville, aged twenty-eight.' He mused a while. 'That's not too far off Royde's age.'

I couldn't see why that was relevant and I didn't believe the 'A' who had met Royde was Mrs Renville.

'That's it, Grace,' he insisted, seeing my doubtful expression. 'Alessia Renville must be 'A'.'

'If she is, it would be highly unusual. If there's no lodger, it's more likely we're chasing someone who never lived at Wysteria Lodge.'

'But why? It would make sense that Alessia was involved with her husband's schemes, and sense that Royde was asked to meet her at Onslow Street. We have his note on the theatre programme.'

'We can't make that jump, Nick. Why would she be in

194

charge of such an important project? She was a middle-class woman, a wife and mother of young children — it would be strange if she were involved in anything other than household affairs.'

'Perhaps this was a particularly enlightened marriage.'

I must still have looked doubtful because he cast around for more ammunition. 'Perhaps she had experience that would make her useful to an architect like Royde. Her name sounds Italian.'

'Maybe.' He had a point and I began to argue it through with myself. 'We know Royde spent time in the Italian states and we know the display space at the Exhibition was to sell Italian goods. It's true, too, that he and Alessia Renville would share a knowledge of Italian culture.' I was beginning to feel a little more confident. 'So if she were Italian — and we can't be sure — it might provide a clue to the unusual arrangement.'

Nick was beaming. 'Great. It's sounding good, so where do we go from here?'

'It could be worth trying the newspapers again.'

'How's that?'

'When I was searching the British Library, I found Edward Renville mentioned in an article published in *The Daily News*. Only his name, but I'm wondering...' Nick leaned towards me, his eyes bright, urging me on. '... he was probably too small a fish to be of major concern to a national paper, but a smaller, local weekly might be interested. Local events, news of important families residing in the borough, and so on. There was a paper for the Holborn district around the mid-century — *The Holborn Times, The Holborn Mercury* — something like that. I think it survived for about ten years.'

'And there'll be records?'

'I'm not sure, but it's worth a try. I'll check online first — we may be lucky. If not, I'll have to take a trip to Colindale.'

'Is that London?'

'Yes, of course it's London — North London to be exact.'

'How would I know?' he said, a tad indignantly. 'It's just another fusty record office.'

'A fusty record office that might provide the breakthrough we need.'

I started to type in the Colindale website while he switched his computer off and came to stand behind me.

'This could save me a long journey,' I told him. The site was complex and it was taking me time to navigate. He leant over me, his lips brushing the top of my hair.

'Do we have to do this right now?' It was another of his rapid mood changes. A minute ago he had been impatient to get on with the search and follow the new clue wherever it led.

'Let's leave it till tomorrow and have fun instead.' His voice was soft and persuasive and I felt him nibbling at my ear. 'We haven't celebrated your freedom yet.'

I wasn't sure how tasteful celebrating the break up of a long-term relationship was, but the occasion seemed to need marking in some way.

'It won't hurt to do a brief search first.' My protest was half-hearted.

'This will be more interesting.' He was nuzzling my neck and his hands had begun their downward journey. 'Much more interesting.'

I gave up and closed the laptop, then followed him through the bedroom door.

\* \* \*

A loud hammering shook me awake and I heard the front door creak beneath the onslaught. Nick groaned and turned over and I was ready to follow suit, but the noise was too persistent. I staggered to my feet and weaved a path to the door, turning the key to the sound of receding footsteps.

The woman turned back. She was a stylist's dream, groomed from head to toe, immaculate from her tweaked pixie cut to her shining Louboutins. She stood looking at me, surprised and no doubt horrified. The picture could not have been very pretty. I was wearing only a bra and pants and both had seen better days. With Oliver huffing downstairs, I'd had to swoop swiftly and my choice of clothes had been eccentric.

My bare legs and arms were pimpling in the cool of early morning, and it *was* early. It couldn't be more than seven o'clock and here was this svelte goddess standing on Nick's doorstep. I couldn't even begin to make sense of it. Then I looked more closely at her face and saw she had the very bluest of eyes. It began to make sense after all.

She smiled uncertainly. 'I'm so sorry to disturb you this early, but I have a hectic day ahead.' The voice was well modulated and clearly embarrassed. 'I was hoping to speak to Nick, but I'll ring him later.'

'No, no,' I stuttered. 'Nick's here. I'm sure he'd want to see you.'

I wasn't sure, after what Nick had said about his family, but I couldn't turn his sister from his doorstep, even at seven in the morning. It wasn't, after all, my doorstep.

'Do come in,' I said. A duchess could not have been grander.

Lucy came in, stepping gingerly across the stained carpet and looking forlornly for somewhere half decent to sit. I was unsure whether she had ever visited here before. From her reaction, it seemed unlikely.

Nick appeared in the bedroom doorway at that moment, his yawns almost filling the space. He glanced across at his sister. 'Ugh,' he said, and stumbled to the sink to fill the kettle.

Strong coffee seemed a very good idea and, while he was banging mugs around, I took the chance to retrieve my jeans and jumper. I couldn't compete with Lucy's elegance, but I wouldn't feel quite so mortified if I were not half naked.

When I reappeared, Nick made perfunctory introductions and Lucy smiled benignly, or at least made a game effort. Very wisely, she refused the coffee and perched daintily on the edge of the least disreputable chair.

'If you've come about the Royde thing, no worries.' Nick had decided to get in first. 'We're almost there.'

Lucy looked across at me enquiringly. 'Grace is an expert,' he said, and then choked slightly from the scalding coffee. 'The report will be with you in two shakes.'

'That's good news,' she said graciously, 'but that's not why I'm here. I would have rung, but I thought it was too important. You might not have picked up my message in time.'

'What's up, Luce?'

His use of the diminutive hinted he was more at ease with his sister than he'd previously suggested. And it was evident she was looking out for him; hadn't she given him the job researching Royde's plans?

'There's an opportunity,' she began, 'a great opportunity. But you'll need to play your cards right.'

He had stopped slurping his coffee and was listening intently.

'*Art Matters* has a staff position going. They're not advertising, but I think you should try for it.'

'How do you know?'

'I'm friendly with one of the directors.' Suddenly she was a little coy. Lucy was sleeping with the man, I thought, and about to call in a favour for her brother.

'And he is?'

'Rodney Finkel.'

I hoped he was nothing like his name, but Nick had fastened on the job rather than the name.

'A staff job, you say. Wow!'

'I've brought some papers with me. They'll tell you all you need to know about the company—its structure, vision, personnel, that kind of thing. You can get quite a bit from the website, but some of this stuff is confidential.'

'Insider trading.'

'Perhaps, but I know you can do the job or I wouldn't be setting up the interview.'

'I've got an interview?'

'Thursday at ten. You'll need to smarten up, though.'

'That could be difficult.'

'I'll bring a few things round tomorrow evening.'

Rodney's, I wondered? How would he react to seeing his wardrobe paraded at the interview? Lucy got up to go and smiled distantly. She was trying hard to remember who I was. 'It's been nice to meet you… Grace.' I was doing her a disservice. You don't get on in PR without remembering names.

'Don't let me down, Nick. It's your big chance.' She clicked her way towards the front door. 'And let me have the Royde report as soon as you can. The Society has begun to breathe down my neck just a little.'

'Sure thing. Thanks a million, Luce, you're a pal.' And he watched her up the steep stairs to Thetford Road. When he turned back to me, his face was ablaze. 'How about that!'

I didn't want to disappoint him, though I felt he should be cautious. 'It sounds good, but you don't yet know what the job is.' I gestured to the file of papers Lucy had left balanced on the table. 'Why don't you have a look while I fight the shower?'

'Great,' he murmured absentmindedly, and I left him to his reading.

When I found him again, his face was blazing even more excitedly. 'It's an editor's job. Grace, an editor! I can't believe that.'

'But you've never been an editor.'

'I've edited my own stuff, haven't I? How difficult can it be?'

'A lot more difficult than working on your own material, I imagine. And there's the whole business of commissioning writers who will make a profit for the magazine.'

'Don't be a pessimist. Wish me well.'

'I do.' I kissed him soundly. 'You know I do. I just don't want you to get your hopes up if you're not qualified for the job.'

'Lucy thinks I am,' he said pugnaciously.

'Lucy is your sister.'

'So?'

'She's bound to favour you. She's got you the interview, but it's you that will have to perform.'

'And I will. Luce was right, this is a chance in a lifetime and I'm going to grab it. I'll spend the next two days reading this stuff and anything else I can get my hands on. I'll be so well primed, I'll be near to exploding — but not before I've got the job.'

'And Royde?'

'What about him?'

'We were going to research the newspaper archives at Colindale, remember?'

'*You* were going to. Let's put Royde to one side. This is more important.'

'Yesterday, it was a priority.'

'Yesterday, I hadn't had this honey drop into my lap.'

His tone brooked no argument. There was nothing I could do but let him get on with it. I thought of carrying on the Royde research by myself, but I was scarily aware that I had fifty pounds in the bank and no way to feed myself once that was gone. I'd already begun to realise that Nick wasn't so carefree about money as he had first appeared, but his eagerness to join the corporate world still surprised me. It also made me determined to find work for myself. Solid work, permanent work, not dribs and drabs of research that never cleared the bills. I was determined I wouldn't be a financial drag on Nick.

\* \* \*

I spent the next two days looking for jobs that didn't exist, traipsing between different agencies and ringing contacts in universities and libraries. I even cold-called a few galleries, but everywhere the same story. It was worrying, but if Nick were lucky enough to get this job, and I didn't discount it happening since Lucy must wield influence at the magazine, it would give me a breathing space. I was still perching here, I knew, still unsure of my direction, but until I found work I had few choices — unless, of course, I was prepared to go cap in hand to Oliver, and I wasn't.

It was extraordinary and rather sad that after long years of being together, I hadn't missed him for a minute. I'd missed the comfort of a beautiful home, the smooth certainty of life in Lyndhurst Villas, but I hadn't missed the man himself.

The path here had begun with that first visit to the V and A. It seemed a long time ago that Paolo had wheeled an overladen trolley towards my reading desk and I thought how good it would be to see him again. He was one of those rare personalities that breathe life into even the most depressing day.

I didn't phone ahead, but timed my visit to the Art Library to coincide with lunch. He was restacking books when I signed in, making sure I substituted my new address, and straight away came over to me, planting kisses on both cheeks.

'I tried to ring you, cara. But no answer.'

'I'm sorry — you must have used my old number.' The day I'd cleared my belongings from Lyndhurst Villas, I had thrown my phone away. I'd wanted to make a complete break from the past. 'But how are you?'

'I am well, but you look a little tired.' He was still holding both my hands in his.

'I'm camping out at a friend's. It's not too comfortable.' It was a kind of truth, and the most I wanted to explain. 'It would be good to catch up, Paolo — could you spare the time for a sandwich?'

'For you, all the time in the world! But perhaps you would like to eat a proper lunch? There is an excellent Italian in Thurloe Place.'

'A sandwich would be easier. I haven't much time.' It was a lie, but my resources wouldn't stretch further.

'Okay,' he said aimably, 'an English sandwich it is.'

We walked out of the museum and towards South Kensington underground. There was an invigorating buzz in the air, and listening to Paolo talking about his latest project — he was tracing a possibly long-lost Masaccio — made me feel I'd rejoined a world I knew.

Once we'd found a table and ordered a sparse lunch, he was eager to know how my research was progressing. 'Tell me, you have found the mysterious A?'

'I wish I could say for certain. I've found an A, but I'm not sure I have the right person. There was an A living in the same house as the man who commissioned the plans, but she is his wife.'

'And that is a problem?'

'It would be highly unusual for a wife and mother of young children to be involved in anything beyond the household.'

'But it could happen? If the circumstances were right?'

'I'm hoping so. Alessia was Italian and the Exhibition space Royde designed was for Italian silks. Added to that, Royde himself spent several years in Italy.'

Paolo eyes brightened. 'There you are then. You have your A.'

I gave a small sigh. 'It's true there aren't any other leads, and if Alessia isn't A, I'm stumped.'

'And if she is?'

'Then I need to find out more about her. It's possible that if she *were* closely involved with the plans, she had her own copies and lodged them somewhere for posterity.'

'It is a good thought. And much more than I've discovered.'

'You've carried on searching? Thank you, Paolo.'

'I am intrigued—like you. I thought I would look through the secondary material you had no time to read, but so far I've found nothing. It is slow going — we are short of staff in the library and I can do only a little at a time.'

This was my chance to venture another concern. 'Talking of staffing, would you know of any posts coming up at the museum?'

'You are looking for a new job?'

'I've begun to, but I'm not finding it easy.'

His face had fallen. 'I am sorry, Grace, but there is nothing, nothing I know of. My fellow intern has had to leave early. The museum is cutting costs.'

'Isn't everyone?' I couldn't help another sigh.

'But this friend you stay with — does she have a job?'

'He.' I had to be honest.

'Ah,' he said, with a particularly Italian emphasis. 'I understand.'

'I'm not sure you do. I'm only staying there temporarily. I'm working with him — or at least supposed to be — to find these missing plans.'

'I'm sure he likes that you stay with him. He would be a crazy guy to let you leave.'

'That's nice of you. But he doesn't have permanent work either. At least, not at the moment,' I amended. 'I've been trying to contact everyone I can think of, but the answer is always the same.'

'I wish I could help.' He pushed the crumbs around his plate and looked mournful. But also a trifle uneasy. I wondered why until he very cautiously broached the subject of Oliver.

'I did hear,' he said with a studied casualness, 'that you worked for Professor Brooke. He is very well known at the museum.'

'You're right. I did work for him. And lived with him for many years.'

'But not now?'

'I decided to quit both jobs.'

He leaned forward. 'And this friend?' His interest in Nick was clear.

'He was the one who got me into the Royde project. We're working on it together, but I'll be leaving Thetford Road as soon as we're finished.' I don't know why I said that since I'd made no actual decision. It seemed, though, I wanted to tell Paolo I was a free agent.

He nodded and filled my cup from the cafetière. 'You must tell me your new address when you move. And your number.'

'Here.' I fished out the new phone and he made a note. 'I'll let you know if I hear of a job, Grace, but I'm only a miserable intern — no influence, no money.'

'Then we're both on our uppers.'

'What is this 'uppers'?'

His perplexed expression made me laugh. 'Never mind. At least you can smile at it. And you'll be returning to Italy soon, I guess.'

'Not for another six months. So plenty of time to see each other — what do you think?'

'See each other?'

'Maybe go to the theatre? I like the theatre — it's good for my English. Or that Italian meal, or a film, or a walk in the park or...'

'Stop!' I wasn't pledged to Nick and he probably wouldn't mind anyway. Ours was a very casual arrangement. 'It would be good,' I said.

# Chapter Twenty-Four

Paolo's smile had been pure sunshine and I tried to keep it in mind as I made my way back to Thetford Road and the dreary apartment. A glass of wine awaited and that was a comfort. But Lucy was waiting, too. The expensive smell of Shalimar hit me as soon as I let myself in. Brother and sister were not speaking but had moved the two armchairs together and were sitting side by side reading from what looked like the same script. Two pairs of intensely blue eyes looked up as I walked into the room.

'Hallo, Grace,' she said pleasantly. 'Had a good day?'

'I've been job hunting and it could have been better.'

Nick got up and gave me a reassuring hug. 'Forget it and come and have a drink. Lucy's compiled some questions and answers for the interview. With a bit of luck, some of them will come up tomorrow.'

Especially if Rodney has been suitably primed, I thought. But really I shouldn't grouse. After my spectacular lack of success in landing any kind of job, it was more important than ever that Nick did well.

Perhaps Lucy guessed something of what was going through my mind because she said, 'We can't depend on Rodney asking these questions, but I know they're the sort of thing he'll want to know. One of my employees went for a job at *Art Matters* last year and remembered some of the stuff that came up.'

I subsided into one of the hard wooden chairs and propped myself against the scruffy table, now overflowing with Nick's reminders for the next day.

'Are you going to learn the script by rote?' I could hardly believe he would, but I wasn't at all sure with Lucy stage-managing the affair.

'It just gives me a flavour of what to expect.' His tone veered towards the defensive. 'And Lucy has got me some togs to wear. What do you think?'

Togs? Where did that come from? It sounded boarding school, country gent, sherry at six; it didn't sound like Nick. I looked over at the suit he'd indicated. It was pretty sharp and the shirt and matching tie had been chosen with obvious care. He was on track to get the prize for elegance, if not for editing.

'You'll look wonderful.'

I tried to sound enthusiastic, but all I wanted was a drink. And that worried me. I hadn't needed alcohol as much since I'd left Lyndhurst Villas. It felt almost like old times. Nick brought me a bumper glass of red wine and I was half way down it before I realised. I saw Lucy eyeing me askance. She was probably deciding her brother's new girlfriend was a lush, and definitely not Heysham family material.

Nick was more forgiving. 'Was it lousy?' he asked, referring to my abortive job search.

'Yes, lousy.'

'You'll find something soon.' He tried to sound cheerful. 'You can't fail. All those qualifications, plus experience.' But his voice tailed off and I couldn't blame him for losing heart.

He went back to his sister's side and waved a crib sheet in the air. 'In any case, there's no mad hurry.'

'You might not get this job.'

'I might not, but there is something I *have* got. We've got.' And once more he bounded out of his seat and came to the table. For a few seconds he rummaged in the litter and then picked out a sliver of paper, which he tossed into my lap.

'Payment for all your hard work, Dr Grace.'

I looked blankly at the slip. It was a cheque for a pretty sizeable amount and was signed by the secretary of the Royde society.

'What's this?'

'What do you think it is?'

'I think it's a cheque from the Royde Society, but I don't understand why. We haven't finished researching yet.'

'*I've* finished researching.'

I must have looked bewildered because he said with some irritation, 'It's done, Grace, over. I banged out a report yesterday while you were out. I detailed all the stuff we discovered and our conclusion that the plans, if they ever existed, were no longer around. Luce got the report to them pronto, and they obliged this afternoon with this nice fat cheque.'

I was so taken aback I simply sat and stared into space while he carried on breezily. 'So no worries, sweetheart. We can eat for a few weeks. And if I get the job tomorrow, even more weeks.'

'But we still had work to do on it.' I finally spluttered into life.

'It wasn't going anywhere. You know that.'

'I don't know it.'

'Oh, come on, Grace, we've got the money. Let's forget it.'

'The Royde Society was delighted,' Lucy put in. 'Disappointed naturally that they couldn't use a replica of the Exhibition pavilion as their venue, but delighted to have all the new information you uncovered.'

A thread of anger had begun its slow, fiery course through my entire body, and I couldn't bring myself to speak.

'Lucy says she might be able to do something for you — jobwise,' Nick added rashly.

'What!' Suddenly I was galvanised.

Lucy rushed in, aware — how could she not be? — of the fury in my voice.

'The Society was so impressed with your work, Grace, that I took the liberty of mentioning your other experience in the field and the fact that currently you're at a bit of a loose end.'

She was trying to be nice, trying to be helpful, but if I heard any more, I knew I would have to strangle them both, and very slowly. Instead, I did the cowardly thing.

'I have a bit of a headache. I need to rest for a while.'

Lying on the uneven bed, staring at the ceiling cracks above, I tried to regain some calm. I was surprised at how committed I felt to this quest, and how angry Nick had made me. Why hadn't he told me he had written the report? He had done it while I was out job hunting, but he could have shared it with me when I returned. But he hadn't. He had kept quiet, gone behind my back, and stitched it up with his sister. He must have known I wouldn't agree to send an incomplete account.

It was a blow to realise he was capable of deception, a blow to realise that the fee was all-important. Once he had the Society's cheque, he was no longer interested in Royde, whereas I was caught in history and felt compelled to find the truth of events a century and a half ago. A discomfiting gap yawned between us.

And it was to yawn even wider. By the time I'd regained a measure of self-control and thought it time to return to the living room, I found Lucy still there and wandering down memory lane.

'You'll never guess who I saw this morning. Charlie Patterson!' she was saying. 'I was crossing Westminster Bridge to go to a meeting at the Marriott and there he was.'

'Charlie?'

'Surely you remember, Nick. He was a friend of Rob's. The one with big feet and a large Adam's apple.'

'Oh, yeah. Always wore drainpipes. What's he doing in the badlands? The last I heard he was running Daddy's business in Gloucester.'

'He was or rather he is. I could only speak to him for a few minutes — running late, as always. He said he was in town to catch up with a few friends. In fact, he'd just been to see Rob. He's in St Thomas's, Rob, I mean — liver disease — and not doing too well, according to Charlie. He looked very down about it.'

'Poor old Rob. Do you remember him at that amazing party the olds threw just before I graduated? Him and Charlie.'

'Of course I remember. Nobody could forget.'

I had been sitting in silence, my face growing blanker by the minute. Lucy tried to help me out. 'They dressed up as the Jack Lemmon and Tony Curtis characters in *Some Like It Hot*. It was killing, Grace. Then Rob fell off his four-inch heels as they were doing a final sashay down the front steps. High as kites, of course. He landed face first in the fountain!'

A fountain? What kind of home did Nick come from? I

tried a smile but it died.

'Charlie tried to haul him out.' Nick was beginning to chuckle. 'And then he fell in, too.'

Lucy gave a shout of laughter. 'His wig fell off and Daddy found it the next day floating somewhere around the bottom. One of the fish had got tangled up in it, and he got very annoyed.'

'The fish?'

'Not the fish, stupid. Well, perhaps the fish, too. It was a great party.'

'The best.'

They eventually stopped laughing sufficiently to wipe the tears from their eyes, but it took a long time. When the last chortle faded, they turned towards me, four intense blue eyes regsitering uncertainty.

'I'm sorry.' Lucy got up from the chair and ineffectually patted the one cushion Nick owned. 'This must be very boring for you, Grace.'

I said nothing. She flushed a little and then said brightly. 'I'll be on my way then. Good luck for tomorrow, Nicky.'

I didn't get up and Nick went with her to the front door. I knew I should have been more amiable, but I couldn't make myself feel sorry.

# Chapter Twenty-Five

'What was all that about?' he demanded, the minute the door shut behind Lucy.

'What?'

'The unfriendliness, the frostiness. Don't you like my sister?'

I shrugged my shoulders. 'I don't dislike her. What I don't like is your going behind my back.'

'I didn't.'

'What do you call secretly writing a report on Royde, passing it to your sister in a private email and pocketing the cheque?'

'That's unfair. I didn't write it in secret. You were out all day yesterday looking for work.'

'And all today, as it happens.'

'Without any luck,' he retorted. 'At least now we've a cheque to bank — the one you've just discarded. It's there for you to take your share any time.' He came over to the table and started searching for it beneath the piles of paper.

I wasn't mollified. 'You didn't tell me what you were doing. You could have shown me the report last night.'

'I could, and you would have asked me not to send it. You'd have insisted on carrying on, and I didn't want a row.'

'I thought you were just as keen to follow the trail.'

'I was, but there has to be a point when you call it quits. We've found out all that's necessary for the Royde Society to go ahead. That was the aim of the project, after all. They don't need any more information, and neither do we.'

I squared up to him and wished, as so often in the past, that I stood taller than my measly five feet three. 'I don't like the 'we' in that sentence. Your motivation may be money, but I have professional pride at stake. I'm determined to discover as much as I can.'

'Meanwhile earning sod all.'

'There's more to life than money.'

'Only if you don't need it. For years you've not had to worry when you'd be paid next. Oliver provided. But I have and yes, money matters.' Now it was Nick who was angry. 'You should stop acting like a spoilt child.'

'Spoilt? You have to be joking. You and your fountain!'

'It's my parents' fountain and what has that got to do with anything?'

I wasn't entirely sure and in response gave an irritable shrug. He saw my hesitation and decided to take the heat down a degree or so.

'Look,' he said in what I imagine he thought was his reasonable voice, 'the Royde Society is happy. They can go ahead with a clear conscience and build their mock Carlyon chapel for the big celebration. That's all they wanted to do from the first. And if you're really bitten by the search, you can always carry on in your own time.'

'What happens when I find something?' I wasn't giving up the challenge quite so easily.

'If, Grace, if. That would be your little bonus. Just don't find the bloody Exhibition plans, that's all. I don't want to have to go back to the Society and make them cry.'

I thought about it. I suppose it made sense. We had some money now to tide us over and if my job hunting continued in similar fashion to the last few wasted days, I would have plenty of time to fill. It wouldn't hurt to keep digging; it might even keep me sane.

'The cheque will give us a breathing space,' Nick was saying, an echo of my own thoughts. 'I've got this interview tomorrow and who knows, I might get the job, and then we'll be home and dry. Plenty of time for you to get sorted.'

He probably didn't mean to sound condescending, but he did. 'What's with the 'if'? Surely Lucy will have fixed it.'

'Why would you say that?' He gave me a steady look and I instantly regretted my words, but there was no going back.

'Isn't that how your family does things?'

'No it isn't, and why are you so sore? You're not content to ignore my sister, now you're suggesting she's corrupt enough to fix an interview. Not nice, not nice at all.'

I had to agree and could only hazard a guess at why I was behaving so out of character. This evening I'd been granted a small glimpse into Nick's family, and it had been as distant from me as life on Mars. I didn't fit into that scene and never would. I'd thought he didn't either. From all he had said, his family was there to avoid. Yet an hour ago, he'd sat a few yards from me, laughing uproariously with his sister and sharing a world I could never join. He had not been the person I'd come to know. That's why, I suppose, I was sore.

'The truth is you've got a real problem with families.' He was aggrieved and intent on pursuing his injury.

'I thought it was a problem for you, too.'

He ignored this and continued accusing me. 'You don't like families because you don't have one.'

I detest cod psychology and my response was curt. 'I have a sister.'

'In name only. She might as well not exist.'

'Nevertheless she does.'

'But you don't contact her.'

'I can't,' I said flatly. 'We don't speak.'

'As a matter of interest, when did you last speak to… Verity, wasn't it?'

He was cursed with a great memory and also annoying tenacity. 'I don't remember,' I lied.

'You broke with the only known member of your family and you can't remember when! I don't buy it.'

I didn't either, but I was determined not to talk about Verity. That part of my life was well and truly dead, and it was going to stay that way.

'If you don't remember when you last spoke, why did you stop speaking? You can't have forgotten that.' It *was* an annoying tenacity.

'There were difficulties.'

'I imagine so. What precisely?'

I felt immensely tired and knew I should keep my mouth shut and hope he would eventually give up. But of course I didn't.

'Her boyfriend attacked me, but she accused me of coming on to him,' I said bluntly.

'And did you?'

He saw my face and swiftly backtracked. 'Okay, so there was a misunderstanding between you, but surely not worth such a dramatic split.'

'You don't understand.'

'Make me.'

'He was the only boyfriend she ever had.'

'Why? Was she so bad looking?' he said crudely. 'I can't imagine so with you as a sister.'

'She was pretty enough — she just didn't socialise. She always said she couldn't go out in the evening because she had me to look after. She worked as a library assistant and the few men around were old or married or both.'

'But she still got her man, apparently.'

'Just after her birthday — her twenty-fifth — she was asked out by a customer she'd been helping. He kept coming into the library, getting her to find information, and then finally he asked her for a date. She brought him back to the house after they'd been going out a couple of weeks and from the first he gave me the creeps. But she could see no wrong in him. It was embarrassing. She was all over him.'

'Another classic case.'

I must have looked fazed. 'Oliver's male menopause? You certainly collect them. Sorry, go on.'

I didn't want to go on. 'Can we leave it, Nick? It's not an edifying story.'

'But it's your story and that's why it matters. To me, at least.'

He came and sat beside me and his hand reached for mine and held it fast. His resentment had gone and when I looked across at him the expression in his eyes held a reassuring warmth. I think he realised my pain was still alive and kicking. A light kiss on the cheek gave me the encouragement to keep talking.

When I began to speak, though, my voice was barely above a whisper. 'One day I came back home early when Verity was still at work.'

He bent his head towards me and stroked my hair. I began again in a much firmer voice. 'It was the last day of 'A'

Levels and we'd finished Latin B before lunch. I was thrilled to have finished my exams and I flew home on wings. Before that I'd had a few glasses of cider with friends and no doubt that helped me on my way. When I got in, I turned on the kitchen radio and started singing along with it. I can remember it so well. It was a really hot day and I'd kicked off my shoes and was dancing around the kitchen table to these sad pop songs feeling better than I had for years.'

'So far, so normal.'

'Yes, but then Verity's boyfriend turned up. I couldn't work out why he'd called — he must have known she was at the library. He was friendly enough to start with, but then he began coming on to me. I told him in no uncertain terms to get off and stay off. But he wouldn't. He pounced on me and by then he'd worked himself into a frenzy. He was like a wild animal and wouldn't let go. He started tearing at my blouse. We'd been allowed to ditch our uniform for the exams, and it was one of those thin broderie anglaise tops the girls were all wearing that summer, and he wrenched it open at the front. I didn't have a bra on — I wasn't very well-developed.'

'Doing better now, though.'

I pulled my hand away. 'Are you never serious, Nick?' I had repressed this horrible memory for so long and for the first time, found the courage to share it. Banter was the last thing I needed.

'Sorry, sweetheart. Just trying to lighten things a little.'

'There is no light. I was in a dark place, very dark. The man was going to rape me. I fought back, but he was far too strong. Then Verity came in. She'd been feeling unwell and excused herself from work. He told her I'd got drunk after the exams and then come on to him, and that he was trying to restrain me. It was ridiculous — he was twice my size — but she believed him, or pretended to. I ran out of the house and didn't go back for hours.'

'Where did you go?'

'I don't know, I was in such a state. I probably just wandered around until it started getting dark. Then I had to go back to the house. He'd gone, but Verity was there. She had been crying — loads — and she was very angry in a tight-lipped way. She never once raised her voice, but her words flayed me. She said she had lost the only boyfriend she'd ever had or was likely to have and it was all because of me. She said I couldn't bear that she had anything of her own, and I'd deliberately set out to wreck her life.'

'That's crazy. She would have met someone else. In any case, this bloke sounds a complete loser. *Did* she meet someone else?'

'No. I don't know. After that, I didn't stay around to find out. She never said another word about the incident, but she blamed me. It was always there in the background. I would catch her looking at me and her face would be twisted with all that resentment bubbling inside.'

'And you never had it out with her, never tried to convince her she was wrong?'

'I suppose I believed that in a way she was right, that it was my fault. Just as my parents' death had been my fault.'

'You were just a kid. She should have realised the damage she was doing in heaping you with blame. It was her job to protect you from the louse, not the other way round.'

'That's what hurt the most. She didn't protect me, instead she believed his lies — and they weren't even clever lies. I couldn't wait to get away. A few weeks later, I finished school and moved out. I went to stay with a girlfriend for the summer and then left for uni in the autumn.'

'And then found your way to Oliver.'

I turned to face him. 'Are you trying to say something? More psychobabble?'

'Common sense, Grace. You ran to him for protection. What happened made you scared of life. That's why you rarely show your claws. You're scared you'll get hurt again.'

'Let's have another drink.'

I fetched the half empty bottle from the kitchen worktop. I was finding the conversation far too heavy. He'd hit the nail on the head, of course. Avoiding conflict, going with the flow, living a kind of half life: that was what I'd done. Ever since I was ten years old, when my parents had quarrelled over me and stormed from the house to their deaths.

I poured a very large measure of wine, but Nick refused the glass I held out to him. 'Can't do. I have to be on top form tomorrow if I've any chance of this job — unless, of course, Lucy really has fixed the interview.'

'I'm sorry, Nick. That was a wretched thing to say.'

He walked over to the battered sofa and held out his hand to me. 'Come here and I might forgive you.'

I tucked myself in beside him and nestled back into his arms. He had a tough day ahead and I should try to help. 'Do you want to practice?'

'Do I need to? I thought we were doing pretty well.'

I poked him in the ribs. 'Practice for the interview.'

'Oh, that. No. But I wouldn't mind an early bedtime. I'm sure there must be a few rough edges we can perfect.' And he kissed me long and deep.

# Chapter Twenty-Six

Lucas calculated it would take the workmen employed by de Vere's at least two weeks, possibly more, to construct the Exhibition space. There was no chance, therefore, of seeing Alessia for many days. Every evening he was tempted to call at the site to check on progress, as though his presence could in itself speed things along. But for what? Once the pavilion was finished, so was their friendship. When he escorted her next to the Exhibition Hall, they would be the last intimate hours he would spend with her.

On the first day of May at the grand opening he would see her, no doubt sit close to her, but she would no longer be for him alone. Her husband would be by her side and all her attention would be his. Edward Renville would strut, proud in his possession of a beautiful wife and a successful business. And there was no question in Lucas's mind as to which meant most to him.

The weather was now a good deal more pleasant and he had no longer to fight the elements in his walk to the office from Red Lion Square. But as spring wakened, his restlessness grew daily. It was well the new project assigned to him was gathering momentum for the heavy workload provided distraction from what was becoming a dangerous obsession. Just when he thought he could no longer resist the temptation to return to the Crystal Palace, he was once more summoned to de Vere's office.

'Do sit down, Mr Royde.'

The great man was unusually friendly and waved Lucas into a comfortable armchair. His employer sat opposite and swung his seat to face him. The familiar melancholy smile was on his face and his fingers steepled in an attitude of thought. Lucas braced himself for bad news, but it was praise that de Vere had in mind.

'I have perused your initial drawings for the Carlyon estate and I like what I see.'

Lucas could not say the same, but he had drawn according to de Vere's wishes. Secretly, he had every intention of attempting to persuade the earl to abandon the design he had created. Boldness, he would tell his lordship, was crucial. Only give his architect *carte blanche,* and the Carlyon chapel would be universally admired for its beauty and originality.

'I think we are at the stage, Mr Royde, when a site visit is in order.' Daniel de Vere's smile grew a little sadder. 'You will go to Norfolk tomorrow. The journey will necessitate you spending two nights there, and you may book yourself a hotel room for the duration. I will not expect you back in the office until Friday morning.'

Norfolk. It was hardly a world away, but the last thing Lucas wanted at this moment was to leave London. He had no choice, though, but to acquiesce.

'Thank you, sir,' he murmured, hating his enforced submission.

De Vere stood up and handed him a single sheet of paper. 'Here are the details of your initial contact at Southerham Hall, a Reverend Waters. You will present the drawings to him and if he is happy with them, he will submit them to the earl for his opinion. I will send a telegram today to alert him of your arrival. I think you will find suitable accommodation at the Royal Hotel.'

'Thank you,' Lucas said again, and edged towards the door, hoping to make his escape. But de Vere had not yet finished.

'You know, Mr Royde, this project is a large affair, very large,' he counselled. 'I am putting you in sole charge and have every confidence you will do it well. The distinction gained from this work and from the Exhibition space you have designed for Mr Renville will prove most helpful to your career. Yes indeed, most helpful.'

'Thank you,' Lucas said for the third time, and bowed his way past the walnut panelling.

\* \* \*

The journey to Norwich was uneventful but wearing, the train proving no better sprung than the coach that had taken him to the Shoreditch terminus. Uncomfortable wooden boards served as the train's seats, and space was at a premium, for every compartment was vastly overcrowded. By the time he walked up the front steps of the Royal Hotel, his head hurt and every muscle of his body ached. He ate supper alone and soon after retired to his room to sift gloomily through the hated plans. The thought of what lay ahead on the morrow only increased his despondency.

The Reverend Waters proved to be a small and fussy man.

He pored over each drawing for an inordinate time, asking questions, raising spurious difficulties, suggesting impossible additions, until Lucas was near to returning to London and asking de Vere to award this prestigious commission to another of his architectural team. A break for luncheon did nothing to lessen the morning's frustrations when he was directed to the servants' hall to take his meal. How fitting, he thought sourly.

He ate as slowly as he dared, but eventually could dally no longer and with reluctance set off for a further encounter with the Reverend. He was soon lost, meeting a labyrinth of unused rooms, narrow passages and stairs that seemed to lead nowhere. At last he opened the door to a room bearing clear signs of habitation and realised he had stumbled on Lord Carlyon's study. He had also stumbled on Lord Carlyon himself.

The earl courteously waved aside his apologies and then caught sight of the papers protruding from Lucas's satchel.

'You must be the architect from de Vere's. The very man I wished to see. If you have a moment, you can take me through the chapel plans.'

'The Reverend Waters…' Lucas began tentatively.

'Ah yes, Hugo Waters. A sound enough chap but likely to take an age explaining the drawings to me. You, on the other hand, look a much better prospect!'

Here was his chance. A private interview with the man he wished to influence. He would show Lord Carlyon the current design, but in the process suggest several adjustments. If he were lucky enough to be granted a second audience, he would recommend further modifications and slowly and subtly bring the chapel at Southerham into line with his own vision.

By the time the Reverend Waters found them an hour later, Lucas felt he had done well in laying the groundwork towards the eventual acceptance of his proposals, and his return to London was accomplished with a happy heart. He would build a chapel of which he could be proud. And if all went well, he would build it in *his* name and not de Vere's.

Most precious of all, he was now three days nearer seeing Alessia and he dared to think his meeting with her might be imminent. He was desperate to discover how far the pavilion had progressed and, although it was late when he finally reached Red Lion Square, he stopped only to divest himself of his luggage before going straight to Hyde Park and the Exhibition Hall. The workmen had laboured hard and effectively and he was delighted with what he saw. His design, their design, flowed before his eyes and he was impatient to share its beauty. But it was too late to call at Prospect Place; he would have to send a message to her the next day.

* * *

He spent that Friday quite unable to work. The hands on the great oak clock had never moved slower, and he waited in a fervour of impatience to hear the chimes of six o'clock. At last he could leave Great Russell Street for the short journey to Alessia's house. She would know from his message that the pavilion was finished and would not be too surprised to see him. Even if her husband were at home, he could explain his presence at the door by the need to make arrangements to escort her to Hyde Park for a final viewing.

It was the pert maid, Hetty, who opened the door to his knocking. A piece of luck, and if his luck held, Edward Renville might still be at his office.

'How good to see you, Mr Royde.'

Alessia rustled forward to greet him and, as she did so, the lace shawl draped across her shoulders slipped sideways to reveal a gown of pale yellow silk, clinging tight and low against the creamy olive of her bosom. He averted his eyes and tried hard to concentrate on what she was saying.

'I received your note a few hours ago. Such wonderful news of the pavilion! And a splendid homecoming for you — I believe you have been visiting Norfolk for your new commission?' He was following her along the narrow hallway as she half turned towards him. 'I trust your trip to Southerham went well. You must be delighted to be working for such an important man.'

'I am flattered to have been given the commission,' he responded a little awkwardly. 'I am hopeful that Mr de Vere will be pleased.'

He would have liked to confess what he was truly about, but dared not risk her disapproval. In any case, he told himself, it would be unfair to involve her in the web he was spinning. She led him to the back of the house, to the garden room, he noted. Did that mean his earlier transgression had been forgotten?

'May I offer you some refreshment?'

'Thank you, but no. I came only to arrange a time with you to view the pavilion.'

'I am so looking forward to the visit.' Her face was glowing with anticipation. 'These past two weeks I have done nothing but think of it, wondering how the work was advancing. I confess that once or twice I was tempted to summon a hansom and go to see for myself.'

'Then I have my own confession to make. I have stolen a march on you, since I visited last night as soon as I reached London.'

'For shame, Mr Royde.'

'I hang my head, but I am ready to escort you whenever you say.' He smiled down at her and she blushed. He realised that his eyes must give him away, even if his speech and actions did not.

'Shall we go now?'

He blinked. It was almost dusk and the lamplighter was already making his way along the neighbouring roads. She sat facing him, her head slightly lowered and her hands clenched a little too tightly.

'You find it a strange request, I can see, but in truth the project has been so important to me that I feel unable to wait another minute.'

The thought of travelling through the night together made his blood rush wildly, but he managed to say in a sober tone, 'I would be delighted to escort you — and perhaps Mr Renville would also wish to accompany us.'

Her face shadowed a little. If he had not been watching her so closely, he would hardly have noticed. But he was always watching when he was with her, watching her every shade of feeling.

'My husband is attending a business dinner in the City tonight. He will not be home for many hours and my daughters are not yet returned. They are having the most interesting time in St Albans and my mother-in-law has asked for them to stay a little longer. So you see, I will not be missed.'

The sadness in her voice caused him to adopt a false cheerfulness. 'We are free to go then! And we can be back easily within the hour.' His mouth spoke the words, but his heart hoped that time would again prove elastic.

# Chapter Twenty-Seven

**A**s they approached Hyde Park, the traffic grew noticeably thicker. A number of heavy vans, pulled by long teams of horses and piled high with machinery or packing cases, were heading in the same direction. The cab was still some distance away when the Exhibition Hall came into view. Passengers crammed on the top decks of nearby horse-drawn buses craned their necks to see as much as they could. It was virtually dark now, but work was continuing by the glow of lanterns and the glare of bonfires built from a mountain of scrap timber. The whole world seemed a blaze of light against which small, dark figures danced here and there. It seemed to Lucas he was entering an enchanted land.

This time, they turned in through huge bronze gates, newly constructed to mark the northern entrance.

'So much activity,' Alessia exclaimed, 'and they are working so very late.'

The small dancing figures had transformed themselves into gangs of workmen labouring at every corner of the building.

'I understand they are toiling day and night to ensure that all is finished on time.'

'And will it be?'

'Consider the number of workmen — there must be thousands. And the building has to be finished for the first day of May. The Queen's honour depends upon it!'

A long queue of wagons waiting to unload had formed in front of the Hall and they decided to leave the cab and walk the rest of the way. While Lucas paid the driver, his companion wandered ahead towards the entrance.

'Lucas, look at these,' she exclaimed.

She was pointing to huge marble and bronze statues wrapped in canvas and standing ready to be rolled into the Exhibition Hall where they would take their place along its nave. Two were life-sized statues of Victoria and Albert on horses. But it was not the statues he noticed. For the first time she had called him by his given name and had been unaware of doing so. This is how she must think of me, he thought deliriously. I am not Mr Royde, architect, I am Lucas, friend. Perhaps even more. He tried to push away the notion even as it found sanctuary within his heart.

They turned towards the spiral staircase that led to the upper gallery, but an army of painters busily decorating the last of the cast iron pillars blocked their passage and they were forced to sidestep a chaos of paint pots and perspiring men. Lucas began to negotiate his way past them, trying to find a clear path to the stairs, but she did not follow. Instead she had veered to the right and her face was alight with excitement.

'Is that where the Queen will sit, do you think?'

He walked back towards her and saw that a magnificent Indian chair covered in crimson velvet had been placed on a raised platform. Workmen were struggling to fit a canopy thirty feet above, each corner of its blue silk decorated with ostrich feathers in the shape of the Prince of Wales's symbol.

'Almost certainly. The opening ceremony promises to be a splendid occasion and Mr Renville is sure to have reserved your places.' He gestured to the rows of seats covered in crimson cloth that were even now being arranged on the long east-west aisle.

'All that is needed then is the royal carpet.'

'No doubt it's on its way. But we should take a look at our own royal carpet. The painters have moved their tools and we can pass now.'

When they stood at the entrance to the Renville pavilion, Lucas said nothing but watched her face intently. She stood motionless, her eyes wandering here and there, noting the little details they had agreed on, taking in the few additions he had felt bold enough to include. She drew an appreciative breath and turned to him.

'It is entrancing. And your tiles look wonderful. Was it your idea to incorporate them so well with this splendid flooring? Yes, of course it was.' She took his hand impulsively. 'It is the added touch that brings everything together.'

The flooring had been a late idea and one he had not shared with her. If she had disliked it, it would have been easy enough to lift the rich rugs and shimmering tiles and return to plain slatted wood. In the event he had chosen right, and at the same time established a window for his private work. She became aware that she was still holding his hand and abruptly let go.

'Would you care to see more of the Exhibition Hall?' he asked, hoping to distract her. A thread of tension had begun to pull tightly between them. 'I believe most of the displays are now in place, and we saw only a small fraction on our last visit.'

'Yes — no,' she said in some confusion. Then more slowly,

'I think I would like to wander along this gallery to its very end and then wander back again. I would like to come upon this space as though I were a visitor, to see and feel how it will appear to someone who does not know it.'

'Then you will have to scrub your mind blank.'

'I will try.' And once more she was smiling, her moment's lapse forgotten.

They walked the length of the gallery, viewing the darkened expanse of the park through huge windows, occasionally looking upwards at the astonishing roof with its three massive elm trees safely enclosed within. Outside the fires were still burning, though beginning to burn lower. A noise of hammering came to them from the far end of the building. People would be working for some hours to come, but their numbers were gradually diminishing.

They slowly retraced their steps, her arm on his, talking together quietly, enjoying their pretence of being uninitiated visitors.

'And what did you think of the American room?' She had been reading her newspaper.

'Interesting, Mrs Renville.'

'In what way, Mr Royde?'

'Any display that boasts a reaping machine, a piano that can be played by four people at once and a stuffed squirrel can rightly be called 'interesting', I feel.'

She giggled and he wished she would take his hand again. But she did not and they continued decorously along the passageway, arm in arm. The park was almost peaceful now with only distant sounds to mar its tranquillity.

Then they were at the Renville pavilion, poised at its entrance. Their eyes locked for an instant before they plunged together through the draped gauzes to gaze silently on their handiwork.

'Is it truly wonderful or am I being dreadfully partial?' Her voice was no more than a murmur.

'It *is* truly wonderful. The pillars gleam as richly as I could ever want and their carvings are beautifully precise. And these silks,' he ran his hand lightly down a sinuous swathe of glowing violet, 'are iridescent.'

And so was she. In the reflected, flickering light of the fires which burned outside, she had never looked more beautiful.

'We have ourselves a triumph, Mrs Renville.'

'I am so pleased,' and her voice shook. A tear slowly wandered down one cheek. She tried to pretend it was not there, but his finger gently wiped it away.

'I am sorry. I am being foolish again.'

'You are being an artist.'

And then quite suddenly she was in his arms and he was kissing her cheek with small, butterfly kisses. It is only for comfort, he thought. But it was not. He felt her tremble and pulled her closer, holding her tight against himself. Then his hands were in her hair and, unresisting, she allowed him to liberate her neatly fashioned locks until they fanned out across the shoulders of her cloak. His lips grazed the shining strands of hair hanging loose around her face, then nibbled at her earlobes and found their way downwards to the softness of her neck.

The cloak fell to the floor and his mouth flitted across her bare shoulders. He needed to taste her. When she offered her mouth to him, it was soft and inviting. His tongue gently parted her lips and slowly began to explore the softness within. He felt her body melting into his, heard her small pants of pleasure. Then his fingers were undoing the tiny pearl buttons of her dress and his lips gliding across the smooth cream of her bosom. He was lighting a fire in her, in them both.

She was breathing quickly and matching him kiss for kiss, stroking his body until it burnt beyond his control. In an instant, he had guided her downwards to lie on the thickest of rugs, covering her body with his. She tore at his shirt, burying her face in his bare throat. He was a lost man. He forgot everything but his need to feel her naked skin against his, the hardness of his body against hers. He would allow himself this one moment.

\* \* \*

They strolled hand in hand along the pathway, as though they glided through a dream. Surely it had been a dream. But no, Alessia walked beside him, the beautiful woman he had so thoroughly loved, walked beside him. He knew he had made her happy, and for the very first time. For himself, past pleasures were not unknown but they faded into nothingness. This was love, not lust. The months with Marguerite had been mere childish fumblings. This was a love that went deep and true. Alessia was his destiny and must be his always.

She spoke and the spell was broken. 'Edward may be home by now.' The hour had lengthened into three. 'I will say that when you called to make an appointment, I insisted you escort me to Hyde Park this very evening.'

Her voice was decided, but he hated the necessity for such an excuse. He wanted to shout to the roof tops that they need make no apology. They were in love and they belonged together. The whole world must see that, the whole world must sing it loudly. But he would not compromise her.

Nor himself, he warned the eager lover within — not at this stage. When the Exhibition was over, when he had made a name for himself, perhaps then…

'I will say nothing,' he reassured her. 'I will leave you to explain your absence.'

But in the event Edward Renville had not yet returned from his business dinner and they had no need to lie. Lucas stood beside her in the open doorway, the street light shading his face. He reached for her hand and brought it to his lips.

'Should we visit the site again before the grand opening, do you think? It might be wise to ensure that all continues successfully.'

She knew exactly what he was offering and accepted his invitation. 'It would be well to do so,' she said demurely.

Well indeed. And so began the happiest three weeks of Lucas Royde's entire life. At every opportunity she would send a message that she would be alone that evening. She sent always to Red Lion Square for he had warned her that Fontenoy, still hopeful of discovering something discreditable, was a danger. It seemed to Lucas that she spent a great many evenings alone and he rejoiced. In those hours she was entirely his. But what could be wrong with Edward Renville, to prefer the company of men — and businessmen at that — to a woman so full of love that he, Lucas, was daily drowning in its bounty.

He supposed his work at de Vere's was still considered satisfactory, but in truth he had little remembrance of what he did from day-to-day. All he could think of were the evenings and their promise. On the few occasions Renville remained at home, Lucas was driven half mad with jealousy and frustration. But the next night they would again lay close on those deep, rich rugs, flickering fire lighting the space and every snatched minute together charged with joy.

* * *

One evening as they were preparing to leave, he was prompted to ask out of the blue, 'Was your husband a successful man when you married him?'

She gave no direct answer, but teased him instead. 'Do you know your eyebrows can be very threatening?'

'Threatening?'

'Yes, even though your eyes say something quite different.'

'But your husband?'

'And so insistent! Why do you ask?'

'I want to know everything about you. I wondered what kind of man he was when you first met, if you had any notion of what your life would be once you married.'

She flushed a little, but her voice was steady when she answered. 'Edward was starting out. He had a very small business, but he was certain he would make a success of it.'

'And you believed him?'

'Naturally.'

They were fully clothed and sitting side by side on the love seat looking out over the darkened park. Half turning towards her, he glimpsed her profile, classical in its beauty, outlined against the shadows of the pavilion.

'Why naturally? Did you know him well?'

'I could see that he had energy and enthusiasm. With more capital, I knew he would make his company a success.'

'And you provided him with the capital.'

She drew herself up, her back stiff. 'Why do you say that?'

'I wondered if that was how it was,' he returned mildly.

'Isn't it always? Women have little say in these arrangements, even now in the middle of the century.' For the first time in their acquaintance, he heard a note of resentment in her voice.

'But your father — was he happy with the 'arrangement'?'

'More than happy.' The resentment had been replaced with bitterness. 'He wished very much for me to leave the family home. A small legacy from my mother was useful in persuading someone to take me off his hands.'

'How can you say that? You are a prize men would risk all to win.'

'You are a romantic, Lucas. That is not the way of the world. But you must not think I was coerced. I was very happy to leave my father's home.'

'Because of your stepmother?'

'Indeed. She was jealous of the affection my father showed me and made my life unendurable.'

'So Edward Renville rescued you — for a price. Somehow I cannot see him as a knight errant.'

'He has done his best. I am probably not the most useful spouse he could have chosen.'

'He got your money.'

'That is very crude.' She jumped up from the seat and strode to the window, looking out at the darkness beyond.

'It was a crude agreement.'

She whisked around to face him. 'You are not kind.'

It was a reproof, and he was desperate to wrap her round with his love. 'I cannot bear to think of you having to submit to a man like Renville.'

'I cannot complain. My husband is devoted to his business and I have a comfortable home. I am permitted to shop alone and visit museums and galleries whenever I wish.

Many husbands, you know, insist their wives stay at home unless they are there to escort them. It is not Edward's fault that we share little understanding of each other's lives.'

'Why did he suggest you become involved with the Exhibition, I wonder?'

'He seems conscious that I need occupation, now the girls are older. I should be grateful for it.'

And so should I, Lucas thought. When Renville decided his wife should oversee the design, he could not have considered the possibility that she would find occupation of a very different kind. A young man without status, a mere junior employee, would not merit a moment's serious concern.

She went on talking, seeming eager to defend her absent husband. 'Edward can be kind — he is very kind to the girls.'

'So you have said, but to you?'

'He is not unkind. He rarely bothers me.'

'In what way?'

Her blush this time was fiery. 'I think you must know.'

'And me?' he asked, his hand caressing her cheek and coaxing her lips to his.

'You, Lucas? You may bother me until eternity!'

# Chapter Twenty-Eight

Two evenings later they were lying together, exhausted from passion, when footsteps sounded outside the pavilion. She made to jump to her feet, but Lucas restrained her with one hand and put the other to his lips to signal silence. It was very dark and with luck the intruder would see nothing if he or she came farther into the room. For a few terrifying moments, the steps shuffled here and there and then slowly retreated towards the staircase.

A man's rough voice shouted to someone on the floor below. 'If we are to do anything useful, we need a light up here. It's as black as pitch.'

The response was inaudible, but the footsteps going down the staircase were clear enough. The man had gone to fetch a light.

They sprung to their feet and hastily dressed. Then very cautiously emerged from the pavilion and made their way to the staircase, hearts jumping, in case the man or his companion had found the light they sought and were about to return. But fortune favoured them and they were down the stairway and out through the entrance, meeting no one other than a lone workman loading surplus glass on to a rickety wagon.

They walked swiftly to Park Lane and managed to find a hansom almost immediately. Neither had spoken since that dreadful instant of near discovery, and they continued the journey in silence, hands held fast. The cab swung round into Prospect Place, and they saw that the windows of number eight were brightly lit. For once the master was home and Lucas felt his lover tremble beside him.

Her voice was hardly steady when she spoke. 'I will tell Edward that some of the draping has not been as successful as we hoped and that you asked me to accompany you in order to approve a different arrangement.'

He wondered if her husband would be deceived by something so patently flimsy. When she grasped the cab door and made to dismount, he stayed her hand, bringing her face to his and kissing her long and deeply. She emerged from his embrace gasping.

'What are you thinking! Here of all places.'

'I am thinking that I love you. We belong together, Alessia, and should not have to adopt such subterfuge.'

'But—'

'No 'buts.' Only let the Exhibition open, and we will be together, I promise.'

'How can that be?'

'I have an idea.'

'Tell me.' The fear had left her face.

'You must go now but trust me. We will soon be together for good.'

She kissed his cheek and the smell of jasmine stayed with him as he walked the short distance to Red Lion Square.

Once in his room, he divested himself of outdoor coat and shoes and lay down on the bed to think. His surroundings seemed to him less appealing than ever. During the day the room attracted the best light in the house, having a skylight to the chimney tops of Holborn as well as a small window on to the street, but at this time of the evening its dark brown paint was gloomy enough to corrode even the most sanguine of souls. He had pushed the small bed tightly against the wall in order to clear space for a desk and his drawing equipment. But apart from a chair and a narrow stand on which perched a tin basin for washing, the room was devoid of furniture. There was no wardrobe and what clothes he possessed remained folded in his trunk. It was not a place to which he could bring Alessia.

He had high hopes of the Southerham commission, but he would need to redouble his efforts. His recent interview with Lord Carlyon had been instructive. The man was good natured but essentially ignorant of architecture. He had seemed to like Lucas, to enjoy his company, and had insisted that when the young man returned for a second consultation, he was to eat his meat with him and not with the servants. Lucas was determined to use this proximity to his advantage. The earl's help would be essential if he were to provide a home for the woman he loved. Divorce was impossible — at least for the moment — though once he became a wealthy man, the situation would be different. But divorce, marriage, none of it meant a jot. All that mattered was to be with her.

He slept little that night, his mind busying itself with visions of a shared future and with the more pressing problem of where in the meantime they could meet. It was clear the Crystal Palace was no longer an option. Tonight they had escaped discovery, but the next time they would not be so fortunate. From now until the Exhibition opened, there would be increased activity in the galleries above:

workmen, contractors, exhibitors would be swarming. There could be no next time, but he had to see her.

He spent much of the night considering alternatives, finally settling on Vauxhall Gardens. Although little of its illustrious past remained, the gardens were still a place where the sexes could meet freely without social constraint. Vauxhall itself had become tawdry, but the neighbourhood of Kennington was newly respectable and he had few qualms in asking Alessia to meet him there. The gardens' greatest advantage was their size: they were very large and, in parts, very dark, enough for them to lose themselves among the crowd and meet in complete secrecy.

* * *

He met her there on his return from a second brief visit to Southerham Hall. For once Alessia's time was unrestricted. Edward Renville had left for Southampton that morning for contract meetings with his carriers, their two daughters remained at St Albans and the impertinent Martha had been given leave of absence to visit her sick mother. They would have the time to talk; only talk, he reminded himself, after their recent alarm.

He had much to tell her, for he had returned from Norfolk in jubilant mood. Lord Carlyon had given his verbal agreement to very considerable modifications to the chapel's design and it was now most definitely a delicate Italianate building, all vestige of the Gothic disappeared. Further encouragement followed when he broached the topic of a private contract and found the earl ready to listen.

Nothing was agreed definitely, but it was sufficient for Lucas that Lord Carlyon had not rejected outright the idea of employing him on a purely personal basis. He had been careful to intimate that after the grand opening of the Great Exhibition, with the Renville commission complete, he would be free to walk from de Vere's unencumbered. He was sure he could negotiate a fee for the work at Souther-ham that would allow him to set up on his own for the very first time, albeit in a small way. Best of all it would enable him to provide Alessia with a worthy home.

He met her by the main gates of Vauxhall. She was heavily cloaked despite the gentleness of the April evening, and he could see immediately that she was unusually nervous. He wondered if it was the unaccustomed meeting place that was disturbing, and whether his choice had been apt. A glimpse of the gardens ahead showed them to be unin-viting, the lamps on the main walk burning dingily amid scrubby trees and the company going in and out of the gates decidedly raffish. But he had important news to tell and he quickly paid their admission.

'You are very quiet, my love,' he remarked, as they strolled down the South Walk. 'Does this place perturb you? Vaux-hall is hardly the Crystal Palace, I grant.'

She looked vaguely around as though she hardly regis-tered her surroundings. 'I am well, Lucas, thank you.' Her voice had lost its rich music.

'Are you sure?'

'Yes, it is really nothing.'

'Which means you are bothered by something. Tell me,' he urged.

She hesitated for some minutes before saying diffidently, 'I thought I recognised someone as I approached the gates. But I must have been mistaken.'

'Who?'

'A woman. She looked like a visitor who once came to

tea with my mother-in-law. But it must be a mistake,' she repeated.

'I think so. I cannot imagine a friend of the elder Mrs Renville frequenting Vauxhall!'

He was cajoling her, quite sure that her nervous state had precipitated these qualms. 'But just in case, we will hide ourselves completely,' and he steered her towards one of the small paths that led away from the main promenade towards what he knew was the Dark Walk. Here the lamps were absent and the company very thin. It was not long before he found a small wooden shelter half way up the Walk, where they could be entirely alone amid thick darkness.

'I have news,' he said, trying to not to betray his excitement. 'The plans I have been pursuing are now almost certain. I hope to be designing the Carlyon chapel as an architect in my own right.'

She looked at him blankly. Her mind still seemed far away and he had to reiterate. 'I will be leaving de Vere's.'

This startled her into words. 'But without a salary, how will you manage? How will you afford your lodgings?'

'Once I am working for the earl, I will be able to afford far superior lodgings. So superior they will be good enough to accommodate you.'

'I will be able to visit you there?'

He clasped her hands tightly between his. 'You will be able to live with me there.'

'You are suggesting I leave my home?'

He could not understand her reluctance, but said patiently, 'We cannot continue to meet like this, Alessia. We must have a place to call our own.'

'But I cannot leave Edward. I am his wife.'

Why did she cling so tenaciously to a life she despised? 'Are you not more my wife than his?' he asked urgently.

'But in the eyes of the church…' Her voice trailed off, disappearing into the night mist.

'What matters most — *our* eyes or those of a distant church?' He was almost fierce in his denunciation.

'Ours,' she agreed unhappily.

'So?'

'But you cannot have thought — my daughters —'

'The proceeds of the Carlyon commission will allow me to rent a substantial house. We will have them to live with us.'

'Edward would never agree.'

'But surely he would not separate them from their mother.'

'They are his children and he will wish to keep them. The law is on his side.'

'I accept that, but if he knows what it means to you to have them?'

'Can you not understand? They are his children, I am his wife. We belong to him. If I should dare to leave, he will do everything in his power to hurt me.'

The eagerness slowly drained from Lucas and he slumped back against the shelter's rough wooden wall. She turned to him in anguish, desperately gripping his shoulders. 'I cannot relinquish my daughters, Lucas. You cannot ask it of me.'

When he responded, his voice held the note of defeat. 'What you are saying is that you will never come to me.'

A long and painful silence descended between them while Alessia slowly twisted into mangled leather the gloves she held. At length, in a voice hardly above a whisper, she said, 'I did not say that.'

The words appeared wrenched from her, but they galvanised Lucas. He leant forward again, all his eagerness returned. 'Then say you will come. Say that you love me enough to do this.'

'Sometimes,' she said slowly, 'I think you do not know just *how* much I love you.'

'Then come to me, my darling.'

'When?'

'As soon as the Great Exhibition has opened, I will be free to work for Lord Carlyon. I will make all the necessary plans.'

'And my children?'

'Once we are settled in our new home, I will request an interview with your husband. I will tell him your need for your daughters and say that everything will be done discreetly. You are not a part of his social world, so who is to know that you no longer live at Wisteria Lodge?'

She shook her head and a look of near despair flooded her lovely face.

'Alessia!' he said urgently. 'It cannot truly matter to Edward Renville whether you live with him or not. It is only his business he cares for. And as for the children, he will see them whenever he wishes.'

Her continued silence moved him to desperation. 'If you love me, you will come.'

'I do, I do,' she said, sobbing into his shoulder.

He put his arms around her and drew her close. Gentle caresses slowly soothed her, but soon his kisses became harder and more insistent. She was like a drug to him; he could not bear to be without her. He needed to feel her body, her heart, her soul, ever close to him. Beneath his touch she was beginning to burn. Her arms embraced him; her lips were on his neck. Then she was undoing his cravat, unbuttoning his shirt. Her kisses were heightening his passion unendurably and crushing all his good intentions into small pieces.

He took her hand and plunged them into the darkness of the gardens. The soft grass beneath their feet provided all the bed they would need. Slowly and thoroughly his hands began to move over her body, undressing her as he went, his mouth following where his hands led. The warm night air caressed their bare skin and together they took fire until every fibre of Lucas's being sang with hot pleasure. His body ablaze, the world around him vanished into nothingness — the soft grass, the distant lights, the white rags of mist trailing the night sky. His world was contained only in this instant and he gave himself up to it. It was as though this was the last moment of true love he would ever know. But that was stupid. In a few weeks she would be his forever and tonight they were free to love until dawn.

# Chapter Twenty-Nine

Nick was showered, shaved and dressed at an unbearably early hour the next morning. When I managed to prise my eyelids open, I looked at him in amazement — and not only because he was up and ready before the clock had struck a bleary seven. In his borrowed clothes, he looked polished and assured, and for a moment I experienced the same sinking feeling as last night, the feeling he wasn't the same person I had grown to know.

But then he made some stupid joke over the cornflakes and I chided myself that he was no different. At least I hoped so. I wished him luck and meant it. The interview was a phenomenal opportunity and though I wasn't confident of his success, I knew it was what he wanted more than anything, and so I wanted it, too.

As soon as Nick had banged the front door behind him, I washed the few breakfast dishes and switched on my laptop. A lot seemed to have happened since my visit to Silver Street, but I hadn't forgotten my uncanny experience there and it continued to play and replay in my mind. The physical reaction I'd had — the prickling, the breathlessness — had been upsetting, but it was the scent of jasmine that haunted me most, so much so that I had stopped wearing the perfume.

Something bad had happened there, I was fairly certain. Job hunting could wait a while; I would finish the work for Leo Merrick and put Silver Street out of my mind for good.

I logged into the Colindale site and searched their records for 1863, choosing *The Daily News* as my first port of call. It had been a campaigning journal, concerned with the poor and likely to contain news coming out of the East End. The search proved almost too easy. A subdued paragraph told me that the Misses Villiers, sisters who had been in joint charge of the girls' elementary school in Silver Street, had been found dead in the schoolroom by a caretaker on his evening rounds, that their family was unknown and that the funeral had been attended by a representative from the School Board. That explained their short tenure and the abrupt change to a male teaching staff.

But what a truly dreadful end for two such young lives. No wonder I had felt disquiet in Silver Street. Even now sitting here, I could feel my body starting to relive the memory, and despite my best efforts, I couldn't shake myself free. It was too vivid. I jumped up and walked into the kitchen, back to the mundane. But it was several cups of coffee later before I felt able to return to the laptop.

This time I checked the 1863 Register of Deaths, and as I suspected, they were recorded as suicides or in official parlance, the Misses Villiers had died from suspension by the neck from a ceiling beam. Aged twenty and eighteen respectively, they had hung themselves. It was a ghastly story and I would have liked nothing better than to have forgotten it there and then, but I knew I would have to tell my client. He had wanted an explanation and here it was, though whether he chose to continue his project after such news was another matter. The newspaper article gave no clue as to what lay behind the women's terrible deaths, why they had decided at such a tender age their lives were unendurable. It was the darkest of mysteries, but it wasn't mine to solve.

What was mine was the mystery surrounding Lucas Royde and the enigmatic Alessia. I went straight back to the newspaper library. I wasn't sure how much material from local papers had found its way online and I was half expecting a journey to the wilds of North London, but I was blessed with an enormous stroke of luck: a copy of virtually every issue of *The Holborn Mercury* for all of its ten years had been uploaded into the library records.

I wondered if de Vere's would be mentioned since they must have been one of the most prestigious employers in the Holborn district at the time. But it was the Renvilles that I was really after and I was determined to be as thorough as I could, beginning the sweep from two years before my target date with the edition dated 7 January, 1849.

*The Mercury* was a weekly newspaper and it proved an arduous business trawling through well over a hundred editions. Half way through the morning I made another large pot of coffee and drank the lot. I needed it. I was already wishing I had started from a much later date and sure enough my hunch was correct. It wasn't until the first week of February, 1851 that I discovered anything of interest. And what interest! Not only a mention of de Vere's, but of Edward Renville, too.

Renville's name appeared in the paper as a local grandee who was making a large contribution to the Great Exhibition. I read the tantalising paragraph over and over again, hardly able to believe my luck. All my questions answered in a dozen lines of text.

*Mr Edward Renville, as readers will know, is a consider-
able personage in Holborn, being a merchant dealing in the
finest silks and fabrics from the Italian states…*

'Yes!' I cried, punching the air in a way I've always dis-
dained.

*… and having a large premises in the City. Mr Renville
has commissioned a pavilion at the Great Exhibition to
display the breathtaking array of beautiful materials that
he regularly brings to these shores. The Exhibition Hall,
currently being constructed in Hyde Park, will be opened
on the first of May by Her Majesty Queen Victoria. One of
Holborn's most prestigious architectural practices has been
commissioned to produce plans for Mr Renville's display
space and a most promising young architect, a Mr Lucas
Royde, will act as chief designer.*

Yes, and double yes!

*Mr Royde has spent a number of years in the Italian
states of Lombardy and Emilia-Romagna and has only
recently joined de Vere and Partners. Mr Renville's wife,
Mrs Alessia Renville, will be assisting with the project. It
is believed Mrs Renville's family originates from Lombardy
and this gives her a particular interest in what will be a
themed display.*

So Nick was right all along. Alessia Renville was our
unknown contact. And she had been given the task of
overseeing the project because she came from Italy, again
just as Nick suggested. I still had problems, though. If she

had been Edward's spinster sister or even a childless wife, I could have better accepted her presence in what must have been a flurry of project design and management. But a married woman with children? It went against everything I knew of middle-class Victorian family life. But it was there in black and white and I had to believe it.

I was making a copy of this wonderful extract when my phone rang. It was Paolo to tell me he had tickets for us both for a gallery opening in the West End the following week. I'd barely taken in the details before I burst out with my news.

'That is brilliant, Grace.' I could feel his smile across the line. 'Maybe now you'll find the plans.'

'I'm not so certain. Given time, I think I could, but first I need a job.'

'While you're looking for one, you could write up your research. Make an article and be paid for it.'

I'd already toyed with the idea of writing a piece that would raise questions about Royde's first design, but now I had something far more substantial to support my theory — and far more interesting.

'I'll think about it. It's a good idea. And thanks for the ticket — the new gallery sounds something I'd like.'

When he had rung off, I wandered into the kitchenette and opened the small fridge. I knew I should have some lunch and then set out on the job trail again, but I was too excited to eat anything and desperate to tell Nick what I'd discovered. I had no idea how long he'd be at *Art Matters* or whether he intended to come straight home after the interview. I imagined he would, either to dance in delight or lick his wounds.

I didn't have long to find out. I was half-heartedly trying to cook toasted cheese on a grill that surely predated the

Renvilles when I heard him coming down the basement steps two at a time. Did that mean good or bad news? One look at his expression and I knew it was good, very good.

'Who's a clever boy then?' His face was one enormous grin.

'You got it?' I was dumbstruck.

'You might at least pretend you're not surprised. Of course I got it.'

And he grabbed me in his arms and pirouetted around the small space, banging into table, chairs and finally the grill, and sending the slice of bubbling cheese flying upward and due south. It landed on the chair that until now had sported the least stains. That was a pity. Now all our furnishings were equally disreputable.

'I got it, Grace! And the interview was tough, no walk-over. No fixing either.' And he looked slyly at me.

'I've already said sorry — endlessly. But you must have shone.'

'I did my best.' He let me go with a smirk on his face. I was finding his pretence at modesty a trifle annoying.

Then he came down from the heights and confided, 'I can't quite believe it's happened. I know I answered pretty well, but there were a couple of stinking questions. The thing is I got the feeling early on they were actually wanting me to succeed. They mentioned the series I wrote for them.'

'The Gorski show?'

'I still owe you for that — not throwing me out of the launch, I mean.'

'You've just repaid the debt by getting a permanent job. It is permanent?'

'Not only permanent, but I get my own office.' He was like a child who had held out his hand for a smartie and been awarded a sherbet dab.

'Anyway…' He took a breath. 'They were very enthusiastic about the stuff I did on Eastern European artists. It was different, they said — 'radical'. How about that? And that's what they want to see more of in the journal. Time to depart from tradition, and they think I'm the right man to commission a new kind of writing.'

He talked on, his tongue running away with him, while I rescued the toast from its sticky resting place and started cooking another slice. He finally ran out of steam as I put two plates of slightly burnt cheese on the table.

'Why are you home in the middle of the day? I thought you were on the job trail again.' He had realised I shouldn't be there.

'I decided to wait until this afternoon.' I had an uncomfortable feeling I should be excusing myself, saying sorry that I wasn't out pounding the streets.

'I guess there's no rush. I start next Monday and it's a big enough salary for us both.'

That made me feel even more uncomfortable, but I said, 'That's wonderful,' and kissed him soundly on the lips.

'More!'

'Later, but now let's eat. I've some news to tell you.'

'How come?'

'I took your advice.' That was stretching the truth only a little. 'I did the newspaper search. I was right about the title, it was *The Holborn Mercury,* and there were online records for all ten years of its life.'

'Good,' he said absently.

I could see the research had become a distant memory. In his imagination he was already sitting behind a large desk in an equally large chair behind a door grandly labelled *Art*

*Matters*. When I didn't continue, he stopped munching his toast and looked across at me.

'Tell me, then. What's the great news?'

It hit me hard that his reaction was so different to Paolo's. The excitement of discovery drained away and I was left feeling disappointed. I didn't want now to share something that was important to me, but meant nothing to him.

'You were right,' I conceded eventually. 'A is for Alessia. And you were right, too, about why she was involved — well, according to *The Mercury*. Her being Italian was deemed helpful to the project.'

'Aren't I just too clever for words?' He was gloating. I was sure this was one of the most glorious days of his life, but he was getting a little carried away and needed a small corrective.

'*I* found the article,' I pointed out.

'Aren't *we* just too clever?'

'Quite clever.' I needed to keep both our feet on the ground. 'The paper mentioned the architect in charge was Lucas Royde and that he worked for de Vere's. But although that backs up our research, it doesn't bring us any nearer the plans.'

'The plans are a complication we don't want, particularly as I cashed the Society's cheque today. Everything is neatly tied up and that's the way it should stay.'

I gave up on the last morsels of my charred offering and, with a sigh, sat back on the chair's hard wooden slats.

'Shouldn't it?' he asked a little too insistently.

'I suppose so.'

'Why only suppose? You've found out what you wanted and now you can concentrate on getting a job.'

'I thought there was no rush'.

'There isn't, but I can't imagine you'll want to sit here and twiddle thumbs for too long.'

'No,' I said slowly. 'It's just I have a hunch there's more to be found.'

'What more can there be? You know who A is and you know the house she was living in no longer exists. So what else can you do? Attempt to trace her descendants?'

'I might. There were two daughters, remember.'

'You would be wasting your time. It wouldn't bring you any nearer finding the plans and remember — we don't, in fact, want to find them.'

He looked fixedly at me and his expression was stern. 'You know what I think? This isn't about the plans any more. It's about you.'

'I have no idea what you're talking about.'

I truly hadn't, but I also knew I didn't want to; he had an uncanny knack of getting to the heart of things. I tried to sound sensible. 'It's nagging me, Nick, that we've come from zero, yet already found so much. There's bound to be something else.'

'Okay, we've made amazing progress, but the search is over. By all means write an article on Royde and try to flog it to some scholarly journal. You've got a new angle with Alessia — Victorian women had more freedom than we thought, etcetera. But then leave it.'

My face must have registered the stubbornness I felt because he reached across the table and grabbed my hands.

'Leave it, Grace,' he commanded.

That was sufficient to make me decide I wouldn't be leaving it.

# Chapter Thirty

It was several weeks, though, before I returned to the story of Alessia Renville. I had begun to drift and seemed helpless to stop. Failure is insidious. It rarely happens in one spectacular surge; instead it destroys gently, and I was no exception. My professional confidence was dented, leaking slowly but certainly away, and undertaking research, even the most basic, seemed beyond me. Nick was in the ascendant, and against the gleam of his success, the struggle to believe in myself became more and more difficult.

He had started work at *Art Matters* the Monday following his interview, and for the next week I had hit the phone or emailed, trying to set up meetings with past contacts. I had given up the agencies as useless. But the contacts proved no more helpful, and I began to wonder if I'd ever work again. Despondency ruled — I had no heart even to begin the article Paolo had suggested. It would be difficult, if not impossible, to break into the magazine market, and poorly paid if I suceeded. I hadn't the energy. I phoned him to cancel the gallery opening, too. It was mean, but I couldn't face it in my present state of mind.

But Nick was prospering. It was as if he was born to wear a suit. To be fair, the work was interesting and his colleagues congenial, but I was still astonished at how well he'd fitted into a world I had never imagined was his. Or perhaps it had always been his and the casual, spontaneous man I'd first met had been an aberration. I suppose that in some way everyone is a prisoner of their family, and to an extent that first experience of the world determines their life thereafter. Mine certainly had. Perhaps Nick, too, had never entirely escaped his upbringing, his bohemian lifestyle a small rebellion against conformity. Now a way had opened to more worldly success and he could compete on equal terms with his siblings, he seemed to have little difficulty in fitting back into the Heysham mould.

One morning after he'd left bright and early — and his willingness to put in the hours was another shock — I'd had enough of pretending to search for an invisible job and decided to do something practical by sorting out the one wardrobe the flat possessed. I wrenched open the slightly tipsy door and the chaos overflowed gently into the bedroom. Instilling order into the tumble of clothes, shoes, bent hangers and discarded carriers would keep me busy for hours, and in a way that was a blessing. It was lunchtime before I could congratulate myself on a job well done and then just as I was closing the door I noticed hidden away at the back of the top shelf a small cardboard box that I was sure I'd never seen before.

Out of curiosity I hauled it over the row of sweaters, now sitting neatly in line, and deposited it on the bed. It contained a pile of folded tee shirts. I unravelled the top one and held it up for inspection: I Drink Therefore I Am, it proclaimed. There was something very sad about the find. The box was testimony to the fact that Nick had discarded his former life almost completely. It made me wonder if along with the tee shirts, he had also discarded the person I'd known.

I should be as ruthless myself. I was carrying a lot of stuff that had come to the end of its natural span and was taking up space, not just in the wardrobe but in my life. Like most women intent on remodelling, it was easiest to begin with hair and clothes. There was a slight problem: I had no money for new clothes and there was little I could do about my hair. I was a natural blonde and would look odd as anything else; the frenzied curls were also severely limiting as to style. Nevertheless the next afternoon I marched off to a cut-price hairdressers I'd seen around the back of Kings Cross station and asked bravely for a short crop. The girl did a good job despite the modest price and for a short while at least I felt rejuvenated.

When I got back to Thetford Road, I looked closely at myself in the mirror for the first time in weeks, but it wasn't the hair that caught my attention. It was the eyes. There are times when my eyes shine a brilliant green and as such they're very noticeable. They were noticeable now but for the wrong reason. They looked huge, out of all proportion. I had lost weight — I often felt nauseous these days and wasn't eating well — and I looked haggard. The rejuvenation took one step back. My problem, I reasoned, was that I was depressed: I had no home, no money, and no job, and Nick wasn't exactly helping.

Almost his first words each night were, 'Any luck?' Tonight he followed the question with a renewed plea that I talk to Lucy since he was sure she could help me find work. 'I don't know why you're being so stubborn.'

'It's called being independent.'

'Independence is all very well, but it doesn't pay the bills.'

'No, you do,' I finished for him.

'Look, Grace, I'm not rubbing it in, honestly. I just think you could make more effort.'

'Are you suggesting I'm not trying to find a job?'

'Initially you were trying hard, but now you seem to have given up.'

He was right of course. I had.

'And I can understand it. God knows, I've been there, too.' He was trying to sound solicitous. 'But a regular salary makes life a good deal easier. So why not give Lucy a try? If we were both working, we could think of moving out of this hovel.'

'Move?' I had almost stopped listening, but at this I was jolted awake.

'I'm not saying we should move immediately. Sort the job first, then we can look around.'

It all sounded easy, but it wasn't. Lucy's offer of help was generous, but I couldn't accept it. It would feel too much like surrendering my liberty. Foolish, I know, but I'd had to dig deep to find the strength to break free of Oliver's sway, and I was stupidly scared of the possibility, no matter how remote, of handing myself over to someone else's control. I had to find the job for myself, and right now a job wasn't there. But the conversation had its effect, spurring me back to the only thing I could do, which was write.

Overnight I decided I would tell the first part of Alessia's and Lucas's story, part fact, part speculation, and even though I felt more queasy than usual the next morning, I buckled down. Getting involved in writing helped me forget just how foul I felt. It also made me forget to make dinner. We had fallen into the age-old pattern of breadwinner and helpmeet, and I had taken on the responsibility of cooking. I was a terrible cook, but either Nick was too tired to care when he got back from work or he considered it was the least I could do to contribute.

I imagine the latter. To say he was irritated by the lack of food that evening was an understatement. 'Couldn't you even get a meal together?' He was huffing and puffing. 'I'm the one who's been working all day.'

'I have, too.'

'You've been to work?' He sounded incredulous.

'That's not what I said. I've been working all day writing an article, and I've an idea where I might place it.'

'I thought for a moment you'd got a real job.'

There it was again: that echo of Oliver. His voice sounded down the weeks, still with crushing effect: *the work you do is nothing work*.

'Sorry. I didn't mean that.' Nick looked ashamed but soon recovered. 'I hope you don't mind, but I've asked Lucy to pop round tomorrow evening and have a chat.'

'About what?'

'She can help you. She meets a huge number of people through her PR business. She rang me today with a possibility. She's met a businessman who's desperate for a PA. He's an entrepreneur from Slovakia, or is it Romania? Anyway his PA got homesick and went back to Bratislava and he can't find anyone suitable. He's willing to pay a pile.'

'I'm not a PA,' I said dangerously.

'You helped Oliver.'

'Oliver was my partner. Your shady dealer from Eastern Europe isn't.'

'How do you know he's shady? You're far too judgmental.'

'And you're far too interfering.'

It was the first time we had come close to a serious

quarrel. I'd been looking forward to talking the article over with him, hoping for some enthusiasm. This could, after all, turn out to be my new career. Instead he'd suggested a questionable job and seemed to think I should be grateful. I didn't even bother with the pretence of making a meal after that and Nick soon trudged off to find the nearest pizza. I was still feeling unwell and glad of the excuse to go to bed early. But I didn't sleep and when he arrived in the room, I busied myself pretending.

'Grace?'

I didn't answer.

'I know you're awake, so speak to me. This is silly.'

I had to agree. 'What is it?'

'I know things have been a bit rough for you lately. In a way I feel responsible. I don't know if you would have left Oliver if I hadn't been around.'

I said nothing because I didn't know either. I preferred not to think about it.

'And I haven't been much help, it's true. I've been working so hard, trying to get my feet under the desk — literally — that I've forgotten how to enjoy myself. What we both need is some fun back in our lives.'

'What do you suggest?' I was cautious.

'We could start small. My senior editor is a really nice guy and we get on well. He wants us to go to dinner at his house. It should be a great evening, very civilised. There aren't any kids — Hughie values his freedom too much. It's just him and his wife.'

'Where does he live?' I imagined at best a small detached on a suburban estate.

'Funnily enough, Hampstead.'

There was nothing funny about that. 'Where in Hampstead?'

'He's got a big house on Millfield Lane, near one of the ponds.'

'And he's in publishing? There must be some mistake.' I hoped I didn't sound acid.

'Inherited money, I think,' Nick said easily. 'Surely it doesn't matter.'

'No, why should it?'

It didn't matter. I had a mild prejudice against inherited wealth because of the unfair opportunities it gave those lucky enough to possess it, but it wasn't what was making me pause. It was the feeling that once more I was being pushed into someone else's world. I'm sure it must be good for couples to share their lives, but this wouldn't be sharing. Nick wouldn't be sharing *my* world because I didn't have one. I only inhabited others' — first Oliver's, now his. I was being unreasonable, I knew, but I'd had enough of glass cages.

'I'll see,' I said, and with that he had to be content.

\* \* \*

Lucy turned up the next evening, her face apprehensive, and darting worried glances at me. She had brought flowers, huge great lilies that looked out of place in the basement's dingy rooms. I put them in the only large container we had, a plastic bucket, and then they simply looked dejected. I was ready for her to start selling me the Eastern European gentleman, but she didn't. She was wary, in fact, of mentioning work at all, so I thought I'd throw her a lifeline.

'I've gained some commissions,' I said brightly.

'That's great.' There was a pause. 'What are they exactly?' She sounded distracted and evidently found me unsettling.

261

'I used to have my own business in property research, heritage stuff you know, and quite by chance met one of my old clients a few weeks ago. He wanted me to do a follow-up on the report I wrote. He phoned me this morning and he's passed my number on to one of his colleagues who's interested in using me.'

'What good news, Grace. I'm so pleased. Does that mean you'll be restarting your business?'

She was just a little too eager. She had been talking to Nick, I was sure, and he'd encouraged her to encourage me. Or was I being paranoid?

'I don't think so — not on a permanent basis. I have other ideas.' I hoped I sounded mysterious.

Nick arrived between us with wine and glasses at that moment, I was spared further interrogation. Not for long though.

'Nick and I were talking on the phone the other day.' So I wasn't paranoid. 'We were saying it was time we went up to Gloucestershire for a weekend to see the parents.'

I nodded absently. The chance of a couple of days alone in Thetford Road was appealing.

'We thought it would be a good opportunity for you to meet them.'

I kept nodding. I was busy deciding just how I would spend my two days free of Nick.

'We could go up by train together,' she was saying, 'or I could drive. That might be the better option. What do you think?'

I suddenly realised she was including me in the plans. 'I'm going to be busy this weekend,' I said quickly.

'It doesn't have to be this weekend does it, Nick?'

Nick shook his head vigorously. He wasn't going to help

me out. 'Next weekend or the one after that is fine. The olds are pretty flexible. You name the day.'

I looked at their beaming faces and felt trapped. If I refused, what would that say about my relationship with Nick? If I prevaricated, they would keep on suggesting dates until they had a definite answer. It was frustrating. He should have discussed the visit with me before letting his sister loose; then I might have been able to explain how I felt, to myself as much as to him. With Lucy smiling benignly a foot away, it was impossible. But I didn't want to go. I didn't want to meet his parents. It was too soon and too difficult.

'Yes,' I heard myself saying, 'why don't we make it the week after next.'

When she had gone, Nick came up to me while I was washing up and put his hands around my waist. 'Thank you.'

'Why?'

'I know you're not crazy about going to Gloucestershire, but thanks for doing it for me.'

More guilt. I was doing it because I had no other option. He slid his hands upwards and started undoing my shirt. I felt sore and tired, but I didn't have the heart to push him away. He was working flat out, keeping the apartment afloat. I abandoned the dishes and allowed myself to be scooped up and carried lopsidedly into the bedroom. We plummeted onto the bed in a tangled heap of limbs, laughing and breathless. This was the person I had fallen for in those strange two days in Dorchester, a person who nowadays disappeared for long stretches of time. I wondered how long it would be before this new man, the one I hardly recognised, returned.

# Chapter Thirty-One

On the following day, I dressed as smartly as I could and sallied forth to meet my client, who had offices in Bloomsbury. It turned out to be a fairly brief meeting and a fairly sparse commission, but at least it was a start and he assured me that his colleague, Jessica Hanley, would be contacting me in the next few days.

With time to spare, I walked to nearby Somerset House hoping to do a small part of the research I'd need to complete the work he wanted done. It would save me a journey later in the week; I was still feeling weary and anything that conserved energy was good. I was beginning to have some unwelcome suspicions and after I had left Somerset House and was on my way to the bus stop, I dived into a pharmacy. If I could get back to Thetford Road before Nick returned, I would have time to do the test today. I didn't want to know the result, but I had to find out. Locked into a string of difficult thoughts, I wasn't looking where I was going.

'Grace!' The man I'd cannoned into was holding out his arms. I blinked. Oliver of all people.

'How wonderful to meet you like this,' he was enthusing. 'I've been trying to get in touch, but I've failed dismally. Your mobile doesn't seem to be working.'

It wouldn't, I thought, not from the bottom of a Hampstead pond. Oliver had no idea where I was living and, without my old mobile, no means of contacting me.

He was still smiling fondly, as though he couldn't quite believe the present he had been given. 'Do come and have a drink.'

'It's three in the afternoon, Oliver.'

'I know, but I've just had lunch at the BBC. They're reduced to bottled water there. Tap water next no doubt.'

I let myself be shepherded into the nearest pub, which smelt so strongly of beer that I almost retched.

'Are you all right?' His face peered anxiously at me. I noticed then that he'd shaved off his beard.

'Yes, I'm fine.' I took a deep breath. 'It's just a bit potent in here.'

'Let's go into the lounge bar, the air might be clearer.'

It was marginally fresher, and I let him order me a fruit juice and hoped I would keep it down.

'Shouldn't you be at the gallery?' I suppose I had an idea of putting him on the back foot.

'Not for an hour, and I'm so pleased to see you.' He looked it and my heart softened. 'So how are you doing?'

'Good.' I was economical with the truth. 'I've decided to continue the business and I've commissions coming in all the time.'

'I'm glad to hear it. I did wonder — you seemed quite adamant about not carrying on.'

I took a cautious sip of the juice. 'Words said in haste.'

'We both said words in haste, and I've been repenting mine ever since.' He reached across the table and took my hand. His long fingers were warm and clasped mine tightly. 'I miss you, Grace.' I was touched, but I needed to steel myself against any false reconciliation. 'I didn't value what I had until it was no longer there. If you would reconsider…'

I shook my head. 'I don't think it's ever a good idea to go back. I'm sorry things didn't work out between us, but very pleased to see you again. I hated parting on such bad terms.'

He clasped my fingers even more tightly. 'I hated that, too. Don't think I don't understand your wish to move on — I do — and I promise I won't pester you to think again. But I want you to know you are welcome back at Lyndhurst Villas any time you care to climb the hill. And on your terms.'

It was a generous offer, but the security he represented no longer looked as enticing. My silence told him that his offer was unlikely to be taken up and he covered the awkwardness by filling me in on the projects he had been busy with since I left. An hour passed before we said goodbye.

'If you would care to give me your new mobile number, I could pass it on to anyone I thought a likely client,' he said diffidently. 'I promise I won't call you myself unless it's business, or you call first.'

It was another stroke of generosity and I gave him the number. I hoped he wouldn't try to resurrect a dead relationship, but he seemed genuinely to want to help. We parted with light kisses and I walked towards Trafalgar Square with a happier heart. The meeting had been valuable in laying the past to rest; now it was the future I had to deal with.

* * *

As soon as I reached the flat, I made for the tiny bathroom. I didn't require much space or much time for what I needed to do, and I had my answer very shortly. Positive. But whose baby was it, Oliver's or Nick's? And what was I to do? I wandered back into the sitting room and collapsed into a moth eaten chair. There was a lot of thinking to do and all without the obligatory glass of wine. No more alcohol for months.

If the baby was Oliver's and I told him, what would be his reaction? He would want me to return to Lyndhurst Villas; he had already asked me to, and if he thought I was carrying his child, he would be insistent. Today's gentle request would become a command. I couldn't go back. Oliver didn't like children, but that wouldn't stop him wanting to control events. I had escaped once, but with a child dependent on me, I was unlikely to manage it a second time.

And it might well not be his: in fact it was far more likely to be Nick's. What would *he* say? I knew instantly — he would say we should get married. I don't know why I knew that, but I did. He had fallen into being conventional man just a little too easily. I think the Nick I'd first met had been an identity he was trying out. The Nick that had emerged in recent weeks looked like the real person, and that person would want to get married. Perhaps 'want' was stretching it — inwardly he'd probably be appalled at the prospect— but he'd feel obliged to. And I'd had enough of obligation.

Strangely, I never considered ending the pregnancy. I was nearing thirty, I wasn't particularly maternal, and I had little in the way of visible support. Yet it never occurred to me that I wouldn't bear this child. Before Nick got back, I rang for a doctor's appointment. The test result might prove a mistake, but I didn't think so. In the meantime, I would keep my counsel.

I got up to make tea and realised I'd left post still lying by the front door. I had been too intent on getting the test done and ringing the surgery to worry about mail. I bent down to rescue the several envelopes and saw the first was marked *Living History*. It was quite thin: either it was a rejection without the return of the manuscript, or it was an acceptance. There was only one way to find out.

Nick came through the door as I spread out the one-page letter. 'It's been accepted!' I waved the sheet of paper in the air.

'What has?'

'My article on Lucas Royde and his collaboration with Alessia Renville.'

He threw his briefcase down on the one empty chair and yawned loudly. 'I didn't know you were writing.'

'I told you.'

'Sorry, other things on my mind.' His tone wasn't exactly dismissive, but suggested quite definitely that my success could only be small beer.

'*Living History* is taking it.'

'That's a general interest mag, isn't it?'

'Yes, why?'

'An academic paper seems more your line.'

'I'm going for the lay reader instead. It should pay better.'

'I guess so, but —'

'But what? The magazine loved it and wants me to do a second article once I've completed the research.'

He didn't respond immediately, but made for the bedroom to change his clothes, though not before I'd seen the fleeting irritation in his face. There was something about the Royde research that annoyed him. Every time the subject came up, he did his best to ignore it. I couldn't fathom what was going on since initially he'd been the one keen to investigate. I wondered if it might be that when we'd started out, I had been in control. My professional expertise had mattered, and he had been the hanger-on. Now our roles were reversed and I had the impression he much preferred it that way.

When he re-emerged, he was wearing faded jeans and Converse trainers — they always made him look good. But his smile had all the appearance of being pinned on.

'That's really good news,' he said a trifle too heartily. 'About the article, I mean. It will certainly help out until you get something more permanent.'

'Permanent' was a word I seemed to hear a lot from Nick these days and it jarred. Nothing about me or my life felt permanent: on the contrary both seemed to be in constant flux. It was depressing to feel so little solid ground beneath my feet, but on occasions the uncertainty could be oddly welcome. Nothing was fixed, everything was open. Different possibilities washed around me, often no more than a shadowy sense of what my future might look like. But that little blue taper was telling me that from now on I needed focus.

Nick began pouring wine into the first of two glasses.

'Not for me, thanks.'

He raised his eyebrows, but made no other comment. Instead he dropped a small depth charge. 'Lucy rang me at work. She'll pick us up at six on Friday.'

I had forgotten about the visit to Gloucestershire, I'd been too busy battling with nausea. Now it was almost upon us, and I couldn't get out of it. If I pleaded ill health, Nick would want to know what was wrong. There was no escape; I was going to have to brave the weekend.

I stayed awake for hours that night while Nick snored gently beside me. I couldn't stop thinking about the baby. Home pregnancy tests could be unreliable, I knew, but I was sure the result hadn't lied. The thought of a baby terrified and elated me in a single breath. A child of my very own, a small scrap to love unconditionally, but a small scrap wholly dependent on me for health and happiness. I had to get a grip; I couldn't continue to stagger blindly from one set of circumstances to another and hope that life might turn out right. When I returned from Gloucestershire, there were important decisions to make.

# Chapter Thirty-Two

The trip to the Heyshams was mercifully brief. In the end Lucy had to see a valuable client on the Friday evening and didn't collect us until the next morning, and by teatime Sunday we were back in Thetford Road. Nick wanted to be bright-eyed for the next day's work.

I had seen the house in my imagination, fountain and all, but it turned out to be even grander than I'd thought, with room after room of high ceilings and expensive antiques. Nick's parents were equally grand but very welcoming. Victor Heysham, or Justice Heysham as perhaps I should call him, had crunched his way across the broad gravel drive even before Lucy's car pulled to a halt.

'Grace!' I was barely out of the vehicle and he had my hand in his and was pumping it vigorously. 'How very good to meet you. And good of you to bring our prodigal son home.'

I was about to deny any responsibility for returning Nick to his ancestral lands when Mrs Heysham emerged from an immense door of studded oak and enveloped me in a cloud of rustling silk.

'Grace! How wonderful you could come.' I was beginning to feel a minor celebrity. The welcome accorded Nick and Lucy was noticeably less effusive.

All three of us were ushered into the sitting room or what I imagined was a sitting room. There were certainly seats, but there were also acres of space, floor to ceiling windows, and a stunning view towards rolling grassland. I balanced uncomfortably on the edge of one of the squashy sofas and sipped my coffee. I was finding it difficult to relax.

'Your job sounds fascinating, Grace,' Mrs Heysham said. 'Do tell us how you got into property research.'

'I studied Art History, Fine Art, too,' I mumbled. 'And it went on from there.'

'How marvellous! And what exciting project are you working on at the moment?'

What on earth had Nick told his mother? I tried to catch his eye, but he had buried his face in his cup while Lucy looked studiously down at her feet.

Mrs Heysham was darting eager glances at me. 'I think it's so wonderful, women having careers — and such interesting careers — these days.'

There didn't seem much to say to that, but I noticed the judge looked a little less eager. 'Even more important for the men, wouldn't you say?' He looked meaningfully at his youngest son. 'Good to see you getting there, Nick.'

Nick flushed with annoyance, and I could feel Lucy about to step in. Protecting her younger brother seemed to be her role in the family, and no doubt she'd been doing it since childhood. This time, though, she didn't have to speak. The sound of a car horn distracted Mr Heysham's attention and sent his wife drifting towards the door, leaving a trail of lavender behind her.

'Martin,' the judge announced in a satisfied tone. 'On time, too.'

There was a flurry in the hall and then a slightly stockier version of Nick put his head round the door and nodded a hello.

'Brought anyone with you?' Victor asked.

Martin looked uncomfortable. 'Just me, Dad.'

'Hmm. We would have welcomed a friend, you know. The door is always open.'

'I know, but your summons caught me on the hop. I didn't have time to ask anyone. Not that I'm not glad to be here. It's great to meet you, Grace.'

I hoped very much that Martin wouldn't feel a similar need to quiz me on my mythical job, but I needn't have worried. From now on, it was legal gossip all the way, and it was only Nick yawning rather too loudly that brought the conversation to an end.

Mrs Heysham smiled brightly. 'We've invited a few friends to dinner this evening, Grace. We thought it more entertaining for you.' Then she turned to her children. 'You'll know all of them very well. Martin, I know you'll be pleased — Judge Dauncey's daughter is visiting. You remember Marianne?'

'And you've invited her?' Martin didn't appear that pleased.

'Naturally,' his father boomed out. 'Couldn't leave her languishing at home, could we?'

I intercepted a conspiratorial smile between the senior Heyshams while Lucy and Nick exchanged a knowing look but said nothing.

'Fine.' Martin's tone suggested a shrugging of shoulders, but he said no more and walked back into the stone-flagged hall to pick up the overnight bag he'd abandoned there.

'What was all that Marianne stuff?' I asked Nick when we

finally escaped to the bedroom.

'It's evident — she's been nominated Martin's partner for the evening.'

I plumped down on the bed and promptly sunk into two feet of goose down. 'He didn't appear too happy with the arrangement, but your parents seem very keen on his having a girlfriend.'

'Lost causes tend to be their speciality.'

'Why lost?'

'Martin is gay, but the olds don't know.'

I gaped at him. 'Why ever not?'

'They would freak, that's why not.'

'They have to know some time.'

Nick threw several tee shirts and a pile of socks into the top drawer of the chest. 'Not necessarily. He lives in London and rarely comes home. They live in Gloucestershire and rarely go to London.'

'But doesn't he want them to know?'

'I doubt it. He didn't want us to know, but Lucy discovered it by accident and told me. Martin got us together in a solemn powwow and made us swear we'd never tell. It was like something out of Enid Blyton.'

\* \* \*

I thought the evening party should prove interesting, but in the event I had little time to watch Martin negotiate the tricky business of keeping Marianne Dauncey at arm's length, while also keeping his parents happy. I was far too busy answering questions. Like their hosts, the Heyshams' guests were kind and welcoming, but a little overbearing. I had the strong sense they were there to inspect me, as much as to make the party convivial.

'Is your family local, Grace?'

'What university did you attend?'

'Would we know your parents?'

'How long have you lived in London?'

'Where did you meet Nick?'

And the killer of them all, 'Do you hunt?'

I forced myself to keep smiling, but at times I felt I was taking part in a mystery audition. It seemed as though a whole corner of Gloucestershire had come out to assess me for a role that was never spelt out, though I had my suspicions what it might be. When they weren't asking questions, they were discussing the relative merits of four-by-fours or the best saddlery to patronise or the disgraceful conduct of the parish council. On and on it went, and I smiled and nodded until my face ached. The last guests lingered, and by the time they left I could barely stand straight to wave them goodbye.

'They like you,' Nick said happily, as we fell into bed around midnight. Apparently I'd passed a test I hadn't expected to sit.

I don't remember much of the following day. Sunday passed in a blur although I do recall some less than subtle comments from Mrs Heysham on how she and her husband were getting tired of waiting for their children to marry and how they didn't want to be too old before they became grandparents. I felt a momentary guilt over the secret I harboured. But the baby might not be Nick's and if it were, I would want the child raised a million miles away. This was such a narrow world, kind but narrow, and ultimately stultifying. I could see why Nick had had to escape, but I could also see why he'd begun to revert to type. The nest was agreeably feathered, undemanding and secure.

'You must visit again, Grace,' Mrs Heysham made a point of saying, when after a monumental Sunday roast, the bags were being stacked into the boot of Lucy's car.

'It's been wonderful to meet you, my dear. You're obviously very good for Nick.' I couldn't see how she had decided that, but it was clear his parents were delighted their youngest offspring had finally confounded expectations. 'It would be nice to see him settled, wouldn't it, Victor?'

Victor growled his approval. 'The sooner the better.'

'Young people these days...' She shook her head. 'It's all so different. We were married in our early twenties, you know.'

This was beginning to feel uncomfortable, but worse was to follow. Mrs Heysham came right up to me and stood very close. 'We're so pleased Nick has found you,' she whispered in my ear. 'We've rather been relying on Martin. He's the eldest after all. But now — well, my dear, we must see.'

* * *

Lucy and Nick chatted all the way back to London, but I contributed very little to the conversation. The Heysham visit had given me a lot to think about, in particular families and the way in which most are dysfunctional to some degree. Nick's family got along well together, almost too well it seemed, but it was a surface relationship and most of what was important was left unsaid.

His parents had no idea their eldest son was gay or, if they had, they would not voice their suspicions. And his father had merely nodded in a satisfied way when Nick had spoken about his new job. He hadn't wanted to know the details, hadn't wanted to know why Nick had suddenly relinquished his alternative lifestyle. I imagine he'd never understood why his son had taken it up in the first place. It was an eccentricity to be airbrushed from the Heysham story. It was all immensely civilised, but it was empty. Nothing objectionable had been said to me, even the question marathon on Saturday evening had been phrased delicately, but the visit had made me surer than ever that I didn't fit in, and more than that, that I didn't want to. A few months ago when I was still content living my own version of the cocooned life, I might have felt differently. But not now.

\* \* \*

Thinking about the Heyshams naturally got me thinking about my own damaged family: two parents dead through a senseless row and a sister estranged by the squalid antics of a pervert. The thought hit me that Verity would very soon be an aunt. Would she want to know? Would I want her to know? Strangely I did. I toyed with the idea of writing to her — eleven, twelve years too late — writing to tell her she was about to gain a niece or nephew. I had no idea whether she still lived in the house our parents left us or whether she'd sold up and moved on. If she had, she would surely have tried to find me to pass on my share of the sale. Perhaps I would write to the old address. After all, what had I to lose?

'Want a glass of wine?'

Nick was standing in front of my chair, bottle in hand. I had been daydreaming so hard I hadn't heard him come out of the bedroom. Every evening he chose the next day's clothes with an almost religious devotion, arranging them on multiple hangers on the back of the bedroom door. And this was the man who for years had seen wardrobe as synonymous with torn jeans.

'Not for me,' I said.

'Have you gone on the wagon?' He had noticed I wasn't drinking.

'Not entirely.' I scratched around for a credible excuse, but ended by sounding limp. 'I'm getting stuck into the freelance stuff in the morning and I need a clear head.'

He looked ruffled. But then he always did when I mentioned writing, so I rarely spoke of it. In a way I had changed places with him. He was now the manicured professional, I was the dropout. Perhaps he didn't like to be reminded of the change.

'Are you still looking at Royde?' His tone wasn't encouraging.

'*Living History* is interested in a second article on him — I think I told you. But I've other ideas, too.' I hadn't, but I was sure they would come.

'The mag will be paying you a pittance.'

'It's a start,' I said shortly.

Over the weekend I had been mulling over whether or not as a freelance I could make a living, or enough of a living to survive alone. Actually, not alone. For the very first time, that truth pierced me — there would be two of us, the baby and me — and for the moment I was struck dumb.

Nick came to stand behind my chair and leant forward to cradle me in his arms. His voice took on a coaxing tone. 'Gracie, why don't you call the agencies again?'

'It's pointless.' I tried to suppress a yawn.

'Then go online, go back to the job sites.'

When I said nothing, he came round to the front of the chair and stood a short distance away. He looked like a schoolmaster, his expression fair but firm. 'The writing is never going to be more than a hobby, you must see that.'

I didn't see it, but I wasn't going to argue and I wasn't going to look at job sites either. Somewhere I heard the sound of glass cracking.

# Chapter Thirty-Three

The next day I went back to the information I had uncovered on Alessia Renville and thought about my next move. I had given up the idea of finding the Exhibition plans: Nick was adamant he didn't want them found, and my instinct, too, was telling me they no longer existed. It was also telling me that Lucas Royde had more to do with Alessia than simply being her partner in design. It was a very odd arrangement and I kept coming back to that. Why would her husband have sanctioned her being part of such an unusual collaboration, and why would she have agreed?

It was possible Edward Renville had encouraged her involvement as a distraction from the loss of a child — premature death was hardly unusual in the period. But the 1851 census showed that she had two children alive and living with her in Prospect Place, so the explanation wasn't likely. Was it because she was Italian, as *The Mercury* suggested? She would have experience of the Italian states, especially Lombardy where Renville regularly traded, but surely her husband would have as much knowledge of the area, if not more, and up-to-date knowledge at that. Was it then a case of speed? Did she help get the display space designed, constructed and opened more quickly and, if so, how closely had she worked with Lucas Royde?

When Nick and I first got back from Dorchester, we had visited Prospect Place or where Prospect Place had once been. Not only was there no Wisteria Lodge, the house named in the 1851 census, but there was no street at all: it had been obliterated by wartime bombing. It was a disappointment, but as Nick had pointed out, the Renvilles might only have lived in the house for a short time. If Renville's business had increased greatly, perhaps as a result of success at the Exhibition, the family could have afforded a more affluent lifestyle in a more prosperous neighbourhood. Prospect Place in the 1850s was respectable but not especially wealthy. Discovering the family's whereabouts after 1851 would bring me no nearer the plans, but it would fill in some missing details.

The first step was to consult the census taken in 1861. For some reason neither of us had thought it worth looking at before. If the family had moved in the intervening ten years, the census wouldn't tell me when they had made the move or even if they had lived in another place in between times. But I needed more material for the second article, and it was certainly worth checking.

I found the family immediately. Ten years later, the Renvilles were still living in Prospect Place. In 1861 Florence was fifteen and Georgina thirteen; Edward Renville was still going strong at fifty-five. But — and I had to look twice at the listing — Alessia Renville's name was not there. She was no longer living with her family. Divorce at the time was virtually unknown and separation most unusual, so could she have died in the interim? If so, it was a premature death, since even in 1861 she would have been no more than thirty-eight. There could have been a tragedy involving childbirth after all, only this time including mother as well as child.

I brought the General Record Office up on the computer and for some reason my hands were shaking slightly. I began a trawl through the index of deaths, working backwards from the last quarter of 1861 towards 1851, a time when I knew she was alive. It seemed sensible to start at the later date since death was more likely at thirty-eight than at twenty-eight. I changed my mind, though, by the time I had reached the beginning of 1856 and there had been no mention of an Alessia Renville. The indexing was alphabetical and the name reasonably uncommon, so skimming the records wasn't difficult, but still tiring.

I broke off to make myself a cup of coffee before once more settling down to the job. If Alessia hadn't died, perhaps she had gone back to Italy, leaving her daughters at Prospect Place? If she had, I would never find her. By why would she have gone abroad and left her girls behind? A father had complete control over his family and could have stopped his daughters leaving with their mother, but if so, something very bad must have happened to make her take off alone.

My nerve endings were bristling and it wasn't just the coffee affecting me. This was something to do with Royde, I was sure. Back and back through the records I went until I reached the last possible quarter of my search, June 1851. And there she was! My hands shook even more when I read what was on the screen in front of me.

Alessia had died in May 1851 at Old Grave Lane in the district of St George in the East. *It can't be the same person*, I thought. In a matter of days she had gone from a healthy young woman living in a respectable family home and overseeing an influential project, to a dead young woman who had breathed her last in an unknown house in one of the poorest boroughs of London. But it had to be the same woman; there was no other by that name. Something very strange and very terrible had happened.

I pushed my cup aside. The coffee was making me feel sick and it had been stupid of me to drink it, but in my excitement I'd forgotten my newly fragile state. So where *was* she living before she died, if not at Prospect Place? Could she have stayed with a friend — was it likely she would have a friend living in such a seedy district as Old Grave Lane? A maternal relative then? That was even less likely. And if I discounted the idea of a friend or a relative, then at her death Alessia was severed from her family without obvious means of support. That indicated only one thing: recourse to the workhouse. The National Archives provided me with the name of the local institution, the Raine Street Workhouse. My stomach was twisting itself into the severest of knots. I knew I was on the brink of discovering something huge, but also something very distressing.

Sure enough the Admission Register for Raine Street recorded that on 8 May, 1851, an Alessia Renville was admitted to the workhouse. I sat and stared at the screen for some time, but then clicked through to the Discharge Book. Here there were lists of all the inmates who had left the institution and precise details of where they were bound.

Alessia was bound for the graveyard: the brutal black strokes of a pen confirmed she had died on the ninth of May. Just one day after being admitted. I hadn't known this woman, yet her fate resonated with me and not just from a common humanity. I felt that in some way she and I belonged together. My heart was leaden as I moved on to

Raine Street's Register of Deaths and learned that Alessia had died at twenty-eight years old from an inflammation of the lungs.

I jumped up from the chair, unable to sit still any longer, and paced around the small living room. It was a totally unexpected find, and I didn't know whether to be glad or appalled at what I had discovered. From a financial perspective, it could be gold dust. I would have no trouble now in selling the new article and I could even bargain for an increased fee. But this was a woman's life, a life that had been torn to shreds by something appalling that I had yet to uncover. Should I go on?

There was only one answer, and when I felt calmer, I went back to the Raine Street Admissions Register and studied Alessia's entry once more. Under the address column were the ominous words: 'No fixed abode.' So she had been homeless, living on the street at the time she was admitted. She must already have been ill when she passed through the workhouse doors, perhaps taken there because she had been found collapsed, unconscious even. What could have occurred to transform this woman's fortunes so dramatically and so tragically?

I needed to share the immensity of what I'd found and knew who to tell. I picked up the phone and called Paolo. It took him a while to answer, and before he spoke I could hear muffled bangs filling the air.

'Sorry for the noise,' he said cheerfully. 'We are moving stuff.'

'I can hear, but can you talk? I wouldn't have called only—'

'Yes, yes.' He had sensed my tension. 'You have found out more?'

I told him then, everything I had discovered, and there

was a long silence. 'That is so sad,' he said eventually. 'How bad you must feel.'

It was the response I needed. I did feel bad —not elated as I'd thought, but dreadfully, dreadfully sad.

A loud crash sounded down the phone line, but Paolo ignored it. 'Will you go on? You could look at a later census, I suppose, see what happened to the family. Maybe there would be a clue as to why this poor lady died.'

'I could, but I'm not sure I should. I can't bring myself to write about it.'

'I understand. But maybe you need to know. For yourself, Grace.'

I was surprised at how accurately he had read my mind. 'You may be right. And sorry again for letting you down over the gallery visit.'

'There will be others — you won't escape!'

I went back to the laptop and pulled up the 1871 census. It was unlikely to tell me what had happened twenty years before, but as Paolo said it could hold a clue to the family dynamics that had led to Alessia's dreadful demise. But when I got to it, the later census contained no Renvilles living at Wisteria Lodge. All three had vanished into the ether. Who was living there now?

I logged into the Land Registry in the hope of tracing a sale. It was always going to be a long shot and cost me money to search, but I was so taken by the chase that I forgot for the moment I was penniless. I knew the Land Registry had been set up in the 1860s, but had been little used at the time since there was no compulsion to register sales of property. I was in luck, though. Wisteria Lodge was there, its first registration under the name of Benjamin Salter, solicitor. He had purchased the property in May 1866 for what seemed a suspiciously low sum.

Another mystery, another link in what seemed to be a chain of disaster. My gut instinct told me that Lucas Royde had been at the very beginning of that chain, that he had somehow been involved in Alessia's untimely death. But it wasn't Royde that bothered me; it was Alessia. I couldn't get her fate out of my mind, and I was desperate to talk about her. Nick would be home soon and I would tell him everything I'd discovered.

That evening he was back later than usual and, by the time I heard his key, I was wound into a tight little spring.

'Guess what?' I bounced out of my seat as he came through the door.

He sauntered into the room, loosening his tie as he walked. 'No idea, but let me take my jacket off first. I've a deal to tell you, too.'

His words distracted me for a moment. 'What is it? Tell me.'

I wanted to get whatever he had to say out of the way before I hurled my thunderbolt. This evening I wanted him to concentrate on Alessia and nothing else.

'Shall I shoot first then?'

'Yes. Quickly though.' I was still fizzing, longing to share my discoveries.

'Here goes then. Hughie — my boss — saw this great little flat just off Hampstead High Street and told me about it. It's currently for rent, but it could be for sale later if we got a joint mortgage. That's not impossible if…'

'If I get a permanent job,' I finished for him.

'That's right.' He looked gratified.

'No.'

'What do you mean, no?'

'I don't want to live in Hampstead. I've already done that.'

'How does that affect anything? It's a nice area. You must have liked it well enough to stay all those years.'

'I did, but I don't want to go back.'

'Because of Oliver? The flat is nowhere near Lyndhurst Villas and I doubt you'd ever bump into him.'

'Oliver is not the problem — I've already bumped into him.'

'You never told me.' It was his turn to be distracted.

'It wasn't important.'

'It might be.' His face was flushed with suspicion. 'Is that what it is? You've started up with Oliver again and you don't want to be living too close.'

'Don't be ridiculous, Nick. If that were the case, living around the corner would be ideal.'

I walked across the room and held out my hands. He took them in a limp hold. 'Oliver means nothing to me any longer. It was a friendly meeting, that's all. I just don't want to go to Hampstead. It would be like travelling backwards. I know it wouldn't be right for me, for us.' He looked unconvinced.

'In any case,' I added with what I hoped would be a clincher, 'Hampstead is far too expensive.'

He pulled away from me quite roughly. 'It's perfectly manageable with two incomes,' he said tersely. 'If you get a job — I don't mean the freelance frippery, but a proper job — we could easily afford a decent place there.'

I was now the one to feel nettled. 'Freelancing was good enough for you up to a few months ago.'

'But it isn't now. And it shouldn't be for you either. You're worth a great deal more. We could make a real success, Grace.'

I suppose I could have done the clichéd thing and asked him to define success, but his blue eyes were wistful. He must have felt he was losing me as surely as I was losing him.

'I simply don't want to live in Hampstead,' I said wearily.

'You're making a mistake. It's a great flat.'

'Only according to Hughie.'

'But he's right. It is a great flat, I've seen it.'

I gaped. 'You've been to see it?'

'Tonight, that's why I'm back late.'

I felt betrayed that he hadn't discussed it first. At the very least he could have rung and let me know his plans. I dug my heels in ever deeper.

'Great little flat or not, I'm not moving there.'

'I've taken it.'

'What!'

'I've signed a year's lease and given notice on this flat. So unless you want to find a place of your own, you better think about moving — to Hampstead,' he added unnecessarily.

It was Oliver all over again: my life governed by someone else's decisions. I felt the glass wall sliding back into place. Over the last few months I had watched Nick change, or rather revert to an older self. I had been hoping that something of the man I'd first met might survive, but I could see now that I'd been naïve. The job at *Art Matters* had brought with it a huge injection of confidence and encouraged his deepest roots to flourish. He was once more a Heysham, warm and amiable, but needing to be in full control, to order life exactly as he directed.

What would happen if I told him about the baby? Not if, when, I scolded myself. He had to know, but I was certain it would provoke trouble. I guessed he would insist we did what he'd term the right thing. Except it would be the wrong thing — for both of us.

There was a tense silence and then he said brightly, 'Well, what's *your* news?'

'Nothing much,' I said. 'It's nothing much.'

I heard my voice, dull as a December dusk. I felt numb, washed out. I had no desire to confide my discoveries, no heart left to tell him. He would trample over Alessia's death without a second thought. And no one must trample on her.

My discovery could make my name in Victorian research, but I decided it wouldn't. I'd have to make my name in other ways. I would go on digging — I needed to know what lay buried deep beneath those bald statistics — but whatever my findings, they would remain mine alone. I wouldn't publish, wouldn't broadcast my news to the world. It would feel too much like a betrayal. Alessia and her tragedy would stay my secret.

# Chapter Thirty-Four

*London, mid-April 1851*

A loud scratching on his door roused Lucas from a fitful sleep. It was barely light and the noise reverberated through the otherwise silent building. He wondered blearily if it was one of his fellow lodgers in need of help, though it seemed unlikely. It must be his landlady, but why she should have mounted three flights of stairs to wake him so early, he had no idea. Quickly he pulled on trousers and shirt and stumbled to the door.

A slight figure, shivering in agitation, stood on the threshold. Her voice when she spoke barely made a whisper. 'You must help me, Lucas. He has said we are to move.'

Lucas was shocked into full wakefulness. Alessia stood in the doorway, her usually neat curls in disarray and her dress half covered by a shawl falling from her shoulders and trailing untidily along the ground. But the shawl did nothing to disguise the richness of her gown nor the glitter of her jewellery. What had his landlady thought when she opened the front door to this visitor? Here he was, a single man, entertaining a woman alone in his private chamber when the rest of the world was barely awake. And not just any woman, but one who came with wealth attached and a wedding ring on her finger. He would be lucky not to be thrown instantly onto the street.

'Help me, Lucas,' she repeated, her voice choking on a sob, and her hands twisting and turning as though they had a life of their own.

He reached out and grasped her by the arm, pulling her into the room and shutting the door with an emphatic click. If Mrs Stonehouse was listening below, and he was sure she was, he had probably sealed his fate, but he could not leave Alessia to stand in the open doorway. In her distress she was likely to blurt out sentiments that would serve only to incriminate them further.

He went to the window and pulled back the fading curtain. In the bleak light of early day he saw that her beautiful face was ravaged. A few steps and he was across the room and had folded her into his arms, one hand stroking her cheek, his lips brushing lightly against her hair.

'Alessia, my darling, calm yourself.'

The gentle words and his slow, rhythmic caresses had their effect. Her breathing steadied and she gained control over her trembling limbs. He led her to the one chair he possessed and kneeled beside her. He had no time to feel ashamed of his meagre dwelling.

'Now tell me — slowly,' he commanded, his arms still wrapped around her. 'Tell me just what has occurred to bring you here.'

'Edward has said we are to move,' she stuttered, and he felt her body once more begin to shake.

'You are to move? But where?'

'He has not said, but I know in my heart it will be a place

far distant.'

'And you are all to go, the whole family?'

'My daughters and I are to leave Prospect Place first. I think that Edward plans to join us later.'

'Had you no idea what was towards?' That was foolish. If she had suspected anything amiss, he would have been the first to know.

'He has been very cold towards me, colder than usual. But I had no inkling of what he intended. Last night he came home from the office very late and summoned me from my bed to tell me.'

'Why would he do this?' Lucas was still trying to grapple with the enormity of the news. 'Why would he suddenly wish to remove from Prospect Place? It is a most convenient location. Surely he cannot mean to go far, his business is in London.'

'I think he intends to stay most of the week in the City and join us when he is not working.'

Lucas rose from his knees and strode up and down the small room. 'It makes no sense, Alessia.'

'It does if he wishes to live at a distance from me.'

'Have you quarrelled?'

'We never quarrel. But I am accused of becoming too independent, too opinionated. He blames the Renville pavilion and says it was a mistake to involve me, and now I should think only of being a wife and mother.'

'You could do that as easily at Prospect Place. It hardly explains his sudden desire for you to leave town.'

He stopped walking and stood close to her, looking down at her bent head. There was something she hadn't said, he was sure. Then it came.

'I fear he suspects.'

Lucas felt his face tighten. 'But how is it possible? We have been circumspect — for the most part,' he added uneasily. He was remembering the risks his passion had sometimes pushed them to.

She looked up at him, her dark eyes misty with tears. 'I am almost sure I was seen at Vauxhall. Do you remember that when we met outside the Gardens, I felt there was someone watching me? Maybe that someone has talked.'

'But you can't be *certain* there was anyone.' He was desperate for her assumption to be untrue. 'Your husband has not confronted you with it?'

'No. He has not mentioned the matter directly.'

Lucas seized on this scrap and began again to pace the room. 'So he may not suspect you of anything other than neglecting your wifely duties.'

'Why else would he want me to go away? His complaint that I have too independent a mind is a pretence. What Edward really suspects is that I have a lover.'

She got up from the chair and moved towards him, stopping him from his constant pacing. She took hold of one of the wide sleeves of the loose white shirt he wore and gripped it hard. 'I know it is so, Lucas.'

Then she turned away, and her voice was once again breaking. 'How am I to face him, knowing he believes I have been unfaithful? I have been a bad wife, a disloyal wife, when he has been as good a husband as he is able.'

'He has not loved you and you should feel no guilt for the past,' he said firmly. 'Instead you must think of the future and that looks bright, my darling.'

She let go of his hands. 'How can that be?'

'We will be together. Whatever Renville's suspicions, they do not involve me. Every day I go to work at de Vere's and not one word has been spoken.'

'What do you mean?'

'That if your husband suspected I was your lover, I would have been immediately dismissed. But I am still there — and devising a golden future for us both.'

'I do not say he suspects *you*. But I am sure he must guess I have someone in my life who is most precious to me.'

'You have not disguised your feelings?'

She looked a little shocked as though for a moment they were talking different languages. 'When you are in love, it is difficult to pretend otherwise. Edward and I have not a close relationship, you know that, but perhaps he has sensed I have moved even further from him. Then whoever spied on me has reported their news and Edward has added things together and decided that even if there is no truth in the story, I am better away from the city.'

'And when are you to go?'

'He has not told me, but very early this morning I heard him give Martha instructions to begin packing for the girls and have all ready by the end of the week. Our departure is imminent.'

His mood plummeted. The shock of losing her so soon left him aghast, and her face told the same story. 'Lucas, my darling, what is to become of us?'

His arms were round her again, soothing, comforting. 'We will survive this. You must leave now, but wherever you go, you must get a message to me. After the Exhibition is launched, I will come for you as soon as I can. But now you must leave.'

'The first of May is still two weeks away. I cannot bear to be separated from you for so long. If we are finally to be together, why not now, at this very moment?'

When he said nothing, she renewed her plea with greater urgency. 'Can I not stay here with you? I have thought much on it and know a way of bringing my daughters. I can steal them from the house when Martha is looking away.'

His face paled. 'That is not possible, my dear.'

'We will not crowd you too badly, I promise. And very shortly you will be in a position to rent better lodgings.'

He relinquished his hold on her and his voice held an unusual severity. 'That day cannot come soon enough, but you must never come here again. The opening day of the Exhibition must come and go before we see each other.'

'But why?' It was a cry drawn from the depths and filled with pain, and he winced.

'My darling, the Renville commission can make me or break me. Think what would happen if even a hint of our story escaped! The architect who stole his sponsor's wife! It doesn't bear thinking of. I would never win another commission, for every potential client would look at me and wonder if I were about to seduce his spouse. I would be forced to leave de Vere's and the Earl of Carlyon would dismiss me from his project. And *he* is our great hope, Alessia. We must be patient.'

'Forgive me, but I cannot understand how waiting will make a difference. You will still be the architect who stole his sponsor's wife.'

'But don't you see, once the fuss over the Exhibition has died, I will no longer be the focus of attention and Renville will no longer be my sponsor. I can fade into the background, fade into the Norfolk countryside. I am likely to be working there for months and you will come with me. We can live quietly together as husband and wife and no one need know the truth. But if your husband learns of our love before the Exhibition opens, he will be intent on making an example of me. His anger will subvert discretion — and he will have a very large audience.'

'So what am I to do?' She sounded tired and frail.

'You are to go home and pretend you are content with your husband's arrangements. Go willingly wherever he decides and wait for me there. In the meantime you must not visit me — it is too dangerous. The woman who opened the door to you is my landlady and she cannot see you here again. For now, I will try to placate her with some story of a sick relative.'

'I cannot bear to say goodbye.'

Her face wore such a distraught expression that he was almost ready to throw caution out of the window and beg her to stay. Almost, but not quite. That way lay the squandering of all his talents and a penurious life for them both.

'As soon as you are able, send me news,' he said urgently.

He was ushering her to the door when an uncomfortable thought struck. 'Will your absence this morning not be noticed?'

'Edward had already left for the docks when I slipped out. He has a large shipment coming into the Port of London today. But Martha will know I have been from home. No doubt she will report it — I am convinced she spies on me.'

'I'm sure your fears are unfounded.' He hoped his voice held conviction, for Martha had seemed to him just the kind of servant who would spy. 'But you will have to think of a reason why you were from home so unseasonably early.'

'I will say I went to the pharmacist for linctus. Georgina is suffering from a cough.'

'Would you not have sent Martha?'

'No, I could not. She was busy tending the fires. It is

important that Georgina has warmth.'

He smiled at her, his blue eyes intense and loving. 'Make sure then that you return with a bottle of medicine.'

She turned to clasp his arm for the last time. 'How will I exist without you?'

'You are a strong woman, Alessia, you will come through.'

'But love has made me weak.'

He fervently hoped these last words had not reached the ears of a hovering Mrs Stonehouse and made to escort Alessia down the stairs to the front door, saying in a deliberately loud voice how grateful he was that his cousin had called and how sorry to learn of their uncle's illness.

When he returned to his room, he washed and dressed for work, hardly aware of what he was doing. The news Alessia had brought was devastating. He was not to see her for weeks, not to know the delights of loving her. The future was hazy. He had no idea what Edward Renville suspected and for all the reassurances he had given, he knew it would not be easy to arrange Alessia's departure from the family home.

Then there was the Exhibition itself. It was imperative that he appear every inch the successful and promising young architect. The Renville pavilion would display his talents to the widest audience and he had to live up to the occasion. But could he trust Alessia to do as he had asked, to pretend compliance and await his arrival? She was in a highly nervous state. What else would have brought her to his rooms at daybreak and unescorted? And a highly nervous woman was liable to do something stupid.

# Chapter Thirty-Five

At a time when a glorious future beckoned, Alessia's news was the worst he could imagine. He was certain his design for Renville would be praised, and he believed that offers of work would follow. He was near to winning a private commission with the Earl of Carlyon, and through his lordship other aristocratic patrons might beat a pathway to his door. It was all there for the taking. And yet, right at the eleventh hour, after years of study and toil, he trembled on the brink of disaster. If Renville's suspicions became certain, if he cast around for a likely culprit and remembered all the time his wife had spent with the young architect, his eyes would fix on Lucas. He must be circumspect in the extreme — at least until the Exhibition opened. Then once he knew Alessia's direction, he would contact her secretly. It was the only way out of this mess.

On the brisk walk to Great Russell Street, his mind continued troubled. The image of his lover, forlorn and broken, gave him no peace, but alongside the pain was a fear that in her distress she would say or do something to ruin all his plans. He could only hope she would master her emotions by the time she returned to Prospect Place. Anxiety had him in its grip and might have spiralled beyond control but for an urgent message that arrived within half an hour of sitting down at his desk.

'You're a real blue-eyed boy, ain't you?' Fontenoy greeted him jauntily. 'First a plum job at the Hyde Park Exhibition, now there's an earl asking for you. What have you got that I haven't, Royde? Apart from the blue eyes, I mean.'

The man had been a constant irritation since the very first day Lucas had joined the practice. This morning there was no bearing him.

'What is it, Fontenoy?'

He barked out the question and his colleague took a step back. Gingerly, he proffered a small sheet of white paper. 'A message from the Earl of Carlyon, like I said,' he mumbled.

Lucas grabbed the missive, his hand shaking just a little.

'Hey!' Fontenoy exclaimed sharply, 'Is it that important?' But he was quick to regain his own desk.

For a moment Lucas thought he had been discovered, that the earl knew of his illicit love and wanted nothing more to do with him. The message would contain his dismissal. But then he steadied himself and read.

*Dear Mr Royde*

*I know that you are not due at Southerham for some weeks, but I wonder if you would do me the kindness of making an earlier short stay. It will take only a few days of your time, and I feel the visit would prove highly beneficial for us both. Please do not go to the bother of reserving a room at the Royal as I hope you will consent to be my guest.*

*Sincerely,*
*Justin Carlyon*

Not a dismissal, but an invitation. Thank God. And to be asked to stay at Southerham Hall suggested the earl was ready to approve the chapel plans, perhaps even confirm him as sole architect. Another reason then to keep from Alessia until his fortunes were settled.

He pushed back his chair in a rapid movement and went to knock at his employer's door. 'May I speak with you, Mr de Vere?'

Daniel De Vere looked up from the drawings he was perusing. 'Of course, Royde. How can I help?'

Lucas felt encouraged. 'The Earl of Carlyon has written regarding the chapel plans.'

'Ah yes, I saw his note,' de Vere replied calmly.

'Then you will know, sir, that his lordship has requested my presence at Southerham in the very near future.'

'Indeed, yes, and I am happy for you to go. You appear to have established an excellent relationship with the earl.' His employer leaned back expansively, his thumbs puckering either side of his floral waistcoat. 'May I suggest you leave for Norfolk tomorrow and are back in the office early Monday morning?'

* * *

Returning to Red Lion Square that evening, Lucas took little time in packing a small valise for the few days he would be away. He folded the reworked chapel plans into his portfolio case and after a sparse supper decided on an early bedtime. He must wake betimes to catch the first train from Shoreditch. But once in bed, he tossed and turned into the small hours. Try as he might, Alessia invaded his mind and his body. He saw her lovely face stained by tears, her dark curls tumbling in disarray, felt her soft form cling to him as if to a rock in rapid waters. He would be there for her, he told himself. Only a few weeks and he would be there for her for the rest of her life.

The next morning was foggy and bleak, the weather alternating now between brilliant spring sunshine and the occasional return to winter. He crawled from bed in a daze and shivered awake as he washed in cold water. He must dress with care for the day ahead. An invitation to the Hall imposed constant watchfulness and Lucas needed to look his most professional.

He turned out of the square along Eagle Street and into Procter Street. At the intersection with High Holborn he was sure to find a hansom that would take him to Shoreditch and the train. He was feeling less burdened today, as though the journey out of London was already casting adrift some of his cares. He had just reached the cab stand when a ragged boy appeared at his elbow and barred his way.

'What is this?' He was puzzled, thinking the child was both too young and too weak to engage in successful robbery.

'This is for you, mister.'

The note Lucas was handed had been written on expensive vellum, but clutched in the child's grubby hand, it resembled a crumpled and soiled napkin.

'For me? Are you sure?'

'I watched yer,' the boy said staunchly. 'Yer come out the 'ouse in the Square, the one wi' the yeller door. That's what she said. Not to go up to the 'ouse but wait till yer left. She said yer'd be carrying a bag, kinda strange shape — like that 'un.' And he pointed an accusing finger at the portfolio case.

Lucas felt his heart plummet. He knew without looking that the message was from Alessia: the fine notepaper, the delicate handwriting. And what other woman would be writing to him? He unfolded the paper and saw there was no address. Was that because she had written in haste? He stood and read her letter with growing alarm.

*Lucas, my darling,*

*Martha has told of my absence yesterday morning. Despite all my protestations, Edward has refused to believe I would go myself to fetch medicine for Georgina, and so early in the day. He was very angry and accused me directly of going to meet my lover. I love you so terribly, Lucas, I could not deny it.*

*He has decided I am to leave London immediately, but that is not the worst. I am not to go to a home of my own, but to my mother-in-law in St Albans. She is to watch over me most strictly and it will be she who has full control of my daughters.*

*I have lost my children! Edward does not say so, but I know this is punishment for my wrongdoing. His mother will turn my girls against me and I will be powerless to resist. I will be a despised prisoner. It is worse than anything I could have imagined.*

Lucas broke off his reading and looked blankly into the distance. He was appalled, remembering Florence Renville all too well. After a minute, he turned his eyes reluctantly back to the letter.

*I am desperate, Lucas. I cannot go to St Albans. I know I*

*would never survive such treatment. It has broken my heart to say goodbye to my darling ones, and now I have nothing left to lose. I have left Prospect Place and taken a room in a lodging house. I have brought nothing here that does not belong to me: a few clothes, a little money and my mother's jewellery.*

*Come to me, my darling, as soon as you are able. I am depending on your great love.*

*Yours eternally*
*Alessia*

His first thought was that anguish had caused a temporary insanity. To have left her family and taken a room in a lodging house! A respectable woman did not do such a thing. But was she any longer a respectable woman? Had he turned her into something else? Contrition gnawed at him.

'You taking this cab, guv'nor?' the jarvey asked, his chin jutting pugnaciously.

'Yes, this minute,' and Lucas threw his bags into the back of the hansom. No matter how dismayed he felt, he could not stay; he had to go to Southerham. The boy had his hand out and he fished in his pocket for a small coin. Then as the driver gathered the reins together, a thought sparked.

'Can you return to the lady and speak to her privately?' There was no time to write and it seemed the boy could be trusted to act discreetly. 'Wait until she leaves her lodgings and is alone and then follow her for a distance. Only approach her when she is well away from the house. Can you do that?'

'What's innit fer me?'

'You will earn a silver sixpence.'

The boy whistled slowly. 'What am I to say, guv?'

'You are to reassure the lady I have her note, but that I must go away for a few days. And you are to give her these,' and Lucas pulled from his pocket his last two sovereigns. 'Tell her she must use this money until I return.'

The boy gave him a cheeky salute and wrapped the coins in a less than clean piece of linen. 'Right guv'nor. I'll do that.'

'Now, this minute.'

'I promise.'

He was unsure how much worth he could attach to the young boy's pledge, but he had to trust him to deliver message and money. The next moment he was in the cab and on a rapid journey to Shoreditch. He shrunk back against the stained leather swabs. Every instinct had urged him to abandon the journey and find her immediately, but reason had said otherwise and reason had won. What good would be served by such a course? The earl would be insulted and his employer angry. All his plans destroyed in one stupid action. No, this was the better way. He would seek her out immediately he returned and hope to have the very best news to tell her.

But there had been no address on the letter! His stomach clenched at the realisation. Why had he not thought to ask the boy for directions? He cursed himself — he had no means now of contacting her. He could only wait for her to write again.

# Chapter Thirty-Six

At Norwich station he was met by the earl's carriage. Its luxury soothed his nerves a little, and once the horses had been set going, he was able slowly to relax into a seat of soft velvet. He was roused from his reverie by the sound of gravel beneath the carriage wheels, and looking out of the window, he saw they had reached Southerham Hall and were sweeping up its driveway, coming to a halt at the pillared entrance. Almost immediately, the huge door of Georgian oak flew open and the butler stood on the threshold, bowing Lucas up the front steps. A footman took his hat and gloves, another footman his bag, and the housekeeper ushered him to his room. It was a large and airy chamber overlooking lawns sculpted years previously by Capability Brown. A fountain played in the middle distance and to one side a quiet river flowed. One of the casement windows was open, and he heard the water's gentle lapping close by.

A knock on the door heralded a curtseying maid. 'May I unpack, sir?'

Lucas felt the first of many discomforts. He had only a small valise with him in addition to his drawings, and the charade he would have to endure while the maid pulled out shirt and trousers, a cravat, his one change of underwear and a set of slightly dog-eared brushes, made him blench.

'That won't be necessary, er…'

'Bennett, sir.'

'Bennett. But thank you.'

And he slipped the girl a sixpence in what he hoped was an accomplished manner. He prayed he would not be called upon to dispense too many tips over the next few days. He had provided himself with all the money he had to hand, but then despatched most of it to Alessia. That at least gave him a warm feeling: it would provide her with comfortable shelter.

He looked around, imagining her here beside him. This was a most elegant house and she would revel in it. It was a natural setting for her, and for him, too. This was what he was destined for. Only manage the next few weeks and they would have their reward, to be honoured guests in an eminent household.

Dressing for dinner was a nervous business. He was forced to wear the same coat in which he had travelled, but donned a pair of newly purchased evening trousers, a stiff white shirt and an expensive white cravat of the finest lace. He blessed Marguerite for the latter.

Drinks were served in the library, and he found the earl waiting for him. 'Come in, my dear fellow.'

Carlyon exuded good nature and Lucas felt his shoulders loosen their tight grip. He realised then how tense he had been, facing an unfamiliar milieu and eager to make a good impression. The earl poured sherry from one of the several crystal decanters that sat in line atop a marquetry console.

'I am delighted you were able to honour me with your presence, Mr Royde. We have much to talk of.'

'Indeed, your lordship.'

Lucas was cautious. He was desperate for Lord Carlyon to endorse the informal agreement they had made on his previous visit, but he needed to tread warily. If the earl had changed his mind in the interim, he would be forced to reiterate his loyalty to Daniel de Vere and swiftly approve his employer's vision for the Southerham chapel. At this moment, he had no clear idea of which way the dice would fall. It was as though he was astride two horses, both blinkered, but heading in very different directions.

'I have been studying your revised plans with care,' the earl went on. 'We will go through them in detail tomorrow of course, but I wanted you to know that I accept them without reservation. In fact, I am delighted with them, my dear chap.'

Lucas glowed. The earl's response was better than he could have hoped.

'Yes, you have done an excellent job. The new design is exactly right for the chapel, respectful of its tradition but innovative, too — and quite beautiful.'

There was a pause while both men sipped delicately from their glasses. 'You must not mistake me, Mr Royde.' Lord Carlyon's tone was thoughtful. 'I respect Daniel de Vere enormously, but in this case I do not feel his suggestions have quite caught the ambience of Southerham.'

It was what Lucas had dreamed of hearing.


Dinner that evening was what the earl described as a cosy affair. They were only two at the table, but despite this Lucas faced a bewildering array of courses: Julienne soup, a turbot in lobster sauce and a red mullet, followed by roast quarter of lamb and Spring Chicken, then by quails and green peas and finally a Charlotte Russe and Neapolitan cakes, washed down with copious glasses of Madeira.

He ate doggedly on, allowing the earl to monopolise the conversation. His lordship liked to talk and Lucas was happy to let him. It meant a chance to think, to turn over in his mind the words of praise he had heard. He hugged them close, arranging them and rearranging them in his head, determining the way he would tell Alessia of his success. There was still the matter of signing a private contract, but by the time the port made its appearance, he had decided not to broach the subject until the morrow. Tonight he would simply relax in the knowledge that he was on his way.

* * *

The next morning he breakfasted alone. Another vast choice of dishes lay resplendent beneath the silver covers, but he satisfied what small appetite he had with a modest plate of scrambled eggs and bacon, leaving untouched the devilled kidneys and smoked haddock in pastry. Then he made his way back to the library and had barely begun a scrutiny of the floor-to-ceiling bookshelves when the earl arrived in a flurry of notes and illustrations. He seemed as keen as Lucas to discuss the intricacies of rebuilding his family chapel, and was soon heavily engaged in deciding with him the number and variety of craft workers, tradesmen and labourers to be hired.

'It seems a complex task,' the earl remarked at one point.

'It is complex,' Lucas admitted, 'but not insurmountable. It would be easier if I were not employed in London.' He smiled winningly, his blue eyes guileless.

'We talked a little, did we not, of your contract with de Vere's?'

This was the opening Lucas needed. 'In fact, your lordship, I have no precise contractual term. I joined the practice in order to learn new skills and, if I am honest, I would have to admit I have now learnt all I can.'

The earl said no more and Lucas decided he must be brave and put his cards on the table. 'Your lordship, may I speak frankly?' The earl inclined his head slightly. 'If you would be prepared to confirm me as your private architect, I would be able to give the project my full attention. I could move to lodgings locally and be on hand to supervise the entire construction.'

Lord Carlyon looked fixedly at the patterned carpet and said nothing. Lucas dreaded that he had gone too far, but he need not have worried.

'I like your proposal,' the earl said at last. 'And I would pay you well.' He mentioned a fee that made Lucas feel faint. 'But I *am* concerned about de Vere. He's a good man, and I wouldn't wish to poach his best employee.'

'He is the best.' Lucas hoped his enthusiasm was sufficiently hearty. 'But I know Mr de Vere would not wish to stand in the way of my advancement. And to work exclusively for your lordship would represent a huge step forward for me.'

'It would be courteous to discuss your change of employment with Mr de Vere as soon as possible.'

'I agree, your lordship, but it might be helpful if we were to postpone our discussion until after the first of May. Mr de Vere needs my aid in seeing through a contract with a difficult client, and I have promised him my fullest support.'

'Your consideration does you credit, Mr Royde.' Lucas had the grace to colour. 'You can be sure I will not contact Mr de Vere until the date has passed. I think I shall go up to London and take the fellow out to luncheon. Easier, you know, to break bad news when you are eating well.'

* * *

Dinner that evening followed much the same pattern as the previous day's, with the exception of an additional guest and even more food. The earl had invited one of his closest neighbours, a Mr Fennimore, to eat with them. Lucas let the two friends talk together but listened with attention. It seemed that Francis Fennimore, though lacking a title, was extremely wealthy, wealthier even than Lord Carlyon. He had recently bought a semi-derelict mansion ten miles the other side of Norwich with the idea of creating a home for his two unmarried sisters. Since he inherited Dereham Abbey on his father's death, he had been forced to house the unhappy women. His wife found their presence a constant irritation and Mr Fennimore himself had grown tired of the continual disputes.

'Justin tells me you have genius in your fingers, Mr Royde.' Lucas modestly denied all claim to genius. 'Do you think an Elizabethan manor house near to collapse would be too daunting a commission for you to undertake?'

'It sounds exciting rather than daunting, Mr Fennimore.'

'In that case, I wonder if you'd care to eat your mutton with us tomorrow. My sisters will be present, and it's them you'll have to please. You can break the ice, see how you like them and they like you. Come for luncheon, drinks at twelve, and in the afternoon my carriage will take us to the property. You'll need to see it before you decide.'

'I can't have you jumping the queue, Francis,' the earl joked. 'Your manor house must take second place to my chapel.'

'I wouldn't dream of suggesting otherwise, my dear

fellow. I've put up with the wrangling for the last five years so another will make little difference.'

Lucas retired a very happy man that night. He could hardly believe his luck that a second possible commission — and a prestigious one at that — had come so close on the heels of the first. The future was indeed golden.

He had intended leaving early Sunday morning, to be back in London by the afternoon, and able to set out in search of Alessia immediately. He was sure that by now she would have written again, only this time giving her address. But delaying his departure for a few hours had to be worthwhile, particularly if Mr Fennimore paid as well as the earl. And why would he not? He was a very rich man; he might even pay better. Warmed by this wondrous vision, Lucas laid his tired head on the goose down pillow and slept the sleep of the contented.

\* \* \*

By the time he boarded his train at Norwich station late on Sunday evening, he was ecstatic. The manor house had proved to be less derelict than his host had forecast, and he could already visualise several solutions for restoring it to a modern and comfortable home without destroying its history. The Misses Fennimore had been amenable, more than amenable. They had taken one look at his slim figure and blue eyes and decided that whatever he said must be right.

Despite his tiredness, the thought of what he had accomplished kept his spirits soaring. There was so much to tell Alessia, and once he reached Red Lion Square he bounded up the stairs two at a time to his small attic room expecting to find her message. But there was none. Why had she not written?

He supposed her note might have been delivered into the hands of Mrs Stonehouse, but quailed at the thought of confronting his landlady. In any case, it was too late to rouse her. He would knock at her door early tomorrow morning before he set off for Great Russell Street. It meant another delay, but Alessia would not worry unduly, he was sure — he had not mentioned the exact day he intended to return — and in the meantime, she was safe and well and living agreeably on the money he had sent.

* * *

Before eight o'clock the next morning, he was knocking at the downstairs apartment.

'Ah, Mr Royde.' His landlady, arms folded, looked him up and down. 'I was wishful to speak to you.'

'How can I help, Mrs Stonehouse?' He hoped his voice did not sound as nervous as he felt.

'You came in very late last night and banged the front door,' she responded accusingly. 'It startled me awake. If you are to continue as my lodger, you will need to show a great deal more consideration.'

Relief pulsed through him. He was not after all to be interrogated over his unwelcome visitor. He was ready to grovel.

'Please accept my apologies, Mrs Stonehouse. I have been away on business and was unable to catch an earlier train from Norwich last night. I am unlikely to return so late again, but if it should happen, I will be sure to close the door more carefully and remove my shoes in the hallway.'

She gave an impatient snort, and he forced himself to annoy her further by asking after a possible message.

'No messages, Mr Royde. Were you expecting one?' She peered intently at him, suspicion writ large across her face.

'My employer thought he might need to contact me last night,' he lied fluently, 'but I was detained in Norfolk and am anxious there has been no problem.' Another impatient snort, and the door closed on him.

He set off for de Vere's feeling perplexed. He longed to tell Alessia his good news and thought it strange she had not again tried to contact him. Perhaps his warning to stay far from his lodgings had hit home and she was acting with extreme discretion. She was a blessed creature.

There would be a message from her soon, he was sure, and in the meantime he would look for new lodgings away from Red Lion Square. He could see now that it would be some weeks before he could make the move to Norfolk, and he could not bear to be away from her a day longer than necessary. He would take lodgings in a false name, making certain there was no way of tracing his real self, and as soon as the Exhibition was open, he and Alessia could dissolve into London's anonymous millions. Weeks later, they would surface in Norfolk, to all intents and purposes a properly married couple.

At Great Russell Street, Fontenoy was as annoying as ever. 'How did your country weekend go, Royde? Make another conquest?'

The teasing slid harmlessly away. He felt as though he was shrugging off a skin he had outgrown. Soon he would be saying goodbye to Fontenoy, the cramped desk, the mindless office routine. He would be his own man and a well-paid one at that.

'It went well,' he said cheerfully. 'Conquests aplenty, but not the kind you have in mind,' and despite all his colleague's efforts to probe, he refused to elaborate further. The last thing he wanted was to jeopardise his meticulously laid plans by making them public too soon.

The week ticked by and still there was no message from Alessia. In a few days, he found lodgings some distance away in Westminster where neither of them was known and hoped she would approve. He felt slightly aggrieved that she had made no attempt to get a note to him, but in the depths of his heart he had to acknowledge there was relief, too. If Alessia had come to his lodgings again or even to de Vere's... His face paled at the thought.

No, it was better to maintain this distance. There were moments when her continued silence made him uneasy and he considered whether he should set out to find her, but in the end he decided against such a search. His questioning would arouse unwelcome curiosity and that was the last thing he wanted. There was just one week left before the opening ceremony of the Great Exhibition and nothing must overshadow his day of triumph.

# Chapter Thirty-Seven

*London, 1 May 1851*

Lucas was awake before dawn. It was not a day to sleep. This morning the great Exhibition Hall, along with its hundred thousand exhibits and seventeen thousand exhibitors, would be formally opened by Her Majesty Queen Victoria. He felt a heady mix of expectancy and apprehension. The spectacle would be amazing, a once-in-a-lifetime experience. He would be helping to make history, but building his own future, too.

His exhilaration, though, was as much that of a lover's as an architect, convinced that today, at last, he would see Alessia. He had received no message still and been plagued by contrary emotions, at first imagining that discretion was rendering her absent, but then finding himself a prey to doubt. She was a woman in love, passionately in love. Was it likely that, free from the tyranny of her marriage, she would not have found a way to meet? He could not think why she had remained silent and shocking possibilities began to chase themselves through his mind.

But then reason took over. There was a simple explanation. It was obvious — she had returned to Wisteria Lodge. At the moment she wrote to him, he was sure she had not found lodgings; there had been no address on the letter. And when the boy returned with money for her expenses, the enormity of what she was proposing must have struck home, and she had turned back to her family. Her letter had said she had left her darlings, but Lucas was certain she would never, ever abandon her daughters. Not when the moment came.

Instead she had decided to follow his advice and appear willing to agree her husband's arrangements, even to the extent of braving St Albans under the gimlet eye of her mother-in-law. She would know that Lucas would come to her rescue. But if she had not yet left to live with the formidable Florence and was still at Prospect Place — and he was convinced this must be the reason for her silence — she would accompany Edward Renville to this morning's opening ceremony. And he would see her at last.

The Exhibition Hall was not open to the general public until nine o'clock, but Lucas intended to be there well before eight. It was important he ensure the Renville pavilion was perfect, and he was hopeful of reserving a good vantage point for himself from which to view the opening ceremony.

Already, as he walked from Holborn towards Hyde Park, the streets were filling. He could see that within the hour every square inch of pavement and grass would be jammed to capacity with visitors from all over the country and abroad. The streets were awash with different languages and different skins. The nearer he drew to Hyde Park, the denser the crowd grew. Many souvenir stalls and refreshment booths had set up business and were already attracting custom.

Crossing Park Lane to the newly constructed Prince of Wales Gate, he glanced down the road in the direction of Buckingham Palace. Guards lined the route the Queen would take later that morning, ready to protect her should the crowds get out of hand. Always the fear of riots, he thought. But the crowd was good-natured, laughing with excitement, occasionally jostling each other, and making light of any discomfort. He walked quickly across the park towards the immense building that filled its southwest corner. Flags on the roof flared in the stiff breeze, and as he drew nearer a shaft of sunlight sent the crystal dancing like shifting diamonds caught in candle flame.

He walked on, hundreds of people on either side of him spread across the grassy slopes. Despite the overnight rain they had kept vigil, sleeping in the park to ensure their place from which to view the Queen. Many of them had brought picnics and were unconcernedly eating breakfast as a regimental band tuned up nearby, their uniforms a splash of vermillion against the brilliant green.

Lucas joined the queue of those waiting to be admitted to the Exhibition Hall ahead of the public opening: not only exhibitors, but members of their families, government officials with their minions, and those charged with the overseeing of the building. Anyone, in fact, who could lay the slightest claim to be there was queuing for admission at the stroke of eight.

Once inside, he saw that in the weeks since he last visited thousands of plants — banks of colourful azaleas — had been positioned along the nave while above large sheets of canvas had been placed over the glass roof to avoid glare and overheating. The curved transept stretching between north and south entrances had been left uncovered, creating the effect of a broad rectangle of sunlight driven through the middle of the building. In turn, the sun's rays hit the crystal fountain and beamed its reflections into every corner.

There was no sign of Edward Renville and no sign of his wife. Now that he was in the building he and Alessia had known so well, her absence made him curiously disinclined to make his way to their pavilion. It would seem wrong, worthless without her. Instead he wandered idly along the nave looking at the various stalls that had sprung up on either side.

He stopped at a large souvenir shop that boasted a stack of printed engravings of Joseph Paxton and the Exhibition Hall. There were sheets of piano music featuring twelve different Crystal Palace Polkas, rows of mugs adorned with the portrait of Prince Albert, and tiers of sweet tins and boxes of soap. A Post Office had been set up nearby to allow visitors to send letters or telegrams postmarked from the Great Exhibition. And the small restaurant where Alessia and he had drunk tea together had vanished, replaced by a vast cordoned area large enough to feed the thousands that would attend that day.

Eventually he walked back along the nave and up the staircase that he and his lover had used so many times. By now it was nine o'clock and the public had begun trickling through the turnstiles. The upper gallery was still empty except for exhibitors and for a moment he paused at the head of the stairs, looking down on the hive of people below, the mass of men's hats and women's bonnets swarming like bees. Tickets for the opening day were prohibitively expensive and only likely to attract the upper classes, but despite that a slow-moving mass of humanity was already winding its way around the ground-floor exhibits, moving from stand to stand with a determined seriousness. Here and there, where a display was proving particularly popular, a bubble of people bulged into the nave.

He was finally at the Renville pavilion and looked around the display space with attention. Nothing was out of place; it was perfect. Emptily perfect. Not a trace of their love remained. And still there was no sight of her. A cough sounded behind him and he whirled around. Not Alessia, but Mr Dearlove, whom he had last seen the day he had collected materials from the Renville warehouse. The day he had first kissed her.

'Mr Royde, isn't it?' Mr Dearlove nodded in his direction and removed his hat, which he placed methodically beneath a love seat. It was a sacrilege Lucas had to ignore.

'Mr Dearlove,' he said in as warm a voice as he could manage. 'I am delighted to see you again. I imagine you are here to help customers choose their fabric.'

Mr Dearlove nodded again, but said no more. He was a man who rationed his words, his volubility saved for the silks he loved. People had now begun to drift into the space through the veils of jewelled gauze, and Lucas forced himself to wear a welcoming smile. Over the next few hours he seemed to do nothing but talk; explaining, describing, answering questions, many of them foolish. One excellent opportunity presented itself, a manufacturer entranced by the Italian tiles that were Lucas's own. If he could interest another half dozen such businessmen, the day would surely be worthwhile. But not without Alessia, a voice in his head whispered distractedly.

The opening ceremony was to take place at noon, and to be sure of a seat he made for the entrance a good thirty minutes beforehand. Here a space had been cleared for the Queen's dais and an auditorium erected for the musicians and choirs. As Lucas retraced his steps towards the central staircase, a heavy shower buffeted the glass walls with a sudden violence that sent people in the park scurrying for cover. It seemed to him that it signalled the end of the morning's bright promise. He shivered but kept walking.

When he reached the rows of red velvet, he saw that most of the chairs had already been taken and was forced to squeeze past a number of stout matrons to secure one of the last seats. Then he wished he had not. Sitting elbow-to-elbow and jammed between two majestic females, he felt stifled. Minutes passed and his frustration mounted. He was unable to see the comings and goings taking place around him and, though he tried craning his neck at an extreme angle, he could not discover whether or not Renville and his wife had joined the gathering.

Guns firing in the distance and deafening cheers nearer to hand heralded the arrival of the royal party. Another stray beam of sunshine lit the entire hall as a diminutive figure alighted from her carriage and made a stately progress towards the assembled throng. Everyone stood and the National Anthem boomed. The Queen was resplendent in pink silk, embroidered with silver and studded with diamonds, and with a matching headdress of diamonds and feathers in the shape of a crown.

Once the royal party had been accommodated, the audience resumed their seats and Prince Albert took his place at the front of the dais. In a voice that lay bare his German ancestry, he read the formal address, setting out the purposes of the Exhibition and listing a mystifying array of statistics that had attended the planning and construction of the Crystal Palace.

When he sat down, the Queen rose to reply briefly with praise for the splendid spectacle they were enjoying. A special prayer for the occasion was offered by the Archbishop of Canterbury, and the massed choirs of St Paul's, Westminster and St George's, Windsor, sang a rousing version of the *Hallelujah Chorus*.

Surely that must be the finale, Lucas thought, but it was merely a pause in the official programme. Everyone remained just where they were while the royal party took a small tour of the Exhibition Hall, first to the north side and then along the southerly stands, before returning to the centre. The tour took no more than thirty minutes but trapped as he was, it seemed a prison sentence. When after half an hour the Queen once more mounted her specially prepared dais and declared the Exhibition opened, his sigh of relief was audible.

A flourish of trumpets, a mass cheering and a waving of handkerchiefs, then another rousing chorus of the National Anthem, and the Queen and her entourage were on their way back to Buckingham Palace. The semicircular clock that dominated the entrance with its stately presence showed the hour as just past one.

As soon as he was able to extricate himself, Lucas hurried back to the Renville display and was greeted by the thin, clipped voice he had come to hate.

'Ah, there you are, Royde. At last! I imagined — evidently wrongly — that you would have thought it proper to remain in the pavilion.'

It was Edward Renville, alone. Which meant that Alessia must even now be sitting in Florence Renville's drawing room.

'I have been here since eight o'clock this morning, Mr Renville. I left only to see and hear the Queen.' He wondered why he bothered to reply. He had no need to excuse himself and this arrogant man would in any case accept no excuse.

Renville tugged at the short bristles of his moustache. 'Now you *are* here, you can be useful. There are several people anxious to discuss with you the process of design, though I am far from understanding why.'

'It could be they have an interest in architecture.' Somehow Lucas managed to keep a measured tone.

The afternoon wore on, Edward Renville immediately assuming charge and quick to demote Dearlove and Lucas to menial status. He was there to meet his public while they were there to answer the questions he chose not to. Visitors were greeted with what Lucas scorned as false bonhomie, but Renville's manufactured smiles were accepted happily enough by an undiscerning audience. More and more people came to view. News of the pavilion's beauty and its daring design had by some mysterious process passed through the building, and by late afternoon there was little room to move and the crowd was spilling out into the passage beyond.

Lucas was exhilarated. Renville's deliberate discourtesy was as nothing. This was his design and clearly a success. He had never doubted it, but he hugged to himself the knowledge that his instincts had not lied.

Several architects from eminent London practices paused to congratulate him and discuss his work at length. He was conscious of Renville's scowl at the attention he was receiving, but he felt elated. Elated that at last his hard work and his mother's sacrifice were to be rewarded. And this was real reward, definite reward, not plans in formation or dreams in the sky, but actual offers of commissions. This was his moment.

Then he saw her. More the shadow of a movement than a flesh-and-blood form. From behind one of the slender marble pillars a flash of blue dress, the very same she had worn when first they had met. But now it carried the grime of the streets on its hem and hung limply from newly thin shoulders. The figure hovered on the very edges of the pavilion and he looked again, hardly able to believe what he saw. She was transformed: gaunt, bedraggled, starved even. Her face had a pallor that spoke illness and in her hand she clutched a white handkerchief that was ominously stained.

She was ill! My God, what had happened? He remained rooted to the floor, unable to move or make a sound. What had happened? What had happened? The cruel refrain beat ceaselessly through every fibre of his body. Her eyes were staring straight into his, their brown depths huge in the ravaged face. The message was clear: come to me.

He wanted to run to her side, to take hold of her, comfort her, kiss her, keep her safe. But at that moment Renville turned and she disappeared from view. He should run after her, but he could not. Her husband stood feet away. The pavilion was full. Too many people to witness a scandal in the making. The end of a career that was only just beginning.

He felt Renville looking at him. There was an odd light in the man's eyes, or was that Lucas's tortured imagination? It would hardly be surprising if the expression were odd. He must look strange himself, wild eyed and distraught. Had Edward Renville seen the slight figure half-hidden behind gauze and pillars? Had he seen his wife? And if so, had he guessed that Lucas was her lover? He could not be sure. Renville did not speak, but turned away once more to direct an excitable woman impatient to import Venetian silk towards Dearlove's expert advice.

Lucas looked back at the pillar, but there was nothing. She had gone, and he knew not where. Agonising minutes followed, one after another, Renville close by and smiling benignly at visitors, Dearlove advising on the manufacture of silk and himself mechanically answering the endless, endless questions on the dream design that had once been the pinnacle of his world. At length, his ordeal was over.

In a pause between visitors, Renville turned again towards him. 'I shall be leaving now, Royde.' His face was expressionless. 'I trust you will continue the good work. And you, too, Dearlove.'

He waved a hand vaguely in the direction of his assistant and strode out into the passageway without a second glance. Lucas gave him several minutes to melt into the crowd and then followed. He pelted down the staircase, searching to his left and right along the ground-floor nave. Then out into the park. He wandered, almost crazed, among the picnicking families, but there was no sign of her. She had vanished, dissolved into the crowds as though she was no more than the wraith she resembled.

# Chapter Thirty-Eight

He walked slowly back towards the Prince of Wales Gate. The frenzy was abating and he knew in his heart that he would not find her here. She had come to their trysting place, come to find him, and he had denied her. His love had been tested and he had failed. But what had happened since he bade her farewell that early morning two weeks ago, and why if she were in such distress had she sent no message? He felt a growing anger towards her, but he knew that it was anger deflected.

Even greater crowds had gathered in the time since he had walked to the Exhibition so full of hope. That had been in another life. Black columns of pedestrians swarmed the pavements and a continuous stream of buses and cabs swept the roads clear. There were people atop roofs and walls, small boys up trees and gas standards. The population had climbed wherever they might to obtain a good view of the royal procession and the glittering glass palace in the distance.

As he began the long walk back to Holborn, he tried to bring his mind under control, to focus on what he must do to find Alessia. She was not staying at the house in St Albans; she was not living at Wisteria Lodge.

But someone there might know something. If he could garner only a small clue, it might lead him to her. He would call and if he were lucky, the friendly maid — Hetty was her name — might help him. Even if it was Martha who opened the door, it was possible he could bribe her to tell him what she knew. He still had a few coins in his pocket and there was one more sovereign secreted beneath the floorboard in his room, destined only to be used in grave emergency. There could be nothing graver than this; he would need the money if he were to search for his love and find her. And he would, he was resolute.

In half an hour he turned the corner of Prospect Place, his breathing erratic and his heart pulsing uncomfortably. This visit was a desperate throw, but it was all he had. Once on the street, he slowed his pace and almost dawdled past the row of gracious Georgian buildings, trying to decide his best approach. He must appear unconcerned, not allow a hint of panic to escape. He would enquire casually after the lady of the house, express a little surprise that she had not attended the ceremony today. And hope against hope there would be a word spoken that would hurry him to her side.

He stood outside Wisteria Lodge and looked up at its windows. They were blank. The house had a newly mournful air as though it were only just getting used to a bereavement. A symbolic bereavement. Blinds were drawn in every room and the door knocker had been taken down. Wisteria Lodge was no longer a home. So where were the daughters? Where was Renville himself living? They had shut up house and scattered to the winds. There was no help for him here.

Tears of frustration stung his eyes. Why had she not waited for him in the Exhibition Hall? If she had been frightened by seeing her husband so close, she could have concealed herself nearby. It would not have been difficult among such a very large crowd. She must know he had understood the message in her eyes; she must know he would come to her. Why then had she not waited, but left him flailing? He trudged heavily back to Red Lion Square and once in his room, flung himself on the bed and wept. This time it was not tears of frustration, but long heaving sobs that shook his frame in a violent assault.

When his emotion was spent, he sat up, dull-eyed. Furious, too, that he had allowed himself to give way to pointless tears. He should be out there, searching every road, every alley, every courtyard, in Holborn and beyond, to find her. Roused to action at last, he lifted the loose floorboard beneath his bed and retrieved his last remaining sovereign. He had reached the door when the first heavy drops of rain began to fall on the skylight above. Clouds, the colour of polished granite, threatened overhead, and he looked around for an umbrella he rarely used. He would need it, for this was likely to be a very long night. He would not rest until he found her.

His umbrella was slumped by the door where he had thrown it weeks before, and as he picked it up, he dislodged the fraying doormat, preventing the door from opening more than a few inches. He bent to replace the mat and a small speck of white caught his eye. He kneeled down and extracted a torn and dirty sliver of paper from under its coarse bristles. He felt a sickening jolt as he deciphered his name on the front of the folded sheet.

*My darling*, he read, *I have taken a room here.*

Where? he thought frantically and scanned the top of the page. There at last was an address: 2a Bluegate Fields. He did not recognise the street name.

*I have taken a room here with the small amount of money I had with me. The landlady is not a trusting woman and demands that I pay in advance. So far I have managed to do so, but now I find myself at a standstill. I have given this woman the few pieces of jewellery I possess, my mother's jewellery, and that has paid my lodging for several more days, but I have nothing left. My darling, I am sorry to ask this, but can you get money to me as soon as possible? More rent is needed and I have nothing for food or medicine. I think I am falling ill.*

*I have asked one of your fellow lodgers to place this note under your door so that I am not seen. Please help me, Lucas, I will not embarrass you or cause you scandal. Please come to me, I beg of you. Please, my darling.*

*Your love*
*Alessia*

His right hand holding the paper was trembling so much that he had to grasp it firmly with the left in order to hold it still. For a while he could manage no other action. Then he urgently scanned the letter again. The date, when had she sent this message? A whole week ago! And he had not responded. She had sent a plea for help and when he had not replied, she must have thought his love dead.

Today she had come to the Crystal Palace — at what personal cost, he agonised. She was ill, but had dragged herself there to make a last effort to reclaim him. And he had denied her again — or so it must seem. It was truly grotesque. He had done nothing but think of her, long for her, make plans for them to be together.

And the messenger he had sent to her, what had happened to him? The boy had appeared trustworthy, but he must have judged the child wrongly. Or perhaps he had been set upon by thieves and relieved of the money he carried. If so, he may have ended too battered to deliver the message, or too frightened to confess to Alessia what had happened.

Lucas stood stock-still for more minutes than he knew, bewildered by the tragedy unfolding in his life. Then spurred into movement, he shrugged himself into his coat, memorised the address at the top of the letter, and ran down the stairs. Out on the streets, the day was slowly winding to its end and crowds of happy, contented people were making their way home. For him there was no happiness, no home. He was running now to the cab stand at High Holborn. He jumped into the first hansom he could find and gave the jarvey the address.

The man looked him up and down, taking in the smart attire he had donned for this memorable day. 'Sure you want to go there, mister?'

'I do,' he said abruptly. Could the place be so bad that a seasoned driver had doubts?

It was. The lodging house was situated deep in the East End and proved to be a bleak tenement building, squatting within a warren of narrow, rotting streets. He stepped out of the cab into a monochrome world, the canyons of blackened brick forever blocking out the sun. His feet were wet from the pools of filthy water that lay everywhere, and the carcass of a dog festered on the cobbles where it had died. And this was where Alessia had been living!

He heard the hansom move off swiftly behind him. The driver was taking no chances, and seeing some of the unkempt youths lolling against the buildings opposite, Lucas could hardly blame him. He felt eyes looking at him from out of broken windows and the small urchins who had been kicking a stone between them at the end of the street had stopped and were watching.

The house to which he had been delivered was by no means the worst in the road, but the paint was peeling, tiles had fallen from the roof and the windows were cracked. At least it had a door on which to bang loudly. No one came and he knocked again. Again no one, and then as he lifted his fist to knock a third time, the door opened noisily on unoiled hinges.

'Yus.'

The woman who stood before him was short and squat. She wore a ragged smock over an even more ragged dress and neither had been washed for a very long time. Thinning hair straggled across a face scored by poverty. Her hand clasping the door was rough and none too clean.

'I believe you have a lady lodging with you,' he began in as pleasant a voice as he could muster.

'No.' She went to shut the door, but he swiftly inserted his foot against its closing.

'I think you do,' he said more insistently.

'I ain't got no female 'ere, mister. More trouble than they're worth. I only takes men.'

'But you had a lady here?'

'Oh 'er.'

At last! But his heart quailed at the knowledge that in truth this was the house in which his lover had found refuge.

'Yes, her. Where is she?'

'Females,' the woman sniffed. 'Like I say, more trouble than they're worth.'

She tried to kick his foot from the door, but he stood his ground, his anger growing into a hard, fiery ball. This was the woman Alessia had been forced to confront, the woman who insisted on payment in advance, the woman who had callously extracted precious jewellery from her sick tenant.

'Where is she?' he demanded, and his voice shook.

The slatternly woman glared at him, her fists clenched. She looked as though she would be capable of striking him. ''ow do I know?' she said, her voice coarsely belligerent.

'Are you saying that she no longer resides here?'

'Reside,' she jeered. 'No she don't. I turned 'er out.'

He paled. 'Why would you do such a thing?'

'Them's that don't pay their rent, don't stay. I ain't a bleedin' charity.'

'But the lady paid you.'

'She paid fer seven days and that's what she got.'

'But she gave you jewellery, precious jewellery, to stay longer.'

'It weren't precious to me. Couldn't sell it nowhere.'

Lucas thought quickly. It was possible the woman was telling the truth. Alessia's jewellery would be obviously foreign and perhaps cause suspicion among the local fences.

'Could you not have waited until she was able to obtain more funds?'

'Look 'ere, me fine gent, I told yer I ain't a charity. Any case she was coughin' so bad I reckoned she 'ad some disease. I don't want nuthin' catchin' in my lodgings. It's a respectable 'ouse.'

So she *was* ill. Dear God, what ailed her and how long had she been without shelter?

'When did she leave?'

'Dunno, four days ago, mebbe five.'

Five days without shelter and food and all the time he had been ignorant of her torment. He had pictured her living safe and warm on his money. He had felt pleased with himself that he had provided for her. Such arrogance, such stupid arrogance.

He became aware of the woman scowling ferociously up at him. 'Yer arsk a deal o' questions, mister, and I ain't getting paid fer any of 'em.'

'Then allow me to pay for the jewellery the lady left with you.'

For the first time in the squalid proceedings, the woman looked interested. 'I ain't got nuthin' but a neckliss. Yer can 'ave that fer a price.' And she shuffled along the dingy passage behind her to a room at the end.

The woman must have sold the other items, Lucas thought, despite claiming otherwise, but she had kept back this one piece, unwilling to let it go. When she returned she had in her hand an exquisite necklace: three delicate strands of lapis lazuli weaved sinuously into a lustrous crescent. No wonder she hadn't wanted to sell it for a few shillings.

'What do you want for it?'

The woman had a crafty look in her eye. 'Two guineas.' It was a ridiculous price for something she could only sell illegally.

'Here,' and he fished in his pocket for the last remaining sovereign. She sniffed when she saw it was far less than she had demanded, but the coin nevertheless disappeared in a trice into the smock's large pocket.

He relaxed his stance as he held the wonderful neck-lace in his hand and imagined its fragile beauty adorning Alessia's sweet neck. The woman took advantage of his inattention and slammed the door shut against his foot. He gazed at the necklace for a moment more, then wrapped it lovingly in the folds of a clean linen handkerchief and placed it in his coat's inner pocket. He would keep it close to his heart forever.

As he stepped back from the door, he became aware that the lolling youths were looking more interested. They had witnessed the woman handing him the necklace and the opportunity for robbery was ripe. He turned swiftly on his heels and made his way as quickly as he could out of the alley and into a neighbouring street, almost as narrow and, if possible, even dirtier. From there he wandered into yet another miserable alley and then to another, not knowing where he was headed, only knowing that he had to keep walking, had to keep moving.

The future, so long in the plotting, so powerfully desired, had receded to nothingness. He could see only this. This was his life: to walk every backstreet and alley, cross every filth-laden yard, scour every crevice of a forsaken city for however long it took. Alessia was here in this maze of misery, and he would find her.

# Chapter Thirty-Nine

'**W**here have you been? I've been waiting an age for you.'

Nick was at my side even before I had the door fully open. He had regained his old Tigger-type bounce and was wearing a tee shirt so well washed that its motto was impossible to decipher. I should be used by now to his mercurial nature, but seeing my original lover resurface before my eyes felt uncanny.

I made my excuses. 'I wanted a walk before supper, that's all.' The late August day had been unusually sultry and hardly walking weather, but he didn't seem to find it odd.

'Anyway, you're back now, and that's good.' He enveloped me in a bear hug. It was getting stranger by the minute. 'We've stuff to discuss.'

I didn't feel at all like discussing stuff; I felt intensely weary. I had been telling the truth about the walk, but an hour strolling by the Caledonian Canal had tired me and done nothing to help me come to a decision. Before that, a doctor's appointment had made clear that I needed to, and quickly.

Nick grabbed my hands and pushed me down none too gently into the sagging seat of an armchair. Half-filled boxes and bags, their contents a jumble, littered every inch of floor space — his attempts at packing had been predictably haphazard.

'Lucy has found this guy, a man with a van, who can move us cheaply. He does jobs for her PR company, and he'll give us a special rate as long as we can fit in with his schedule. I've fixed it for this Friday, if that's okay.'

Friday was only four days away; decision time was coming fast. It was not that I hadn't given thought to where I should go. Ever since Nick had thrown out his challenge, I had been toying with the idea of taking on the lease of Thetford Road. The flat was cheap enough to manage on a small income and work was definitely beginning to look up. I had been offered a monthly column with *Living History,* and over the weekend Jessica Hanley had phoned to discuss a possible commission that looked substantial. Just today while I had been walking by the canal, a message from Oliver had arrived to say he'd recommended me to a contact, who he was sure *would benefit from your expertise.* Text messaging and Oliver were never going to be a cosy fit.

The lease was due to run until the end of this month and I could easily request the landlord to substitute my name for Nick's, but the thought of bringing up a child in such bleak surroundings was more than depressing. I'd also thought of leaving the city entirely, somewhere near enough London to travel in for business meetings, but considerably cheaper. The South coast, I thought, a nicely rundown seaside town. But I had been feeling too sick to begin the search, so Hampstead still beckoned. The old siren of security was sounding again, even louder now I had another to think of, and when I pictured the struggle ahead, I was tempted. Nick, after all, was expecting me to move with him; why wouldn't he be when my two suitcases stood ready packed with all I possessed? I was ready to go — somewhere.

'Friday, then?'

'That's fine.' I agreed without really hearing him, my mind busy elsewhere.

'While she was on the phone, Lucy mentioned she'd been up to Gloucestershire again.' I nodded, still in dream mode. 'My father's written his memoirs. Did I mention that? He wouldn't trust the manuscript to the post, so Lucy went to collect it.'

It sounded pretty antiquated, but I went on nodding. Then I thought I should be polite. 'I hope they're keeping well.'

'Yes, they're good.'

He had sat himself down opposite me and was studying my face rather too intently. His eyes were the most extraordinary deep blue, bluer than I had ever seen them, almost navy. They were eyes that meant business.

'They asked after you, Lucy said. They really liked you, Grace.'

I couldn't imagine why — I had said so very little. Perhaps that was why.

'Good.' I tried to sound hearty in the best Heysham tradition, but it wasn't easy. I was still feeling nauseous much of the time, and Nick's odd manner was disturbing.

'The thing is…'

I had started to slip back into my dreamy state, but when he didn't go on, I jerked awake again. What on earth was the matter with him? I had never seen him so awkward.

'The thing is, the olds were hoping…'

'Yes,' I said encouragingly. I was hoping myself — that I could soon find my way to the shower. It was hot and sticky in the flat, and I'd done myself no favours with an hour's walk in the sun.

'Why don't we do the decent thing and get married?' he rushed out.

No wonder he was wearing clothes from a past life: they were to give him courage. And no wonder he'd appeared so strange. It was a startling declaration and it made my life ten times harder. I had always thought that if he knew about the baby, Nick would insist on getting married. But here he was, without obligation, offering to be a husband. Did he really love me then, love me deeply enough to make a marriage work? Or was it that he loved me sufficiently and wanted to make his parents happy?

I was bewildered. I wasn't at all sure I loved him. I wasn't at all sure I wanted to marry anyone. Yet he was offering me a way out of my difficulties: a pleasant enough flat in an attractive area, a little part-time work while he brought in the solid money, shelter and security for the small being I was carrying. It was tempting, more than tempting.

I had no idea how to answer, so I didn't. Instead I took refuge in a cowardly, 'Why?'

His blue eyes lightened. They registered surprise, as though it was the last question he'd expected to hear. 'A new start, I guess, a new page. Hughie says that he and his wife moved into their place the same week they married. It sounded good to me.'

Ah yes, Hughie, who values his freedom too much to have children. I must have grimaced without realising because Nick reached out for my hands and clasped them so tightly it hurt. 'I know you're not keen on the idea of living in Hampstead, but I'm sure that once we get there, you'll really like the flat. I wish you'd been to see it. You'd know then that moving will make a big difference to us. It's a place we can put down roots.'

'In a small London flat?'

'It's a start,' he said defensively. 'Why knock it?'

'I don't mean to, but I'm finding it difficult to picture you settling for something so conventional.'

In fact, I wasn't finding it that difficult. Not any longer. But somehow I felt the need to pretend an earlier Nick still existed. It stopped me from having to confront the truth of my situation.

He grinned, the rueful grin that had once swayed my heart. 'It happens to everyone, doesn't it? Sad but true.'

He got up and took hold of my shoulders and shook them gently. 'You, too, Grace, if you're honest. What was all the stuff with Oliver but your wanting to settle down? That didn't work out, but this will.'

I couldn't decide where he was most wrong. My life in Lyndhurst Villas hadn't been about settling down; it had been about fear, panic that I had to grasp whatever security was on offer. Putting down roots implied growth, but I had been stultified, merely clinging on with my fingertips. And now his assumption that all was going so well between us that marriage was a question he hardly need ask, made me squirm.

He got up and produced a paper carrier from behind the fridge.

'Bubbles — to celebrate! Or are you still on the wagon?'

I accepted a glass of what I knew was very expensive champagne. With luck, he would soon feel too hazy to work out just what we were supposed to be celebrating — I hadn't agreed to either a wedding or a house move. And surely one glass wouldn't hurt. It might even help dim my feeling of being a fraud. I'd begun to believe I could depend on myself alone, but Nick's offer had revealed that as illusion, a disguise for my very real lack of guts. If I'd had courage, I would have rejected his suggestion outright, but I hadn't. I hadn't even voiced my doubts. It seemed I was ready to fold without a fight.

He downed his glass in minutes and was already pouring a second when I thought it time to lob my own grenade. 'While we're talking of the future, Nick, there's something I need to tell you.'

He stopped drinking. My tone of voice must have bothered him. His eyebrows were question marks that demanded an answer, and I took a deep breath.

'I'm pregnant.' There was no way of saying it gently.

He gaped at me, his mouth slightly open and his eyes those of a startled hare. 'You can't be.'

'I am.'

'But…' No congratulations, no smile. 'We've been very careful.' He ran agitated fingers through his hair. 'I just don't see.'

'We weren't careful the first time,' I reminded him.

'Yes, but one time.'

'Once is all it takes.'

'I don't need a biology lesson.' He was almost angry.

He was not reacting as I had imagined. After that proposal, I thought he would have leapt on the news and had me half way up the aisle before the day was finished. But he was finding the idea of fatherhood difficult to accept. It turned out that he didn't accept it at all.

'It could be Oliver's.'

'It isn't.' I was as certain as I could be that Nick was the father. 'And 'it' is a baby.'

'It, the baby, could be Oliver's. You can't know for sure.'

'And how does any of this alter the fact of my pregnancy?'

'It doesn't, but…' There was that 'but' again. 'Grace, this could mess us up.'

He came and sat close to me again and took both my hands in his. His eyes were very blue again and seemingly very sincere.

'Look, we've got this chance of a new start in Hampstead — a great little flat, two good jobs — I'm sure you'll land on your feet soon. We could be living a comfortable life.'

'Without a baby?'

He looked at me gratefully. 'Babies are good at the right time,' he soothed, 'but this isn't it.'

'And when would the right time be?'

'Later, when we've got ourselves sorted. We've only known each other a matter of months after all.'

'But long enough for you to suggest we get married.'

'A wedding first, babies later — much later!' Sensible, pragmatic. You couldn't quarrel with the sentiment. But something visceral had taken hold of me, and I did.

'What you're saying is that you want me to have a termination.'

'I'm not saying I want it. It's hardly something you want. But in the circumstances…'

So many unfinished sentences were muddying my thoughts. Was he pushing for an abortion because the baby might be Oliver's, or because he was intent on moving to a new flat near a new friend and a baby would cramp his style? Or was it both? He wanted to marry — that would fit neatly with Hughie — but he didn't want more.

'I know this is difficult,' he was saying. 'I don't want to force you into something you'll regret, I really don't. It's just I would rather we have a clear run. A few years to settle as a couple before we get into the grown-up stuff.'

It was all sweetly reasonable, but reasonable was not how I felt. Protective, yes, possessive, yes. I was already a defender.

'It's for the best, Grace.' His voice was soft and persuasive. And if I didn't do what he clearly wanted? No doubt he would prove a true gentleman and shoulder the unwanted burden, but it was hardly the most encouraging way to begin a marriage.

'It's not too bad these days, I believe. You can't be far gone, and it will be over before you know it.'

When I didn't reply, he said more urgently, 'I'll go with you, I'll be there to support you.'

'I need to think,' I said, like the coward I was.

# Chapter Forty

The next morning, he was slightly the worse for wear and for the first time since starting at *Art Matters*, he stumbled into work late and heavy-eyed. Last night's momentous question didn't resurface and I wondered if he was regretting his impulsive proposal, particularly in the light of my pregnancy. I couldn't be sure. I couldn't be sure of myself either.

This morning, I felt a good deal better despite the glass of champagne. For the moment at least, I was free of the debilitating sickness I'd suffered for days. My new found health, though, was making me restless, and a compulsion to lose myself once more in the past, took hold. It seemed perverse when I was facing the most critical moment of my life, but I was plagued by unfinished business — the sale of Wisteria Lodge and the disappearance of all three of its inhabitants.

I went back again to the trusty *Holborn Mercury*. I had barely brought up the index when there was a loud knocking at the door. Lucy again? I thought I'd put to rest her attempts at finding me gainful employment. But, of all people, it was Paolo who stood on the threshold.

I blinked at him. 'What are you... how did you... ?'

'My apologies, Grace. I found your address in the library

register. And as you wouldn't come to me, I decided to come to you! I shall cook you the best meal you've eaten outside Italy.'

I hadn't noticed the basket at his feet. 'You've brought food.' I sounded dazed still. Then I began to laugh.

'Why do you laugh? I am a good cook. My porcini and spinach risotto is the very best.' He looked affronted.

'I'm sure it is, Paolo. But you haven't seen what passes for my kitchen, have you? Come and take a look at the challenge you've given yourself.'

He took a look and it was his turn to blink. But he squared his shoulders and gave a brave smile. 'It will do. And I will feed you well — you are too thin and too pale, cara.'

'Not for much longer. I'm pregnant.' I was determined to be honest.

His smile faltered a little, but he came over to me and gave me a big hug. 'That is very good news, no?'

'Maybe. I'm not entirely sure at the moment.'

'But the baby?'

'I want her,' I said. I couldn't have been more certain.

'And your…' he stumbled over what exactly to call Nick since I'd been insistent he was no more than a friend.

'Nick has asked me to marry him. Can I make you a coffee?'

'Yes, coffee would be good. And you have agreed?'

'No, not yet.'

He looked around him, taking in the bleak walls and drooping furniture. 'It is true this place is not good for a child. But if there is love…'

'That's the problem — love or rather lack of it.'

'Then don't do it, cara.' He was decisive. 'Don't marry.' He clinked his coffee mug against mine in a show of solidarity.

'So where are you going now with the research? Are you making progress still?'

'I was about to take another look at the *Mercury* when you knocked. Edward Renville was a prominent resident of Holborn and the paper took an interest in him. I thought it might help if I could trace what happened to his house.'

He nodded agreement and sat down with me at the table. I scrolled through several editions of the paper and within minutes had found the picture I was looking for in the nineteenth May edition — a solid Victorian villa with, yes, wisteria twining itself on either side of an arched door.

'A very nice house,' Paolo said.

'It is, but look at the banner above the picture: Sold by Auction. Why would a prosperous man like Renville auction his house rather than sell privately? An auction would mean public exposure, perhaps even a loss of dignity.'

'Is it possible he'd get a better price in an auction?'

'Maybe, or maybe he needed a quick sale.'

We ploughed on through the paper. There had been scant details accompanying the picture, but just when I thought we'd discover nothing further, Paolo pointed to a small article tucked away at the bottom of the next to last page. It was headed **Prominent Citizen goes to Queen's Bench**. I read on astounded.

Paolo jabbed his finger at the paper. 'What does this mean? This Queen's Bench?'

'It was in Southwark and replaced the Fleet and the Marshalsea. They were two notorious debtors' prisons. It means that Edward Renville was in debt! Whatever money he raised at auction must have been insufficient to cover everything he owed.'

'But the article says he is in prison. How is this?'

344

'Debtors who couldn't pay went to prison — until 1869. How on earth could a man with so much end up with so little?'

I tabbed down the article. It was coy on detail, but it seemed Renville's hold on his business had slipped drastically over the years, and from a highly successful concern, the firm had gradually withered. The collapse of a bank holding the firm's few remaining assets — and there were plenty of collapses in the 1860s — had been the last straw.

'The poor man seems just to have crumbled,' Paolo remarked.

He had, crumbled to final ruin. Had Alessia's death set him on this disastrous path? Had he been overwhelmed by the responsibility of caring for his children, or felt himself in any way to blame for his wife's dreadful end? Whatever the truth, it appeared he had been unable to continue life as normal — and had paid the price. His daughters, too. The very last sentence of the brief account read: *Miss Florence and Miss Georgina Renville are to devote their lives to the poorer inhabitants of our city. They will go as schoolteachers in the district of Bethnal Green.*

I stopped. Then I clutched at Paolo's arm. 'Look at this.' I pointed to the lines I had just read. 'Florence? Georgina? Two sisters, two teachers, Bethnal Green — Silver Street.'

Paolo looked bewildered. 'The dates are spot on, their ages and the time they served at the school match Leo Merrick's ghosts,' I said wildly.

'Ghosts?'

'I've been chasing spirits for a client,' I tried to explain. 'The name in the paper is Villiers, but they are Renville's daughters all the same. They must have changed their name.' I was working it out as I spoke. 'And gone to teach as

Florence and Georgina Villiers.'

'If they did, you could not blame them. Their father is in prison.' Paolo laid back as far as the wooden struts of the chair would allow and stretched his arms high above his head. 'So now you have solved every piece of the mystery. Perfect.'

'Not so perfect. I wish it could have had a different ending. Those poor girls hung themselves less than two miles from the place their mother died. She must have been in their hearts as they taught through every long day.'

Of course, the handkerchief, I thought. The handkerchief with the delicately embroidered letter A, still lying in the pocket of my coat. It had been Alessia's, I was certain.

'You would like more coffee?' Paolo collected the cups and made for the kitchen.

I shook my head. 'I've made great strides today drinking one cup. I won't risk another. You know, Paolo, I can understand why the girls chose to teach at the Silver Street school — it was in Raine Street originally and that's where their mother died. And I can understand why they chose to devote their lives to the poor — Alessia died in a workhouse. But why, after only nine months, did they abandon their grand plan and opt for death themselves?'

He paused with the kettle in his hand. 'It was a shocking thing to do. How young they were!'

'There must have been a trigger. Their father, perhaps? Something happened to Edward Renville?'

While Paolo stirred his coffee, I went back to the laptop and brought up the Register of Deaths. It didn't take long to find what I needed.

'Here it is — the record of Edward Renville's death. He died in the Queen's Bench prison from bronchial pneumonia in May 1866. That must have been the trigger. It was a month before his daughters took their own lives.'

What must those girls have felt on hearing their father would never leave the prison except in a hearse? How much more could they suffer? Not much, it seemed. As young children, their mother had died ill and friendless, their father left to retreat ever more into himself and away from them. The comfortable home they had known had gradually disintegrated until Renville's ultimate fall from grace, his imprisonment for debt.

They had struggled bravely, true daughters of Alessia, struggled to free themselves of a scandal that was not theirs, but their attempts to make a different life under a different name had faltered then failed. When Edward Renville breathed his last, it had been the finale in an endless paean of sorrow.

Paolo sat down again and covered my hand with his. 'It's very sad, Grace, but you mustn't let it darken your life.'

'I know you're right, but I'm finding it difficult. I'm too involved, I think.'

He looked at me expectantly and I struggled to find the words to explain. 'It can't be coincidental I took on two entirely separate searches that turned out to be very much connected — a haunted schoolhouse in the East End and a missing set of plans for the Great Exhibition.'

'I agree it's odd they are tied together, but why do you feel so involved?'

'Both projects landed in my lap at the very same time and I'm convinced that wasn't a coincidence. The research has sucked me in — it's as though my future is being shaped by what I find.'

The story I'd uncovered could be my story, though how

and why was still unclear to me. Since I'd discovered Alessia's shocking fate, I'd thought of her every day, unable to shake off the sadness, unable to let her go. At the outset, I'd been eager to follow Lucas Royde's story, to find out what lay behind the mysterious gaps we'd uncovered: the absent blue plaque, the name excised from the Exhibition Catalogue, the missing man in the family photographs. But slowly Royde's story had faded into the background and Alessia had stepped into the spotlight. For me, she had become the only actor.

'I need to find Alessia Renville,' I said.

# Chapter Forty-One

The workhouse records had given no details of Alessia's burial, but the only graveyard in the East End likely to have had room for a pauper was Tower Hamlets. It was one of the 1841 cemeteries authorised by Parliament because burial conditions in London had become so deplorable. The workhouse would probably have had a contract with Tower Hamlets for the burial of its inmates.

'Will you come with me, Paolo? To the East End?'

'You want to go now?'

'If you don't mind postponing the greatest Italian meal ever.'

He grinned. 'I will come, of course. At least we'll have a good appetite when we return — in cemeteries you must walk far.'

The weather had turned and autumn was most definitely in the air as we walked from Mile End station to Southern Grove and the main gates of Tower Hamlets cemetery. The sky was overcast and a stiff breeze was swirling fallen leaves along the kerbside. It was a suitably sombre day for a pilgrimage. I had never before been to the burial ground, but even from the road I could see it was huge.

'Certainly much walking.' Paolo surveyed the area. 'The

cemetery must stretch for miles.'

'I think we should make for its farthest corner. From my experience, that's where we'll find the pauper graves.'

He tucked my arm in his and together we strolled down the main walk, past the ranks of elaborate monuments to the Victorian dead, until we turned off onto one of several narrow footpaths, leaving the winged angels and over-plump cherubs behind. The size of the grave plots gradually grew smaller, plinths assumed more modest dimensions and crosses became less pretentious.

But once more we turned off the path we were following, this time into an even narrower track with grass growing untidily on either side. It led us towards the farthest reaches of the cemetery, where the headstones were battered and listing at a drunken angle, their inscriptions largely illegible.

Paolo wandered from grave to grave, trying to make out the badly degraded epitaphs. 'We're looking for a space that lacks headstones,' I said. 'In the case of paupers, the dead are mere bumps in the ground.'

We walked on towards a broken wall and a cluster of overhanging trees, and it was there we found what I was looking for. Paolo left me to wander among the small hillocks of grass and earth, the resting place of so many, but seeming like a battlefield at the close of combat. The sky was now leaden, threatening but not yet delivering rain. The breeze had stiffened further and the dried reeds lining the small stream beyond the boundary wall began to chime in harmony. The light shifted, quite subtly, but enough to highlight one solitary stone in the midst of this desolation. I walked towards it, my heart beating somewhere in my throat. The dark rectangle of the grave was stark and unadorned, discoloured by time and by the ivy that wound its rapacious path through the entire graveyard. As I drew nearer, I could see the commemorative stone tilting a little to one side and partly covered in lichen, but still clearly elegant: slim, beautiful, and made of shining granite. I knew it was Alessia's.

I went up to it and put out my hand to clear the lichen. It was damp in this part of the cemetery and the lichen moved easily. I bent down and peered at the inscription, tracing the faded gilt with one finger. There it was — my instinct had not lied.

*Alessia* (no Renville I noted)
*1823–1851*
Then a line of Italian.
*Nessun Altro Amore*. No Other Love.

Not for the dead woman certainly, extinguished years before her time, and perhaps because of the very love this gravestone celebrated. I would never truly know why Alessia had left her home. I could only guess at an illicit affair: Victorian depictions of the fallen woman came graphically to mind.

And it was an open question who had erected the stone. A penitent husband who had cast her out? Unlikely. He would have had her removed from this unhappy resting place and reburied in the family plot. Instead he had locked himself within his four walls and been slowly eaten thin by remorse. An immigrant Italian then, who felt sorry for his countrywoman? Even less likely.

Or an architect who spoke Italian? I was as certain as I could be that Lucas Royde had erected the headstone. But if

Royde had been her lover, why had he not rescued her from the shadows that threatened, why had he allowed her to die in such miserable circumstances? They were questions that would go unanswered. If Royde had belatedly searched for his lost love, he had found her not on the fetid streets of London, but here in this weeping graveyard. He had stood on this very spot and tasted the bitterness that was death.

I knew now that Royde's plans for the Great Exhibition would never be found — I was sure their architect had destroyed them. He and Alessia had worked together on the Renville pavilion. They had been partners in all senses of the word, I guessed, and after her death he must have distanced himself from any happiness he had known, from his entire life in London. That was the reason there was no blue plaque on the wall of number eight Red Lion Square and why there was no mention of de Vere's as contributing architects to the Exhibition. Royde must have used his later influence to obliterate any connection to the Crystal Palace.

It would not have been that difficult. If the Renville pavilion had been a late design, it would not have been listed in the official Catalogue. And from his exalted position, Royde could have engineered the disappearance from print of any mention of his work before the Carlyon chapel. That was more than possible — the newspapers of the time were nothing if not deferential.

He had needed to erase every memory because he could not bear to think of the woman he had loved and lost. I wondered how well he had succeeded. Not greatly, it seemed. He had never married and biographies contained little of a personal life. 'No other love' had turned out to be a mantra for him, as well as for the woman for whom he grieved.

The breeze was blowing even more strongly now, forcing

the reeds into an angry jostle, their voices strident, as though exhorting the paupers to rise in revenge from a forlorn rest. I shivered. I was becoming fanciful and it was time to go. But I would never forget Alessia. How could I when I'd been on the same journey? We shared more than a perfume, it seemed.

Standing by her deserted grave, I knew why I'd been chosen to uncover her story. Why I'd felt such delight in her necklace — the lapis lazuli was almost certainly hers — why I'd felt impelled to lift the lid of that school room desk, why I'd kept searching until I found her. She had shown immense courage in forsaking her only security, in walking away from a bad marriage and reaching out for the life she wanted. Her fight had been valiant, but had broken her. She had died because she could find no way through the walls of glass that held her prisoner. But if I were brave enough, I could find that way. Alessia's quest was over, mine was not: I had choices she could never have imagined.

I retraced my steps, feeling a glow that was very like joy. 'I've made my decision,' I told Paolo. 'I'm not going to marry.'

'That's a big decision. Are you sure?' He looked concerned.

'Completely sure — for the first time in my life! I was confused. Nick gatecrashed my world at the perfect time, he was the catalyst for change. But I wasn't in love with him; I never have been. He doesn't want this baby, and I do.'

Alessia had lost her beloved girls forever. They had been sacrificed, she had been sacrificed, to one man's pride and another's ambition. But *my* daughter — and I was as certain as I could be that she was a daughter — would live and breathe free. My years of scrabbling for security were over. Like Alessia, I was ready to walk through the glass, but unlike her, I'd walk into a world of my own making.

'And Nick?' Paolo asked delicately.

'Nick will always be a friend. He'll be welcome whenever he cares to visit. But I'm strong enough to follow my own path now.'

'I think you always were. I knew it the moment we met.' He looked at me for a long moment, his dark eyes warm with affection. Then he cleared his throat and said, 'So now we return to Thetford Road?'

'We do — my brilliant kitchen awaits. But if you can bear another minute in this forsaken place, I'd like to take a keepsake.'

I walked back to Alessia's grave, fumbling in my pocket for my phone. I would cherish this photograph for ever. As I pulled the phone free, a letter I'd been carrying with me for days fell to the ground. It was an invitation, a very special invitation, and it came from my sister. It seemed that Verity was still living in the family home, still single, still alone, but hoping for a visit from the only relative she had in the world. How remarkable that she wanted to see me. Remarkable, too, that I wanted so much to see her and the house I'd once fled.

'I'm going home,' I said, when I reached Paolo's side again. I liked the sound of the phrase. 'For a while, at least.'

'But you'll come back to London, I hope? I'll still be here.'

'That's good to know. And don't worry, I'll be back.' I held out my hand to him. 'Now about that risotto — the one like no other I've ever eaten…'

# Before you go …

I hope you enjoyed reading *House of Glass*, and if you did, I'd love it if you'd leave a review on your favourite site. Authors rely on good reviews – even just a few words – and readers depend on them to find interesting books to read.

If you'd like a sneak preview of another timeslip novel, *House of Lies*, just flip to the next page for a taster.

In the meantime, Happy Reading!

# House of Lies

How do you survive when your world falls to pieces? When Megan Lacey's lover dies in a car accident, she retreats to a small coastal town certain, she will never recover from his loss. Until, that is, she discovers everything she'd thought real has been an illusion.

Grappling with a series of catastrophic events, Megan finds herself walking back into the past to an older story of love and betrayal.

Slowly and and irrevocably, she is drawn to Sophia, a Victorian woman who once occupied the same cottage and who, in so many ways, is her counterpart. But centuries later, can she help the woman escape her fate? And can the past help Megan herself find happiness?

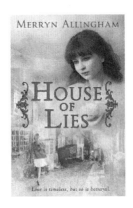

# Chapter One

*London, October, 1849.*

Through the window, a new world awaited. If she craned her head around the lifted sash, she could see the brougham at the very end of the street, the horse standing silent in the dawn mist. The time had come to leave. She opened the closet door and pulled from its depths the valise that for several days she had been packing in secret, then gathered up the very last item – the heart-shaped trinket box of Bristol blue glass that her mother had given her as a small girl. She laid it reverently between the few dresses she possessed and glanced around the room; there was nothing more to do but fasten the valise.

But now the moment was here, she was beset with panic. She had made a decision that would change her life for ever; after this, there was no going back. If only her parents had not insisted she renounce him. She loved them dearly, but she loved him more.

She pulled her woollen cape from the peg behind the bedroom door and slipped it on. The carriage would be draughty and there would be many hours of travel before they reached the south coast. Very carefully she inched the door open. Not a sound. But why would there be? She had betrayed nothing of what she intended, and in the room across the landing her mother and father slept untroubled. She was about to creep downstairs when she remembered, and went swiftly back into the room. Scrabbling under the bed, she tugged clear a square-shaped parcel, packaged in brown paper and string. Then, parcel in one hand and valise in the other, she made her way down the staircase, step by step, avoiding the last from the bottom. Its creak would surely have woken her sleeping parents.

She left the valise and the parcel in the hall while she stole into the parlour. From her pocket she drew a letter and propped it against the gilt mirror that sat above the mantelpiece. Seeing it there, its black and white characters dancing before her eyes, her heart swelled with tears. If only she could have made them understand that when they commanded her to give him up, they were asking her to give up life itself.

She stood for too long, caught between the letter on the mantelpiece and the valise that waited in the hall, but a glimpse of her mother's fine Chinoiserie clock brought her to her senses. Its ornamental hands showed half past four and she knew she must go. She reached for the large iron key and the front door opened noiselessly to her touch. Thank goodness her father was meticulous in the oiling of locks and bolts. A lump formed in her throat when she thought of him, but then she was out in the chill of an autumn dawn and her lover was walking towards her.

# Chapter Two

**I**'d been wrong to come. The conviction had grown on me as I'd walked from the station, and now standing outside the cottage, I knew it for truth. I shouldn't be here. I fumbled for the key that Deepna's uncle had given me, but my hands were so cold from the freezing rain that it slipped from my grasp and fell with a jangle onto slippery stone. There was more fumbling before I could fit key to lock and push open the heavy wooden door, then gingerly back down the front steps awash with water to collect my small case. The small case said it all. I must have known I wouldn't be staying.

But it was a relief to find shelter, even though the hallway was dark and narrow and there was an unpleasantly fusty smell of a house still deep in its winter sleep. *Uncle Das has no bookings until June,* Deepna had said, *and he's happy for you to have the house on a low rent.* Hopefully June would prove more clement for Uncle Das's visitors: I'd walked through sheets of almost horizontal rain to get here.

I abandoned the case in the hall and turned into what was an attractive room. It was lighter here, but the overcast sky and driving rain still cast a gloom. An ornamented cast iron stove took up a large part of one wall, the blackened bricks on either side testifying to its age. I guessed it must be the cottage's sole form of heating and felt lucky it wasn't the middle of winter. I walked over to the bow window. It looked out on a line of black railings that climbed the entire length of the narrow street, seeming to guard the cluster of timber-framed houses. The buildings' white plastered walls and sloping ceilings, unchanged for centuries, made me feel I had entered another world.

I sank wearily into a chair. I must go back tomorrow – catch an early train and be in Hampstead well before midday. I'd leave the key at Mr Patil's as I passed, telling him there was some kind of emergency in London and I'd had to return.

Deepna would be a more difficult proposition. She had been so certain and so persuasive that I needed time away from the shop, away from the flat. *Somewhere completely different*, she'd said. Somewhere, she meant, with no link to Dan. *It will be new for you, peaceful and quiet. You can talk to people or be alone, and I'll make sure the shop runs smoothly. I'll have Julia around for anything difficult*. She was a dear girl, an irreplaceable assistant, but she had never lost someone she loved as suddenly and as brutally as I'd lost Dan. He had been torn from my life and she didn't understand, couldn't understand, the limbo in which I'd been left.

I would have done better to stay in London and keep myself busy at Palette and Paint. I'd made mistakes lately, I knew, silly mistakes. Ordering too many easels, delivering a canvas to the wrong address, forgetting to send Zac Martin his supply of Venetian Red. It was why Deepna had offered to run the shop single-handed while I sorted myself out. She didn't actually say those words, but that's what she meant. I wasn't going to sort myself out, though, sitting in a musty cottage in the middle of a strange town.

I wasn't going to sort myself out anywhere, since nothing was likely to erase that night from my memory. Dan had left shortly after five – I remembered looking at the clock – and after a scratch meal I'd watched some television, half asleep. Then washed up the last dishes, changed the water in the cat's bowl and taken myself to bed as I'd done a thousand times before. But the phone call in the middle of the night hadn't happened a thousand times before. Nor the waiting police car, its blue light chopping at the darkness. Nor the morgue and Dan's body covered with a sheet – there had been internal bleeding they told me – covered except for his feet and the manila coloured label attached to one toe.

The image haunted me still and I got up quickly and walked to the back of the house. It felt far less welcoming, the passageway dark and oppressive. It seemed as though it should lead somewhere but instead ended in a completely blank wall. At one time, I could see, there had been a doorway on the right, perhaps to an unused cellar. A tingle of unease made itself felt and I wheeled sharply to the left and into the small kitchen. An old ascot boiler clung to the wall, but an attempt had been made to give life to what was a dreary space, the worktop glowing bright blue and the cupboards painted a startling yellow.

The refrigerator had been stocked with butter and milk and a small pack of supermarket cheese. A bottle of white wine had been added, too. Thoughtful, but nothing I could make a meal of. I bent to look through the small window at the little courtyard beyond. A blue painted table and slatted chairs had survived the rigours of winter, and when the sun shone would make a pleasant place to sit. But not today, though the rain had almost stopped and the sky was marginally less grey.

Reluctantly, I picked up my handbag again; I would have to go in search of food and I'd seen a pizza shop on the seafront. It was the best I could do. There was a time when I'd looked forward to the evening meal, but now eating had become purely a means to stay alive. Dan enjoyed cooking and I enjoyed eating what he cooked. It was a civilised oasis, that moment in each day when we shared our lives over chopped vegetables and a bottle of wine. A moment to feel warm and secure.

I was checking my purse for money as the door knocker sounded. Deepna's uncle? When I'd collected the key, he had apologised profusely that he couldn't accompany me. But by now he would have closed his antiques shop and be here to discover what I thought of his cottage. When I opened the front door, though, it was a young girl who stood on the threshold.

'Hello, I'm Lucy.' Her voice brimmed with life. 'Well, actually, Lucia Martinez, but that's too much of a mouthful.' A smile spread across her face. 'I work with Das, Mr Patil.' Both her hands were gripping a swathe of tea towels. Whatever was underneath looked heavy.

'Come in – please – and put that down.'

'Phew, thanks. I was hoping I'd find you in. I didn't fancy toting this round Hastings for too long. I'll put it in the kitchen, shall I? All you need do is heat it up when you're ready to eat.'

'How nice of you.' For a moment I was taken aback by this simple act of kindness arriving so unexpectedly. It made me feel guilty I'd already decided to abandon ship.

'Think nothing of it. Look, if you're hungry, I can light the stove for you. It can be a bit temperamental. There's a knack to it, but you'll get the hang soon enough.'

'I am hungry.' And for once, it was true. It must be the sea air. 'I was going in search of a pizzza.'

Lucy pulled her mouth down. 'I hope you'll think this is better. Gil says the only pizza worth eating is in Italy. He's my brother, by the way.'

'And Gil is Italian? And you, too, of course – your name…'

'Spanish. Kind of. Argentinian really and then only half. Mum is English, but our father's family come from Buenos Aires. We lived in Spain for years before we moved to England. Then Dad inherited a ranch in Argentina. Can you believe it? Neither of us fancied life on the pampas, so we stayed.'

'In Hastings?' I was curious. Lucy's background seemed altogether too exotic for this small town.

'London first. I moved here when Gil got a job in the art gallery. He's the chief curator.'

'Hastings has an art gallery?'

'It has two! Gil's is small but perfectly formed. Das said you're in that line, too. That you sell artists' supplies.'

'I do. I've a shop in Hampstead. Deepna is my assistant.'

'That must be exciting, working in such a smart area.'

If nothing exciting ever happened to me again, it would be too soon. My face must have shown what I was thinking because she said, 'Deepna told me a little of what happened. I'm so sorry – such a dreadful thing.'

'Thank you. It is dreadful but I'm coping.' I wasn't, but Lucy didn't need to know that.

She'd opened the oven door and was kneeling on the floor in order to wave a match at the stove. As if by magic, it took light. 'There, give it half an hour and it should be piping.'

'It's very kind of you.' I felt obliged to keep thanking her.

'That's okay, Megan. It's all right to call you Megan? Deepna said you needed feeding up.' She stopped, aware she had betrayed a confidence.

'I know Deepna has my best interests at heart,' I was quick to say. I didn't want this bright, bubbly girl to feel bad.

'She really does. She thought you would love Hastings – it's a haven for artists, you know.'

'Is it?' I was surprised.

'There's an art school here and the town is full of students. And a lot of established artists come to paint as well. It's the quality of light – and the seascape.'

When we walked back into the sitting room, the air had cleared sufficiently to glimpse a small wedge of sea from one side of the bow window. The water was no longer an angry froth of metallic grey, and there was beauty in the way a shaft of light played across the tips of the waves.

'I can see the attraction.' And I could now. The water and the hills and the old town itself were natural subjects.

'There are masses of great views. East Beach is at the bottom of your street and, if you turn left before you get there, that's the way up to East Hill. Or you can take the funicular railway. Do you paint yourself?'

Instinctively, I covered my hand. 'No, not any more. But I enjoy walking and I'm sure I'll find plenty to interest me.' Why was I saying this when I had no intention of staying?

'You'll love Gil's gallery, too. Just say the word, and Das will let me off for an hour and I'll walk you round.'

I smiled faintly. This was getting way too difficult, but Lucy seemed to sense my reluctance and made for the door.

'Don't forget – come and visit me at the shop.'

When she'd gone, I wandered back to the kitchen and rooted through the cupboards to find plates and cutlery. A cruet of salt and pepper had survived the damp of winter, and a bottle opener was placed handily on a lower shelf. Mr Patil rose in my estimation. The chicken casserole turned out to be delicious and I savoured each mouthful. So delicious I allowed myself a glass of wine. It was the first time I'd drunk wine since… I'd thought the crash might have been due to Dan drinking, and that had put a stop to any desire for alcohol. He had been drinking a lot more than usual in the few months before he died, but the police had assured me there was no evidence to suggest alcohol had been to blame. It was plainly an accident, they said, an accident on an unlit country road. He'd swerved to avoid a deer, they thought, the tyres spinning in the mud, and then the vehicle hitting a submerged rock at the side of the road. It was as simple and as devastating as that. But why he'd been on that road, I had no idea. It wasn't the most straightforward route to Winchester.

But I must shut my mind down – its constant harrying was exhausting. I would have an early night and be up and away soon after dawn. I climbed the steep, narrow stairway, plastered white like the rest of the house, and chose the bedroom directly above the sitting room. It was the larger and brighter of the two with a solid oak beam running across the ceiling and a small, rough-hewn fireplace that stood bare and empty. I dropped my case onto the bed and rummaged for pyjamas. Lucy had been so friendly I couldn't face telling her I wouldn't be staying. Before the shop opened tomorrow, I'd post the key through the door with a note. Then back to the busyness of Hampstead, though in my heart I knew it would make little difference. There would still be a dreadful emptiness filling every minute, every hour, every day.

Losing Dan had been devastating, more so for the sense I had of something not completed. In the weeks before the accident, we'd had several disagreements – low level affairs – my mother's operatic nature had taught me to run scared of massive rows and he was too easy going to get deeply embroiled. But the disagreements were a cover for what was beneath, the feeling we were slowly growing apart. I'd wondered if he were unhappy, but I wasn't brave enough to ask. I'd meant to talk to him but I hadn't had the conversation. It seemed to me now that if I had, it might have stopped him from dashing to that conference on the spur of the moment. Stopped him from being on that country road, miles from help, alone and dying.

# Chapter Three

Since the accident, I'd hardly slept and tonight was destined to be no different. If anything, my sleep was more fitful. The small hours saw me in a tangle of rumpled sheets, throwing myself from one side of the bed to the other desperate to find rest, the image of a mangled car, a mangled body, as always colonising my mind. But there was something else, too, something new. Voices. Whispers really. Unfamiliar noises I couldn't get out of my head. I was in a strange bed, I reasoned, in a strange room, and had lived through a difficult day – it wasn't surprising I was disturbed.

Whatever the reason, by the time my travel clock showed six in the morning, I'd had enough. A bright sun was washing the room and when I pulled back the thin curtains, I saw a sea transformed. Today it was laced with diamonds and the colour of indigo. I had an urge to walk out and discover. It was unlikely I'd get a train for several hours; meanwhile I could stretch aching limbs, pick up some breakfast on the way, and still be in time to collect my case and get to the station by nine o'clock.

Once out of the front door, I remembered Lucy's words and turned left, down the hill for several yards and then another sharp left until I reached the bottom of a long flight of steps. The sandstone cliff – East Hill, I think, was the name she'd given it – towered over me. This was going to be a long climb. The gradient turned out to be as steep as it looked and I was soon breathing hard. If the funicular had been running this early, I would have been tempted. Half way up the twisting set of steps, I stopped to take in the view.

The drop from the cliff to sea level appeared almost vertical and immediately below me, at the mouth of the valley, a wide shingle beach stretched itself to the sun. It was dotted with fishing boats, and several more arrived into harbour as I watched. Despite the early hour, a fish market was in process, already heaving with activity, the daily catch being bought and sold at a spanking pace.

The seascape was magnificent, and newly enthused I began to climb again. It was worth every step since at the very top, I found a vast grass-covered space and the most stunning vista of hills and open downland to my right and below, the grand sweep of the English Channel. I don't know how long I stood looking, but I felt my heart lighten. There was a buzz in my head, an itch to my fingers. The possibilities were endless: the Old Town, the beach, the hills, the cliffs eroded by storm into magical shapes.

But I had a train to catch and forced myself to turn back. I was half way down the hill when a voice, coming out of nowhere, startled me. 'It's a great view, isn't it?'

I'd thought myself alone, but then a man emerged around one of the turns in the steps, a few feet below me. It was a solitary spot at this time of the morning and instinctively I shrank back..

'Have you seen the fish market? It's in full swing.' The man arrived at my side and pointed to where the beach had again come into view.

'I noticed it on my way up. It's something quite new to me.' He didn't appear threatening – average height, hair a soft brown and a face that was pleasant enough. It seemed safe to talk.

'New to most people who don't know the town, but the Stade has been used for over a thousand years.'

'The Stade?'

'The beach directly below us.'

'A thousand years is quite a history. Are you a fisherman yourself?'

He gave a small laugh. 'Sometimes I wish I were.'

'But you live in Hastings?'

'I'm no native, though I've been here three years. How about you? Is this a holiday?'

'Yes. No. I'm here for the summer.' Why had I said that when I'd already decided to leave?

'You'll love it, I guarantee. Where are you from?'

'London.'

'Where else?' He smiled at me and for the first time I noticed his eyes. They were grey with a hint of green, or was that blue? They were smiling, but they held a discernment, a shrewdness, that surprised me. I doubted you'd ever be able to lie to them.

'I ought to be going,' I said rather too quickly. There was something about those eyes that made me feel a fraud.

'Then be sure to come again. And early. It's the best time of the day and the view is worth the climb. Be careful going down. The steps get steeper towards the bottom and they're still wet from yesterday's storm.'

'Thanks. I'll be careful.'

I started back down the steps, travelling as fast as I could but on my guard for slippery stone. I'd been far longer than I'd intended; my watch was already showing eight o'clock. Somehow, though, once I reached the road, I found myself slowing, legs lagging, feet dragging. There was no real rush, was there? Nothing to make me hurry back to Hampstead. My assistant was expecting to run the shop for weeks and I knew she'd do it every bit as well as me. I might stay – a few days. Deepna would be delighted if I did. Julia, too.

When Hastings was first suggested, I'd been worried she would think I was running away, refusing to accept the truth of my new life. Julia was strong and would face loss, if it came to her,  far more robustly than I had. The night of the accident I'd phoned her, hoping, longing, she would go to the morgue in my stead. That's how feeble I was. She was at a party with friends I didn't know and had been drinking heavily. It was too far away, she said, to call a cab. She'd have to stay over, but promised she'd be with me in the morning. And she was. She always kept her promises, and in the days that followed she'd been my strength. Along with Deepna, she'd encouraged me to pack my case. *Give Hastings a try,* she'd urged. *I'll call every day and see how things are going.*

She hadn't phoned last night, but I could guess why. She'd had to travel down to Bath the day before I left and she must still be there. She'd been hoping to stay only one night, but Nicky was her son, after all, and deserved to see his mother on his birthday. I knew she wouldn't want to speak to me in front of others – right now, I could be unpredictable – but she'd call as soon as she got back to London.

The first thing that hit me as I neared the cottage, was the large box sitting on the doorstep. My first thought was that a carrier had made a wrong delivery, but the parcel seemed familiar, and then it came to me. These were my artists' materials. I'd packed them up and sent them ahead days ago and, now I'd decided not to stay, I'd have to make arrangements to send them back.

I heaved the box inside – how much had I packed! – and left it in the sitting room, meaning to make a cup of tea. I was parched after the walk and in my rummagings last night had found an old box of teabags left by last summer's visitors. But when I got to the sitting room door, an intense desire to unpack my paints and brushes and easel took a grip. I wanted to get those colours down. The sea and the hill. But first the street outside – the red brick, the white plastered walls, the dark wood beams, the black iron railings. It was all there. On the spur of the moment, I tore off the packaging and ripped open the box, unfolding the easel and setting it up in the bow window.

'So you do paint?' It was Lucy. In my struggle with the box, I'd left the front door open.

'Only a little. Nothing I'd want to admit to.'

'Far better than I'd ever manage, I'm sure. I hope you slept okay? I thought you might like some breakfast. The café down the road does a good scrambled egg unless you prefer something posher.'

'No, I was...' I trailed off. How could I tell this engaging girl that I had no time for breakfast, in fact I'd have to run if I were to catch the train I intended? It wouldn't be kind. And it would be illogical. I'd set up an easel – why would I be catching a train?

'That's a great idea,' I heard myself say. 'Thanks for stopping by.'

The cafe was a five minute walk along the seafront and already busy. With practised ease, Lucy got our order in before a gaggle of office workers arrived for their take-away coffees. She sat me down at a small table overlooking the beach and smiled out at the sparkling scene a few yards distant.

'Brilliant on a day like this, isn't it?'

I had to agree and told her of my hike up the East Hill, and how wonderful the air had been and how exciting the view of sea and sky.

'Hastings is going to keep you busy,' she teased. 'You'll never leave your easel.'

I didn't want to disappoint her so I nodded and reached for my coffee cup. I saw her eyes fix on my scarred hand.

'An accident years ago,' I explained. 'It means I'll never be able to paint professionally.'

Her young face filled with concern. 'What a dreadful thing to happen.'

Another dreadful thing. Perhaps there are people who are destined to take on the dreadful things of the world and so protect everyone else.

'It was bad at the time,' I agreed, 'but I've been lucky. My fingers have regained enough movement over the years to be able at least to hold a paint brush.'

'So were you going to be an artist?' she ventured.

'Instead of running a shop for artists?'

'Yes. I mean… We all change our minds, don't we?' She was trying rather awkwardly to be kind. 'I still don't know what I want to do. My job with Das is only temporary.'

'*I* knew what I wanted.' My voice carried conviction. I'd known since I was a young child, but the accident had put paid to any career in art. A saucepan of boiling water tends to do that. 'But I had to drop out of college. The scar tissue tightens, you see, and you lose dexterity.'

She made sympathetic murmurings and we drank our coffee in silence. I didn't mention that my mother had hurled enough water to send me to a burns ward for weeks.

The scrambled egg arrived and Lucy set to with a will. 'I suppose you couldn't paint with your left hand?' she asked in a muffled voice.

'My tutors suggested I try, but it was just too difficult and I gave up. Now I use my hands to sell instead – it's easier.'

'And more lucrative, I imagine.' She threw back her head and laughed. 'Have you had your shop long?'

The scrambled egg was as good as she'd promised, soft and buttery, and sitting on nicely crunchy toast, and I took my time to reply. 'Five years now. And it's worked well. At first I was a bit dubious I'd enjoy dealing with artists when *I* couldn't paint, but I like them and it helps me feel I've kept a little of my old self.'

And a little of my old self-esteem. It had taken a long time to get to that point. For months after the accident, I'd been drained of confidence and filled with mistrust for everyone and everything. I'd been lost and rootless in what had become a dangerous world.

'It sounds like the shop idea was a success.' She gulped down a mouthful of coffee.

'It was. It is. Palette and Paint is probably the best thing I've ever done. It was a step in the dark at first – a gamble moneywise – but we've made it work. I guess the shop opened in the right place at the right time.'

'You share it with someone else then?'

The 'we' had slipped out automatically. Julia was as much a part of Palette and Paint as I was. 'Julia is my partner. Julia Fallon. She's been with me since the beginning. She's my financial guru, a whizz at the books. She's also my best friend.'

'I hope I can meet her.' Lucy stabbed the last piece of toast with her fork and chewed vigorously. 'She'll be down to visit you, I expect.' She said it with certainty.

'If she does, we must have a meal together – my treat after that wonderful chicken last night.'

'I'm glad you liked it.' Her cheeks flushed with pleasure. 'To be honest, it's the only thing I can make. Gil is a much better cook than me.'

'One dish is all you need. I could eat that casserole every evening.'

'Oh lord!' She jumped up suddenly, clasping her watch and banging her knee on the underside of the table. 'I should be at the shop. You must give us a look-in when you have a minute. Some of the stuff is tat but don't tell Das I said so. Some of it's genuine, though. Antiques, you know.'

'Some time this week, perhaps?'

'That's great. I'll look forward to it. I can take you along to the gallery afterwards.'

She lunged to the floor and retrieved a small backpack, then with a wave of her hand she was out of the door and heading in the opposite direction from the way we'd come. Had I just made a false promise? I thought of her bright, friendly face. Thought of the easel I'd set up in the sitting room. I wouldn't be false, I decided. I'd stay, but not for long, certainly not as long as Deepna envisaged. But long enough. And I would paint every day I was here.

My heels had a gentle spring in them and, retracing my steps along the seafront, my shoulders felt looser and lighter. I reached the cottage in record time and spent a good half hour unpacking my box of goodies, disentangling every item from layers of bubble wrap and arranging them as best I could on the small table that sat beneath the window. The light had retained its earlier purity, but grown warmer as the clock moved on to midday and the street was bathed in sunlight. That's what I would paint – the view from this window. Yesterday, I'd seen the possibilities and today I'd make a start. I looked around the room. The walls were bare except for one small picture hanging in the furthest corner. I could paint a canvas for this room, a present for Uncle Das for allowing me to stay at a peppercorn rent.

A street scene, though, might not complement the sole image Mr Patil had thought to hang. I'd taken only vague notice of it before, but now I went up and looked closely. I was surprised. It wasn't a painting at all, but an embroidery. The image of a child, a young girl, embroidered in fine stitches and subtle hues. The girl wore a figured blue gown, its motifs picked out in a deeper blue silk, and its voluminous sleeves boasting small frilled cuffs. A bodice, white and tiny, was decorated with a brooch in the shape of a silver butterfly. It was exquisitely sewn. The girl's hair was a rich auburn and flowed loosely down to her shoulders, her complexion clear and creamy, with the slightest tinge of pink, an echo of the pink lilies half hidden in a background of dark green leaves.

How wonderful to be the mother of such a child! The thought hit me without warning, and a longing, as strange as it was powerful, swept through me. There had been a time when I'd dared to suggest a baby to Dan, but he had looked so horrified I never mentioned it again.

I gave myself a shake. This was getting me nowhere. But when I turned to go, something drew me back to the picture. It was the child's eyes that made me prisoner. Eyes of dreamy blue, eyes that were innocent yet searching. They pulled me in, making me look ever deeper, as though I were walking into the picture itself, as though I were walking through it. The eyes sought something from me and I struggled to understand.

And struggling, I lost all focus. The air became dense and the embroidery seemed to swirl in a mist and vanish from view. I tried to fix my gaze on the wall where it had been, but the wall was bare. And the room itself was changing – fading into sepia, returning and fading again. I was ill, I must be. For some reason, the picture had stirred hurtful memories of Dan and I was suffering the breakdown I'd feared. I must keep it at bay. I'd escape the room, go upstairs and rest, and the madness would subside. But then I heard the noise. Whispers, the whispers of the night, but this time louder. Sounds coming nearer. A man's voice close by, then a woman's low laugh and the door opening.

# Other books by Merryn Allingham:

*The Buttonmaker's Daughter* (2017)
*The Secret of Summerhayes* (2017)

*The Girl from Cobb Street* (2015)
*The Nurse's War* (2015)
*Daisy's Long Road Home* (2015)

# About The Author

Merryn Allingham was born into an army family and spent her childhood moving around the UK and abroad. Unsurprisingly it gave her itchy feet, and in her twenties she escaped an unloved secretarial career to work as cabin crew and see the world. The arrival of marriage, children and cats meant a more settled life in the south of England, where she's lived ever since. It also gave her the opportunity to go back to 'school' and eventually teach at university.

Merryn has always loved books that bring the past to life , so when she began writing herself the novels had to be historical. She finds the nineteenth and early twentieth centuries fascinating to research and has written extensively on these periods in the Daisy's War trilogy and the Summerhayes novels.

*House of Lies* and its companion volume, *House of Glass*, move between the modern day and the mid-Victorian era.

For more information on Merryn and her books visit http://www.merrynallingham.com/

You'll find regular news and updates on Merryn's Facebook page:
https://www.facebook.com/MerrynWrites
and you can keep in touch with her on Twitter @MerrynWrites

Sign up for her newsletter at www.merrynallingham.com and receive *Through a Dark Glass*, a FREE volume of short stories

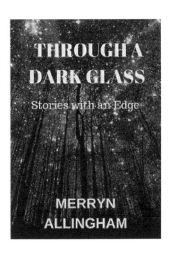